# CLIVILIUS
## WHERE CREATION MEETS INFINITY

© 2024 Nathan Cowdrey. All rights reserved.
First Edition, 13 March 2024
ISBN 978-1-4461-1371-4
Imprint: Lulu.com

Step into Clivilius, where creation meets infinity, and the essence of reality is yours to redefine. Here, existence weaves into a narrative where every decision has consequences, every action has an impact, and every moment counts. In this realm, shaped by the visionary AI CLIVE, inhabitants are not mere spectators but pivotal characters in an evolving drama where the lines between worlds blur.

Guardians traverse the realms of Clivilius and Earth, their journeys igniting events that challenge the balance between these interconnected universes. The quest for resources and the enigma of unexplained disappearances on Earth mirror the deeper conflicts and intricacies that define Clivilius—a world where reality responds to the collective will and individual choices of its Clivilians, revealing a complex interplay of creation, control, and consequence.

In the grand tapestry of Clivilius, the struggle for harmony and the dance of dichotomies play out across a cosmic stage. Here, every soul's journey contributes to the narrative, where the lines between utopia and dystopia, creator and observer, become increasingly fluid. Clivilius is not just a realm to be explored but a reality to be shaped.

Open your eyes. Expand your mind. Experience your new reality. Welcome to Clivilius, where the journey of discovery is not just about seeing a new world but about seeing your world anew.

*Also in the Clivilius Series:*

*Gladys Cramer (1338.205.1 - 1338.214.3)*

In a world frayed by tragedies, Gladys Cramer seeks solace in wine, her steadfast refuge amid life's turmoil. Tethered to a man ensnared by duty and love, she stands at a pivotal crossroads, her choices poised to weave the threads of her fate. Each glass of wine deepens her reflection on the decisions looming ahead and the silent vows brimming with untold consequences. Amidst tragedy and secrets, with wine as her guiding light yet potential harbinger of misstep, Gladys's journey veers onto a path set for an inevitable collision.

*Luke Smith (1338.204.1 - 1338.209.2)*

Luke Smith's world transforms with the discovery of a cryptic device, thrusting him into the guardianship of destiny itself. His charismatic charm and unpredictable decisions now carry weight beyond imagination, balancing on the razor's edge between salvation and destruction. Embracing his role as a Guardian, Luke faces the paradox of power: the very force that defends also threatens to annihilate. As shadows gather and the fabric of reality strains, Luke must navigate the consequences of his actions, unaware that a looming challenge will test the very core of his resolve.

*Jamie Greyson (1338.204.1 - 1338.209.3)*

Haunted by shadows of his past, Jamie Greyson navigates life with a guarded heart, his complex bond with Luke Smith teetering on the brink of collapse. When Jamie is thrust into a strange new world, every moment is a test, pushing him to confront not only the dangers that lurk in the unknown but also the demons of his own making. Jamie's quest for survival becomes a journey of redemption, where the chance for a new beginning is earned through courage, trust, and the willingness to face the truth of his own heart.

### *Paul Smith (4338.204.1 - 4338.209.3)*

In a harsh, new world, Paul Smith grapples with the remnants of a hostile marriage and the future of his two young children. Cast into the heart of an arid wasteland, his survival pushes him to the brink, challenging his every belief. Amidst the desolation, Paul faces a pivotal choice that will dictate where his true allegiance lies. In this tale of resilience and resolve, Paul's journey is a harrowing exploration of loyalty, family, and the boundless optimism required to forge hope in the bleakest of landscapes.

### *Glenda De Bruyn (4338.206.1 - 4338.209.4)*

Dr. Glenda De Bruyn's life takes a perilous turn when her link to a government conspiracy forces her to flee. Thrust into Clivilius, she confronts medical crises and hints of her father's mysterious past. As danger and discovery entwine, Glenda's relentless quest to uncover her family's secrets propels her into the unknown, where every clue unravels the fabric of reality as she knows it.

### *Kain Jeffries (4338.207.1 - 4338.211.2)*

Kain Jeffries' life takes an unimaginable turn when he's thrust into Clivilius, far from the Tasmanian life he knows and the fiancée carrying their unborn child. Torn between worlds, he grapples with decisions concerning his growing family. Haunted by Clivilius's whispering voice and faced with dire ultimatums, Kain's resolve is tested when shadowy predators threaten his new home. As he navigates this new landscape, the line between survival and surrender blurs, pushing Kain to confront what it truly means to fight for a future when every choice echoes through eternity.

*Cody Jennings (4338.204.1 - 4338.212.1)*

In a world cloaked in secrets and prophecies, Cody finds himself at a crossroads between heart and honour. As his affection for Gladys deepens, their lives become entwined with a Guardian destined to alter their reality. Navigating through a maze of loyalty, betrayal, and hidden dangers, Cody is driven by a quest to protect and uncover the truth. With every decision shadowed by consequence, his journey tests the bounds of sacrifice and courage. But as the threads of destiny converge, a single moment changes everything.

*Karl Jenkins (4338.209.1 - 4338.214.1)*

Plunged into Tasmania's most chilling cases, Senior Detective Karl Jenkins confronts a string of disappearances that entangle with his clandestine affair with Detective Sarah Lahey. As a dangerous obsession emerges, every step toward the truth draws Karl perilously close to a precipice threatening their lives and careers. "Karl Jenkins" is a riveting tale of suspense, where past haunts bear a perilous future.

*4338.205.1 - 4338.211.7*

# BEATRIX CRAMER

**CLIVILIUS**
WHERE CREATION MEETS INFINITY

*"In each antique, I discovered a whispered narrative, a soulful connection that momentarily filled the echoing void in my heart with echoes of forgotten lives."*

- Beatrix Cramer

*4338.205*

*(24 July 2018)*

# FAMILIAR SENSATIONS

## 4338.205.1

I lay on my bed, the soft duvet moulding to the contours of my body, offering a small comfort in the solitude of my room. The walls, a pale shade of blue that once felt calming, now seemed to echo the monotony of my days. I could hear the muffled laughter and banter from the living room, where my parents were engrossed in the latest reality TV spectacle. The sounds, distant yet piercing, served as a reminder of the chasm between their world and mine. I had never found solace in the flickering images of television screens; they seemed to me like windows to a world fabricated for amusement, far removed from the complexities and textures of real life.

I sighed deeply, a sound that seemed to carry the weight of my restlessness. It wasn't the kind of sigh that escapes when one is burdened by an immediate sorrow or discomfort. Rather, it was born out of a contemplation, a quiet mourning for the zest of life that seemed to have slipped through my fingers. *How did life become so mundane?* The question lingered in the air, an uninvited guest in my room of introspection.

My thoughts meandered through the corridors of the past week, a tapestry of days woven with the threads of routine and predictability. Even the fleeting moments of entertainment at work felt like brief interruptions to an otherwise unremarkable narrative. There was nothing that sparked the desire to share, to connect. And yet, the human soul craves connection, does it not? Despite my tendency to retreat into my shell, the thought of reaching out to someone, anyone, flickered like a candle in the wind. My sister, Gladys perhaps. She was always there, a beacon of familiarity in the tumultuous sea of life.

With a sense of resignation, or maybe it was hope—sometimes it's hard to tell the difference—I extended my arm, the motion languid, and retrieved my mobile phone from the nightstand. Its screen came to life at my touch, a portal to the outside world resting in the palm of my hand. I navigated to the messaging app, the blank canvas of a new text message staring back at me. My thumb hovered over the contacts, each name a story, a potential bridge to a moment of connection. Yet, as I scrolled, indecision wrapped its tendrils around me. *Who to reach out to? Who would welcome the intrusion into their evening?*

In that moment of hesitation, the device seemed to pause, as if contemplating with me. And then, as though guided by an unseen hand, the screen froze for a heartbeat, bringing Gladys's name into focus. It stood out amidst the sea of contacts, a name that carried with it memories of laughter, of shared secrets, of a bond that time and distance had strained but not severed. For a moment, I was transfixed, caught in the web of emotions that the sight of her name evoked.

"Oh," I moaned into the emptiness of my room, the sound more of a lament than a complaint. "No, I really can't be bothered," I declared to the phone, my voice tinged with a mixture of apathy and frustration. With a lack of grace that mirrored my dwindling patience, I pushed the home button and let the device slip from my fingers, watching disinterestedly as it landed back on the nightstand. It felt like a symbolic gesture, relinquishing any last thread of the desire to connect.

Rolling onto my other side, I sought distraction in the familiarity of my surroundings. My gaze settled on the wall opposite me, the only one adorned with wallpaper. It was a peculiar source of comfort, this wall. Unlike the bare, unadorned surfaces that made up the rest of my room, this one held a pattern that captivated me. The geometric dance of grey hexagons intertwined with smaller octagons was both intricate and mesmerising. My parents, with their taste rooted firmly in the past, had surprisingly managed to select something that resonated with me. In these shapes, I found an odd sort of solace, their complexity a welcome reprieve from the monotony of my thoughts.

As my eyes began to betray the weariness I felt, fluttering shut in a moment of surrender to the impending sleep, they snapped open at the intrusion of my phone's shrill ringtone. "Really?" I found myself questioning the universe, or perhaps just the empty space that filled my room with a palpable sense of loneliness. The caller ID flashed Gladys's name, a beacon of unexpectedness in the night. The temptation to dismiss the call was strong, an instinctive reaction to shield myself from whatever lay on the other end. But something, perhaps a whisper of intuition, urged me to pause, to consider the rarity of this moment.

With a hesitant swipe, I answered the call, the action feeling almost rebellious against my initial impulse to isolate myself further. As the phone barely grazed my ear, a sensation, uncannily familiar yet always startling, raced through me. The fine hairs on my arms, like sentinels reacting to an unseen presence, stood on end. A shivery tingle, cold yet electrifying, shot up my spine, a harbinger of something beyond the ordinary. It settled at the base of my skull, leaving a residue of anticipation mingled with apprehension. This sensation wasn't new to me; it was the physical manifestation of a prelude to moments that had the power to alter the course of my narrative. It was a feeling I had come to associate with significant, sometimes life-altering, interactions.

Two years ago, life had a different hue, tinted with the naïve optimism that comes from creating something with your own hands, something you love. Alone, yet not lonely, I poured my heart into the old town church Brody and I had transformed into a haven for antiquities. Our antique store was more than a business; it was a dream sculpted into reality, each piece within its walls a testament to histories untold and stories waiting to be discovered. The air was thick with the scent of old wood and the subtle musk of aged paper, an aroma that spoke of timelessness and the quiet dignity of the past.

That same foreboding feeling, a prelude to tragedy, had visited me once before, its icy fingers running down my spine, leaving a trail of unease. It was a sensation so distinct, a herald of impending doom, that when it gripped me, I knew the fabric of my reality was about to be torn apart. Moments before Gladys burst through the door, the air seemed to thicken, as if anticipating the storm that was about to break.

Tears streamed down her face, unchecked, painting trails of sorrow on her cheeks as she ran towards me. Her embrace was desperate, a lifeline thrown in a moment of despair. The sight of her, so vulnerable, so utterly shattered, spoke volumes before a word had even passed her lips. Our relationship had never been easy, fraught with the tension and rivalry that sometimes plagues siblings. Yet, in that moment, all barriers dissolved under the weight of shared grief.

"Brody has been in a serious accident." The words spilled from Gladys, raw and jagged, cutting through the stillness of the shop. "He didn't make it." Each word was a blow, a wave of agony that knocked the breath from my lungs. I collapsed into her, my body no longer able to support the weight of my own despair. Yet, in the midst of this emotional tempest, I found myself void of tears. The pain was so acute, so all-consuming, that it scorched the very possibility of tears from my eyes, leaving behind a barren wasteland of shock and numbness.

In the months that followed, my world crumbled into ash. The antique store, once a beacon of our shared dreams, became a mausoleum of our failed aspirations. My spirit, broken by loss and betrayal, could no longer sustain the business we had built together. The bank's cold indifference as they reclaimed the church and its contents was a final, cruel blow in a series of defeats. The battle over Brody's estate with his family added layers of bitterness and resentment to my already heavy burden.

Moving back in with my parents was a retreat, a white flag raised against the relentless siege of life's cruelties. Defeated and diminished, I returned to the starting line, carrying the scars of my battles and the weight of my losses.

Now, as Gladys's voice cracked through the silence, a familiar sensation of change whispered through the air. It was a whisper laden with the promise of upheaval, a harbinger of transformation. This call, this moment, was a pivot, a fulcrum upon which the scales of my life would once again tip.

"Hey, Gladys," I responded, my voice a calm counterpoint to the storm of emotions raging within. I held the phone to my ear, a lifeline cast across the chasm of our past conflicts, reaching out to whatever future lay on the other side of this conversation. In that instant, I stood at the threshold of change, braced for the unknown, my heart a fortress against the tide of memories and the shadow of loss that lingered at the edges of my consciousness.

# THE CRAZY!

## 4338.205.2

*What does Gladys want now?* The thought echoed through my mind, laced with a mixture of irritation and concern. My sigh filled the room, a tangible manifestation of my fatigue and the emotional toll of the day. Gladys's voice on the phone had been laced with urgency, yet the details she provided were frustratingly vague, leaving me to navigate the uncertainty of her cryptic message. It was a small comfort, at least, to know that she was alive and, by extension, that my parents were too, ensconced in their usual evening routine of consuming mindless television. Their world seemed untouched by Gladys's call, a stark contrast to the storm of thoughts whirling through my mind.

The urgency in Gladys's voice was undeniable, a rare seriousness that couldn't be ignored. She wouldn't summon me without good reason, knowing all too well my disdain for unnecessary drama. Her offer to come and collect me, though made with good intentions, was swiftly declined. The idea of being confined to a car, making small talk while my mind raced with possibilities, was less than appealing. Besides, the short walk from my parents' house promised a moment of solitude, a chance to breathe and gather my thoughts under the cover of night.

I slipped into my grey trackies and pink joggers, the comfort of the familiar fabric offering a small shield against the chill of the evening and the unease that settled in my chest. "Don't wait up for me," I called out to the living room as I passed by, my voice steady but my pace quick, eager to escape into the night. I didn't stop to see if my parents had heard me, nor did I glance their way. The possibility of getting drawn into a conversation, of having to fabricate a reason for my abrupt departure, was a detour I couldn't afford.

The evening's breath was a mix of cool whispers and unseen movements, a gentle reminder of the world's quiet stirrings beyond the confines of day-to-day life. I found myself easing into the rhythm of the night as I transitioned from a casual walk to a steady jog, the motion a physical manifestation of my attempt to keep pace with the racing thoughts within. The world around me blurred into a backdrop of shadowed outlines and silhouetted forms, each step bringing me closer to a destination fraught with uncertainty.

Less than a kilometre around the corner, the familiar silhouette of Gladys's house loomed into view, its imposing structure a stark contrast to the simplicity of our childhood home. Standing at the edge of the property, I couldn't help but marvel at the life Gladys had carved out for herself. The house, with its sprawling lawns and commanding presence, seemed too grand for a woman whose only companions were two cats. It was easy to jest about her becoming the archetypical crazy old cat lady, a character from a child's cautionary tale, her eccentricity a shield against the world's prying eyes. The thought teased the corners of my lips into an almost smile, a brief flicker of amusement in the moment.

Yet, as I approached, the weight of anticipation pressed heavily upon me, an invisible cloak woven from the threads of our shared history and the unknown future. The air seemed charged with the electricity of impending revelations, each step towards the front door amplifying the sense of a threshold about to be crossed.

Before I could gather my thoughts or prepare myself for what awaited, the door burst open as if on cue to my tumultuous inner state. Hands, firm and insistent, reached out, seizing my arm with an urgency that allowed no room for hesitation. I was propelled forward into the entryway, the door slamming shut behind me with a finality that echoed ominously through the house.

"Shit, Beatrix. What took you so long?" Gladys's voice, tinged with impatience and a trace of relief, cut through the tension like a knife as she hauled me unceremoniously across the threshold of familiarity and into the heart of her home. Her grip on my arm was unexpectedly strong, a testament to the urgency—or perhaps the desperation—behind this summoning.

"Don't 'shit' me," I retorted, half-hearted in my attempt to wriggle free from the iron clasp of sisterhood. There was a peculiar comfort in our bickering, a reminder of countless childhood squabbles that had somehow always found their way to reconciliation.

As we stumbled into the kitchen, the scene before me was one of controlled dystopia. The counter was cluttered with the detritus of what appeared to be a frenzied attempt at culinary therapy or perhaps just the aftermath of trying to drown worries in wine. "Here," Gladys pronounced, extending her arm towards me with a flourish that was both carefree and slightly forced. She pushed an already-filled glass of wine into my grasp, the crimson liquid sloshing perilously close to the rim.

As I took it, the weight of the glass felt oddly comforting, a solid reality in the midst of swirling emotions. I couldn't help but observe Gladys's glass, cradled loosely in her other hand. It held barely more than a residue, a few sips at most, glistening under the harsh fluorescent light. The deep burgundy of her drink was almost gone, absorbed by her stress or perhaps her need for solace. And judging by the slightly unfocused gleam in her eyes, it was clear this wasn't her first glass of the evening.

"Looks like the crazy has really come out tonight," I quipped, my voice laced with a wry amusement that I hoped would cut through the tension. The words tumbled out, louder than intended, echoing off the tiled walls.

"Beatrix, stop it! You know I hate that word," Gladys shot back, her tone a mixture of irritation and weary resignation. It was a dance we'd performed countless times, a balancing act between her sensitivity and my blunt observations.

I couldn't suppress a chuckle, a sound that bubbled up from deep within, tinged with a hint of cynicism. In the midst of our chaotic family dynamics, I found a strange solace in these exchanges. They were familiar, a reminder of our shared history and the complex bond that tied us together, for better or worse.

I took a gulp of the red wine, allowing the rich, velvety liquid to coat my throat, a brief escape from the impending conversation. "So, what is it that you have summoned me here for so desperately, my dear sister?" I asked, my tone softening slightly, infused with a genuine curiosity and a hint of concern. There was an underlying seriousness to my question, a readiness to peel away the layers of sarcasm and face whatever truths needed to be addressed.

"Jamie is gone!" Gladys blurted out, her voice cracking under the strain of panic. The words sliced through the tense air of the kitchen, as sharp and unexpected as shattered glass.

"Gone?" I echoed, my confusion mirrored in my furrowed brow. "What do you mean, gone?"

"He's gone. He's in Clivilius and he can't get back out," Gladys shrieked, the pitch of her voice climbing with each word. It was a sound I associated with abject terror, a primal fear that seemed to permeate the very walls around us.

"Clivilius?" I probed, a frown etching deeper lines into my forehead. The mention of that name sent a jolt through me, a mix of surprise and an unsettling sense of foreboding. *How the hell does Gladys know about Clivilius?* The thought hammered in my mind, echoing with the intensity of a warning bell.

"Yes! Clivilius," Gladys confirmed, her voice breaking on the name. "He went in there with Luke and Paul, and now Clivilius has them!" Her words tumbled out in a torrent of hysteria, painting a picture of desperation and despair.

"You sound like you've got Clivilius," I mocked, a weak attempt to diffuse the tension. I hoped that injecting some levity into the conversation would steer us away from the edge of panic. But my heart wasn't in it. The mention of Clivilius, a place shrouded in mystery and fraught with danger, gnawed at my sense of calm, unveiling a well of concern I wasn't ready to acknowledge.

In response, Gladys's hand darted out, seizing an empty plastic water bottle from the counter, and with a kind of frantic urgency, she hurled it at me.

"What the hell, Gladys!" I yelled, startled, the wine in my glass sloshing dangerously close to the edge. The water bottle hit the floor with a hollow thud, rolling away in silent accusation.

"Read it," Gladys instructed, her voice a mix of desperation and insistence. It was a command, not a suggestion, laden with an urgency that brooked no argument.

"Read what?" I asked, my irritation giving way to confusion. It was just a water bottle, an ordinary, inconsequential thing. I'd seen plenty of them before, discarded remnants of our daily lives, not carriers of cryptic messages.

"Just read it," Gladys pressed, her gaze locked onto mine, a fierce determination etched into her features. It was a plea, a silent entreaty for understanding.

Humouring my sister, I steadied my glass on the kitchen bench, its contents a dark, still mirror to the turmoil unfolding between us. I bent to retrieve the water bottle from the cold tile floor, rolling it between my hands, a mundane action offering a momentary distraction. The label, with its standard font and familiar branding, offered no hint of the extraordinary. It was just a water bottle, identical to countless others I'd discarded without a second thought.

And then, as if the world had shifted under my feet, I saw it. Hidden beneath the guise of normality was a message that froze my blood. My breath caught in my throat, and I looked up at Gladys, the bottle slipping from my grasp as if it had suddenly turned to ice. "What the hell, Gladys? Is this some sort of cruel joke?" The words tumbled out, laced with disbelief and a rising tide of anger. *How could she play with such grave matters?*

"I almost wish it were," Gladys replied, her voice a whisper of its former hysteria, a haunting resignation in her eyes. She seemed smaller somehow, weighed down by the gravity of the secrets we were unearthing.

I began to repeat the words aloud, driven by a compulsion to understand, to confront the reality laid bare before me. "Brody's death wasn't..." The words felt foreign on my tongue, a dark incantation unlocking a door I wasn't sure I wanted to open.

"Beatrix, don't!" Gladys screeched, cutting through my recitation with a sharpness that made me flinch. "Never say those words aloud," she demanded, her eyes wide with fear. It was more than a request; it was a plea, a warning of dangers I couldn't begin to comprehend.

I paused, a great lump forming in my throat, a physical manifestation of the fear and confusion swirling within me. Despite my sister's reaction, a morbid curiosity, a need to understand the depth of the abyss we were staring into, propelled me forward.

Regaining my composure, I whispered the rest of the message, as if saying it softer could somehow lessen its impact. "Brody's death wasn't an accident. I know why he was murdered. And so does Beatrix!" The words hung in the air, a spectre of accusation and revelation that wrapped around me like a shroud.

My eyes closed involuntarily, as if to shield me from the weight of my own thoughts. Images of that dreadful day surged forward—a cascade of memories I had tried to lock away. Jamie's warning, cloaked in urgency and fear. The unexpected visit from a man whose eyes spoke of violence, a knife glinting in his hand as he issued threats veiled in venom. The announcement from Gladys, a prelude to this moment of unravelling.

A single tear escaped, tracing a solitary path down my cheek. It was a testament to the chaos of emotions within—grief, fear, disbelief, and a burgeoning resolve. In the silence that followed, the kitchen felt like a sanctuary and a prison all at once, holding me in a moment suspended between past horrors and the uncertain promise of revelations yet to come.

"I think we'd better sit and talk," I suggested, my voice steadier than I felt. The room seemed to tilt slightly, the water bottle's label now a symbol of the unravelling deception.

Gladys, seemingly unfazed, or perhaps just seeking solace in the familiar, poured herself another glass of wine. The bottle made a soft glugging sound as the dark liquid flowed into her glass. I'd only had a single sip of my own drink, yet somehow, in that moment, I found myself holding my glass out for a top-up too. It was an automatic gesture, one born from a desire to share in whatever semblance of normality we could muster.

I followed my sister into the living room, the wine glass cradled carefully in my hand. On a whim, I snatched the almost empty bottle of wine from the bench before I left the kitchen. The weight of it felt reassuring, a tangible connection to something other than the impending conversation about realms and secrets I was not sure I was ready to face.

Only once we were settled on opposite ends of the plush, white leather couch did we allow the silence that had cocooned us to break. The couch, a stark reminder of simpler times, felt like a chasm between us now. "So, tell me about Clivilius," I said, the curiosity gnawing at me. My voice betrayed a hint of the apprehension I felt, curious to know what my sister knew of this place that seemed more like a myth than reality.

Gladys glanced over at the almost empty bottle of wine sitting on the floor beside us, her expression unreadable for a moment. "I think we might need another bottle," she remarked, a half-hearted attempt at levity that didn't quite reach her eyes. With that, she got up and left the room, her movements sluggish, as if weighed down by the gravity of our situation.

I rolled my eyes and shook my head lightly, a wry smile tugging at the corners of my mouth despite the tension. I shouldn't be surprised, really. It was so like Gladys to seek refuge in the predictable, even when faced with the unfathomable. The gesture, simple and so quintessentially her, offered a brief respite from the heavy cloak of uncertainty that had settled around us.

As I waited for her return, the living room seemed to close in around me, the walls echoing with the silent screams of my unspoken fears. The plush couch, once a haven of comfort, now felt like a stage set for confessions, for revelations that could alter the course of our lives forever. And yet, amidst the turmoil, a part of me was grateful for this moment of pause, this breath before the plunge into the unknown depths of Clivilius and the secrets it held.

"So, tell me about Clivilius," I pressed, the weight of my curiosity grounding me as Gladys resettled herself on the couch, her movements deliberate. The fresh bottle of wine she brought back seemed like an unspoken acknowledgment of the long conversation ahead, its presence on the coffee table a testament to the mysteries of what we were about to unravel.

"Well..." Gladys began, her voice hesitant, as if the words she was about to utter were foreign to her, too large and complex to be comfortably vocalised in the cozy confines of her living room.

As Gladys unfolded the narrative of her last twenty-four hours—her interactions with Luke, the discovery of the Portal, the unimaginable realities it implied—I found myself sipping from my glass more frequently than I intended, the rich, bold flavour of the wine a sharp contrast to the complexity of emotions swirling within me. Each mouthful was a brief respite, and I felt myself being pulled deeper into the intricacies of a world I had only glimpsed through Leigh's guarded admissions.

My participation was minimal, a question here and there to steer Gladys back when her story meandered too far into the technicalities or when she seemed to lose herself in the recounting. But mostly, I remained silent, a sponge soaking up every detail, every nuance of her experience. It was a lot to take in, a testament to the depth and breadth of the secrets that had been kept from me.

Occasionally, Gladys would mention something—a specific detail—that sent a shiver down my spine, the hairs on my arms standing on end as if reacting to a cold draft. Each time, I found myself mechanically smoothing them down, a physical attempt to calm the storm of emotions these revelations stirred within me. These details resonated with eerie familiarity, echoes of conversations I'd had with Leigh. Leigh, who I knew to be a Guardian, had always been a fortress of secrets. The danger of his position was something I had come to accept, but the full extent of his Guardianship, the depths of the world he was entwined with, remained shrouded in mystery. He had shared with me the burdens of his duty, the weight of the responsibility he carried, but always there was a line he wouldn't cross, a boundary he wouldn't allow me to step over.

The Portal, a miracle of existence that Leigh was privy to, remained beyond my grasp. My desire to witness its wonders, to understand the full scope of its power and significance, was a longing Leigh consistently denied. "It's not something to be played with," he'd say, a note of finality in his voice, a barrier erected not from a lack of love, but from a deep, abiding sense of protection.

As Gladys spoke, the pieces began to fit together, a puzzle taking shape, but with each piece, the image that emerged was more daunting, more overwhelming than I could have imagined. The realisation that there were aspects of this world, this reality, that were so far beyond my understanding, yet so intimately connected to the people I loved, was a heavy burden. I was caught in the crossfire of an unseen war, a bystander in a battle that had chosen me, rather than the other way around.

We sat there, enveloped in a silence that seemed to stretch and warp the space between us, a tangible manifestation of the tension and uncertainty that had taken root. The living room, with its soft lighting and the occasional creak of the white leather couch beneath us, felt like a cocoon, isolating us from the rest of the world. My mind raced, grappling with the revelations Gladys had just shared, each word a puzzle piece in a picture that was simultaneously terrifying and mesmerising.

It seemed, from Gladys's account, that her understanding of Clivilius and the Portals was nascent, shaped by a whirlwind of events and Luke's explanations within the last day. She had witnessed the Portal, yes, but the awe of that experience might have blinded her to the true nature of its power, the dangerous allure of its energy that beckoned so seductively, promising wonders but harbouring untold perils.

I took another sip of wine, the rich liquid momentarily grounding me. Then, drawing in a deep, steadying breath, I braced myself for the plunge back into our conversation. "Well, I'm still not completely convinced," I ventured, my words deliberate, a mask to conceal the depth of knowledge and fear that churned within me. It was a gamble, keeping Gladys in the dark about my own encounters and insights into the Portals, a decision borne out of a protective instinct.

Gladys's reaction was immediate, her expression a mix of shock and disbelief. "Beatrix, how…?" she trailed off, her voice a mirror to the confusion that flickered across her face.

"I'm kidding," I laughed, the sound lighter than I felt. It was an attempt to inject some semblance of normality into the conversation, to step back from the edge of the precipice we were inching towards. "There's no way that anyone but Jamie could have known what was written on that bottle," I continued, grounding my jest in truth. For a moment, I allowed the conversation to drift away from the dark allure of Clivilius, seeking refuge in the more immediate mystery of Jamie's note. "I'd be very surprised if even you knew it."

Gladys's response was tinged with relief, but a shadow of concern lingered. "I had no idea at all," she admitted, her vulnerability laid bare. "Why didn't you tell me?" Her question, softly posed, carried the weight of our shared fears and the unspoken bond that strained under the secrets we kept.

*Why didn't I tell her?* The question echoed in my mind, a reflection of my own doubts. The truth was, I had been navigating these treacherous waters alone. To share that burden with Gladys meant acknowledging the depth of the darkness I faced, and perhaps I wasn't ready to do that—to admit to myself, let alone to her, the full extent of the role that I had played in Brody's death.

I shrugged, a nonchalant gesture that belied the turmoil churning within me. "It doesn't matter," I said dismissively, though every fibre of my being screamed that it did, in fact, matter immensely. I cast a probing glance at my sister, "Does anybody else know?" My question was laden with an underlying concern about how far the tendrils of our conversation about Clivilius had already reached. Gladys, bless her, had a reputation for being as secure as a sieve when it came to secrets.

"About the bottle?" Gladys queried, a hint of confusion lacing her words.

"No, about Clivilius, stupid," I replied, my tone a mixture of playfulness and exasperation. It was a dance we had performed countless times, a balancing act between jest and seriousness.

"Oh, no, I don't think so," Gladys answered, her voice carrying a tremor of uncertainty. "But Beatrix, you mustn't breathe a word of this to anyone," she implored with a sudden intensity that caught me off guard. "You must keep this a complete secret."

"People have a right to know," I countered, feeling the weight of responsibility press down on me. This wasn't just about us anymore; it was about the potential fate of humanity itself. My assertion felt hollow, even to my own ears, a parroted line from a debate I wasn't entirely convinced I believed in. Yet, I needed to gauge the depth of Gladys's understanding, to see if she grasped the enormity of what Clivilius represented. Leigh's words about Clivilius being a key to altering the course of human evolution lingered in my mind, a stark contrast to Gladys's apparent lack of awareness.

"Escape?" Gladys fired back, her disbelief palpable. "Absolutely not!"

The conversation hung between us, a delicate thread stretched to its breaking point. I was struggling not only to understand Gladys's perspective but also to reconcile it with my own burgeoning awareness of Clivilius's significance. Leigh's warnings echoed in my mind, a haunting melody of caution and revelation. I knew that Gladys and I were standing at the precipice of something monumental, a revelation that could unravel the fabric of our reality or weave it into something entirely new. And in that moment, the weight of our shared destiny felt both terrifying and exhilarating, a paradox that defined the very essence of our human experience.

"But Gladys..." I began, my voice softening, a plea for her to listen, to really hear me. I was trying to pierce through any walls she had erected, to reach the part of her that might understand the stakes we were dealing with. This wasn't just about keeping a secret; it was about understanding the potential ramifications of that secret.

Gladys cut me off with a sharpness that reverberated through the tense air between us. "There's more than one thing about you, Beatrix, that I could share with our parents if you open your mouth and you can kiss goodbye your free rent," she warned, her voice laden with an unspoken threat that hung between us like a guillotine blade, ready to sever the fragile peace we had maintained.

"Whatever. As if they'd believe you anyway," I retorted, my words coming out more defensively than I intended. Despite my outward display of indifference, a knot of anxiety tightened in my stomach. In the darker corners of my mind, I knew Gladys held a certain power over me, a catalogue of misdemeanours that could easily unravel the semblance of stability I had fought so hard to maintain. There had been incidents, brushes with authority that I had narrowly skirted, convincing myself of my own innocence with rehearsed lines and justifications. *That expensive silverware accidentally slipped into my handbag as I left the restaurant table,* I silently rehearsed the excuse, a mantra that did little to quell the rising panic at the thought of those episodes coming to light. *I had no idea that it was in there, officer, honest.* The words echoed mockingly in my head, a reminder of how close I had come to getting caught.

Gladys's glare did not waver, her eyes piercing through my defences as if they were made of glass. "And I'm not talking about the stolen silverware," she declared, her voice cutting through my flimsy rebuttals with surgical precision. The water bottle she held aloft was not just a container for liquid; it was a vessel for secrets far more damning than any petty theft. It was a tangible manifestation of the precarious edge upon which I teetered, a reminder of the deep, dark abyss of guilt that threatened to engulf me.

"Fine," I conceded, the word tasting like ash in my mouth. My face was a mask of tension, the muscles taut as I tried to maintain a veneer of composure. The confirmation I had been seeking, albeit not the one I had hoped for, was clear. Gladys was not yet prepared to delve deeper into the enigmatic and dangerous waters of Clivilius, and perhaps, neither was I. With a sense of resignation, I poured myself another glass of wine, the ruby liquid swirling in the glass a reflection of the tumultuous emotions swirling within me.

As I took a sip, the wine did little to quench the dryness of my throat or the thirst for answers that gnawed at my soul. The conversation with Gladys had opened a Pandora's box of implications, each more foreboding than the last. The realisation that we were caught in a web of secrets and lies, with stakes far higher than any of us could have imagined, was a struggle to wrap my head around. The weight of what remained unsaid pressed down on me, a silent spectre of the challenges that lay ahead. In that moment, the wine tasted of both surrender and resolve, a paradox that epitomised the complexity of our predicament.

❖

A full bottle later, the edges of our reality had softened, blurred by the wine's insistent whisper that all could be forgotten, if only for a moment. The decision to destroy the label—a tangible piece of evidence of the unimaginable—felt like a rite of passage, a step into a pact of silence that bound us tighter than blood. Standing side by side at the kitchen sink, there was a solemnity to our actions, a silent acknowledgment of the permanence of what we were about to do.

I held the label delicately between my fingers, its edges crisp against my skin, a stark contrast to the fluid uncertainty that had characterised our evening. Turning to my sister, I found a resolve in her eyes that mirrored my own. "Do it, Gladys," I commanded, my voice steady, betraying none of the turmoil that churned within. It was more than a command; it was a plea for finality, for an end to the questions that threatened to consume us.

Gladys struck the match with a precision that belied the amount of wine we had consumed, the small flame a beacon of defiance against the shadows that lurked at the edges of our understanding. My gaze was transfixed by the bright glow, the way it danced and flickered with a life of its own. As she set the label ablaze, the fire took hold with a hunger that seemed almost personal, as if it too understood the necessity of its task.

I held onto the label for as long as I dared, the heat licking at my fingertips, a tangible reminder of the destructive power of secrets. And then, with a final act of will, I let it drop into the sink, where we watched in silence as it shrivelled into ash, the last physical proof of my secret reduced to nothingness.

"Nobody else needs to know," Gladys slurred, her words thick with the wine's influence and the weight of our decision. There was a finality in her statement, a closing of ranks that left no room for doubt or dissent.

I nodded, the gesture heavy with unspoken thoughts. If only Gladys knew the half of what happened that day, our current reality might be irrevocably altered. The secrets I harboured, the truths left unspoken, lay between us like ghosts, their whispers a constant reminder of the distance that secrets could create. In that moment, as we stood watching the last remnants of our secret turn to ash, I realised the precarious nature of our bond. It was strengthened by our shared silence, yet simultaneously strained by the weight of the unsaid.

❖

Another half-bottle down, the evening had devolved into a series of mindless chatter, a desperate attempt to skirt around the enormity of what we had just done. The wine, once a facilitator of courage, now felt like an anchor, dragging my thoughts through a haze of incoherence. Gladys, ever the pragmatic one despite our earlier indulgences, decreed that I was in no state to navigate my way back home. "You're staying here tonight," she insisted, her voice brooking no argument. In my current state, the prospect of arguing seemed as daunting as a solo climb up Everest.

Grasping the side of the couch for support, I made an ungainly attempt to stand, my coordination betrayed by the wine's lingering embrace. The room tilted alarmingly, a carousel of furniture and shadows spinning before my eyes. I didn't bother with a protest; Gladys's suggestion, for all its imposition, was a lifeline I was all too ready to grasp.

Staggering towards the spare room felt like navigating an obstacle course designed by a particularly sadistic mind. Each piece of furniture, each doorway, presented a challenge, a barrier between me and the blessed oblivion of sleep. I was dimly aware of Gladys's presence, a silent sentinel ensuring I didn't succumb to gravity's mocking pull.

Crossing the threshold into the spare room, I barely registered the space around me. The details of the room, usually noted for their quaint charm or Gladys's unique sense of style, blurred into insignificance. Without a backward glance or a word of thanks, I closed the door with a quiet click, a barrier between me and the world, between me and the weight of our shared secret.

The bed welcomed me like a long-lost friend, its soft mattress a gentle reprieve from the night's turmoil. Collapsing into it, I barely had the energy to rid myself of my shoes before exhaustion claimed me. My head throbbed, a dull ache that seemed to pulse with every beat of my heart, a testament to the evening's excesses and the emotional rollercoaster that had accompanied them.

As sleep crept closer, drawing a veil over the whirlwind of my thoughts, I found myself adrift between awareness and oblivion. The significance of what we had done, what we had decided to keep hidden, loomed over me, a shadow that promised to stretch long into the future. Tonight, however, it was just Gladys and me, two sisters bound by a secret that was as much a curse as it was a bond.

# A WHISPERED NAME

## 4338.205.3

The night had transformed while I slept, the early evening's tranquility usurped by a tempest that raged outside. A thunderclap, sharp and commanding, shattered my slumber, pulling me from the depths of uneasy dreams. The wind's howl, a mournful lament that seemed in tune with the turmoil within me, pushed branches against the house with a persistence that spoke of unseen forces at play. It felt almost poetic, as if the natural world mirrored the storm of emotions and secrets that swirled within the confines of Gladys's home.

A familiar tingling sensation, a prelude to heightened awareness, spread across my skin, setting every nerve alight. It was a sensation I had come to associate with moments of significance, a bodily response to the unseen and the unknown. Despite the comfort of the bed and the lure of sleep's escape, curiosity and concern propelled me forward.

Moving with a quiet deliberation born of necessity, I approached the bedroom door. The carpet underfoot muffled my steps, a silent ally in my nocturnal exploration.

The door opened with a caution that spoke of my reluctance to disturb the night further. Peering down the hallway, the soft glow of ambient light painted the walls with a ghostly luminescence. It was in this half-light that I heard it —a whisper, sharp and urgent. "Cody," Gladys's voice cut through the silence, a name unfamiliar yet charged with an intensity that demanded attention.

Halted by the sound, I stood, a silent observer caught between curiosity and caution. The name 'Cody' echoed in my mind, a puzzle piece without a picture, a story untold. Leigh had never mentioned a Cody, and the unfamiliarity of it added layers to the mystery that already enshrouded our evening.

Continuing my cautious advance, I followed Gladys into the living room, only to find her stopped, a silhouette of confusion and perhaps fear. Seizing the moment, I voiced my confusion, my annoyance tinged with concern. "What the hell are you doing, Gladys?" The question hung between us, heavy with implications. "Who's Cody?" The name felt foreign on my tongue, a key to a lock I hadn't known existed.

Gladys's response was a study in evasion, her words a poorly constructed barrier against the truth. "Umm, nobody. I had a nightmare. Must have had too much wine," she offered, the lie as transparent as the wine glasses we had emptied. Her breathing, heavy with the residue of her supposed nightmare, told a story her words sought to conceal.

I didn't press further, recognising the futility of interrogation in the face of her determined obfuscation. The time for truth, for unravelling the night's enigmas, would come, but not now. Now, the weight of unanswered questions and unshared secrets pressed heavily upon me, a burden compounded by the wine's lingering fog.

Retreating to the spare room, I sought solace in the bed's embrace, though sleep now seemed an elusive ally. My mind raced with speculation, with the shadows of half-formed thoughts and the ghost of the name 'Cody'. The night had deepened, not just in hours but in mystery, each unanswered question a thread in a tapestry of secrets that Gladys and I were weaving.

As I lay there, the storm outside mirroring the tumult within, I realised that the night had irreversibly changed something between us. The secrets we shared, and those we kept hidden, had drawn a map of our relationship, a terrain now altered by the whisper of a name in the dark.

*4338.206*

*(25 July 2018)*

# MOUNTING QUESTIONS

## 4338.206.1

The morning light, filtered through peach-coloured drapes, cast a warm but unwelcome glow across the room. I burrowed deeper into the blankets, seeking refuge from the day that lay ahead. The events of the previous night hung over me like a cloud, the memory of our secret conversation, the burning of the label, and the mysterious mention of 'Cody' weaving through my thoughts like threads of a complex tapestry yet to be unravelled.

Despite my efforts to find solace in sleep, Gladys's early morning activities had jolted me from a restless slumber. The alcohol we had indulged in offered no comfort, serving only to sharpen the edges of my unease. My body ached from the fitful hours spent tossing and turning.

A gentle tap on the door, soft yet insistent, sliced through the remnants of sleep that clung to me. "Beatrix," came the soft call, a voice tinged with a note of urgency that the morning light had no right to hold. "Are you awake yet?"

"Oh," I moaned, the sound muffled by the pillow as I turned my back to the door, a feeble attempt to ward off the intrusion. "Go away, Gladys. It's too early to get up." The words were a plea for a few more moments of escape, a brief reprieve from the reality that awaited beyond the confines of the soft, enveloping blankets.

The door creaked open, the sound a herald of the end of my resistance. I let out a heavy sigh, resigning myself to the inevitable as the warmth of the room was slowly infiltrated by the chill of the morning air.

Gladys, undeterred by my reluctance, rushed to my side with a determination that spoke of matters pressing. "Come on, Beatrix. Get up," she insisted, her hands grasping my shoulders with a force that bordered on urgency. Her touch, though meant to rouse, felt jarringly out of place in the soft dawn light, too harsh for the delicate balance of my frayed nerves.

I rolled over to face her. "How the hell are you even functioning this early?" The words left my mouth before I could temper them with kindness, my own exhaustion and frustration bleeding into the tone. Her presence, so alert and determined, stood in stark contrast to the weariness that enveloped me. "Oh wait," I added hastily, a sarcastic edge creeping into my voice as I answered my own question, "I forgot. Of course, you'd be fine."

"What's that supposed to mean?" Gladys snapped, the tension between us crackling like a live wire.

Raising my eyebrows, I met her challenge with a pointed question, "Do you really need me to explain that?" The words hung heavily between us, a reminder of the unspoken grief that had taken root in the aftermath of Brody's death. "I swear, sometimes you are more messed up by Brody's death than I am." It was an accusation, a reflection of the complex web of grief and guilt that entangled us both, but it was also an admission of my own inability to fully grasp the depth of her pain.

The change in Gladys was palpable, her lips pressing into a tight line, a physical barrier against the hurt my words had inflicted. "That's not fair, Beatrix," she protested, her voice a mix of anger and vulnerability.

"Well, it's true," I pushed, unwilling or unable to retract the barb, even as I saw its impact.

Gladys's response was a raw, guttural shout, "You're not the one who found him lying in his own blood!" The words echoed in the room, an unwelcome reminder of the horror she had faced alone, a burden I had unwittingly forced upon her shoulders.

The sharpness of her outburst cut through my defensiveness, leaving a bitter taste of regret. I bit my lower lip, chastened by the realisation of the depth of her suffering. My mind raced with guilt, the knowledge of my own complicity in Brody's fate a heavy chain around my heart. I had known the danger he was in, yet I had chosen inaction, lost in my own world, blinded by the distractions of our antique store.

Guilt gnawed at me, a relentless reminder that I had allowed Gladys to shoulder the burden of our loss alone, letting her believe Brody's death was a tragic accident. The police, unaware of the true nature of the threat, had offered no closure, leaving a gaping wound in our lives that had festered into a source of unending torture for Gladys.

I inhaled deeply. "So, why do you want me up so early?"

Gladys's expression shifted, the shadows of our previous altercation giving way to a semblance of normality. "I thought you might like to come and visit Luke with me," she offered with a casual shrug, as if extending an olive branch. "I have to go round to collect the small truck I left there yesterday."

"Oh," I replied, a bit taken aback by the sudden shift in focus. My hand instinctively went to my eye, brushing away the remnants of sleep that clung stubbornly to the corners. "Sure. But I need a shower first, and coffee."

Gladys's soft chuckle was a sound I hadn't realised I'd missed until that moment. "I'll take you home first," she said, her voice lighter now, as if our plans for the day had momentarily lifted the weight from her shoulders. "Come on, get up," she urged, patting the bed in a gesture that spoke of reconciliation, or at the very least, a temporary truce.

Closing my eyes tightly, I willed my body to cooperate, to move beyond the inertia that gripped me. Rubbing my eyes with closed fists, I sought to erase the vestiges of sleep and the deeper weariness that pervaded my spirit. Opening my eyes, I took a deep breath, filling my lungs with the resolve to face the day. "Okay, I'm coming," I acquiesced, swinging my legs over the side of the bed in a mechanical gesture of readiness.

As I prepared to follow Gladys, a sense of apprehension mingled with the mundane anticipation of the day's errands. Visiting Luke, collecting the truck—these tasks were simple on the surface but carried an undercurrent of complexity given the layers of unsaid things between us. Each step felt like a move on a chessboard, a negotiation of space and understanding in the wake of our shared and individual traumas.

❖

As I opened the car door and slid off the passenger seat, the cool of the concrete driveway kissed my bare feet. My sneakers, a familiar weight, dangled from my left hand, swaying slightly with each step I took.

"I'll be back in an hour to collect you," Gladys's voice called out from behind me.

I didn't turn around. Instead, I offered a short wave over my shoulder, a silent acknowledgment of her words. Speaking felt superfluous; our actions spoke volumes more than casual farewells ever could. With each step towards the front door, the distance between me and the car grew, alongside a subtle yet palpable shift in my demeanour. I was transitioning from the passive passenger to the protagonist of my own morning saga.

Entering the house, the act of closing the front door behind me was soft, almost reverent. This threshold was a boundary between the world outside and the sanctuary of home, though today, it seemed more a gateway to a scene of domestic disarray. The smell of burning toast, sharp and accusing, invaded my senses, a telltale sign of the morning's tardiness. *Father must be running late for work again*, I mused, a thread of concern weaving through my thoughts. Nearing his sixtieth birthday, his mornings had become a battleground of his own making, a struggle against time and his diminishing capacity to juggle the demands of the day.

Retirement was on the horizon for him, a mere few years away, yet each day I wished it were closer. Watching him, this man who had always seemed larger than life, succumb to the inexorable march of time was becoming increasingly difficult. It felt as though his vitality was ebbing away with each rushed morning, each burnt slice of toast, a poignant reminder of the fragility of human strength and the relentless passage of time.

Curiosity piqued, I peeked into the kitchen, half-expecting to find another casualty of his morning routine. To my surprise, the toast sat on the breakfast bar, perfectly browned, a small victory amidst the usual morning defeats. The plate, white porcelain, gleamed under the kitchen lights, an island of calm in the sea of morning drama. Father was nowhere to be seen, likely caught up in the next task in his Sisyphean attempt to leave for work on time, but at least, for today, the toast was spared. A small smile tugged at the corner of my mouth, a silent cheer for these little triumphs.

"You didn't come home last night," my mother's voice cut through the morning silence like a cold draft, startling me from my thoughts. Her presence loomed behind me, a palpable tension in the air.

"I was with Gladys," I replied, my voice steady but my heart not so much. I reached for a small knife in the kitchen drawer, its metal cool against my fingertips, a distraction from the conversation. As I spread the butter over the toast, each stroke felt like an attempt to smooth over the unease that lay between us.

"How is she?" my mother probed, her concern genuine but laced with an undercurrent of something else—fear, perhaps, or disappointment.

"She's fine," I found myself saying, the lie slipping off my tongue too easily. The butter clung stubbornly to the knife, mirroring my reluctance to reveal the truth. I knew well the burden of worry that weighed on my mother, her nights spent in tearful vigil, fretting over Gladys's well-being. To confess the depth of Gladys's struggles would only add to that weight.

I couldn't fathom why my mother couldn't see Gladys for what she truly was—a functioning alcoholic, though the 'functioning' part was increasingly debatable. It seemed easier, somehow, to maintain this façade than to confront the painful reality.

Nibbling the corner of the cold, buttered toast, I grimaced. The texture was unappealing, the flavour lacking. It was a poor substitute for the warmth and comfort I longed for.

"Morning, sweetheart," my father's voice broke through my reverie as he entered the kitchen. His presence was a balm, a familiar and comforting force in the midst of our family's silent battles.

"Morning, Daddy," I responded, setting the toast down with a lack of appetite.

He kissed my forehead lightly, a gesture of affection that felt like a lifeline. "You're not going to finish that?" he inquired, noticing the abandoned toast.

"I'm full already," I lied, offering a shrug that was meant to be casual but felt more like a surrender. The lie was a thin veil over the truth—that my appetite for this morning's offerings, both culinary and conversational, was nonexistent.

"Full?" My father scoffed, his laughter a brief respite from the morning's heaviness. "Even a mouse would eat more than you," he joked, his chuckle echoing softly in the kitchen.

Mum's fingers, deft and deliberate, plucked the doctor's appointment reminder card from beneath a fridge magnet. The card fluttered slightly as she held it up. "I have to go into town for an appointment at eleven. Do you want to come for a ride?" she asked, her voice carrying a hint of hope, perhaps for a bit of company or maybe just for the chance to spend time together outside the confines of our home.

I shook my head, the decision quick but weighed down by the anticipation of the day ahead. "No thanks. Gladys and I are going to visit Jamie and Luke this morning. She's coming to collect me in an hour," I explained, trying to sound more upbeat about the plan than I felt.

Mother's gaze shifted, a sideways glance that felt like it could see right through me. "Don't they have work today?" she asked, her inquiry seemingly innocent but laden with an underlying concern. Without waiting for my reply, she pressed on, "Actually, doesn't your sister have work today?" The questions came rapid-fire, interrupting my thoughts and leaving me scrambling for answers that would ease her mind.

"Gladys has the week off, remember?" I replied, my voice steadier than I felt. Focusing on Gladys was a diversion, a way to steer the conversation away from the murkier waters of Jamie and Luke's circumstances. Yet, as I spoke, my mind couldn't help but wander to the very questions my mother hadn't asked but which hung in the air like a heavy fog.

*What is Luke doing about work?* The thought nagged at me, an itch I couldn't scratch. *Has he quit?* The possibility loomed large, a sign of the upheaval that seemed to follow Jamie and Luke around. *And if Jamie really is gone, how is Luke planning to cover for him?* The questions spiralled, each one leading to another, painting a picture of uncertainty and curiosity.

"Sounds like a marvellous idea, honey. Maybe your mother and I should tag along too," my father's voice broke through the morning routine with an unexpected suggestion, his tone light, teasing even, as if proposing an adventure on the spur of the moment.

"No," I responded with a bluntness that echoed more sharply than I intended. The word hung in the air between us, a barrier as solid as the breakfast bar that separated our spaces.

Father's eyebrow arched in response, a silent question at my abruptness.

"You do have work today, remember," I teased, trying to soften the blow of my refusal with a playful poke to his shoulder. It was a light touch, an attempt to bridge the gap my sharp 'no' had created, to bring back the easy banter that usually filled our mornings.

"Yes, he does," my mother chimed in, her voice carrying the weight of authority, tempered with a hint of amusement. "In fact, you'd better go and finish getting ready, or you'll be late again," she continued, her firmness belied by the affection in her eyes. It was a familiar dance of nudges and reminders that underpinned their marriage.

Father's gaze met mine from across the breakfast bar, an unspoken understanding passing between us. "The master has spoken," he declared, his grin wide, infusing the moment with a light-heartedness that felt both comforting and necessary. His words were an acknowledgment of my mother's role in our family, the quiet orchestrator of their daily lives.

The air snapped as my mother flicked a checked tea towel with precision, a playful threat that cracked like a whip between us. "Hurry up, or the master won't miss next time," she warned, her voice steady but her eyes sparkling with mirth. It was a rare glimpse of her playful side, a reminder that beneath her composed exterior lay a well of warmth and humour.

I watched as the corner of her mouth turned up, a wry smile that spoke volumes. It was in these moments that I saw the source of my own ability to mask my emotions, a trait inherited from the woman who navigated the world with a poker face. This skill, this ability to conceal, had served me well, though not without its consequences. My thoughts darkened as I remembered Brody, a shadow of regret passing through me at the memory of how my actions, my little habit of slipping things, nonchalantly, into my handbag on many an occasion, had led to irreversible outcomes.

Jumping down from the stool, I sought to shift the mood, to pull me back from the brink of those heavier thoughts. "Hey," I started, my gaze shifting between my parents, seeking to engage them in lighter conversation. "Do either of you know anyone called Cody?"

Father's head shake was immediate, a gesture of ignorance or perhaps disinterest. "No," my mother echoed, her response succinct, tinged with curiosity. "Should we?"

"Hmm, probably not. I heard Gladys mention the name last night. He's probably just a work colleague," I replied, my tone casual, brushing over the surface of my deeper concerns. The mention of Cody was a pebble tossed into the still waters of our morning, a name that held significance yet remained just out of reach, its implications as unclear as my feelings towards the unfolding day.

❖

I found myself lost in contemplation, gazing through my bedroom window as the familiar sound of the car made its way into the driveway. The precise timing of Gladys's arrival, almost exactly an hour after she had left, was noted with a quick glance at my phone. It was oddly satisfying to see something go according to plan, even if it was just the punctuality of an expectation.

Sitting on the edge of my bed, I wrestled with the first sneaker, pulling it over my foot in a mechanical motion. The abrupt sound of the car horn, a long, impatient honk, shattered the morning's quiet. *Gladys is more impatient than usual this morning*, I noted with a twinge of annoyance.

"You took your time," Gladys's voice carried a mix of impatience and accusation as I settled into the passenger seat. Her words, meant to be a casual greeting, felt more like a veiled critique.

*Seriously?* I couldn't help but think, *What is Gladys's problem today?* The question echoed in my mind, a silent query amidst the growing tension.

"I had to put my shoes on," I retorted, my response laced with a coldness that mirrored my growing irritation. Glaring at Gladys, I reached down to tie the last shoelace, my movements deliberate.

"Doesn't look like you've even finished that yet," she observed, a note of sarcasm in her voice that did little to ease the atmosphere.

Gladys was being especially irritating this morning, her comments sharper, more pointed than usual. As my foot accidentally clinked against a glass bottle rolling around at my feet, frustration bubbled to the surface. "Why do you have a bottle of wine in the car, again?" I asked, lifting my gaze to meet hers. The question was more than a query; it was a silent expression of my concern, my confusion at her choices.

The car jostled us as it rolled over the lip of the driveway, the familiar bump serving as a physical manifestation of the turbulence I felt. The wine bottle clinked against my foot once more, a tangible reminder of the complexities and contradictions that defined my relationship with Gladys.

"It's good to have one nearby. You never know when a good bottle will come in handy," she answered, her voice carrying a nonchalance that belied the gravity of her words.

I exhaled a heavy sigh, the weight of my concerns for my sister pressing down on me like a physical burden. *My sister really needs help*, the thought was a constant echo in my mind, a refrain that grew louder with each passing moment.

"I know what you're thinking, Beatrix. Stop it," Gladys warned, her voice sharp, cutting through the silence of the car. It was as if she had read my thoughts, a feat that wouldn't surprise me given the years we'd spent navigating each other's moods and silences.

"Stop what?" I asked, opting for a feigned ignorance. It was a defensive play, a way to deflect from the tension that was building.

"You know what," she replied, her tone laden with a mix of frustration and resignation. "We got a little carried away last night." Her admission hung in the air between us, a testament to the unspoken worries that had been accumulating like storm clouds.

I scoffed lightly, the sound more of a reflex than anything else. *That was an understatement*, I thought, the reality of the situation far more complex than her words suggested.

Gladys continued, her voice taking on a defensive edge, "I've only had one or two glasses a week for the last three months." Her attempt at reassurance felt more like a plea for understanding, for validation of her efforts to control what I feared was spiralling beyond her grasp.

My eyebrow raised in surprise, skepticism colouring my reaction. "Really?" I asked, the disbelief evident. It was hard to reconcile her claim with the evidence that seemed to suggest otherwise.

"Yes, really," Gladys defended, her indignation palpable. The pouting that followed, a childlike gesture of defiance, unexpectedly drew a giggle from me.

"What?" Gladys inquired, her focus remaining on the road ahead, the seriousness of her demeanour untouched by my amusement.

"It's nothing," I replied, the laughter fading as quickly as it had appeared. The brief moment of connection dissolved into silence once more, leaving us enveloped in our own thoughts.

And the car fell silent, a quiet that was both a respite and a reminder of the complexities of our relationship.

As the landscape outside the car window blurred into a monotonous stream of greens and greys, a sudden thought pierced the silence, compelling me to reach for my phone nestled in my bag. The screen lit up under my fingers, a beacon of potential answers in the midst of uncertainty. I initiated a new message, my thumbs hovering with purpose over the digital keyboard.

**Beatrix:** *Hey Leigh. Do you know anyone called Cody?*

The question, simple yet loaded with implications, hung in the digital ether as we continued our drive, the silence in the car stretching out like the road ahead of us. Two minutes passed, each second ticking by with the weight of anticipation.

**Leigh:** *No. Why?*

Leigh's response, almost immediate and to the point, mirrored the urgency of my query. I found myself hesitating, my fingers poised to type a reply. The words formed and then disappeared as I deleted them, caught in the throes of indecision. *What reason could I give?* The question loomed large in my mind, a reminder of the delicate balance between seeking answers and protecting those involved. Leigh had warned me about the dangers of sharing names or details, advice that resonated with a newfound significance in the wake of the Brody incident. Though I was certain Brody's situation was unconnected, the memory served as a haunting reminder of how quickly threats could escalate.

**Beatrix:** *What about Luke Smith?*

**Leigh:** *Everyone knows Luke Smith.*

The response elicited a soft gasp from me, a reaction that I quickly stifled. I darted a glance at Gladys, relieved to find her ensconced in her own thoughts, oblivious to my growing alarm. The simplicity of Leigh's reply belied the complexity of the emotions it stirred within me—surprise, curiosity, and a hint of fear.

# THE DELIVERY GUY

## 4338.206.2

Gladys brought the car to a gentle halt at the edge of the curb, the engine's low hum coming to a stop. My gaze followed hers to the small delivery truck occupying the driveway, its presence an anomaly in the otherwise familiar scene.

"That's odd," Gladys murmured, her eyes narrowing as she peered through the front windscreen, her curiosity piqued by the sight.

"What's odd?" I inquired, my interest equally aroused as I pushed the car door open.

"I'm sure that's not the same truck I brought around yesterday," Gladys replied, her voice laced with a mixture of confusion and suspicion. Her statement sent a ripple of unease through me, my heart rate accelerating as I considered the implications.

"Perhaps someone else is helping him?" I suggested, trying to sound hopeful yet feeling the grip of apprehension tighten. The possibility of another person involved added layers of complexity to an already uncertain situation.

"Perhaps," Gladys conceded with a hint of reluctance, her skepticism mirroring my own. She opened her door, stepping out into the open air.

As we walked towards the driveway, I cast a cautious glance at Gladys, seeking reassurance in her familiar presence. The sight of the house's open front door, juxtaposed against the eerie quiet that enveloped us, heightened my sense of foreboding. It was as if the silence itself was a prelude to a revelation we were yet to discover.

Gladys, perhaps sensing my unease, offered a noncommittal shrug in response before raising her voice, "Hey, Luke," her call breaking the quietude with a note of expectancy.

Compelled by a mix of curiosity and trepidation, I moved towards the side of the truck. Its back door was ajar, hanging open midway as if interrupted. The sight of it, vulnerable and exposed, seemed to encapsulate the uncertainty of our visit. The open door was an invitation, a silent beckoning into the unknown, and as I stood there, the air thick with unasked questions, I couldn't shake the feeling that we were on the cusp of uncovering something significant.

The moment I swung the other side of the truck open, an involuntary scream tore from my throat, raw and filled with shock. "What the fuck, Luke!" My voice was unrecognisable to my own ears, charged with panic and disbelief.

Gladys, responding to the urgency in my scream, raced to my side in an instant. Together, we were confronted with a scene so grotesque, so utterly unexpected, that my mind struggled to accept it as reality.

My gaze was locked onto the young man lying motionless on the floor of the truck, his form surrounded by an expansive pool of blood that seemed to seep into every crevice of the metal floor. The sight sent my vision swimming, the world tilting dangerously as I fought against the rising tide of nausea.

Luke's face, lifted to meet ours, was a mask of horror and confusion. I clamped a hand over my mouth, a futile attempt to stifle the gag reflex triggered by the ghastly scene before me. A torrent of terrible questions raged through my mind, each one more horrifying than the last. *Why the fuck is Luke covered in another man's blood? And in the back of a truck, no less?* The possibility that Luke could be responsible for such a scene was unfathomable, yet the evidence was laid out before us in the most brutal and undeniable form.

"No, no, Luke, no," Gladys's voice broke through my shock-induced paralysis, her words laced with despair and disbelief. She paced in tight circles before vanishing around the corner of the truck, unable to face the reality that unfolded.

Rooted to the spot, I could do nothing but stare at Luke, my eyes wide with horror and accusation. Words failed me, yet my gaze screamed the questions I couldn't voice, each one a silent plea for an explanation, for some shred of understanding in the midst of unfathomable brutality.

"I didn't do it," Luke blurted out, his voice defensive yet tinged with a desperate plea for belief. "I swear, it wasn't me." His words, meant to be a defence, hung heavily in the air, a fragile claim of innocence against a backdrop of undeniable violence.

Drawing in a deep, steadying breath, I willed the chaos swirling within my mind to subside. The sight of the bloodied body before me was not my first encounter with death, a grim reminder of the darker aspects of my life's narrative. Leigh's tales of Portals and Guardians had painted a world where such scenes might not be uncommon, preparing me, in a way, for moments just like this.

"Who is he?" My voice was steady, a testament to the calm I had forced upon myself, as I approached the edge of the truck, driven by a need to understand, to piece together the story that had led to this tragic end.

"Fuck, Beatrix! Don't touch anything!" Luke's hiss was sharp, a panicked plea that arrived a moment too late. My curiosity had already propelled me forward, my hands pressing into the metal bed as I hoisted myself inside the truck. "Sorry," I shrugged, an apology that held an edge of defiance. "I can't help it. I'm curious."

"Curious!" Luke's disbelief was palpable, his voice a mix of astonishment and anger. "I'm covered in a dead man's blood and you're fucking curious?"

"Well, yeah. A bit." My response, simple and honest, underscored the disconnect between my own grim fascination and the horror of the situation.

"You're fucking nuts, Beatrix!" Luke accused, his voice climbing with each word, a crescendo of frustration and disbelief at my reaction—or perhaps, the lack thereof.

"We need to call the police," Gladys interjected, her voice cutting through the tension as she returned to the scene. Her words, though logical, seemed distant to me, my focus locked on the grim tableau within the truck.

I brushed aside her suggestion, my gaze riveted on the lifeless form before me. The urge to understand, to uncover the story behind the blood and despair, overrode the logical part of my brain that screamed for caution and procedure.

"You've got to be fucking kidding me," Luke's exasperation was directed at Gladys, but his words felt distant, muffled by the intensity of my curiosity.

The scene before me was like a puzzle, each detail a piece waiting to be understood and placed. Despite the horror, despite the danger, I felt an undeniable pull towards the mystery, a drive to look beyond the blood and the fear, to understand the how and the why of the young man's fate. It was a compulsion, perhaps a flaw in my character, that led me down paths others might fear to tread.

The sight that met my eyes as I peered closer was both horrifying and mesmerising—a clean slice through the young man's throat, so precise it seemed almost clinical. "There's so much blood," I murmured, the words slipping out as I took an involuntary step back. It was only then that I truly noticed the arterial splatter painting the side of the truck, a grim canvas that told a story of violence and sudden death.

"We can't, Gladys," Luke's voice cut through my shock, a note of desperation in his tone.

"Why not?" Gladys demanded.

I found myself momentarily torn away from the grim fascination of the scene before me, my attention now fully on Luke, eager for his explanation. His response came swiftly, laden with a bitterness that underscored the seriousness of our situation.

"Well, that'll look great, won't it," Luke said, his voice heavy with sarcasm. "I'm covered in blood, your sister now has her fingerprints all over the crime scene and you're just standing there, drinking wine out the bottle."

His words, sharp and accusatory, jolted me back to reality, prompting me to glance down at my own hands. The instant realisation of my actions—or rather, my lack of caution—struck me with the force of a physical blow. In my curiosity and haste to uncover the story behind the young man's fate, I had unwittingly implicated myself within the crime scene. My fingerprints, a silent testament to my presence, now littered the truck and its grisly contents.

Luke's frustration boiled over in a sudden, violent outburst, his fist colliding with the side of the truck with a force that reverberated through the air. The sound made me flinch, a reflexive jump at the unexpected noise. My heart raced, adrenaline surging through me as I turned my attention back to the grim scene, only to notice another disturbing detail—a vile pool of vomit, just feet away from the deceased's head.

"Spew," I murmured under my breath, the word barely a whisper as I crouched down for a closer inspection, the acrid smell assaulting my senses.

"What happened to him?" I pivoted towards Luke, seeking answers. "Is that yours?" My question, pointed and direct, aimed at the mess on the ground.

"It is," Luke's admission came softly, a stark contrast to his earlier anger, his voice carrying a mix of defeat and resignation.

"What are you going to do with him?" Gladys's voice, tinged with anxiety and curiosity, broke the tense silence, even as she sought solace in the wine bottle.

"I don't know," Luke's response was laden with uncertainty. "I was thinking of taking him through the Portal."

I stared at Luke, my mind racing to piece together the reality that had just unfolded before me. *So, Gladys had been telling the truth last night. Luke really did have a Portal Key.* The realisation that he might also be a Guardian, as suggested by his possession of such an artefact, added layers of complexity and intrigue to the situation.

"Shit," Luke's curse was a succinct summary of our predicament.

"Don't worry," I found myself saying, an attempt at reassurance as I tapped him lightly on the shoulder. "Gladys already told me about your Portal."

The glare Luke directed at Gladys was sharp, filled with a mixture of betrayal and exasperation. Despite the gravity of the situation, I couldn't suppress a giggle. The chaotic scene before us, dark and fraught with tension, somehow brought out a mischievous part of me that relished in making my sister squirm. It was a twisted form of amusement, finding levity in moments of crisis.

"Sorry," Gladys's whisper was barely audible over the sound of her drinking, her apology mingling with the clink of the bottle against her lips.

"Can I see it?" The question tumbled from my lips, carried by a blend of curiosity and eagerness. My heart raced at the thought, the prospect of witnessing something Leigh had spoken of with such fervour, yet remained shrouded in mystery to my eyes.

"I don't know," Luke's hesitation was palpable, a cautious restraint that bordered on reluctance. His uncertainty served only to fuel my curiosity further.

"Oh, come on," I pressed, my brain quickly sifting through arguments to bolster my case. "You have to get rid of this body anyway, so you may as well," I insisted, a sense of satisfaction washing over me as I found a plausible reason to sway him.

Luke stood frozen for a moment, lost in thought, the weight of the decision evident in his expression.

*Come on,* I silently urged, my internal plea a testament to my desperation. Despite all of Leigh's talk of Portals, the visibility of such phenomena remained just beyond my grasp, a tantalising mystery I was now on the cusp of seeing with my own eyes. *Please.*

"How are the two of you being so calm about all of this?" Luke's question, voiced in a mix of bewilderment and accusation, momentarily pulled me from my thoughts.

"Calm?" Gladys echoed, her tone laced with incredulity as she gestured with her bottle of wine—a visual representation of her own method of coping.

Luke's gaze shifted to me, searching, perhaps, for some semblance of reason in my response.

I shrugged, a noncommittal gesture that belied the turmoil of thoughts swirling within me. Leigh had been adamant about the dangers of sharing his secrets, a caution I had taken to heart until this moment. But faced with Luke's evident connection to the same clandestine world, my resolve wavered. "I don't know," I admitted, the words a half-truth that masked the depth of my knowledge and curiosity.

Luke sighed, a sound heavy with resignation and the burden of what lay ahead. "I need to clean up first," he announced, his voice resigned yet tinged with a determination to address the immediate crisis. His gesture for me to follow him away from the truck was an implicit invitation, a bridge between the grim reality we faced and the possibility of peering into a world I had only dared to imagine.

"Sure," I agreed readily, my feet hitting the ground with a sense of purpose. The chance to witness a Portal firsthand, to validate the stories that had captivated my imagination, was a temptation too strong to resist.

"What are you doing?" Gladys's voice cut through the tense silence, her query sharp with confusion.

"Huh?" I responded automatically, my body pivoting towards her voice. Realisation dawned a moment later that her question wasn't meant for me. "Oh," I muttered under my breath, my focus shifting back to the scene unfolding before us.

"I need to move him forward," Luke's voice was strained, his explanation pragmatic in the face of the gruesome task at hand. "His foot is stopping the door from closing properly." The simplicity of his statement, juxtaposed against the macabre reality of adjusting a corpse to shut a door, sent a chill down my spine.

Luke grunted, his efforts to reposition the body evident in the tensing of his muscles and the grim determination etched on his face. I couldn't tear my eyes away, the morbid fascination mingled with a growing sense of horror as the body was dragged through the mingling mess of blood and vomit. *You're screwed now, Luke*, my thoughts accused silently, the severity of his situation becoming painfully clear with each passing moment.

"So, who is he anyway?" Gladys's question pierced the heavy air. "Did you know him?" Her voice seemed to echo louder than intended in the sombre quiet of our surroundings.

I scrutinised Luke's expression, searching for any sign of deceit or evasion. "He's just the delivery guy," he responded after a moment, his voice betraying a hint of defensiveness.

*That's bullshit!* My inner voice screamed in disbelief. *You totally know more than that!* The skepticism churned within me, urging me to press for the truth. "Who?" I demanded, my gaze locked on Luke, seeking the honesty his initial answer lacked.

Luke's demeanour shifted then, a vulnerability breaking through as his eyes filled with tears, one spilling over and trailing down his cheek. "His name is Joel. He's Jamie's son," he confessed, each word heavy with a sorrow that seemed to deepen the tragedy of the situation.

"Shit," was all I could manage, the revelation striking me with the force of a physical blow.

The sound of shattering glass snapped me back to the immediate aftermath of Gladys's shock, her wine bottle crashing onto the concrete, the liquid spilling out like a mirror to our scattered emotions. "Oh dear," she murmured, her gaze locked on the broken bottle, a trivial loss, yet symbolic of our collective fracture.

"What the... how... when did...?" My questions faltered, words failing me as I attempted to navigate the torrent of confusion and disbelief.

"I had no idea. No idea at all," Gladys repeated, her voice echoing the shock that had rendered us momentarily speechless. She moved her gaze between me, the body, and Luke, as if trying to piece together a puzzle that had just become infinitely more complex.

Luke's hasty departure from the truck was abrupt, his movement so sudden that he collided with Gladys, the impact of his clumsy landing sending a jolt through the tense atmosphere that had enveloped us.

"Luke! Where are you going?" My voice echoed after him, a mix of confusion and concern threading through my words.

"Don't leave us here with him!" Gladys's voice joined mine, her plea tinged with a mix of fear and disbelief. The idea of being left alone, in the shadow of such a grim discovery, seemed to magnify the surreal nature of our predicament.

Without a word, Luke's silence hung heavily between us as we trailed behind him into the house, his actions dictating our course. He moved with a purpose that seemed to cut through the lingering shock, leading us decisively across the living room toward the hallway.

"Hey! Where are Duke and Henri?" Gladys's inquiry broke the heavy silence, her observation highlighting the absence of the two Shih Tzus that were staples of warmth and welcome in the home. Their usual enthusiastic greeting was conspicuously missing, adding another layer of unease to the already strained atmosphere. Without missing a beat, she navigated to the kitchen cupboard, procuring a wine glass with a familiarity that spoke of her attempts to find some semblance of normality in the abnormal.

"Oh," Luke's response was almost an afterthought, his attention momentarily pulled back from whatever thoughts consumed him. "Henri accidentally ran through the Portal earlier this morning and I accidentally took Duke with me." The casualness with which he delivered such a fantastical explanation was jarring, the reality of Portals and missing pets mingling with the day's darker revelations.

"Can they get back out?" Gladys's question, laced with concern, seemed to momentarily bridge the gap between our grim reality and the concern for the well-being of the pets.

"Nope," Luke's reply was succinct, his tone resigned. "We tried that already." The brief pause that followed seemed to carry the weight of his resignation.

"Anyway, I'm going to shower," he announced abruptly, his decision to retreat from the conversation, from us, marking a physical and emotional withdrawal into the solitude of his thoughts and the privacy of the shower.

As Luke disappeared up the hallway, the reality of the situation settled heavily upon me. The house, once a place of warmth and laughter, felt hollow, its corners filled with shadows of unanswered questions and the echo of footsteps walking away.

"Poor Duke and Henri," I murmured to myself, a tinge of sadness colouring my voice as I contemplated their fate. *Clivilius, with its constant dangers and harsh environments, was no place for pets,* a thought that weighed heavily on me. The very idea of those innocent animals lost in a realm so far from their home filled me with a deep sense of unease.

Gladys's movements brought me back to the present, the clank of her wine bottle against the kitchen island punctuating the silence. "Why are they poor?" she queried, her curiosity piqued as she rummaged through the cupboard above the rangehood with practiced ease. It didn't escape my notice how well she knew the boys' hiding spots for their alcohol—a small, yet telling detail of our intertwined lives and shared spaces.

"Oh," I stuttered, caught off-guard by my own slip of the tongue. My mind scrambled for a plausible cover, aware that I had inadvertently revealed more than intended. "No particular reason," I offered lamely, hoping my vague response would be enough to deflect further probing. I retreated to the sanctuary of the black leather couch, casting my gaze around the room in a feigned interest that I hoped would discourage any more questions.

The silence that followed was a welcome reprieve, allowing my thoughts to drift and wander through the complexities of our current predicament and the implications of what lay ahead.

"Here," Gladys's voice broke through my reverie, her hand extended towards me with a glass of wine. Gratefully, I accepted it, allowing the rich aroma of Chardonnay to fill my senses, a small comfort. "Thanks," I whispered, the word a soft exhale of appreciation.

Gladys took her place beside me, her presence a silent solidarity that I found both comforting and necessary. Together, we sat in quiet contemplation, the world around us momentarily paused.

The sudden sound of water rushing through pipes jolted us, a brief reminder of Luke's presence elsewhere in the house. But as quickly as it came, the noise faded, leaving behind a profound silence that seemed to envelop everything.

# UNINVITED

## 4338.206.3

"Gee, you were quick," Gladys remarked, her tone a mix of surprise and relief as Luke re-entered the living room, now dressed in a fresh pair of jeans and a clean t-shirt.

"Do you want to see this Portal or not?" Luke's direct question snapped me back to the present. He held a small device in his palm, its significance unmistakable.

I barely managed to disguise my gasp as a random hiccup, my mind racing. *That has to be the Portal Key*, I realised with a jolt of excitement mixed with disbelief. It looked identical to the one I had inadvertently discovered falling from Leigh's pocket. The brief moment I had held it, feeling its weight and texture, had left me with more questions than answers. The sudden interruption of the shower turning off had spurred me to hastily replace it, convincing myself that Leigh would reveal its secrets in due time.

Luke's next action held my complete attention, a mix of anticipation and apprehension coursing through me. He pointed the device towards the living room wall, a seemingly mundane gesture that I knew was anything but.

The room was momentarily illuminated by a small ball of energy that emanated from the device, darting across the space between us and the wall. The impact was immediate and mesmerising—a burst of colourful energy exploded upon contact, unfurling into pulsating waves that danced across the wall's surface. The spectacle was unlike anything I had ever seen, a vivid display of power and beauty that transcended the boundaries of my understanding.

My eyes were wide, captivated by the display before us. The swirling energies painted the room in hues of possibility and wonder, a proof of the stories Leigh had woven and the secrets he had guarded. In that moment, the reality of Portals and Guardians shifted from the realm of fantastical tales to tangible truth, a revelation that both thrilled and terrified me.

"It's so pretty," slipped from my lips, a whisper of wonder breaking the intense focus I had on the mesmerising display before me. The vibrant energy swirling on the wall had captured my entire attention, its beauty transcending the surreal nature of the situation.

Luke, perhaps emboldened by my reaction or driven by his own curiosity, moved closer to the wall, his actions signalling the beginning of something even more extraordinary.

*That's a good idea*, a thought flashed through my mind, prompting an impulsive decision. "Take this for me," I called out to Luke, tossing a cushion in his direction in a playful test of the portal's reality.

The cushion, however, never reached Luke's hands. Instead, it vanished into the colourful energy with a fluid ease that left me momentarily stunned. "Shit. That's incredible," I whispered, my voice filled with awe. The cushion's effortless disappearance through the wall was nothing short of incredible, a tangible confirmation of the portal's existence and function.

"I have another idea," Luke said. Retrieving Duke and Henri's small beds and box of soft toys, he prepared to send a piece of home through to the other side, a thoughtful gesture that bridged the gap between our world and wherever the portal led.

"Good idea," I echoed, my mind still grappling with the implications of what I was witnessing.

"Oh yeah," Gladys said, her voice casual as she produced a small envelope from her handbag. "Can you give this to Jamie for me?"

"What's this?" Luke's curiosity was piqued as he eyed the envelope.

After a brief hesitation, Gladys's response was tinged with a mix of resolve and vulnerability. "It's a letter for Jamie," she admitted.

"You wrote him a letter?" My question laced with sarcasm.

"Yeah, well, I figured I can't exactly talk to him," Gladys retorted, her defensiveness masking the genuine effort behind her action.

"Oh yeah, I see your point," I conceded, the sarcasm giving way to a sincere acknowledgment of her thoughtfulness. In a situation as unfathomable as this, such gestures of connection held a newfound significance.

With a resolve that seemed to solidify with each passing second, Luke stepped through the swirling mass of colours, disappearing from our sight and leaving Gladys and me alone with our wine and a silence that spoke volumes.

❖

As I sat there, transfixed by the spectacle before me, the wall of swirling colours seemed to transcend mere visual beauty, becoming a living, breathing entity of its own. The sparks of electric energy that erupted in mesmerising collisions sent shivers down my spine, each burst of light a testament to the incredible power housed within the portal.

"It's incredible, isn't it," I found myself saying, the words barely a whisper as I rose from the couch, drawn inexorably closer to the display. It felt like stepping into a dream, one where the rules of reality were rewritten by the whims of magic and science intertwined.

Gladys murmured in agreement, her attention momentarily torn between the wine at her lips and the spectacle before us. Her casual affirmation belied the depth of wonder that the scene inspired.

The longer I watched the energised particles dance across the wall, the more I felt their energy resonate within me. It was a call that went beyond curiosity, touching something primal and instinctual. I felt alive, more connected to the universe and its mysteries than I had ever thought possible.

Driven by an impulse I couldn't quite understand, my hand reached out, fingers stretching towards the vibrant display. With each step closer, the air around me seemed to hum with energy, the boundary between my body and the portal's force blurring. I was so close now, close enough to feel the vibrational energy pulsate against my skin, sending waves of shock through my fingertips.

"Don't touch it, Beatrix!" Gladys's warning sliced through the air, her voice sharp with urgency.

I whirled around to face her, the sudden movement causing the last of my wine to swirl tumultuously in my glass. "I know what I'm doing, Gladys," I retorted, my voice laced with a confidence I wasn't entirely sure I felt. The sheer proximity to something as formidable as the Portal had emboldened me, yet Gladys's cautionary shout reminded me of the razor-thin line I was treading.

Gladys's eyebrow arched, skepticism and curiosity mingling in her gaze. "You do?" Her question, simple yet loaded, hinted at the layers of secrecy and knowledge that lay between us.

I shifted awkwardly, moving to the side as the reality of Gladys's warning sank in. "I... uh..." My voice faltered, betraying my sudden uncertainty. *Surely Gladys doesn't suspect that I already know?* The thought raced through my mind, a whirlwind of panic and speculation. Leigh had been explicit about the dangers of the Portal, warning me of the irreversible consequences of making contact with its energy. Clivilius owned them, he had said—a haunting reminder of the Portal's power and the finality of the choice to cross its threshold.

Taking a nervous sip of wine, I attempted to steady my nerves. Standing mere feet from the mesmerising display of colours, the significance of Leigh's warnings weighed heavily on me. The beauty of the Portal, with its dancing lights and ethereal glow, belied the danger it posed. The realisation that a stray spark could irrevocably alter my fate sent a shiver of apprehension down my spine. If I were to inadvertently come into contact with its energy, I could be swept away, forced to leave behind everything and everyone I knew.

The tension of the moment, the balance between curiosity and caution, left me standing at a crossroads. The allure of the unknown beckoned, yet the stark warnings of the consequences held me back, a tumultuous internal conflict mirrored in the swirling energies before me.

The sudden reappearance of Luke, emerging from the Portal with a purposeful stride, startled me, a jolt of surprise coursing through my body. The shift from the otherworldly scene back to the practical concerns of our reality was abrupt, snapping me back to the moment with an almost physical force.

"How long did you say you've hired that other small truck for?" Luke's question was directed at Gladys, his tone business-like, a sharp contrast to the ethereal experience we had just witnessed. His immediate dive into logistics felt almost jarring.

Gladys's response was hindered by a sudden coughing fit, the wine going down the wrong pipe. "Until Sunday," she managed to say after regaining her composure, her voice laced with a mixture of surprise and confusion at Luke's line of questioning.

I couldn't help but let out a soft chuckle at the situation.

Luke was relentless, outlining a plan that seemed to have been formulated in the moments he was out of sight. "We're going to do a truck swap. Move the truck onto the road for me, would you Beatrix?" His instructions were clear, his movements towards the front door signalling the urgency of the task at hand. "I'm going to bring Gladys's truck back from Clivilius. You'll need to reverse your truck back into the driveway once I have left. Then I'll reverse mine in front."

A wave of anxiety surged through me at his words. *What is Luke up to?* The question echoed in my mind, a blend of curiosity and trepidation. The sound of my glass clinking loudly against the kitchen bench punctuated my nervousness as I placed it down more clumsily than intended.

"The keys are still in the ignition," Luke's voice floated back to us, a final piece of instruction before he disappeared outside.

"Beatrix, you can't be serious!" Gladys's exclamation was a mix of disbelief and concern as she rose from the couch, her actions mirroring my own urgency as we both headed towards the front door.

Ignoring Gladys's exclamation, I slid into the driver's seat with a sense of purpose, my hands steady as I turned the key in the ignition. The engine's roar was immediate, a powerful rumble that filled the air and resonated with the newfound determination swelling within me. A smile crept across my face, a silent acknowledgment of the control now at my fingertips. The steering wheel vibrated under my hands, sending a thrilling surge of power up my arms, a tangible connection between me and the machine.

The truck began to creep forward slowly, each movement deliberate, a testament to the control I wielded. I couldn't help but grin, the temptation to unleash the truck's full power battling with the responsibility of the task at hand. With a disciplined ease, I pressed the brakes as I reached beyond the driveway, the truck coming to a gentle halt.

Then, in the rear-view mirror, a second small truck appeared, heralding Luke's return from Clivilius. He jumped from its cab with an urgency that matched the pace of the day's events, quickly moving to the side of the truck I was in. "Reverse the truck back a little," he called out, his voice carrying a blend of instruction and anticipation.

"Sure," I responded, my voice steady, a reflection of my confidence.

Luke positioned himself at the rear of the truck, his hands gesturing directions, guiding me as I began to reverse. The process was surprisingly smooth, the truck responding to my every command with ease. My experience with larger vehicles, particularly my own four-wheel drive, had prepared me well for this moment. Handling the small truck felt almost second nature to me, each motion fluid and assured.

When the vehicle came to a stop, I swiftly exited the cab, my movements fuelled by the urgency of our task. Luke, with a sense of purpose that bordered on recklessness, flung open the back of the truck, his actions eliciting a sharp rebuke from Gladys, who observed us from her perch on the front step.

"What the hell are you doing, Luke?" her voice pierced the air, a mix of concern and incredulity lacing her words.

"We need to move the remaining goods into this clean truck," Luke responded, his hand giving the side of the truck an affirming slap as if to punctuate his intention. His response, simple yet decisive, offered a glimpse into his strategy.

*Ahh*, a moment of relief washed over me. *So, Luke really does have a plan*. The realisation brought a fleeting sense of stability, a rare commodity in the whirlwind of tragedy that had engulfed us.

Gladys, her equilibrium clearly compromised by the wine, made a wobbly attempt to rise, her hand clutching the handrail for support.

Luke, undeterred, proceeded to the second truck, swinging its back doors open with a similar disregard for caution. "Okay, Beatrix, come help me move this stuff," he beckoned, his gaze assessing the contents. "Looks like there are only a few smallish boxes left." His words, a call to action, spurred me into motion, ready to contribute.

"What about me?" Gladys's voice, tinged with a mix of defiance and vulnerability, floated towards us as she managed a tentative descent from the steps.

"Shit, Gladys. You can barely stand," I couldn't help but scold her.

"I can so," she countered, her determination manifesting in the deliberate release of the handrail and the painstakingly slow, yet deliberate steps she took. Her actions, though fraught with potential peril, spoke volumes of her unwillingness to be sidelined, a testament to her spirit and the complex web of emotions and loyalty that bound us together in this extraordinary undertaking.

Watching Luke as he clambered his way into the back of the truck, I was momentarily overwhelmed by the grimness of our task. The air was thick with an unpleasant stench, an unwelcome reminder of the body that lay within, now a source of decay. Instinctively, I held my nose, trying to shield myself from the odious smell. Flies, drawn by the scent of death, buzzed frenziedly between the corpse and me, their presence a grotesque testament to the situation's severity. A cold shiver of revulsion ran down my spine at the thought of these flies, possibly transferring particles from the corpse onto my skin. The disgust that washed over me was palpable, a visceral reaction to the violation of nature's laws we were witnessing.

"Here, Beatrix," Luke's voice cut through my horror. He handed me the first box, a physical anchor pulling me back from the brink of my revulsion.

I accepted the box, my mind still reeling from the scene before me. "Gladys, come get this box," I demanded, my voice sharper than intended. The urgency of our situation, coupled with the discomfort of our surroundings, frayed my patience. "And for fuck's sake, hurry up!"

"Beatrix!" Gladys's rebuke was swift as she snatched the box from my grasp, her tone scolding yet laced with the same undercurrent of stress.

I glared at her, my frustration boiling over. "Just put it in the other truck," I instructed, my words terse. The urgency of removing ourselves from this macabre scene lent a harshness to my voice I hadn't foreseen.

In what felt like a whirlwind, the three of us managed to transfer all the boxes in a mere three minutes. "I think that's all of them," Luke announced, his feet hitting the ground as he jumped from the truck. He began to walk around the side, his movements signalling the end of one ordeal and the potential beginning of another.

❖

Curiosity leading my steps, I circled around to join Luke from the opposite side, the passenger door announcing my approach with a loud, attention-grabbing squeak. Luke's head shot up, his surprise at my sudden appearance clear in his widened eyes.

"What are you looking for?" I inquired, leaning in as Luke resumed his frenetic search through the cab's interior, his focus narrowing as he sifted through the assorted detritus of daily vehicle use.

"The delivery manifest," he responded after a moment, his voice carrying a hint of frustration mixed with determination. His answer, simple as it was, sparked a flurry of questions in my mind. *What could Luke possibly need with the delivery manifest at a time like this?*

My curiosity only intensified as Luke reached across to the glove compartment, his movements deliberate. I found myself drawn in, my head inching closer to get a better look at the items he unearthed: a pair of sunglasses, a box of band-aids, and several unused condoms. The assortment was eclectic, each item painting a picture of life's unpredictability. *It's an interesting mix indeed*, I mused, my interest in the mundane contents momentarily distracting me.

"Shit," Luke muttered under his breath, a soft exclamation of either disappointment or frustration.

Seizing the moment, I pressed further, hoping to uncover the reasoning behind his search. "What for?" I asked.

Luke, however, remained focused on his task, seemingly oblivious to my probing. He continued to pull papers from the compartment, unfolding and then dismissing each with a quick glance before carelessly tossing them aside.

Compelled by a mix of curiosity and a desire to understand Luke's intent, I reached for the discarded papers as they landed. Unfolding each one carefully, I scanned the contents, searching for any clue that might reveal why Luke deemed the manifest so important. Yet, as I went through them, I found myself echoing Luke's silent assessment. There was nothing particularly interesting about them at all. Each piece of paper, once filled with potential significance, now lay inert in my hands, their secrets either too mundane to decipher or simply beyond my grasp.

"Well?" My patience was wearing thin, the unease of being kept in the dark by Luke gnawing at me. It was clear he wasn't divulging the full extent of his plans, and my frustration was mounting with each evasive manoeuvre.

Luke's response was to forcefully close the glove box, his actions marked by a finality that drew my full attention. When he looked up at me, our faces mere inches apart, I met his gaze unflinchingly, determined to find the truth in his eyes. "You and your sister are going on a road trip," he declared, the corners of his mouth lifting in what he probably intended to be a reassuring grin.

I gasped, disbelief and apprehension mingling within me. *Luke can't be serious, surely?* The idea of embarking on a road trip under these circumstances, especially with Gladys in her current state, seemed absurd. My gaze drifted outside, where Gladys was leisurely inspecting the flax plant beside the front steps. A soft sigh escaped me, the resignation in my voice barely concealed. "Please don't make me take Gladys," I pleaded, turning back to face Luke, hoping for a reprieve.

However, Luke's expression shifted to one of seriousness, his earlier amusement fading. "But we need that manifest," he stated plainly, underscoring the importance of the document with a gravity that made it clear there was no room for negotiation.

"But why?" Gladys's voice suddenly intruded, her presence announced by her head pressing against my thigh as she squeezed her way into the conversation. The unexpectedness of her proximity and the directness of her question caught me off guard.

My hands instinctively pressed against Gladys's head, an attempt to gently but firmly push her away, but she persisted, pushing back with a stubbornness that was all too familiar. With a roll of my eyes and a huff of exasperation, I realised the futility of resisting. The situation, already complex, was made all the more challenging by the dynamics between us.

"The company are going to report the driver and the truck missing. There's nothing we can do about that. But we can at least make it look like he went missing after he finished his deliveries. The police shouldn't have any reason to suspect us then," Luke's explanation unfurled with a logic that was both chilling and reassuring. His plan, while grim, was rooted in a practicality that aimed to shield us from undue suspicion.

"Oh," Gladys's response came slowly, a dawning understanding reflected in her voice. "I see. Good call."

Luke's gaze shifted back to me, seeking affirmation. In response, I mouthed a silent, "No," my head shaking gently in dissent. The hope that Luke would reconsider, that he might see the folly in our actions and find another way, clung stubbornly to the edges of my thoughts. I wanted to believe there was another path, one less fraught with deception and moral ambiguity.

Luke's reaction was a shrug, an acknowledgment of my plea that carried with it a finality of indifference. Without another word, he quickly exited the truck, leaving me to grapple with the reality of our plan and its implications.

"Ooh, condoms," Gladys's voice, light and oddly out of place, broke through my reverie. She had picked up one of the unopened packages, examining it with an almost childlike curiosity that belied the distress of our circumstances.

I sighed, the weight of our situation pressing down on me once more. With a loud grunt, born of frustration and a desperate need for space to think, I pushed Gladys firmly away. The physical distance I created was as much about preserving my own sanity as it was about distancing myself from the absurdity of the moment. Our predicament demanded serious consideration and careful planning, yet here we were, caught in a surreal pause, momentarily distracted by the mundane in the midst of trauma. The contrast between our actions and the severity of our situation underscored the complex web of emotions and decisions that lay before us, each choice laden with consequences we were only beginning to comprehend.

"Beatrix," Luke's voice, urgent and slightly strained, cut through the tense atmosphere from behind the truck.

"Yeah," I responded, my steps hesitant as I moved towards him, the weight of his request already looming over me.

"I need you to help me roll him." The words hit me like a physical blow, the implication of what he was asking sending a shockwave of disbelief through my system.

"Roll him!" My own voice sounded foreign to my ears, laced with shock and a rising tide of panic. "Hell no. I ain't touching him." The very thought of coming into contact with the deceased, of crossing that final, irrevocable line, was more than I could stomach.

"Beatrix, please," Luke's plea carried a desperation that I knew warranted consideration. "I need to check his back pockets." His rationale, however logical it might have been in any other context, did little to quell the turmoil churning inside me.

"Uh-uh," I retorted, my head shaking as if I could physically dispel the reality of what he was asking.

"Beatrix," Gladys's voice suddenly intruded, her head peeking around the corner of the door, her sudden appearance startling both Luke and me.

"What?" My response was terse, the coldness in my tone a reflection of the turmoil I felt at being pulled deeper into this nightmare.

"Help him. I don't want to go to jail," Gladys sobbed, her words striking a chord that resonated with the fear and desperation we all felt to some degree.

My eyes rolled in frustration. I clenched and unclenched my fists, each movement a battle against the anger and revulsion threatening to overtake me. "Fine," I finally spat out, the words forced through clenched teeth, a reluctant agreement born of necessity rather than willingness.

Crouching beside Luke, I pressed my hand against my mouth, an attempt to shield myself from the reality of what we were about to do. The curiosity that had once driven me to seek out the unknown was now replaced by a visceral understanding of the ungodly task at hand. *Dead bodies are rather gross*, I concluded grimly, a thought that did little to comfort me as we prepared to cross yet another line in the sand.

"You ready?" Luke's voice was steady, but I could sense the urgency behind the question.

I shook my head, the motion more a reflex of my inner turmoil than a conscious decision.

"On three, I need you to grab onto his waist and pull him towards us," Luke instructed, his tone attempting to bridge the gap between necessity and my hesitance.

My response was another vehement shake of the head. The sight of blood staining the jeans was too much; the very idea of touching it, of being so intimately involved with the aftermath of death, made my stomach churn.

"It just needs to be a few seconds. Just long enough for me to feel inside his pocket," Luke persisted, trying to coat the grim task with a layer of reassurance.

But his words did little to assuage my fear. The reality of what we were about to do, the physical act of disturbing the deceased, felt like a violation of both the body's peace and my own principles.

"One. Two. Three. Roll!" Luke's command broke through my reluctance.

A grimace twisted my features as, driven by a mixture of adrenaline and Luke's counting, my hands acted on their own. I gripped the driver's waist with a strength I didn't know I possessed, pulling the body towards us with a firm yank. The roll was accompanied by a sickening squelch that echoed my worst fears.

"Aargh!" The sound tore from my throat as I lost my footing, my backside hitting the metal floor hard. My hands, still clamped onto the blood-soaked jeans, inadvertently dragged the body along with me.

Luke, caught off guard by the sudden movement, couldn't evade in time. The body rolled completely, ending up at his feet. "Shit, Beatrix!" His exclamation was a mixture of shock and frustration as he too lost his balance, falling beside me with a thump that sent a spray of blood airborne.

My heart raced, pounding against my chest as if seeking escape from the horror of what had just transpired. In a desperate attempt to put distance between myself and the scene, I scrambled awkwardly across to the other side of the truck.

Gladys's grip on her glass loosened in her panic, and it crashed to the concrete, shattering with a sound that seemed to echo the chaos of our situation. "Get it off me!" she screamed, her hands frantically scratching at her face in a desperate attempt to rid herself of the imagined contamination.

"Gladys! Shut up!" My voice was a harsh whisper, fear sharpening its edges. "Someone will hear you." The possibility of drawing unwanted attention to our already precarious situation filled me with dread.

"I think it's too late for that, Beatrix," Luke's voice, resigned yet calm, cut through the panic. "We've already made too much noise." His statement, a grim acknowledgment of our situation, only served to heighten the tension.

"Get it off! Get it off!" Gladys's screeches continued unabated, her terror oblivious to our attempts to calm her.

Crossing back to her side, I reached out and gently wiped her face with the back of my sleeve, attempting to soothe her distress. "It's all gone," I assured her, my voice softening as I removed the last traces of red from her cheek.

Meanwhile, Luke's focus remained undeterred. Carefully, he leaned across the body, his movements deliberate as he searched the right back pocket. My anticipation grew, watching closely as he finally pulled out a single piece of paper. The tension between us was palpable, a shared breath held in waiting.

"Is that it?" My question was barely a whisper, my body unconsciously moving closer to Luke's side, drawn by the importance of what that piece of paper represented.

Luke's sigh was like a release valve to the pressure that had built up within us. "Yeah," he confirmed, his voice carrying a weight of relief so profound it momentarily displaced the fear and tension. "We got it."

"Thank God," I breathed out, the relief in my voice mirroring Luke's. The sentiment was more than just gratitude for finding the manifest; it was a beacon of hope in the darkness, a slender thread to grasp onto as we navigated the murky waters of our predicament. In that moment, despite the tragedy, the fear, and the moral ambiguity of our actions, we had achieved a small victory, a piece of leverage in a situation that seemed increasingly out of our control.

Luke carefully folded the manifest, his actions precise and deliberate, before handing it over to me. The weight of the paper in my hands felt heavier than it should, a tangible symbol of our predicament and fleeting hope.

"Gladys, get your ass into the truck," I commanded, my tone more authoritative than usual as I jumped down from the back, the manifest flapping slightly in my grip. The urgency of our situation left no room for hesitation or delay.

"But... but... the glass," Gladys stammered, her concern for the broken glass momentarily overtaking the need for our escape.

"Forget about the glass," Luke interjected quickly, his voice firm yet reassuring. "I'll clean it up." His readiness to take care of the aftermath, to ensure our swift departure, was a small comfort.

"Come on, Gladys. We have to go," I urged, my hand gripping her arm, trying to pull her along with me. The need to leave, to put as much distance between us and the scene of the crime, was pressing.

Gladys hesitated.

"Come on," I insisted again, this time nudging her more firmly with my hip in an attempt to spur her into action. The physical encouragement was gentle but insistent, a reminder that we had no time to waste.

Gladys reached for the manifest, her voice taking on a sudden determination. "I'll hold it," she declared. Then, with a swift motion that caught me off guard, she swiped it from my hands.

"Ahh! Gladys!" I hissed, dodging her retaliatory nudge. The exchange, while brief, was a cautious reminder of the tension that bubbled just beneath the surface of our forced composure. In that moment, the manifest became more than just a piece of paper; it was a lifeline, a point of contention, and a reminder of the lengths we were willing to go to protect ourselves and each other.

❖

"Wait!" Luke's command halted our lighthearted retreat towards the truck's cab.

"What now?" Gladys's impatience was evident, her frustration manifesting in the way she brandished the manifest through the air like a flag of defiance.

I couldn't help but send Gladys a disapproving glance, her flippant attitude grating on me given the severity of our predicament. "What do you need, Luke?" I inquired, striving for calmness in the storm that seemed to perpetually surround us.

"We need to move the body," Luke stated, his voice carrying a weight that felt like an anchor dropping me off the edge of a cliff.

"Hell no!" Gladys screeched.

"I can't move it by myself," Luke countered, the plea in his voice underscored by a stark reality that demanded action, however unsavoury it might be.

"Gladys," I intervened, my tone cool despite the turmoil churning inside me. "We're already involved now. We may as well keep going." The harsh truth of our complicity in the day's events was a bitter pill to swallow, yet undeniable.

Luke's smile, fleeting and tinged with gratitude, did little to alleviate the burden of his request. Deep down, I wished he had never asked, never pulled us further into this morass.

"Are you going to take him through the Portal?" I ventured, clinging to the hope of a solution that would neatly resolve our dilemma.

Luke's negative response dashed that fleeting hope.

"Why the hell not?" Gladys demanded.

I turned my gaze back to Luke, my curiosity piqued despite the dire circumstances. "Then what?" The question hung between us, a silent plea for an alternative that wouldn't drag us further into the mire. Luke's reluctance to use the Portal, to dispose of the body in a manner that would forever elude the authorities, was a gamble that placed us all at risk. The stakes were high, not just for Luke, but for each of us now irrevocably tied to the fate of the young man in the back of the truck. The realisation that we were all potential accomplices in a crime we hadn't committed was a heavy burden to bear, a vivid reminder of the precarious edge on which we now balanced.

Luke's sudden gulp was a clear sign of his apprehension. "Jamie isn't ready for the news yet. We can keep the body in the shed at the back of the yard for now," he proposed, a plan that seemed to skirt the edges of practicality and desperation.

*An odd move, indeed*, I mused silently. The idea of storing the body temporarily felt like a temporary bandage on a gaping wound. "And the truck?" I pressed, seeking clarity on the fate of our other cumbersome piece of evidence.

"I'll clean it out and bleach it while you are gone. Then I'll drive it through the Portal," Luke's response was methodical, outlining steps that seemed counterintuitive at first glance.

"But... if you are taking it through the Portal, why bother cleaning it first?" I couldn't help but question the logic. It seemed an unnecessary step if the ultimate destination of the truck was to be beyond our world, hidden from the prying eyes of our Earthly reality.

"I'd rather not raise any suspicions with Paul and Jamie," Luke explained, his rationale highlighting a concern for the broader implications of our actions on our compatriots in Clivilius. His decision, while perplexing, was rooted in a desire to maintain as much normality as possible under the circumstances.

"Fair call," I conceded, recognising the futility in arguing further. Although I found his reasoning somewhat tenuous, the underlying intent to shield Paul and Jamie from additional stress in an already alien environment held merit. *Perhaps Luke is right not to bombard them with the body of Jamie's dead son*, I reflected. The complexities of our situation, the delicate balance of decisions made under pressure, were becoming all too apparent.

Luke's next move was to climb back into the truck, his actions signalling the transition from planning to execution. "We need a blanket," he stated, a practical consideration for the task at hand.

"Gladys," the unexpected deep male voice calling from the front of the driveway instantly spiked my adrenaline. "Shit," I muttered under my breath, a wave of panic sweeping over me. *Who the hell is here?* The question ricocheted through my mind, escalating my fear. *What if it is the real killer?* My eyes darted around, desperately seeking any viable escape routes, preparing for the worst.

"Gladys, everything okay here?" the man inquired, his tone laced with concern yet carrying an undertone of curiosity that did little to alleviate my apprehension.

Peering around the corner of the truck, Gladys's face lit up with recognition. "Cody!" she exclaimed, her voice a mixture of surprise and relief.

*Cody!* The name echoed in my head, a sudden connection clicking into place from the snippets of drama involving Gladys that had unfolded last night.

"Who the fuck is Cody?" Luke's confusion was palpable, his question punctuated by a mix of irritation and urgency. His reaction, sharp and demanding, underscored the precariousness of our situation.

Gladys, now fully visible to Cody, maintained her façade of normality. "Yeah, everything is great here," she lied smoothly, her voice betraying none of the turmoil that churned beneath the surface.

"Get rid of him. Now!" Luke's hiss was a sharp command, a clear indication of the danger Cody's presence posed to our already fragile cover story.

"Why don't we..." Gladys started, her sentence trailing off as I cut in, an idea taking shape in my mind—a devious plan that could potentially leverage Cody's unexpected arrival to our advantage. The gears in my mind turned rapidly, weaving together fragments of possibility into a strategy that could divert suspicion, manipulate perceptions, and perhaps even provide us with an unexpected ally or a scapegoat, depending on how the cards fell.

"Wait," I found myself whispering sharply.

Luke's reaction was immediate, his glare piercing through the tension between us. "What?" he mouthed, his impatience palpable in the silent exchange.

My mind raced, thoughts tangling and untangling as I tried to weave together a plausible strategy. "I think he may be able to help us," I finally voiced, the idea crystallising despite the myriad of doubts clouding my judgment.

"Help us?" Luke's incredulity mirrored the absurdity of the notion. "How?" His skepticism was a tangible barrier, one that I knew I needed to dismantle with careful reasoning.

For a moment, I wondered whether my calculated assumption could possibly be correct. *Was I wise to suggest it? I feared Leigh would be at risk if I did. But what other choice do we have?*

"I think he is like you," I confessed to Luke, the revelation slipping out almost against my will.

Luke's gasp was a sharp intake of breath, a physical manifestation of his shock. The implications of my statement hung heavily between us, charged with potential and peril.

"But shh," I quickly hushed, pressing my index finger to my lips in a gesture calling for silence. "I don't think Gladys knows yet." My words were a whisper, a conspiracy shared in the shadow of uncertainty.

"But how does Gladys know him?" Luke's question was logical, seeking to untangle the web of connections that had ensnared us all.

"They're dating," I replied, venturing a guess at the nature of their relationship. It was a shot in the dark, but the pieces seemed to fit together in a narrative that made an odd sort of sense.

"Dating?" Luke echoed, the word hanging in the air like a question mark. "This is getting bizarre," he muttered, a hand running across his shaved head in frustration.

"Gladys," I hissed, my voice a sharp command cutting through the confusion. "Bring him here."

"Huh?" Gladys's confusion was evident as she peeked back around the truck, straining to catch my words. "What'd you say?"

"Bring him here," I repeated, firmer this time, my determination steeling my voice.

The colour drained from Gladys's face at my insistence, her complexion turning ashen. With a gentle push on her forehead, I nudged her back into action, a silent directive to follow through with my request.

"Cody, wait!" Gladys's voice carried a new level of insistence as she called out to him, her words a lifeline cast into the unknown as we prepared to confront the unforeseen consequences of our actions. The stakes were high, and with each passing moment, the intricate dance of decisions and revelations drew us deeper into a maze of uncertainties and potential alliances.

Cody's approach up the driveway was marked by a casualness that quickly evaporated the moment the full tableau of the truck and its grim contents came into his view. "What the fuck!" His exclamation cut sharply through the air, a visceral reaction to the scene that unfolded before him.

Luke's response was to meet Cody's gaze, an unspoken challenge passing between them as they stared into each other's wide, terrified eyes. The tension was palpable, a tangible force that seemed to freeze time itself.

"Who the fuck is that, Luke?" Cody's demand for answers was laden with a mix of fear and accusation, his eyes flickering between the body and Luke, seeking an explanation for the horror that lay before him.

"Wait," Luke's reply was hesitant. "You know who I am?" The confusion in Luke's voice mirrored my own, a twist in the unfolding drama that neither of us had anticipated.

"Of course," Cody answered, his tone shifting to one of matter-of-fact assurance. "We've been waiting for you." His statement, simple yet laden with implications, sent a shiver down my spine. *We?* The word echoed in my mind, a puzzle piece that refused to fit. *Either Leigh was lying about not knowing Cody, or there were more Guardians than even he was aware of*, I concluded silently.

"Waiting for me?" Luke echoed, his confusion giving way to a dawning realisation that we were caught in a web far more complex than any of us had imagined.

Cody, however, seemed unfazed by the exchange, his attention quickly returning to the more pressing issue at hand. "What happened to him?" he asked, his gaze settling on the body as he climbed into the truck beside Luke. "Throat looks like it has been slit. Any idea who did this?" His questions were direct, demanding answers that none of us were fully able to give.

I leaned in closer, my own curiosity piqued, trying to catch Luke's response. But his voice was a murmur, too soft to discern from my vantage point.

"We don't have time for this now, Luke," Cody pressed, his urgency a clear signal that our window of action was rapidly closing. "I need to know who he is and what happened. We don't have much time." His insistence on understanding the situation was a command that brooked no delay.

Luke faltered, words failing him in the face of Cody's demands.

"His name is Joel," I found myself speaking up, cutting through the hesitation. "He's Jamie's son." The admission felt like a betrayal, a revealing of truths that we had hoped to keep hidden, yet the necessity of the moment dictated our actions. The revelation hung heavy between us, a new layer of complexity added to an already convoluted situation. The interplay of relationships, secrets, and loyalties was becoming increasingly tangled, each new piece of information reshaping the landscape we navigated.

"Is he—" Cody's question hung in the air, his nod towards Luke heavy with unspoken implications.

"No. I don't think so," I found myself responding quickly, understanding the depth of his inquiry. Cody was probing into whether Joel had been a Guardian, a role that seemed far too perilous and profound for someone as young and seemingly inexperienced as Joel. The notion that Joel's lack of experience could have led to his demise was a chilling thought, one that added a layer of complexity to our already tangled situation. *Or perhaps his inexperience is what got him killed?* The thought was a grim speculation, casting a shadow over the tragic events.

"What happened?" Cody's persistence reflected his need for clarity, for some semblance of understanding in the tragedy that had unfolded.

I could only offer a shrug, a gesture of my own confusion and lack of information. The truth was, we were all grappling with pieces of a puzzle that refused to fit together easily.

"I'm not sure," Luke finally spoke, his voice breaking the heavy silence that had enveloped us. "He delivered a few tents here this morning. I took the opportunity to take them through the Portal while he was in the toilet. Then the boys accidentally ran through." Luke's explanation was a recount of the morning's events, a series of unfortunate accidents that had spiralled into the current predicament.

"The boys?" Cody's confusion was evident, his brow furrowing in an attempt to understand Luke's cryptic reference.

"Dogs," I jumped in, offering a quick clarification. A sense of pride flickered within me for being able to keep pace with the conversation, for contributing to the unravelling of our story in front of Cody. My interjection, while minor, felt like a small victory in maintaining some control over how much we revealed and to whom.

"And did he see?" Cody's question cut straight to the heart of the matter, his focus on the crux of our predicament.

"Yeah," Luke confirmed with a nod. "I'm pretty sure he did. And when I returned, I found him like this." The implication of his words was clear, casting a shadow of guilt and consequence over us all.

"Shit," Cody muttered, beginning to pace back and forth

"Oh my God!" Gladys's exclamation pierced the tense atmosphere, her fear palpable. "We've both seen the Portal too," she said, gesturing frantically between herself and me. "Does that mean we are going to die too?" Her question, born of panic and a newfound understanding of the stakes, echoed ominously in the air.

"Not today, Gladys. Not today," Cody's response, while meant to be reassuring, carried an undercurrent of foreboding, a reminder of the precariousness of our situation.

"I am really confused," Luke admitted. "Who are you again? And how do you know me? Did you have a dream too?" His questions, layered with the need for explanations, hinted at a deeper connection, one that seemed to bridge the gap between reality and the inexplicable.

*A dream?* His mention of a dream sparked a flurry of questions within me, a curiosity about the connections binding us together. *But now is not the time to ask them. We have a murder to cover up, after all.* The grim reality of our task refocused my thoughts on the immediate need for action. "I think Gladys and I had better finish making those deliveries," I said, turning my attention to Luke. "I'll call you later. When we're done." The decision to continue with the deliveries, despite the unanswered questions, was a desperate bid for normality, a way to distance myself somewhat from the body lying in the back of the truck.

Luke's nod was a silent acknowledgment, a mutual understanding of the roles we each had to play in the unfolding saga.

"Be careful. Both of you," Cody's parting words were a solemn benediction, a reminder of the dangers that lay ahead.

"We will," I assured him, my determination steeling my voice as I pushed Gladys towards the other truck. The weight of Cody's warning settled over me, a sobering reminder of the precarious path we were about to tread. As we moved to carry out the remaining deliveries, the reality of our situation —a tangled web of secrets, revelations, and unknown dangers—loomed ever larger, a shadow from which we could not escape.

# COVER UP

## 4338.206.4

### Part 1: The New Norfolk Delivery

"Oh, just keep moving, would you!" The words escaped my lips more sharply than I intended as I nudged Gladys towards the truck, my patience fraying at the edges.

"I am moving!" Gladys retorted, her voice laced with irritation that mirrored my own.

The front door of the truck protested with a loud squeak as I yanked it open, a sound that seemed to echo the strain of the moment. Hoisting myself into the front seat, I took a moment to adjust the mirrors and seat, movements that were precise and deliberate, an attempt to impose some control over our hasty departure. Each adjustment was a small assertion of order, a minor victory in the battle against the disarray that threatened to overwhelm us.

The sound of the passenger door slamming shut jolted me from my thoughts, a harsh punctuation to Gladys's entry beside me. I turned to glare at her, the frustration boiling over. Her carelessness seemed to symbolise the broader discord between us. If she continued in this vein, the journey ahead loomed as an ominous prediction of conflicts yet to surface. "Sorry," she offered, a word that felt hollow in the expanse of the truck's cab.

I rolled my eyes and turned away, facing the road ahead as I muttered under my breath, "No, you're not." The words were barely audible, a whispered testament to my skepticism. I knew all too well the dance of apologies and accusations that we had mastered over the years, a choreography of conflict and reconciliation that seemed destined to repeat.

The truck's engine churned and sprang to life with a rattle that seemed to echo through the very core of my being. It was a sound laden with foreboding, a harbinger of the uncertain journey that lay ahead of us.

"Do you really think we should?" Gladys's voice pierced the heavy silence that had enveloped us, her words laced with doubt and fear. I could hear the tremor in her voice, a clear indication of the inner conflict she was grappling with. It mirrored my own apprehension, the gnawing uncertainty that threatened to consume me.

I gulped, a physical manifestation of my resignation to whatever fate now awaited us. The weight of the decision pressed down on me. *What choice do we have?* The question echoed in my mind, a rhetorical reminder of the dire situation we found ourselves in. *Luke was right. We're involved already.* The realisation settled in with a chilling finality, the knowledge that our involvement had irrevocably entangled us in a web from which there was no easy escape. *If we don't cover it up, we'll end up in prison for sure.* The thought was a stark one, filled with the cold dread of a future marred by bars and the loss of freedom. *Even if we managed to persuade the police we had no involvement in the murder,* the logical part of my brain reasoned, *there was no plausible explanation we could offer for not contacting the authorities immediately.* The implications of our inaction were as damning as the act itself.

"We have to," I told Gladys, my voice steady despite the storm of emotions raging inside me. The words were simple, yet they carried the weight of my grim resolve. It was a declaration of the path we had chosen, fraught with risks and moral ambiguity, yet seemingly the only avenue open to us.

The small truck rolled effortlessly out of the driveway, the motion smooth and almost eerily serene. We moved down the street, each turn of the wheels taking us further from the life we once knew, towards a destination unknown. As we approached the first T-junction, my actions mirrored the decisiveness of our choice. Without indicating, I pulled sharply to the right. The absence of the turn signal was a small rebellion, a minor deviation from the rules that mirrored the much larger transgression we were embarking upon.

"Beatrix!" screeched Gladys, her voice slicing through the hum of the truck's engine like a knife. "Where are you going? You're going the wrong way," she accused, her tone heavy with exasperation. I could feel her eyes on me, wide with incredulity, as if I had suddenly decided to drive us off a cliff.

"Huh?" I shrugged, feigning ignorance. "Wasn't Claremont on the list?" I asked, my voice laced with a hint of defiance. I knew exactly what I was doing, steering us away from New Norfolk, but I wasn't ready to dive into the whys and wherefores of my avoidance.

"Yeah, but we should be going to New Norfolk first," Gladys replied, waving the manifest around like it was a map to buried treasure. Her insistence on following the plan to the letter was both infuriating and admirable in equal measure.

I was well aware that New Norfolk was on the list too, but I couldn't muster the enthusiasm to head that way. Not since I lost the antique shop in a gamble that seemed foolish in hindsight. The thought of revisiting the area, laden with memories of what used to be, filled me with a profound sense of loss. "But Claremont is closer," I insisted stubbornly, clinging to any excuse to delay the inevitable.

Gladys's expression morphed into one of seriousness. Yet, I couldn't help but chuckle softly at the sight. My sister, trying to adopt a stern demeanour, often resembled a squirmy fish out of water. It was a look that was more endearing than intimidating, betraying the warmth and concern that lay beneath her surface of seriousness.

"Technically, yes," Gladys began, her voice adopting a tone of reluctant concession. "But if we go the back way to New Norfolk first, we can loop around along the river, do Claremont, and then continue down for the Moonah delivery," she explained, her smugness evident in the lift of her eyebrows. Her strategy, laid out with such confidence, was irrefutably logical, a fact that irked me more than I cared to admit.

Reluctantly, I steered the truck into the next roundabout, feeling a mix of frustration and resignation as I completed a full circle to exit the way we had come. I sighed heavily, the sound filled with a mixture of defeat and begrudging respect. I hated to admit it, but Gladys's logic made sense. Her ability to navigate both the physical roads and the emotional landscapes of our relationship with such deftness was a constant reminder of the delicate balance we maintained as sisters.

"Hey, look!" yelled Gladys, her voice slicing through the tense silence that had enveloped the cabin of our truck. Her sudden outburst jerked me from my reverie. "The truck is gone. Luke must have taken it through the Portal already."

I leaned forward instinctively, my head turning toward Luke's house as we passed. The mere mention of the Portal sent a thrill of fear and anticipation coursing through me. It was a reminder of the thin veil between our world and the unknown that we were flirting with. As my gaze drifted, so too did the truck, veering dangerously to the left with my diverted attention.

"Beatrix!" screeched Gladys, her voice sharp with panic. The urgency in her tone snapped me back to the present, but my reaction came a fraction too late. I pulled the truck sharply back to the right, an attempt to correct my lapse in concentration, but the damage was done. The corner of the truck clipped the side mirror of a parked car, detaching it with an ease that belied the gravity of the mistake.

"Shit," I muttered, a mixture of frustration and resignation in my voice. Through the rearview mirror, I watched the detached mirror fly down the road, tumbling into the ditch in a sad ballet of consequence. My foot hit the brake instinctively, the truck decelerating quickly under my command, but Gladys's next words halted me further.

"No. Don't stop," she said, her eyes wide with panic, darting erratically as if the act of looking could somehow alter our reality. "I don't think anybody saw us," she added, her voice a high-pitched whisper of hope and fear.

"I really think—" I began, my mind racing with thoughts of accountability and the potential for redemption, but Gladys cut me off.

"Beatrix, you have blood on your clothes. We can't stop!" Her words were a cold splash of reality, jolting me with the awareness of our appearance and the dire implications it carried. I glanced down at my jeans, the evidence of our earlier ordeal stark against the fabric. Gladys was right. Again. The visual confirmation of my stained clothes was a visceral reminder of the stakes at play.

"Watch the road!" yelled Gladys, her command snapping me back to the immediate danger. The truck swayed beneath my hands as I fought to regain control, each movement a battle against the weight of our actions and their consequences.

"Gee, you're such a terrible driver," mumbled Gladys from the passenger seat, her words wrapped in the thick tension that had settled between us like an unwelcome fog.

"Me! A terrible driver?" I snapped back, the edges of my patience fraying as my nerves wound tighter, a coiled spring ready to snap under the weight of our impending actions. The irony of her accusation, given our current predicament, sparked a defensive fire within me. "I'm not the one who knocked down a dozen motorcycles," I teased, my words laced with a forced levity I hoped might diffuse the growing pressure simmering beneath the surface of my composure.

"I did that once," defended Gladys, her voice tinged with indignation. "And that was a long time ago." Her protest, a mix of defiance and embarrassment, was a feeble attempt to salvage her pride from the wreckage of past mistakes.

"Hmph," I scoffed loudly, allowing my skepticism to colour the moment. "It was last year." The reminder served as a barbed retort, a verbal jab meant to puncture the seriousness of our situation with a momentary distraction. Yet, the humour fell flat, overshadowed by the weight of our current escapade.

"Just keep going," said Gladys curtly, her command slicing through the remnants of our banter with the sharpness of a blade.

I bit my lower lip, a physical barrier to the thoughts clamouring for release, thoughts that, if spoken, would only serve to deepen the chasm of our anxieties. *They wouldn't have helped our plight*, I reminded myself. "Okay," I accepted with a resigned sigh. "We'll keep going." The acknowledgment was heavy with the weight of our shared burden. We had, after all, been involved in far worse crimes already today to worry about a broken side mirror. The magnitude of our earlier actions cast a long shadow over the triviality of traffic misdemeanours, a compelling reminder of the dark path we had chosen to walk.

We continued our way along the back road, the journey marked by an oppressive silence that enveloped us like a shroud. The only interruption came when we stopped to allow Gladys to throw up in the ditch. The act, so raw and human, served as a visceral reminder of the stress and fear that gnawed at our insides. Watching her, a pang of sympathy mixed with my own roiling discomfort. The tension, the fear, and the uncertainty of what lay ahead were not just abstract concepts but had manifested in the most tangible of ways.

As Gladys returned to the truck, wiping her mouth with the back of her hand, the silence resumed, a silent pact to press on despite the turmoil that churned within us. The road stretched out before us, a narrow ribbon of asphalt that seemed to lead further away from the life we once knew.

"Welcome to New Norfolk," Gladys announced, a hint of irony in her voice as she read aloud the town's welcoming sign. My response was far from welcoming, though. I swallowed hard, the action more of a struggle than it should have been. Strong tingles raced up my arms, an unwelcome sensation that heralded the onset of jitters threatening to overtake my mind. My relationship with New Norfolk had become strained, to say the least, ever since the antique shop had closed. It was a place teeming with memories, both good and bad, and now, even the sight of the welcome sign felt like a visceral punch to the gut.

Watching Gladys's fingers become increasingly fidgety, tearing tiny pieces off the corners of the manifest in minuscule portions, did nothing to ease my growing discomfort.

"What's the address?" I managed to ask, my voice steadier than I felt.

"Oh... um..." Gladys hesitated, her distraction evident as she tried to smooth the crumpled sheet of paper against her thigh. The sight of her struggling with the manifest, a simple piece of paper now embodying our shared anxiety, was enough to fray my already thin patience.

"Gladys!" I snapped, the corners of my mouth pulling into a tight pout. My frustration wasn't just with her, but with the whole situation, with the tangled web of emotions that New Norfolk evoked within me.

"27 Bettong Road," Gladys blurted out suddenly, her voice a mix of haste and surprise.

"Shit!" The word escaped my lips before I could stop it. It was like a bolt of lightning, illuminating the dark corners of my apprehension with stark clarity.

Gladys gasped, her reaction echoing my own shock. "Isn't that Uncle Lance's house?" she asked, her voice tinged with disbelief.

"Yeah," I confirmed, my voice heavy. "It is." Uncle Lance, our mother's brother, loomed large in our family's history, a figure associated with both warmth and conflict. I hadn't seen him for nearly eighteen months, not since that fateful Christmas before last. The memory of that holiday was vivid in my mind, a chaotic blend of festive joy shattered by vehement disagreement. Uncle Lance and Aunt Amy's quarrel with our mother had been explosive, the kind of family drama that leaves scars long after the shouting has faded.

Gladys and I had tried to remain neutral, to stay out of the fray, but the aftermath had been unavoidable. After Uncle Lance and Aunt Amy had stormed out, our mother's edict had been clear and non-negotiable: we were to cut all contact with them. And I, at least, had complied with her demands, a decision that now seemed both a lifetime ago and just yesterday, all at once.

The realisation that our delivery would take us directly to Uncle Lance's doorstep was a jolt back to reality, a reminder of the complex web of family ties and the emotional landmines they often entailed. It was as if fate, with a sense of irony, had decided to thrust us back into the very heart of unresolved family tensions, forcing us to confront the past we had tried so diligently to avoid.

Gladys glanced across at me, her eyes flickering with a mix of hope and desperation. "Maybe we can leave their package in the letter box?" she questioned.

"I don't think so, Gladys," I replied, my voice steady, but my frown deepening as I considered the logistics of her suggestion. The packages we were dealing with were far too large for any standard letterbox, a reality that seemed to escape Gladys in her quest for a simple solution. "I don't remember seeing any packages small enough to fit in a letterbox," I added, hoping to gently steer her towards the reality of our situation.

Gladys sighed, a sound heavy with resignation. "We'll just sneak up and leave it on the front doorstep then," she said, her tone suggesting that this was the next best plan, however flawed it might be.

"We?" I scoffed, unable to hide my amusement at the thought. "I think you mean you," I smirked, shifting the responsibility squarely onto her shoulders. It was a playful jab, but one that carried an undercurrent of serious expectation.

"What!" Gladys retorted, her voice rising to a pitchy shriek, a mixture of shock and indignation at my suggestion. It was clear that the idea of approaching Uncle Lance's house alone was not what she had in mind.

As we neared our destination, my attempt to bring the truck to a more dignified stop failed spectacularly. The front wheels bounced up the curb as they turned, sending a jolt through the vehicle that rattled both of us. The truck shook sideways when the wheels rolled back down, a less than graceful move that did little to calm my nerves.

"What are you doing? I'm sure his house is further down the road," said Gladys, her confusion evident as she struggled to make sense of my erratic driving.

"It is," I agreed, my voice calm as I finally brought the truck to a stop, albeit in a less than ideal location. My admission did little to clear the confusion from Gladys's expression.

"Then what?" she asked, her confusion deepening into frustration.

I sighed. "Well, if we're trying to cover up a murder, I'm not going to pull a truck up outside the front of their house. That's way too obvious."

Gladys glared at me, her frustration turning to anger as the implications of my plan—and our actions—began to sink in. I met her gaze, unflinching.

I nudged her towards the door, my gesture firm but not unkind. "Just do it, Gladys," I commanded her, my voice carrying an authority that brooked no argument. It was a directive born of necessity, a reminder that the stakes were far too high for hesitation or half-measures.

Reluctantly, Gladys opened the passenger door, her movements hesitant as if each step took a monumental effort. She slid her way to the ground, her posture betraying a mixture of apprehension and resolve. "What kind of parcel is it?" she looked back at me, her eyes searching for some reassurance or perhaps seeking to share the burden of our current endeavour.

"I don't know," I replied, my voice tinged with a mixture of frustration and resignation. "Read the labels."

Gladys stalked away with a huff, her silhouette framed against the backdrop of our grim undertaking. Her departure left me alone with my thoughts, a solitude that felt both oppressive and liberating in its silence.

As I sat in the truck's cabin, my gaze drifted across the cab, out through the still open passenger door, an unwitting portal to the world outside that seemed both close and infinitely distant. The metal door of the truck's back groaned as Gladys pulled it open, a discordant symphony to accompany our clandestine mission.

I waited, the seconds stretching into what felt like an eternity, before returning my gaze to the front, my attention now drawn to my phone. It sat perched in its console, an inanimate witness to the turmoil that churned within me. The device, so often a lifeline to the outside world, now seemed like a beacon of uncertainty. *Should I message Leigh?* The question echoed in my mind, a tantalising temptation to reach out, to seek solace or perhaps guidance in this maelstrom of disturbance I had found myself in. *Is it wise for me to tell him what had happened?* The dilemma gnawed at me, a battle between the desire for connection and the fear of exposing ourselves further, of unravelling the fragile thread that held our secret together.

The weight of the decision lay heavy on my shoulders, a burden that felt both personal and shared. To involve Leigh was to widen the circle of our conspiracy, to potentially draw another into the web of deceit and danger we had woven. Yet, the isolation of our plight, the overwhelming sense of being adrift in a sea of moral ambiguity, made the prospect of confiding in someone else all the more tempting.

The passenger side door closed with a resounding bang, jolting me from my reverie like a gunshot. I cringed involuntarily, my heart skipping a beat as I witnessed Gladys's clumsy misstep over the gutter and onto the footpath. My body sighed deeply, as despair clutched me. Watching her stumble, it became painfully clear—there was no way Gladys was going to be able to make this delivery without drawing attention to herself, without risking everything we were so desperately trying to keep hidden.

Leaning across the cab, I reached for the passenger side window, winding it down with a sense of urgency that mirrored the racing of my heart. "Hey, Gladys," I called out, my voice carrying a blend of concern and caution. Gladys stopped in her tracks, turning to face me, her expression a mix of confusion and anticipation.

"You can't be seen. You're supposed to be a man, remember?" The words tumbled out, partly in jest, but underlined by a grave seriousness. The disguise, the masquerade we had concocted, was fragile at best. The entire premise of these deliveries hinged on maintaining the illusion that Joel had completed them, a threadbare veil of deception that stood between us and catastrophe. If anyone were to spot two women undertaking Joel's rounds, our cover would be irrevocably shattered, leaving us exposed to the relentless gaze of police scrutiny—a prospect that sent shivers down my spine.

As Gladys resumed her cautious trek down the street, my foot tapped a staccato rhythm against the brake pedal, a physical outlet for the nervous energy that thrummed through me. My gaze flickered back to my phone, resting innocuously in its console. The temptation to reach out, to send a message to Leigh, gnawed at me with renewed intensity. *Should I do it?* The question circled in my mind like a bird of prey, its talons poised to strike. My hand crept closer to the device, drawn as if by a magnetic pull.

The phone's screen burst into life, vibrating agitatedly against the plastic console, a sudden intrusion into the tense silence of the truck's cabin. My eyes widened in surprise, and my heartbeat quickened, the unexpected buzz slicing through the fog of my anxiety like a knife. It was a message from Leigh, his name flashing across the screen in stark, unyielding letters.

Glancing quickly out the front windscreen, I noted that Gladys was still absent, her figure swallowed by the distance. My breathing deepened, each inhale sharp and each exhale shuddering, as I reached out with a trembling hand to pick up the phone. Swiping the screen, I hesitated for a heartbeat before pressing the notification, the action fraught with a mix of fear and anticipation.

**Leigh:** *We need to meet up. Urgently.*

I gasped, my heart rate spiking as a thousand thoughts raced through my mind. *Does he know about Joel? Does he know what we are doing right now? Am I in danger?* The questions tumbled over one another, each more unsettling than the last. Taking a deep breath, I held it, my fingers hovering over the keyboard as I attempted to compose a reply that betrayed none of my inner turmoil.

**Beatrix:** *Sure. What's up?*

*Too casual?* I second-guessed myself, the words on the screen suddenly seeming inadequate, too light for the weight of the situation. The possibility that Leigh's message was unrelated to our current predicament loomed large, yet the risk of tipping him off to our dire circumstances was a gamble I wasn't sure I was ready to take. With a mixture of resignation and defiance, I pressed send, inhaling another deep breath as I awaited his reply, my anxiety a tangible presence in the cramped space of the truck.

**Leigh:** *Usual @ 2*

A loud whoosh of air escaped my cracked lips as I exhaled, though the relief was short-lived. His reply, cryptic and devoid of detail, did nothing to quell the storm of worry brewing within me. My fingers danced over the keyboard, the word "Danger?" taking form before I quickly erased it, fearing it might reveal too much, might invite scrutiny we could ill afford.

**Beatrix:** *Okay*

I settled on the simplest of responses, a single word that carried the weight of my apprehension and the echo of my resolve.

The sudden swing of the passenger door broke the tense silence like a clap of thunder, startling me from my anxious reverie. My hands, already jittery from the day's stress, fumbled in a desperate attempt to secure my phone, which slipped from my grasp and landed with a thump at my feet—a minor calamity in the midst of our ongoing storm.

"Let's get out of here," Gladys panted, her voice laced with a breathlessness that spoke volumes of the urgency she felt. The door slammed shut with a finality that echoed ominously within the confines of the truck.

Hastily scooping up my phone, I wedged it tightly between my thighs, a makeshift safeguard against further mishaps. With my heart pounding a frantic rhythm against my ribcage, I turned the key in the ignition, and the truck lurched forward, a mechanical beast spurred into motion by our dire circumstances.

"No," Gladys interjected firmly, her tone brooking no argument. "Turn us around and go the other way."

Her sudden directive, delivered with such conviction, sparked a surge of suspicion within me. *Has Gladys done something that will compromise us?* The question wormed its way through my mind, a seed of doubt taking root amidst our escape. Her insistence on avoiding a particular route, on eschewing the path that lay before us, suggested a knowledge—or an action—she was keen to keep hidden.

"Safer not to drive past their house," Gladys offered by way of explanation, her words sparse and shrouded in a vagueness that did little to assuage my burgeoning fears. Her reluctance to elaborate, to offer any semblance of detail, only served to heighten the tension that vibrated between us like a taut wire.

In that moment, a decision presented itself, as clear as the road that stretched out ahead. I chose not to press my sister for answers, to not delve deeper into the potential mire of her actions. Perhaps ignorance was a form of bliss, a shield against the full brunt of our predicament. Besides, the practicalities of our situation loomed large; Gladys was essential to the completion of our mission, to the delivery of the parcels that were our burden to bear. *I'd better not send her over the edge completely,* I reasoned, a pragmatic voice cutting through the fog of my apprehensions.

❖

**Part 2: The Claremont Delivery**

The truck's tires hummed against the asphalt, a steady rhythm that accompanied our journey as the road unfurled alongside the river. I clung to this semblance of tranquility, eager for any respite from the storm of thoughts swirling in my mind, especially those provoked by Leigh's messages. However, the constant, nervous twitching of Gladys's hands, a silent symphony of anxiety, persistently invaded the edge of my vision, a relentless reminder of our shared tension.

Unable to ignore the distraction any longer, my patience frayed to its limit, I finally snapped. "Would you stop that already?" The sharpness in my voice cut through the cab's quiet like a knife.

"Sorry," Gladys murmured, her voice a mixture of apology and stress. "I'm just a bit anxious."

"I know! I've been watching your hands fidget for the last ten minutes," I retorted, my frustration evident. The air between us was charged with an unspoken understanding of the gravity of our situation, yet acknowledging it only seemed to amplify the anxiety.

Gladys exhaled deeply, the sound heavy with apprehension. "Do you think it'll actually make any difference?" she ventured, her question hanging between us like a spectre of doubt.

"What do you mean?" I probed, genuinely puzzled by her line of inquiry.

"Well... I mean... If these people are finding their packages outside their front door, what are they going to tell the police?" Gladys's query was laced with a newfound clarity, her words painting a picture of our efforts as potentially futile.

"Huh?" I responded, still struggling to grasp the full implications of her point.

"I mean if nobody actually sees Joel, then there will be no evidence that he actually made the deliveries," Gladys elaborated with a hint of frustration. "So, really, this whole exercise doesn't get us in the clear at all." Her logic, once laid bare, cast a shadow over our meticulously laid plans, suggesting that our actions might be in vain.

My heart skipped a beat, a silent acknowledgment of the validity in Gladys's words. *Is Gladys right? Is this actually helping us?* Doubt gnawed at the edges of my resolve, yet a deeper intuition suggested that our current predicament was merely the precursor to more significant challenges. Regardless, my gut told me that we were going to find ourselves in far greater trouble than this before the police were on our trail.

"Hopefully it will keep them distracted," I replied, opting for a response that masked my own burgeoning fears. It was a half-truth, offered in the hope of providing some solace, even as my mind raced with the possible outcomes of our actions.

And with that, the cab returned to silence, a thick, palpable stillness that enveloped us as we continued our journey.

As we approached our next destination, mirroring the cautious distance we had maintained in New Norfolk, I brought the truck to a halt a safe hundred metres away from the expected target.

"Can you do this one?" Gladys turned to me, her voice laced with a plea that tugged at my heartstrings. Her eyes, wide and beseeching, sought refuge from the task at hand, a reprieve I found myself unable to grant.

"No," I replied, the word sharper than I intended, a blade cutting through the fragile atmosphere between us. I softened, attempting to cloak my refusal in a veneer of support. "Look, all you have to do is leave it on their front doorstep and come straight back. I'll be here waiting for you," I assured her, my tone a blend of encouragement and desperation.

Gladys swung her door open with a force that spoke volumes of her frustration, and jumped down from the truck. "I still don't think it'll matter," she retorted with a snark, her words a reflection of the hopelessness that seemed to shadow our every move.

"Hey," I called out, an instinctive response to her defeatism. Gladys looked up at me, her face etched with seriousness, a pout forming that was more a mask of her inner turmoil than any childlike sulk.

"Either way, delivering these packages is better than us being stuck with them," I reasoned, my words carrying the weight of our grim reality. I mustered a smile, though it felt as brittle as thin ice, a fragile barrier against the cold depths of our predicament.

❖

## Part 3 - The Moonah Delivery

"Last one," I announced, managing a smile that felt like a small victory, a light at the end of a long, dark tunnel.

"Thank God for that," Gladys echoed, her relief palpable as she buckled her seatbelt, her movements deliberate, as if securing herself for more than just the drive.

"You haven't enjoyed playing delivery girl then?" I couldn't resist teasing, an attempt to inject a moment of levity into the surreal situation we found ourselves in.

Gladys's response was a glare, sharp enough to cut through the tension, yet I caught the underlying fatigue in her eyes.

"So, that's a no," I said, a half-hearted chuckle escaping me as I answered my own question, acknowledging the absurdity of finding humour in our dire circumstances.

"Just drive, Beatrix," Gladys sighed, the weight of her exhaustion evident in her voice. It was a resignation, an acknowledgment that our ordeal was far from over, even with the deliveries almost behind us.

A smug smile momentarily crossed my face as the truck pulled away from the curb, a fleeting sense of accomplishment. However, as we travelled in silence, that smile gradually faded, replaced by a furrow of concern that creased my forehead. My mind, unbidden, drifted back to the messages from Leigh that I had been trying so hard to push to the back of my mind. *Why did Leigh want to meet so desperately?* The question gnawed at me, unsettling in its urgency. Leigh's usual precision with words meant that his use of 'urgent' couldn't be anything but significant.

I stole a glance at Gladys, noting how she sat motionless beside me, her hands clasped tightly in her lap as if holding onto the momentary peace the silence afforded us. Her gaze was fixed through the window, lost in the blur of the world passing by.

"You'd better send Luke a message and let him know that we're almost done," I suggested, the words carrying a mixture of relief and anticipation for the end of our task.

Gladys, lost in her own thoughts, offered no verbal response. Instead, she reached for her phone with a sense of resignation, her fingers moving swiftly over the screen. "Done," she announced, placing her phone back in the console before resuming her silent vigil out the window.

Within minutes, the shrill ring of Gladys's phone cut through the cab's silence, an unexpected intrusion. She answered with a promptness that betrayed her eagerness for any distraction. "Hey, Luke. What's up?" Her voice, tinged with a forced cheeriness, contrasted sharply with the weariness etched on her face.

I stole glances at Gladys, torn between the need to focus on the bustling road ahead and the curiosity piqued by Luke's call. I was on the verge of asking her about the conversation when Luke's voice, amplified by the phone's speaker, filled the truck.

"Hey, Gladys. I forgot to ask you earlier. Can you and Beatrix please collect me a large supply of shelving?" His request, so mundane under normal circumstances, now seemed like an insurmountable task, another weight added to our already burdened shoulders.

"In our truck?" Gladys's voice held a note of disbelief, as if the reality of our situation had suddenly become even more absurd.

"Yes. That's probably the best idea," Luke's reply was practical, oblivious to the sighs of resignation it elicited from us.

Gladys paused, the hesitation in her voice mirroring the hesitation in her heart. "I don't have any more money to spare, Luke. I have the next mortgage payment coming out in a few days," she confessed.

"Don't worry. I have money," I blurted out, louder than intended, a rash offer spurred by a desire to keep things moving, to prevent any further delays in our already complicated situation.

"How do you have money?" Gladys turned to stare at me, her surprise evident.

"Never mind that," I replied quickly, regret lacing my words the moment they left my mouth. The offer had been instinctual, a knee-jerk reaction to the immediate problem, yet it had opened a door to questions I wasn't prepared to answer. "Let's just get this shit done," I concluded.

Gladys gave an indifferent shrug, as she turned back to her phone. "Yeah, Luke. Beatrix has money. She'll pay for it," she declared.

"Anything else?" I yelled out before I could stop myself.

"I also need you to print me some simple instructions for pouring a slab of concrete for a shed," Luke replied.

"Huh?" Gladys asked, her face baked in confusion.

"Gladys!" I couldn't keep the snap from my voice. "The Bunnings store will be able to give us something. We'll ask them while we're there getting the shelving."

"Oh yeah," Gladys finally conceded, ending the call without another word to Luke, her social niceties forgotten in the whirlwind of our day.

"You're not going to say goodbye?" My chuckle was half-hearted.

"Huh?" Gladys's confusion was almost comical, a brief interlude of levity. "Oh," she realised her mistake too late, shouting an apology to the already silent phone.

My eyes rolled for what felt like the hundredth time that day. "Gee. You sure you have the volume loud enough?" The tease was light, but it carried an undercurrent of the stress we were both navigating, a stress that seemed to manifest in petty irritations and snappy exchanges.

Gladys's response was to pout and turn away, her face once again lost to the passing scenery outside her window, a silent retreat into her thoughts.

"What was that?" I asked, straining to catch the mumbled words she had directed out the window, away from me.

"Nothing," she called back, her voice a mix of defiance and resignation. The word hung between us, a placeholder for all the unsaid things, the worries, and fears that we were both trying so hard to keep at bay.

# THE UNEXPECTED DELIVERY

## 4338.206.5

"Next please," the woman at the special service counter of the large hardware store called out, her voice echoing slightly in the cavernous, dimly lit space filled with the scent of sawdust and metal. The fluorescent lights above flickered, casting an industrial glow over the aisles of tools and materials that stretched out behind me.

Stepping forward, I approached the counter, my sneakers scuffing against the concrete floor. "Hi," I began, trying to inject a note of friendliness into my voice. "I'm after some information on pouring concrete, please." I clasped my hands in front of me.

"Just a minute," the woman replied, her attention already drifting to the computer beside her. She began typing away furiously, her fingers a blur against the keys. I watched, a mixture of impatience and anticipation churning in my stomach. "There we go," she said after a moment, turning the screen in my direction with a flourish.

I leaned in, squinting at the screen, but found myself hesitating. I didn't even bother to read the top line. *What do I care for concrete, really?* It was a means to an end, a necessary component of Luke's grand design. "Great. Can I get that printed please?" I asked, forcing a smile, though it felt like stretching a thin veneer over my frustration.

"We don't do printing," the woman replied bluntly, her voice flat, as if she'd had this conversation a thousand times before.

"Oh, come on! It's what, two pages?" I retorted, my patience fraying. I could feel my cheeks flush with irritation, the absurdity of the situation gnawing at me.

"Company policy," she replied with a shrug and a turned-up nose, as if to signify the end of the discussion. Her indifference stung, a sharp contrast to the burning stubbornness I felt to progress regardless.

"Well, that's a shit policy. Look, I'll even pay you to—" My protest was cut short as a young man stepped in, his presence like a sudden breeze in the stifling atmosphere of the store.

"Just print the damn pages for her, Lara. It'll take you two seconds," he told her, his voice firm yet carrying an undercurrent of warmth. His intervention felt like a lifeline, a moment of unexpected solidarity in the face of bureaucratic indifference.

Lara released a loud, defiant huff, resonating through the sterile air of the store like a thunderclap in the quiet. But before I could muster a retort, her hand shot to the left, her movements sharp and brusque. She snatched several pages from the nearby printer with an air of resigned irritation and pushed them across the counter in my direction. The papers slid towards me, a tangible result of my persistence and, unexpectedly, Jake's intervention.

Eyes narrowing at the woman, not just in anger but also in a silent promise of remembered grievances, I collected the papers. Turning my attention to the man who had stepped into the fray, I felt a mix of gratitude and embarrassment. "Thank you," I said, my voice carrying a note of genuine appreciation. I paused momentarily as my eyes flicked to his name tag, seeking out the name of my unexpected ally. "Jake," I finished, smoothing over the moment with as much grace as I could muster.

"No problem," replied Jake, his voice light, tinged with amusement. "Enjoy your concrete," he said, his smile kind, reaching his eyes and softening the harsh fluorescent light that framed him.

I didn't mean to, truly. The guy was nice, genuinely so, but my eyes rolled instinctively anyway. "Yeah," I replied, the word laced with a lack of enthusiasm that belied my internal appreciation. Before turning to leave, I gave Lara one last glare, a silent parting shot that said more than words ever could.

"Rude bitch," I heard Lara mutter under her breath as I walked away, her voice low but unmistakably venomous. The words, meant to wound, only served to tighten my grip on the papers. My fist clenched tighter, the edges of the paper crumpling under the pressure

But no, I reminded myself, I wasn't going to give the cranky woman the satisfaction of another round, of seeing me unravel. With every step I took away from the counter, I forced myself to breathe, to unclench my fist and smooth out the papers, each step a conscious effort to shed the negativity that attempted to cling to me like a second skin.

I soon found myself navigating through an aisle crammed with an extensive array of shelving solutions, each one promising organisation and ease, a stark contrast to the disarray of my current search for Gladys. The shelves loomed large around me, casting long shadows that seemed to mirror my growing concern. But amidst the metal and wood, there was no sign of Gladys. I frowned to myself, a crease forming between my brows. *Surely, I hadn't taken that much longer than her.* The thought nagged at me, an unwelcome guest in my mind.

"Excuse me," I said, my voice slicing through the relative quiet. I approached another servicewoman who was in the midst of changing over several price tags, her movements methodical and precise. She paused at my interruption, turning towards me with a look of open curiosity.

"How can I help you?" the young woman asked, her tone kind and inviting. There was a genuineness to her demeanour that eased the tightness in my chest, a welcome change from my previous encounter.

"I'm looking for my sister. I was supposed to meet her here to get an assortment of shelves," I explained, my voice tinged with a mix of hope and frustration. The details of our plan, so meticulously arranged, now seemed to be unravelling at the edges.

"About this high, with reddish-brown hair down to here?" asked Melissa, her name badge glinting under the store's fluorescent lights. She used her hands to describe Gladys's height and the length of her hair quite accurately, painting a picture in the air between us.

"That'd be her," I replied, a smile breaking through my concern. The relief was immediate, warming me from the inside out. At least it sounded like Gladys had actually been here, a small victory in the grand scheme of things.

Melissa laughed softly, a sound that seemed to carry a lightness, a shared moment of amusement in the otherwise mundane setting. "She had quite a large order. Jarod went to help her take it outside," she explained, her smile broadening.

*No surprises there*, I thought, an internal chuckle breaking through my earlier annoyance. "Thank you, Melissa," I said, my gratitude genuine. Her assistance, so readily given, was a beacon of helpfulness in the vast sea of shelves and aisles.

With a renewed sense of direction, I headed towards the exit, the information Melissa provided guiding me. The weight of my earlier irritation began to lift, replaced by the anticipation of reuniting with Gladys.

I stalked across the asphalt carpark in a huff, the sound of my footsteps harsh against the sprawling expanse. Near the far end of the carpark, I could see Gladys thanking a young man—whom I assumed must be Jarod—before opening the driver's side door of the truck.

"Gladys!" I called out, my voice cutting through the cool air, as I ran the last distance across the car park. My heart was pounding, not just from the run, but from a mix of frustration and the pressing need to confront her before she could take control of the truck.

"Did you get it?" asked Gladys, her voice betraying a hint of excitement, oblivious to the storm brewing within me.

"You didn't have to leave me there!" I cried, waving the crumpled paper in my hand like a flag of my frustration. The paper, once a symbol of progress, now felt like a testament to my annoyance.

"I didn't leave you there," replied Gladys, her tone defensive as she climbed into the front seat. "Jarod offered to help," she added, her words meant to soothe but only fuelling my irritation. And then, the door closed, a definitive sound that seemed to echo my thwarted intentions.

I turned my back to my sister, a silent protest. *Gladys knew I wanted to be the driver!* It was more than just a position; it was about control, about being the one to navigate us through this venture, literally and metaphorically.

A thin, tall man caught my attention from across the car park, pulling me out of my frustrated thoughts. He was lurking in the shadows near the corner of the building, his presence ominous and unsettling. I was certain he had been watching us, the way his posture was angled, the intentness that seemed to emanate from him. A cold shiver ran down my spine, a primal reaction to the perceived threat. I looked away, trying to dismiss the unease that clung to me, but from the corner of my eye, I could see he was still watching, a silent observer to our discord.

"You getting in then?" Gladys leaned out the window and asked, her voice breaking through my apprehension.

Just then, a large, white van stopped behind us, momentarily blocking my view of the building's corner while the driver waited for a nearby car to reverse. It didn't stop for long, but when the van moved along, my heart skipped a beat—the watcher was gone. Vanished as if he had never been there, leaving a lingering question of his intentions.

Forgetting about my stubbornness to drive, the urgency of the situation propelling me forward, I opened the passenger side door and climbed inside. "Let's get out of here," I ordered Gladys, my voice carrying an edge of command. I closed the door firmly and locked it, a small barrier against the unease that the stranger had instilled in me.

The engine started with a clunky rattle, a reminder of the truck's age and the journeys it had weathered. As Gladys manoeuvred us through the carpark, I couldn't shake off the feeling of being watched, the image of the lurking figure etched into my memory.

My phone beeped quietly, a subtle intrusion into the tense atmosphere of the truck. With a sense of foreboding, I pulled it from my pocket. The message displayed was succinct, its brevity doing nothing to ease the sudden knot in my stomach.

**Leigh:** *Change in plans. Package on your bed – needs delivery. You'll get address soon.*

"No!" I said loudly, the word bursting from me with more force than I intended. Gladys, who had been navigating the truck towards the exit intersection, glanced at me, her expression a mix of surprise and irritation. "I need to go home," I told her bluntly, the urgency of the situation rendering me incapable of softening the demand.

Gladys glared solidly at me, her eyes sharp and questioning, clearly not appreciating the sudden change.

Ignoring the honk of the horn from the car approaching from behind, she cut across the driver's path with a decisiveness that was both alarming and impressive, and took the truck left, away from our original direction.

As we veered onto the new path, I felt another vibration from the phone in my hands, which I clutched even tighter, as if the device were a lifeline in the swirling uncertainty that had suddenly enveloped me.

Slowly, with a reluctance born of apprehension, I glanced down at the new message, the digits on the screen searing themselves into my memory.

**Leigh:** *655 Main Road Berriedale @ 7.15pm*

# BLACK DRESS: CHARITY

## 4338.206.6

As I entered my room, the sight that greeted me was both mundane and laden with expectation—a small, plain brown cardboard box perched innocently on the bed. Its simplicity belied the complexity of its origin and the implications of its presence. I knew, without a shadow of a doubt, that it had to be from Leigh. He had once explained to me, with an earnestness that was both fascinating and slightly unnerving, how he had activated his Portal in my room. This act of registering the location in his Portal Key, a device of profound significance to a Guardian, enabled him to traverse the distance between our world and Clivilius at will.

Initially, the thought had unsettled me deeply. The idea that Leigh could come and go into my personal space without my knowledge or consent had struck me as invasive, a violation of a boundary I hadn't realised I valued so fiercely until it was trespassed. The notion had been creepy at best, and at its worst, it teetered on the edge of predatory. Yet, as time passed and our interactions grew in frequency and depth, my perspective had shifted. Understanding blossomed from the seeds of trust and shared confidences. His reasons, once a source of disquiet, now resonated with a sense of necessity and duty that I could not fault.

Reflecting on this evolution of trust, I couldn't help but recall the instances where I'd returned home to find Leigh waiting for me. Each memory was tinged with the surreal quality of stepping into a scene I hadn't known was set for me. The realisation of these moments, in hindsight, sent an odd tingle down my spine, a shiver that was part intrigue and part apprehension. There was something undeniably more unsettling about the thought of him materialising in my absence rather than during it. It suggested a level of forethought and deliberation that felt, in a way, more intimate and invasive than any casual encounter within the confines of my home could be.

I stared at the dull package resting inconspicuously on my dresser. No larger than a shoebox, it sat there, unassuming yet somehow ominous. Lifting it, its weight surprised me, heavy and dense, as if it contained more than just physical objects—perhaps the weight of the unknown, or the heaviness of responsibility.

Upon closer inspection, a name scrawled in black permanent marker caught my eye—Charlie Claiborne. The letters, uneven and hastily written, seemed to pulse with a significance I couldn't yet grasp. "Hmm," I mused aloud, the name unfamiliar, a mystery wrapped within the cardboard confines. "This should be interesting." My mind spun with questions about the package's contents and its intended recipient. Leigh's reliance on me for this task puzzled me. I understood the necessity of his precautions, the layers of security he wove around his existence, but at times, it felt like overkill.

Placing the box down on the dresser, my attention was drawn to a small envelope, an afterthought taped to the side. Its detachment revealed a minor tear in the cardboard, a small wound in the box's side that I smoothed over with a touch.

*DRESS NICE*, the message scrawled across the envelope in the same hasty handwriting, was a directive that filled me with dread. My heart sank. *What the hell is Leigh expecting me to do?* The ambiguity of the message, coupled with the formality of the request, left me feeling out of my depth. It wasn't just a package delivery; this was something more, something that required a role I felt ill-prepared to play.

Taking a deep breath, I steeled myself and extracted the small, thick piece of card from the envelope. The invitation that lay before me was elegant, its heavy cardstock a tactile promise of the event's exclusivity. A black-tie charity fundraiser cocktail event at MONA, the Museum of Old and New Art. The words seemed to leap off the card, each one a hammer blow to my escalating apprehension.

"Shit no," I exclaimed, the words escaping in a loud huff of disbelief. *Leigh knows I don't do events like this*. The very idea of me, mingling in a crowd of philanthropists and art aficionados, dressed in finery I barely owned nor desired, was ludicrous. Leigh's expectations seemed to clash violently with the reality of who I was, a chasm that felt too wide to bridge.

Grabbing my phone in a flurry of sudden determination, I navigated through the clutter of notifications to the last message I had received from Leigh. The weight of the impending event was a tight knot in my stomach, a silent testament to the anxiety bubbling just beneath the surface. With a shaky breath, I tapped out my response with a mix of defiance and desperation. *Sorry, can't do it,* I typed, my fingers hesitating just a moment before I pressed send. A part of me hoped for relief, for an escape from the daunting task ahead.

The spinning blue processing circle then appeared beside the unsent message, a digital purgatory holding my fate in balance. My head tilted, eyes locked on the screen, as irritation began to seep into the edges of my patience. The seconds ticked by, each one stretching out longer than the last. *I don't normally have reception problems in my room.* The thought was a whisper in my mind, a murmur of confusion amidst the growing frustration.

Finally, the relentless spinning halted, but not with the resolution I had hoped for. Instead, an exclamation mark boldly took its place, the words *Message Undelivered* flashing beneath it like a neon sign in the dimness of my room. "Shit," I huffed into the silence, the word a burst of exasperation that did little to alleviate the tension coiling tighter within me. "He's cancelled his number again." The realisation sank in like a stone, heavy with implications.

With a flicker of hope, yet shadowed by doubt, I tapped the screen to resend the message, my heart holding onto a sliver of possibility. But the digital verdict was swift and unchanging. *Message Undelivered,* it declared once more, a finality that echoed in the quiet of the room. The small screen, usually so vibrant and alive with connection, now felt like a barrier, isolating me further in my quandary.

I looked back at the package sitting on my dresser, its plain brown surface a constant reminder of the dilemma I was facing. The weight of the decision pressed heavily on me, a tangible representation of the choice I had to make. *Was not delivering it worth the risk?* The question echoed in my mind, a persistent whisper that refused to be silenced. Leigh's words, often spoken with a gravity that bordered on solemn, reverberated through my thoughts. *Every action has an impact. Every decision has consequences.* Or some shit like that. Despite my attempts to dismiss his advice as overly dramatic, the sincerity in his voice, the earnestness in his eyes whenever he said it, made it impossible to completely disregard. He genuinely believed in the weight of those words, and over time, so had I.

The phone on the dresser shattered the silence, vibrating loudly against the wood, its sudden noise making me jump. "Leigh?" I murmured to the empty room, a flicker of hope igniting within me. Perhaps, I thought, clutching at straws, I'd still have a chance to bail on this entire situation.

The screen lit up with a message, but it wasn't from Leigh.

**Gladys:** *Holding a memorial service for Joel at Luke's house 11pm tonight. I'll pick you up.*

A surge of frustration washed over me as I read the message. My fingers, short and adept, flew over the screen in response.

**Beatrix:** *No I'll come get you at 10:50*

The decision to take control, even in such a small way, was a fleeting comfort in the whirlwind of obligations I found myself caught in. I rolled my eyes, a gesture of resignation to the series of events unfolding before me. "Looks like I'm going to some shitty charity function," I huffed out loud, my voice filled with a mix of irritation and defeat.

❖

"Not bad," I murmured to myself, the words barely a whisper as I stood before the full-length leaner mirror. The reflection that stared back at me was one of composed elegance, a telling contrast to the turmoil that churned beneath the surface. I executed slow, half twirls to either side, my gaze critically assessing the fit of the dress. The sweeping skirt, with its gentle cascade from the gathered and fitted waist, fell just below my knees, the fabric moving with a grace that belied my inner restlessness.

My hands traced the contours of the floral lace that adorned the tailored bodice, marvelling at the perfection of its fit against my skin. The elbow-length lace sleeves had required some adjustment, their ties now redone to hug my arms just so. With a side turn, I checked the corset tie at the back, ensuring it was laced properly, a final nod to the meticulous attention to detail that the occasion demanded.

Returning to a full frontal view, my hand brushed my cheek in a soft caress, a tactile memory that transported me back to a day shrouded in grief. The sheer black dress, now a symbol of sombre elegance, had last been worn at Brody's funeral. The weight of that day pressed down on me, a cloak of sorrow that I hadn't fully shed.

*Am I being callous by wearing this again?* The question echoed in the silence of the room, a spectre of doubt amidst the ritual of preparation. "No," I answered softly, a reaffirmation spoken to the reflection that held my gaze. I could almost feel Brody's presence, his hands on my waist, his eyes locked with mine as he offered reassurance in the face of my insecurities. "Brody would have told me that I was beautiful."

Exhaling loudly, I acknowledged the passage of time, the distance between those days and the present. The dress, though a relic of a mournful past, felt fitting for tonight's function—simple, yet elegant, a bridge between the person I was and the one I needed to be this evening. *And besides*, I reasoned with myself, a brief glance at my phone revealing no miraculous reprieve from the night ahead, *After the day I'm having, I feel like I'm about to attend my own funeral.*

The thought, morbid though it was, carried a thread of grim humour, a momentary lightness in the sombreness of my preparations. Dropping the phone into the small, matching black purse, I turned away from the mirror, from the reflection that held both memories and possibilities. The room I left behind was a silent witness to the transformation, a space that had seen me at my most vulnerable and now, at a moment of forced resilience.

As I stepped out, the dress a soft whisper against my legs, I carried with me not just the physical weight of my attire, but the emotional weight of the evening ahead. The function, with its promise of social niceties and forced pleasantries, loomed large, a trial of endurance in the face of my own personal grief.

❖

Taking my place at the end of the short queue outside the venue, I pulled out my phone and dialled the last number I had for Leigh, my heart holding a sliver of hope for connection. The familiar, sterile voice of the automated reply cut through the night, stark against the buzz of anticipation from the crowd around me. "Your call could not be connected." The words, blunt and devoid of empathy, echoed a sentiment that was becoming all too familiar.

Despite the chill that wrapped the night air around me, a warmth born of anxiety blossomed in my palms, moisture gathering against the cool surface of my phone. This wasn't the first time Leigh had vanished into the ether, changing numbers like one might change clothes, yet the timing couldn't have been worse. Right now, my focus had to shift; I had a charity event to navigate, a package to deliver to Charlie, and a desire to escape the evening's obligations as quickly as possible.

Goosebumps danced along my exposed forearms, a testament to the cold that seeped into the fabric of my dress, piercing the armour of composure I had carefully constructed. The box I carried, an unwelcome companion for the evening, prevented any attempt to warm myself, its presence a constant reminder of the task at hand. A task that, under the gaze of the harsh and unpredictable Tasmanian winter night, seemed even more daunting.

I cast a rueful glance at the sky, cursing my own optimism—or perhaps stubbornness—in choosing attire over practicality. The perfect little jacket that would have complemented my dress lay forgotten, a victim of my rushed departure and a testament to my underestimation of the season's cruelty. A frown etched itself deeper into my expression as I lamented the oversight, the cold biting a little sharper with the regret of my choice.

"You look a bit cold there," echoed a deep, familiar voice, breaking through the evening's chill and the murmur of the crowd. The voice, unexpected yet unmistakably recognisable, prompted an involuntary shiver that wasn't entirely from the cold.

I spun around, my reaction a mixture of surprise and something akin to relief. "Jarod," I acknowledged, my voice steadier than I felt. My gaze travelled upwards, taking in the full six feet and more of him. Jarod always had a way of filling the space around him, his presence somehow both imposing and comforting. "What a surprise to see you here tonight," I added.

Jarod's response was a smile, one that transformed his face, exposing freshly bleached teeth against the backdrop of the night. "I think it is I who should be more surprised to see you. And at a black-tie event no less," he remarked, his tone carrying the light touch of humour and disbelief.

I managed an awkward smile in return, a gesture that felt as forced as my attendance at this event. The social dance of pleasantries we were performing seemed almost a parody of genuine interaction, a reflection of the masks we all donned for occasions such as these.

"Here," Jarod said, his actions cutting through the pretence. He removed his black suited jacket with a fluidity that spoke of his comfort with the gesture. "Take mine." His offer was both a kindness and a reminder of past moments shared, a history that lingered in the space between us.

Accepting the jacket gracefully, I allowed Jarod to slip it over my shoulders, his movements careful and considerate. The warmth that enveloped me was immediate and profound, the fabric of the expensive garment holding the residual heat of his body. It was a sensation that was familiar, comforting in its intimacy. This wasn't the first time I'd found refuge in the embrace of his jacket, nor was it the first time I'd been caught in the subtle cloud of his distinct and memorable Creed cologne.

"Thank you," I murmured softly, my gratitude genuine but my gaze averted, avoiding the dark eyes that sought mine from beneath carefully manicured, yet full eyebrows. In that moment, with the warmth of his jacket wrapped around me, I was reminded of the complexity of our past encounters. *You haven't changed a single bit, Jarod James.* The thought was both an observation and an unvoiced question, wondering how someone so familiar could still remain such an enigma.

"Which charity are you supporting tonight?" Jarod's question sliced through the ambient noise, catching me unprepared as I stood amidst the glittering array of attendees.

"Oh," I stumbled for a moment, the question pulling me back from my thoughts, which had drifted away from the immediate surroundings. "Bonorong," I answered more quickly than I intended, my voice carrying a hint of surprise at my own response.

"Bonorong?" Jarod echoed, his interest piqued, his brow arching in a blend of surprise and curiosity. "I didn't realise Wildlife Parks were charities."

As Leigh's gaze lingered on me expectantly, I offered a casual shrug, desperately attempting to conceal the sudden tightness in my chest. "There's always a few exceptions," I replied, the words slipping out with forced nonchalance, despite the weight of insincerity that hung in the air. My mind raced, scrambling to undo the unintended commitment I had just made, regretting the hasty response that now threatened to entangle me in a web of deceit.

Before Jarod could delve any deeper, a welcome interruption materialised in the form of Mrs. Enid Pennicott, her presence as commanding as her voice. "Jarod! It's so lovely to see you again," she declared, her tone filled with genuine warmth as she approached to kiss Jarod's cheek.

Internally, I breathed a sigh of relief. *Thank God for that!* The sentiment was a silent prayer of gratitude for the escape she offered. As I rolled my eyes and edged away, using the moment to put physical and emotional distance between Jarod and myself, I couldn't help but acknowledge the complexity of my feelings towards him. *That man has only ever caused me trouble.*

Since Brody's death, I had been living in a self-imposed exile from the world we once shared, a world that Jarod was undeniably a part of. Avoiding him, along with everyone else from those days, had been my method of coping, a way to shield myself from the pain and memories that seemed to linger in every corner of my old life.

"Oh well," I muttered under my breath, a whispered concession to the evening's unfolding events. Pulling Jarod's jacket tighter around me, I sought comfort in its warmth, a physical barrier against the chill of the night and the emotional turmoil swirling within. The package, a tangible reminder of my purpose here, felt heavier in my arms, its significance growing with each step towards the front of the line.

The queue moved swiftly, a steady progression towards the heart of the event, each step forward a step further into a world I had once known so well yet now felt alien and intimidating. Holding the package close, I prepared myself for what lay ahead, the weight of the night's expectations pressing down on me with an intensity that was both familiar and wholly new.

"You're not going to ask about mine?" Jarod's question cut through the hum of conversation around us, his return to my side pulling me back from the edge of my thoughts.

"I wasn't going to," I admitted, turning my head to face him once more. There was a certain defiance in my tone, a resistance to play into his hands. "I'm sure you're about to tell me anyway," I added, a hint of sarcasm lacing my words as I observed his mouth open, ready to spill his secrets or, more likely, his well-crafted illusions.

"Umm, no. As a matter of fact, I'm going to keep you in suspense about it," he retorted, his voice laced with a playfulness that I found both irritating and mildly amusing. His attempt at light-heartedness felt out of place, a stark contrast to the depth of my disinterest.

"I think there needs to be a bit of interest before there can be suspense," I shot back, my words tinged with a coy tease yet underpinned by a serious current. My interest in Jarod's charitable affiliations, or lack thereof, was nonexistent. It was clear to me that his presence here, like mine, was driven by motives layered in complexity and self-interest. Any claim of support for a charity was, in my eyes, merely a façade, a strategic move in the social chess game he played so well. In his mind, these manoeuvres towards charity likely served a greater purpose, though I doubted the sincerity of such actions. Others, too, I imagined, would view his gestures with a healthy dose of skepticism.

Mrs. Pennicott's laughter broke through the tension, a hearty sound that filled the space between us. "Oh, Beatrix, you always were a funny one," she declared, her amusement evident. Her white-gloved hand fluttered through the air, a gesture that seemed both dismissive and endearing. "How are you doing, my dear?" she inquired, her attention shifting towards me with a genuine concern that felt like a warm blanket in the chilly evening air.

"Fine, thank you, Enid," I responded, my reply polished with the veneer of politeness that such occasions demanded.

"And your parents?" she continued, her interest extending beyond the immediate, a probe into the well-being of my family.

"They're fine too," I answered, keeping my response brief yet courteous.

"Next, please," beckoned the young woman stationed at the arrival desk, her voice cutting through the low hum of conversation and the rustle of evening attire. I excused myself from Enid with a polite nod.

Stepping up, I presented my invitation with a practiced ease, despite the internal churn of apprehension at the formalities ahead. "Your name?" the woman inquired, her attention shifting from the paper in my hand to her meticulously organised list.

"Beatrix Cramer," I announced, maintaining a façade of calm I scarcely felt.

"Cramer, Beatrix," she echoed, her index finger tracing the names on her list until she found mine. "Yes," she confirmed with a small tick of approval next to my name, a simple gesture that felt disproportionately significant in the moment.

"And your charity of support?" she continued, the question lobbed at me like a test I hadn't studied for.

*For fuck's sake!* The question irked me more than I cared to admit, a reminder of the charade these events often were. "Bonorong," I replied, forcing a smile that I hoped conveyed confidence rather than the irritation brewing beneath.

"Bonorong," she repeated, her brows knitting in confusion as she consulted a second list. The pause that followed, filled with her scrutiny, felt longer than it probably was. "I'm sorry," she finally said, her eyes meeting mine. "Bonorong doesn't appear to be on the approved list."

The small package under my arm felt suddenly heavier, a physical burden echoing the weight of my task. With a gamble that felt more like a leap of faith, I offered her a warm smile. "Just add them to the bottom of the list. Charlie will take care of it from there," I suggested, the name 'Charlie' wielded like a talisman, hoping it carried enough weight to bridge this unexpected hurdle.

"Of course," the woman acquiesced, perhaps swayed by the confidence in my tone or the implied authority of Charlie's name. She scribbled something down, then handed me a receipt, a token of my passage through this checkpoint.

As I was motioned to move along, the two young men in shiny tuxedos at the door appeared like gatekeepers to another realm, the large, double glass doors behind them a portal to the evening's unknowns. Each step forward was a step into a meticulously choreographed dance of appearances and alliances, a world where my presence felt both incongruous and necessary. The weight of the package, now officially smuggled into the event under the guise of charity, was a constant reminder of the real reason I was here, a mission that lay hidden beneath the surface of pleasantries and polite smiles.

After taking several steps forward, the weight of Jarod's jacket on my shoulders felt like a tangible link to a past I was trying to navigate around, not through. With a decision made more out of necessity than desire, I slid the jacket from my shoulders and extended it back to Jarod. *I don't need to give him a reason to follow,* I reasoned silently, the gesture a symbolic severing of the immediate connection he offered.

"You don't want to keep it?" Jarod's voice followed me, a mix of surprise and something unidentifiable in his tone. I didn't turn to face him as he continued towards the check-in desk, where his presence would be officially acknowledged.

"Events like these are always too hot inside," I called back, the excuse rolling off my tongue with practiced ease. A light wave of my purse-clutching hand served as a casual goodbye, a nonverbal punctuation to a conversation I was eager to leave unfinished.

As I approached the entrance, the two young gentlemen tasked with greeting the guests pulled open the doors, their movements smooth and practiced. The lobby beyond them beckoned, a sprawling space filled with the murmur of voices and the subtle undercurrent of anticipation.

*That gamble paid off,* I mused internally, a small smirk playing at the corners of my mouth as I stepped into the warmth of the lobby. The mention of Charlie's name at the check-in had been a shot in the dark, an attempt to navigate through the bureaucracy of the event with the least friction possible. Whoever this Charlie guy is, he must wield some significant influence within these circles. The thought was both reassuring and a reminder of the complexities of the social labyrinth I found myself in. The acceptance of Bonorong as a charity of support, despite its absence from the official list, was a testament to the power of names in this environment—a power I intended to leverage to the fullest in order to fulfil my obligations for the evening.

❖

Immediately upon entering the lobby, I made a beeline for a tray of sparkling bubbles being navigated through the crowd by a diligent server. Grasping a glass, I bypassed the opportunity for idle chatter, my mind singularly focused on locating Charlie Claiborne amidst the sea of guests. The task felt akin to finding a needle in a haystack; after several futile spins, scanning faces in the hope of a recognisable one, the absurdity of my endeavour became painfully clear. Name tags, it seemed, would have been a blessing.

With a sigh bordering on exasperation, I took a generous sip from my glass, the bubbles offering little in the way of solace for my mounting frustration.

"Need help finding your table?" Jarod's voice, unexpectedly close, prompted me to turn with a start.

"Table?" I echoed, the word feeling foreign in the context of my current predicament. The concept of a predetermined seating arrangement hadn't even crossed my mind amidst my preoccupation with the package and its intended recipient.

"There's a table and seat number on the receipt they gave you before you entered," Jarod explained, his tone imbued with a patience I hadn't expected.

"There is?" I stammered, feeling suddenly like a kangaroo caught in headlights.

"You know it's a dinner function, right? It would be advisable to sit for such occasions," he continued, his jest only amplifying the sense of mortification that washed over me.

*A kangaroo that's about to become roadkill*, I thought, my stomach feeling like it had just flopped out of my body, landing on the floor for everybody who was anybody, or nobody, to trample over.

"Oh," was all I managed to muster, my voice a faint echo of its usual certainty. Hastily, I rummaged through my purse, fingers seeking the crumpled receipt I had dismissed so carelessly upon my arrival.

Jarod's swift action of taking the crumpled receipt from my grasp felt like an intrusion into my personal chaos, his fingers deftly straightening out the paper as if he were smoothing away the complications of the evening. "Must be fate," he declared, his grin wide and unabashed, as if he'd been awarded a grand prize. The implication of his words sent a fresh wave of dismay through me, confirming my worst suspicion without need for further clarification. *We have been seated beside each other.*

His arm extended towards me, an invitation, a gesture from a bygone era of our acquaintance that now felt oddly out of place. I stared at him, the stern pout on my face barely masking the whirlwind of emotions stirring within. *Seriously?* The incredulity of the situation was not lost on me, yet here we were, about to navigate an evening that fate, or perhaps a mischievous seating planner, had thrown our way.

"Come on. You used to enjoy this, remember?" His voice held a hint of teasing, a reminder of past moments shared with a levity that seemed foreign in the current context. His elbow nudged me gently, a physical prompt that broke through my hesitation.

"I've tried to forget," I retorted, the words slipping out tinged with a mixture of sarcasm and a subtle acknowledgment of our shared history. Despite the resistance in my voice, I found myself linking arms with him, a concession to the unspoken truce his presence offered. As we began to move towards our designated table, a surprising zing of excitement fluttered through me, betraying my outward show of reluctance.

The memories of our past interactions, once buried under layers of time and circumstance, began to surface with an intensity that caught me off guard. *Jarod was right, I did enjoy it.* The realisation was both unsettling and oddly comforting, a reminder of a time when the complexities of life hadn't yet clouded the simplicity of such moments. The contradiction of my feelings was a testament to the intricate dance of human emotions, where past and present often intertwine, leaving us to navigate the delicate balance between what was and what could be.

"So, who's your gift for?" Jarod's question, accompanied by a curious tilt of his head towards the nondescript package I clutched like a lifeline, momentarily caught me off guard. His casual inquiry felt like a probe into a part of my evening I was desperately trying to keep under wraps.

"Charlie Claiborne," I managed to say, my voice steady despite the inner turmoil. We were moving away from the safety of the lobby, descending the staircase into the heart of the evening's event, each step taking me further into unknown territory.

"A gift for the organiser. I'm impressed," Jarod remarked, a note of genuine surprise in his voice. His words echoed in my mind, magnifying my anxiety. *Organiser?* The realisation hit me with the subtlety of a sledgehammer. *Fuck!*

"Yes," I found myself responding, mustering every bit of faux composure I could. "I thought it would be a thoughtful thing to do." The words felt hollow, even to my own ears, a thin veil over my burgeoning panic.

"Thoughtful," Jarod echoed, his approval evident. "Now you have me twice-impressed." His praise, though likely meant to reassure, only served to heighten the pressure. The façade of confidence I was desperately clinging to felt more fragile with every passing moment.

As we entered the dimly lit function room, warmth enveloping us in sharp contrast to the cool precision of the lobby, I found myself leaning closer to Jarod. "Except I don't actually know what he looks like," I confessed, my voice a whisper barely loud enough to breach the distance between us. In that moment of vulnerability, I questioned my own judgement, pulling back as the realisation dawned on me. *He is making me sloppy.* The thought was a jolt back to reality, a reminder of the need for vigilance. *Or maybe I have simply lost my skills.*

Jarod's reaction was a sideways glance, a mix of confusion and curiosity, before his attention shifted, drawn away by a sight across the room. His expression changed, a recognition sparking in his eyes. "Charlie!" he exclaimed, his voice carrying across the space.

Pulse racing, a tumultuous mix of fear and relief coursing through me, I found myself at a crossroads of emotion. Part of me, driven by a visceral, almost primal urge, wanted to pull Jarod back, to halt this unexpected rendezvous and maintain control over the situation. Yet, beneath the surface layer of fear, there was a recognition of opportunity. This was the moment I had been both dreading and longing for—the chance to deliver the package and extract myself from the evening's commitments with a semblance of grace.

"Charlie. Good to see you again," Jarod greeted, his voice carrying a warmth that seemed to cut through the formal atmosphere of the function room. The ease with which he unlinked from me and approached Charlie, extending a hand for a firm handshake, spoke volumes of their familiarity.

"It's been a while," Charlie responded, his tone echoing Jarod's sentiment. "Glad you could come along."

"Thank you," Jarod replied, his manners impeccable as always. Then, with a gesture that felt both grand and inevitable, he turned towards me. "Charlie, I'd like to introduce you to Ms. Beatrix Cramer," he said, making the introduction with a flourish that left little room for hesitation.

"Nice to meet you, Ms. Cramer," Charlie said, his greeting accompanied by an outstretched hand, a bridge across the chasm of our unfamiliarity.

The moment teetered on the edge of disaster as the small box I held, a silent testament to my mission, began to wobble precariously. My attempts to juggle it alongside my purse felt like a metaphor for the evening itself—a delicate balancing act fraught with potential for error. Just as the box threatened to escape my grasp, Jarod, ever observant, reached out to steady it, his quick reflexes saving me from what could have been a minor catastrophe.

I afforded Jarod a short, appreciative smile, a silent acknowledgment of his timely intervention. With the box now securely in his care, my hand was free to meet Charlie's. The handshake, a formal exchange in an evening filled with calculated interactions, felt like a pivotal moment.

"You've got an incredible set-up down here," I remarked, allowing my gaze to wander across the room. The tables stretched out before us, dressed in fine white linens that seemed to glow under the soft light of the candles. Each set of four seats was complemented by small, tasteful arrangements of blue and white flowers, creating an ambiance of understated elegance.

Charlie's laughter, hearty and sincere, filled the space between us. "I can't say I can take the credit for any of that," he admitted, his humility punctuating the air. "But yes," he continued, a note of pride in his voice, "Mr. Bedding and his crew have done a spectacular job."

His acknowledgment of the effort put into the evening's preparations allowed a smile to break through my previously guarded demeanour. *Perhaps I could allow myself to enjoy tonight after all. Even if just a little,* I thought, a flicker of optimism threading through my apprehension.

"I must say, Ms. Cramer," Charlie then turned his attention directly to me, his gaze appraising. "That is a stunning black dress you have on. I'm sure Sandra would love to see it."

"His wife," Jarod's voice came in a soft whisper, close enough for only me to hear. His brief interjection served as a guidepost, illuminating the social landscape I was navigating.

"I'll let her know when she's done gossiping," Charlie added, his voice dropping to a softer chuckle. The comment, light-hearted on the surface, hinted at the layers of interaction and relationship dynamics at play within the event. It served as a reminder of the complex web of social cues and expectations that surrounded us, a dance of communication and appearance.

"Oh, this is for you," Jarod's voice cut through the hum of conversation, his hand extending the small, brown package towards Charlie. "It's a gift from Beatrix," he added, his tone imbuing the moment with a significance that felt both exaggerated and necessary.

"A gift?" Charlie's response was laced with surprise, his eyebrows lifting as he accepted the package. His reaction, a mix of curiosity and unexpected delight, echoed loudly in the charged atmosphere of the event.

"It is your charity event. I thought it might be the charitable thing to do," I found myself saying, trying to infuse my words with a blend of sincerity and casualness. Despite my efforts, Jarod's reaction—a poorly concealed smirk—betrayed his skepticism. His disbelief was palpable, yet it mattered little to me. My focus was solely on Charlie's acceptance of the gesture.

"Thank you," Charlie responded, his smile genuine and warm, cutting through the tension I felt. "If you'll excuse me, I'll just go and pop this over at my table. Save me carrying it around." His practicality, framed by politeness, offered me a graceful exit from the interaction, a momentary reprieve from the evening's complexities.

"Of course," I replied, the words automatic. "It was nice to finally meet you," I added almost reflexively, instantly regretting the addition. The phrase, so commonly exchanged in such settings, now felt like an awkward appendage to the conversation, one I wished I could retract as soon as it had been uttered.

Charlie's response was an awkward nod, a nonverbal acknowledgment that perhaps he too felt the strangeness of the moment. Yet, as he began to walk away, he paused, turning back towards me. "Thank you again, Ms. Cramer," he called out, lifting the gift slightly as if to underscore his appreciation.

My reply was an awkward wave, a gesture that felt inadequate in the face of Charlie's graciousness. Watching him disappear into the crowd, I let out a sigh of relief, the weight of the interaction lifting as he melded with the ever-growing throng of guests.

"Well, that was a bit—" Jarod's voice trailed off, prompting me to fill in the blanks with a guess that felt uncomfortably accurate given the circumstances.

"Stalkerish?" I offered, the word hanging between us like a cloud about to burst.

Jarod took a deep breath, an audible sign of his attempt to choose his words carefully. "I was going to say clumsy, but yeah, stalkerish will do nicely," he conceded. His agreement, meant to be lighthearted, only served to amplify my growing sense of unease.

"Shit," I whispered under my breath, a succinct summary of my thoughts. The situation, already tangled, seemed to knot tighter with each passing second.

"Don't worry about it. I'm sure the Sergeant didn't think anything of it," Jarod tried to reassure me, but his words had the opposite effect.

"Sergeant?" I echoed, my voice barely above a whisper as my heart skipped into overdrive. The title added a layer of complexity I hadn't anticipated, transforming an awkward social interaction into a potentially precarious situation.

"Yeah, Sergeant Charlie Claiborne, Hobart's most decorated officer," Jarod replied, his grin suggesting he found some amusement in the revelation. But for me, there was nothing amusing about it. The information jarred, sending a ripple of panic through me. *Shit. What the hell was Leigh thinking?* The question echoed in my mind, a silent scream for clarity in the midst of confusion.

*It's time to enact my exit strategy. Now!* The thought was a clarion call, a directive that brooked no delay. Yet, before I could formulate any semblance of a plan, Jarod's voice broke through my thoughts.

"Come on," he said, his hand finding my arm again, guiding me with an assurance I felt slipping from my grasp. "Let's go find our seats."

I grimaced, my feet moving of their own accord, following Jarod towards our designated seating, each step a reluctant march into an evening that promised to be anything but straightforward. The fear that it was going to be a very long evening wasn't just a premonition; it felt like a guaranteed prophecy.

❖

As the evening's formalities drew to a close, the atmosphere in the room shifted from structured to a more relaxed mingling. Jarod, ever the social butterfly, seemed energised by the prospect. He grabbed his glass of beer with a casual ease, the liquid gold reflecting the dim lights of the function room. "I'm going to mingle. Care to join me?" he asked, rising from his seat with a readiness that contrasted sharply with my own feelings.

"Not particularly," I replied without hesitation. The dinner, while pleasant, hadn't done much to alter my desire for solitude—or at least, a respite from the forced socialisation the evening demanded. My response was honest, albeit blunt; the prospect of further conversations, especially under the guise of casual socialising, held little appeal.

Jarod's reaction was immediate, his lips forming a playful pout—a look I remembered well from our past interactions.

"Suit yourself then," he said, the lightness in his voice doing little to mask his disappointment. With that, he turned and walked away, no doubt in search of those who were more amenable to the evening's social opportunities.

I couldn't help but give a little scoff as I watched him go. *He always had been the more social of us,* I mused, a hint of envy intermingled with my relief at being left alone. It was a familiar dynamic, one that had defined much of our interaction over the years.

Allowing myself a moment of respite, I casually glanced at the watch on the wrist of the man seated beside me. The action was instinctive, a habitual check on the time, but the result was a jolt of panic. "Shit," I mumbled under my breath, the word slipping out before I could catch it. It was already ten-thirty. The realisation hit me with the force of a physical blow. *I have to collect Gladys.*

The once orderly room, with its carefully arranged tables and chairs, had transformed into a bustling, animated space. My objective remained singular: to find a discreet opportunity for escape without Jarod noticing. I caught sight of him at the centre of a small group. His engagement with animated gestures and the rapt attention he commanded, were all too familiar. *Centre of attention as usual.*

With a decisive motion, I pushed back my chair, its legs scraping softly against the floor. My movements were swift, a silent excuse me whispered as I navigated through clusters of guests, each absorbed in their own bubble of interaction. My destination was clear—the staircase in the far corner of the room, my escape route from the evening's obligations.

A final, sweeping glance across the room confirmed that Jarod's attention remained firmly anchored away from me, his back to my stealthy retreat. This observation bolstered my resolve, ensuring he wouldn't notice my departure. With that assurance, I quickened my pace, ascending the stairs with a blend of relief and urgency.

Upon reaching the lobby, the contrast was stark. The space, though not as congested, still held guests in scattered groups, their conversations a muted echo of the din I'd left behind. My strategy was simple: keep a low profile, avoid engaging, and make a swift exit. My gaze was fixed on the floor, a deliberate attempt to avoid any accidental eye contact that might delay my departure.

As I passed through the lobby, the presence of the ushers, now familiar figures in their shiny tuxedos, marked the threshold to freedom. Their doors held open were like gates to the outside world, a world I was eager to rejoin. A quick, barely perceptible nod was all I could afford them in my haste—a silent gesture of thanks for their unnoticed but essential role in the evening's choreography.

Stepping through those doors, the brisk night air was an immediate contrast to the buzz and warmth I had just left behind in the function room. As I navigated through the small, dimly lit carpark with a sense of purpose, the silhouette of my 4WD became a beacon in the darkness, urging my steps to quicken.

"Psst, Beatrix," came a soft, unexpected whisper, cutting through the silence like a knife. My reaction was instinctive, a mix of surprise and defence, as I spun around, my purse swinging through the air as a makeshift shield.

Before I could register what was happening, a long arm emerged from the shadow of my vehicle, pulling me in close with a familiarity that was both startling and oddly comforting. "You really think hitting someone with that thing is going to make any difference?" Leigh's voice, tinged with a mix of amusement and rebuke, grounded me back to reality.

"What do you want?" I hissed, the irritation clear in my voice, my heart still racing from the unexpected encounter.

"Did you deliver the package?" Leigh's inquiry, still whispered, carried a weight of urgency.

"Yeah," I replied, my frustration mounting. "So, why me? Why couldn't you do it yourself? And why make me come here?" The questions spilled out, each one underscored by a growing sense of irritation and confusion over his motives and the night's events.

"I just wanted to see you dressed up all pretty," Leigh quipped, his attempt at humour ill-timed and poorly received.

His comment, intended or not, ignited a spark of anger within me, prompting a reaction that was both immediate and visceral—a solid whack with my purse. "Seriously!" I exclaimed, the volume of my voice a reflection of my annoyance.

"Shh," Leigh insisted, a finger pressed to his lips, his eyes scanning the surroundings with a caution that suggested the need for discretion.

"Then why?" The question burst from me, a mix of curiosity and rising irritation, as I struggled to maintain a whisper. The night had taken a turn towards the surreal, and with each word Leigh spoke, the depth of the intrigue seemed to grow.

"I couldn't do it myself. Their eyes and ears are everywhere. Besides, he's seen me before. I needed someone he didn't—" Leigh's explanation was cut short by my sudden realisation, a piece of the puzzle clicking into place, albeit with a few edges still missing.

"Hang on," I couldn't help but interrupt, the implications of his words dawning on me. "You mean he knows who you are? He knows about your... thing?" My voice trailed off as I pointed subtly at his pocket, the location of his Portal Key—a secret that felt too volatile for the openness of our current setting.

A coy small smile crossed Leigh's face, and I recognised my slip of subtle innuendo.

Reacting to his immaturity, I gave him another hard whack across the arm with my purse, an action driven more by impulse than any real expectation of answers. "What was that for?" he asked, his voice tinged with amusement, a slight chuckle breaking through.

"You know what," I growled back, my frustration no longer contained. "I was trying not to say Portal—" My words were abruptly silenced by Leigh's hand, which covered my mouth with a swift, cautionary motion.

"Best you don't say them now," he advised, his voice low, a serious undertone cutting through the lightness of his previous demeanour. As he removed his hand, the gravity of his expression matched the weight of his words. "And no. I don't think he knows that much. He is connected somehow, I just haven't been able to work out how yet," Leigh continued, his brow furrowing in thought.

"So, what was the package? Why so important? And why here?" The questions spilled out of me, a torrent of curiosity and concern that I could no longer contain.

"Haven't you ever heard of hiding in plain sight?" Leigh countered, a hint of a smile playing at the corners of his mouth, as if the answer was obvious to anyone willing to see it.

"Ah," I responded, the pieces beginning to fit together in my mind, albeit slowly. "I get it. I think. But it would make more sense if you answered my other questions." My insistence on understanding the full scope of the situation was driven by more than mere curiosity; it was a need to grasp the potential consequences of my actions.

"I will," Leigh assured me, though his response offered little in the way of immediate comfort.

"You're not even going to say goodbye?" Jarod's voice, carrying across the carpark, interrupted our hushed conversation. The casual call out, laden with an undercurrent of jest, felt jarringly out of place in the tension of the moment.

Leigh's reaction was immediate, crouching even lower, a clear indication of his desire to remain unseen. Instinctively, I mirrored his action, ready to blend into the shadows alongside him.

"No," Leigh hissed. "Stand up. Go," he whispered, urging me into the open with a gentle push. His insistence, firm yet fraught with an unspoken urgency, left no room for protest.

"But..." I stammered, my glare a silent accusation of his sudden decision to abandon me, alone and adrift in the aftermath of unshared secrets.

"Tomorrow," Leigh promised, his voice a whisper of assurance. "I'll find you and explain." The promise hung between us, a lifeline thrown in the uncertainty of the night.

Reluctantly, I acquiesced, stepping out from behind the safety of the vehicle to face the remainder of the evening alone. My heart raced as I moved to open the front door of my 4WD. Jarod's proximity was a surprise, his figure looming unexpectedly close in the dim light of the carpark. The sudden transition from the secrecy of Leigh's company to the potential scrutiny of Jarod's presence sent a jolt of adrenaline through me, a stark reminder of the delicate balance between the night's hidden agendas and the façade of normality I was compelled to maintain.

"No," I replied sharply to Jarod, the firmness in my voice belying the tumult of emotions roiling beneath the surface as I opened the car door. His plea, however, was unexpected and struck a chord within me, disarming my resolve momentarily.

"Come to Wrest Point tomorrow night. For old time's sake," he implored, his hands clasped together in a gesture that spoke volumes of our shared past, of risks taken and moments lived on the edge of adrenaline and chance.

The suggestion, audacious as it was, cracked the stern façade I had maintained throughout the evening. A cheeky smile involuntarily split my clenched jaw, a reaction that surprised even me. Butterflies fluttered in my stomach, a sensation I hadn't felt in what seemed like ages. The thought of returning to the casino, the very place that had been the foundation of Brody's and my venture into the antique store, sparked an unexpected thrill. The funds we had "acquired" there had been the start of something new for us. *Or rather, I'd taken them.*

"You have to admit we made a fine team, you and I," Jarod continued, his voice laced with nostalgia. "You have quick, deceptive hands."

"And you have a fine, deceptive mouth," I scoffed softly, the retort slipping out with a mix of fondness and reproach. Memories of those reckless nights—filled with laughter, the clink of glasses, and the thrill of discreetly disappearing chips—flooded back, painting a picture of a past life that seemed worlds away from the present.

"We never did get caught. We didn't have to stop," Jarod mused, a hint of regret, or perhaps wistfulness, colouring his words.

"Yes, we did have to stop. You know we did. It was all about the numbers. We knew that from the start," I reminded him, my voice steady, a testament to the lessons learned from those heady days. "As easily as we helped people to misplace their chips without them even knowing, we could have easily been caught," I added, the weight of my unspoken confession —*I did get caught!*—hanging heavily between us, unacknowledged yet palpable.

"Just one more time?" Jarod tried again, his request a siren call to a part of me I thought I had left behind.

I bit my lower lip, a gesture of hesitation and the weight of memories long buried but never forgotten. The casino, a place of exhilarating victories and bitter truths, hadn't seen my shadow since the day before Brody's life was cruelly snatched away. He had confronted me, his eyes filled with a mixture of disappointment and disbelief, about the origins of the money that had seemed to appear out of thin air. Brody never fully understood the depths of my talents—or perhaps, more accurately, my deceit. But he knew enough to be troubled, and that knowledge had been a dividing chasm between us, one that we never had the chance to bridge.

"Fine," I finally conceded, the word escaping me like a sigh of resignation. "But not tomorrow. Let's do Friday night." There was a part of me, perhaps the reckless part that I thought I had left behind, that couldn't outright refuse the lure of the past, even though it was wrapped in danger and draped in the shadows of what once was.

"Deal," Jarod responded, his grin spreading wide across his face, a mirror to the excitement I remembered so well. He extended his hand, an offer of agreement, a pact of sorts that felt both familiar and foreboding.

I rubbed the goosebumps that prickled along my arms, a physical testament to the cold that seeped into my bones and the unease that nestled into my heart. "It's freezing out here. I need to go," I stated bluntly, the need to escape the night, Jarod, and the flood of memories overwhelming me. Slipping into the car, I brought the engine to life, its hum a welcome barrier against the night's chill.

Jarod stood back, offering a cheery wave that seemed so at odds with the turmoil churning inside me. I took a deep breath, an attempt to steady the riot of emotions and the drumming of my heart against my ribs.

As I drove past the grapevines, their rows standing sentinel along the large property's main road, a glance in the rearview mirror revealed Jarod still in the carpark, his figure a solitary silhouette against the dim lighting, staring after me. The sight of him there, alone yet undeterred, sent a shiver down my spine. *He was going to get me into more trouble than I needed.* The thought was a cold whisper, a premonition that danced dangerously close to certainty.

"Shit!" The exclamation burst from me as I slammed on the brakes, my heart leaping into my throat at the sudden appearance of a small wallaby on the road. The headlights caught the creature in a stark, frozen moment before it, with seeming reluctance, moved on to the vines on the other side. The incident, brief as it was, served as a jarring reminder of the unpredictability of life, of the dangers that lurked in the shadows, and of the fine line I was walking—once again—on the edge of disaster.

# BLACK DRESS: MEMORIAL

## 4338.206.7

I gave the car horn another long press, the sound slicing through the quiet of the night, marking the exact time of ten-fifty. Impatience bubbled inside me as I tapped the steering wheel, my legs jiggling uncontrollably beneath it, a physical manifestation of my growing anxiety. "What the hell are you doing in there, Gladys?" I muttered to no one, the words dissolving into the cold air of the car's interior.

Finally, the front door of the house swung open, and Gladys emerged, her movements hurried yet somehow still causing me to startle in my seat as the door slammed shut with a definitive bang. My heart skipped, not prepared for the sudden noise in the quiet evening.

"You're all dressed up," Gladys observed as she opened the car door and slid into the passenger seat, her voice carrying a hint of surprise—*or was it accusation?*

"And you're not," I retorted, my irritation spilling over as I took in her casual attire of jeans against my own carefully chosen black dress. The contrast between us was obvious, highlighting the differences in our approach to... well, everything.

"Do you want me to get changed?" Gladys snapped back, her hand already on the door handle, ready to act on my critique.

"Don't worry about it," I huffed out, my frustration deflating as quickly as it had inflated. "No time for that now."

"You're in a mood," Gladys scoffed, her voice laced with that sibling knowingness that managed to be both infuriating and comforting in equal measure.

Choosing to ignore her comment, I focused on the road ahead, pulling away from the house as we began our journey. The silence that settled between us was a familiar companion, the unspoken words and tensions hovering like ghosts of our shared history.

Gripping the steering wheel tightly, I tried to steady my hands, the tremors a silent testament to the turmoil within me. The decision to meet up with Jarod loomed over me like a dark cloud, intensifying the sense of impending doom. *It would only cause trouble,* I chided myself, the thought echoing through my mind like a warning bell. Over the past few years, I'd painstakingly managed to curb the impulsive stealing habits that once defined me—a feat made easier, perhaps, by my self-imposed isolation from the very situations that tempted those darker impulses.

"Did you get anything for the memorial?" Gladys's voice cut through the heavy silence that had settled in the car, her question pulling me back from the edge of my thoughts.

"No," I replied, the word sharp, a reflection of my current state of mind, where the memorial seemed like just another drop in the stormy sea churning inside me.

"I got some scented candles," Gladys continued, undeterred by my terseness. She rummaged through her large handbag, her movements deliberate as she produced several small candles. "We can say they're from both of us, if you like?" Her offer, made with a genuine intent to include me, felt like a lifeline, albeit a flimsy one in the grand scheme of things.

I responded with a small shrug, the gesture laden with a mix of gratitude and indifference. The truth was, scented candles and their symbolic gesture of remembrance were the least of my concerns, dwarfed by the weight of the evening's earlier dealings that had taken place.

The car fell back into its awkward silence.

"Did you bring any spirits?" I found myself asking, the need for something, anything, to dull the sharp edges of my anxiety becoming overwhelming. A shot or two of liquid courage seemed like a necessary evil at this point.

"Cody is bringing the whiskey," Gladys responded, her voice carrying a note of casualness.

"Cody is coming?" The surprise in my voice was unmistakable. The addition of Cody to the evening's equation was a wildcard I hadn't anticipated.

"Yeah," Gladys confirmed. "He said he'll meet us there."

Several minutes later, as the car rolled to a stop in Luke's driveway, the solitude of the scene was marked by the lone presence of Jamie's car, its silent form the only other vehicle in the vicinity. The quiet seemed to underscore the purpose of our arrival.

"Let's wait for Cody," Gladys suggested, her hand clasping firmly around my arm as I reached for the car door.

The insistence in her voice grated against my already frayed nerves, prompting a visceral reaction. I yanked my arm free from her hold, the need for action, any action, overriding the patience she advocated. "I'm not waiting," I declared, a mix of determination and defiance colouring my tone. Exiting the car, I slammed the door behind me, the sound echoing in the quiet of the driveway like a definitive end to the argument.

Standing on the small front porch, I took a moment to breathe, to allow the cool night air to wash over me and temper the storm of emotions that threatened to overwhelm. *This is Joel's night now,* I reminded myself, the mantra serving as a focal point, a centring thought amidst the earlier promises of the evening. It was a moment of tribute, of remembrance, and my personal conflicts had no place here.

Gladys quickly joined me on the porch. The front door's squeak seemed louder in the quiet atmosphere, a herald of our entrance. "Hey, Luke," we both said together, an unplanned chorus that momentarily lifted the heavy air.

The sound of a shot glass clattering against the stone benchtop marked our greeting, a sharp contrast to the softness of our voices. Cody's laughter, deep and hearty, filled the space, a brief respite from the evening's undercurrent of grief.

"You two couldn't even wait for us?" Gladys's voice carried a mix of mock indignation and genuine surprise, her words directed at Cody's premature libation.

"How rude," I chimed in, the words lighter than my heart felt, trying to inject a bit of levity into the room.

"I was just cheering Luke up," Cody defended, his tone light but his eyes avoiding ours.

"I'm sure," Gladys retorted, her skepticism thinly veiled, a protective edge sharpening her words.

Approaching the bench, I observed as Luke methodically arranged his glass among the others, each one a silent testament to the night's intent. Cody filled the line-up without hesitation, his movements deliberate, perhaps a distraction from the evening's weight.

"So how—" I began, the question hanging in the air, unfinished, as Luke cut me off.

"I really don't want to talk about it," he said quickly, a weariness in his voice that belied the strength it took to utter those words. "I'm really tired."

"Or drunk," Gladys couldn't resist adding, her observation sharp, yet not without concern.

For a moment, Gladys and I shared a glance, a rare instance of silent agreement in our often discordant interactions

Luke's response, "Not yet," was both a concession and a defiance, a recognition of his state and a declaration of his intent to find solace in whatever way he could. The simplicity of the exchange, the interplay of concern, sarcasm, and tired resignation, painted a picture of our shared history, of connections forged in better times and tested by the worst. As we stood there, in the kitchen that had witnessed countless moments of joy and now, profound sorrow, the realisation that we were all grappling with loss, each in our own way, was both a comfort and a challenge.

"We've brought the candles," I announced, a declaration that momentarily shifted the focus from the tension hanging in the air. Encouraging Gladys, I watched as she lifted her handbag onto the bench, an unspoken signal for me to delve into its depths. My hands worked through the assortment of candles she had thoughtfully packed, their varied colours and sizes a small testament to her effort to bring warmth to the night's sombre occasion.

Luke, moving with a purpose that seemed to momentarily dispel the cloud of sorrow enveloping him, began rummaging through the kitchen drawers in search of the gas lighter. I took the lighter from him, a silent exchange of understanding passing between us, and began the methodical process of lighting each candle.

"Are you sure you have enough candles?" Cody's chuckle, meant to lighten the mood, instead felt like an intrusion into the solemnity of the moment. My response was a glare, a silent reprimand for the levity in a time that demanded reverence.

"Turn the lights off," I instructed Luke, my voice carrying a soft but firm command. There was a power in the act of extinguishing the artificial light, a symbolism in embracing the candlelight that spoke more eloquently than words could.

Within moments, the house fell into darkness, save for the flickering candlelight that now held dominion over the space. The shadows danced around the kitchen and living room, cast by the gentle flames, transforming the familiar surroundings into something ethereal. In the soft, undulating light, the room took on a different character, one that seemed to bridge the gap between the here and now and the eternal.

The four of us stood in a tight circle around the island bench, the solemnity of the moment enveloping us like a shroud as Cody passed out the shot glasses. The ritual felt ancient, a way to honour a life that had brushed ours only briefly, yet left an indelible mark.

"Do you have a picture of him?" The question escaped my lips before I could think better of it, my curiosity a faint attempt to connect with the person we were about to honour.

Luke's response was a gentle shake of his head, his voice barely above a whisper. "No," he admitted. "We only learnt about him a few months ago." The regret in his voice was palpable, a silent acknowledgment of the lost opportunities to know the person whose absence we mourned.

Gladys's expression mirrored the grief that suddenly filled the room, her question voiced with a tenderness that spoke volumes of her compassion. "Does... does Jamie know he's dead yet?" she asked, her voice laced with a delicacy born of understanding the weight of the news we were withholding.

I found myself biting my bottom lip, an unconscious reaction to the tension that tightened around us with Luke's subsequent denial. "No," he confirmed, his head shaking in a silent negation that felt final. "And he won't ever find out. Cody took care of it," he added, a glance towards Cody laden with a mixture of gratitude and sorrow.

"Yeah," Cody affirmed, though his gaze remained fixed on the row of shot glasses before him, as if the answers to the unspoken questions lay hidden in their depths. "I took care of it."

"It's so sad," I couldn't help but whisper, the reality of the young life lost washing over me in waves of disbelief. "He looked so young."

"He was," Luke agreed, the pain evident in his voice. "He was only nineteen."

"Tragic," Gladys murmured, wiping away a tear.

Then, as if driven by a force greater than ourselves, Luke raised his shot glass, a silent summons for us to join him in this act of remembrance. We all followed, each of us holding our glass like a torch in the darkness, a beacon of memory for a soul gone too soon.

"What do we say?" Gladys's voice broke the silence, her question echoing the uncertainty that hovered around the edges of our gathering. "We never really knew him."

"You say whatever is in your heart to say," Cody's answer came, a simple directive that somehow made the impossible task before us seem bearable.

And so, standing in the dim candlelight that transformed the familiar into a place of sacred memory, we prepared to honour a life that had intersected with ours in the most unexpected of ways. With Cody's words as our guide, we ventured into the territory of the heart, ready to give voice to the unspoken, to the grief and the gratitude that intertwined within us.

"I'll go first," I declared, a sense of resolve steadying my trembling hands as I grasped my glass and held it before me. My intention was clear, yet when the moment came to speak, my voice faltered, words caught in the web of emotion that had woven itself tightly around my heart. I leaned towards Luke, seeking reassurance in a whisper. "What's his name again?" The question was a lifeline, my mind grappling with the tumultuous mix of nerves and the solemnity of the occasion.

Luke's response was a gentle smile, a beacon of warmth in the cool, shadowed room. "Joel," he whispered back, his voice a soft echo that carried the weight of unspoken stories and unwritten futures.

Turning back to face the bench, the word felt more solid, more real, as I spoke it aloud. "Joel," I began again, this time with a firmer voice, though it quivered with the effort of keeping my emotions at bay. "We never had the chance to know you. But we love Jamie. And you are his blood." The words were a bridge, linking us to Joel, to each other, to the very essence of what it means to be connected by unseen bonds. As I spoke, the image of Brody filled my vision, a poignant reminder of another life touched by tragedy, another soul whose absence was a constant presence.

With a deep breath, I pushed through the ache in my chest, determined to honour Joel with the dignity he deserved. "And so, we love you too." The declaration was a testament to our collective capacity for love, extending beyond the confines of direct acquaintance to embrace a young life taken too soon.

"To Jamie's son," I announced, lifting my shot glass as a salute to a life we wished we'd known, to the fragile threads that tied us to Jamie, and through him, to Joel. The liquid burned its way down, a fiery tribute to the memory of a boy who had become part of our story in the most haunting of ways.

"To Jamie's son," the others echoed, their voices a chorus of solidarity. Together, we raised our glasses, a silent vow to remember, to mourn, and to celebrate the ties that bound us, however tenuous they might seem. The glasses were drained and returned to the bench.

Gladys took her glass from Cody with a steadiness that belied the emotion behind her words. "Joel," she began, her voice carrying a mix of sorrow and hope, a heartfelt wish for a connection never made. "May your soul one day know your father and know the good man that he is." Her words, simple yet profound, struck a chord, resonating deeply within the silent spaces of our gathering.

Blinking quickly to ward off the tears that threatened to spill, I found myself reaching up to dab at my eyes. The emotion of the moment, coupled with Gladys's poignant toast, overwhelmed the barriers I had meticulously built around my heart.

"To Joel," said Gladys, her voice a beacon in the dimly lit room as she raised her glass of whiskey.

"To Joel," we echoed in unison, each of us participating in the ritual, allowing the whiskey to burn a path down our throats.

In the silence that followed, we waited, a collective breath held in anticipation for Cody to refill our glasses and continue the cycle of tribute. But instead, Cody paused, his glass held aloft as if it were a chalice of memories and unspoken words. His gaze, fixed intently on the empty vessel, seemed to search its depths for answers or perhaps solace. In the soft, undulating light cast by the candles, his eyes glistened, a visible sign of the emotion he too was grappling with.

"Joel," Cody began, his voice carrying the weight of the moment, heavy with emotion. "You met unfortunate circumstances. But—" His words faltered, a visible struggle against the tide of emotions that threatened to overwhelm him. "But—" he tried again, his voice catching, a raw display of vulnerability that was both heart-wrenching and sincere.

Beside me, Gladys and I found ourselves caught in the wave of Cody's grief, our sniffles breaking the charged silence in almost perfect unison.

"Death is but a mere process, and when we learn to master that process, we will master death itself," Cody continued, his gaze intensely fixed on Luke. The words, though cryptic, resonated with a depth that was both unsettling and profound. They hung in the air, a solemn mantra that seemed to bridge the gap between the tangible and the unknown.

The room fell into a heavy silence, the kind that envelops you like a cloak, thick with thought and reflection. A cool shiver traced my spine, the words echoing in my mind. I didn't fully grasp their meaning, yet they stirred something within me, a yearning for understanding, for closure. I found myself wishing Brody were here; he would have understood, would have found solace in Cody's words, or perhaps even challenged their premise with his characteristic insight.

"To Joel," Cody intoned once more, lifting his empty glass as though it were a vessel filled with memories and unspoken farewells.

"To Joel," we echoed, our voices a chorus of respect and remembrance.

As the moment passed and we each retreated into our personal reveries, I found myself distracted by a loose thread on the lace sleeve of my black dress. My fingers toyed with it absently, the action a metaphor for the unravelling thoughts and emotions that the evening had stirred. The irony of the situation was not lost on me—I was here, mourning the loss of a young man involved in a murder I hadn't committed but had helped to conceal. And this, mere moments after agreeing to revisit the very habits that had indirectly led to the downfall of my greatest love.

This dress, a silent witness to both Brody's funeral and now this solemn gathering, seemed to carry the weight of my guilt and grief. *This dress is cursed,* I mused darkly, the decision forming in my heart with a resolve born of the night's reflections. *And when I get home, I'm going to burn it.* The thought was a silent vow, a promise to myself to shed the tangible reminders of the past, to perhaps find a way to begin anew, even as the complexities of my current choices loomed large, a poignant reminder of the cyclical nature of decision and consequence.

*4338.207*

*(26 July 2018)*

# ANTIQUE

## 1338.207.1

After multiple failed attempts, the black dress remained draped over me, a fabric shroud that seemed to cling tighter with each moment that passed. When I'd finally arrived home after Joel's farewell, the intention had been clear: rid myself of the dress, of its memories, of its curse. Yet, I'd only managed to unlatch the sleeves, my reflection in the mirror becoming an audience to the raw, unbridled emotion that spilled forth. My body trembled, waves of tears flowing freely, a floodgate opened after years of restraint. The guilt over Brody's death had been a constant shadow, a spectre that haunted my every step, embedding itself deep within, burying my emotions so far beneath the surface that I feared they might never resurface. The ensuing battle with his parents had siphoned away what scant reserves of emotion I had managed to keep intact, leaving me hollow.

And now, here I was, drawn as if by some unseen force, to the remnants of a past life. Standing barefoot across the road from our long-closed antique shop, the pre-dawn silence enveloping me like a cold embrace. The clock had crept around to five in the morning, a time when the world lay in slumber, unaware of the small dramas unfolding in its shadow.

Re-lacing the sleeves of the dress, I braced against the chill of the dark, frigid morning air, a physical discomfort that barely registered against the turmoil within. Stepping off the curb, my foot plunged into a near-frozen puddle, the icy water a sharp shock to my system, momentarily grounding me back to the present. The drizzle from a few hours earlier had left its mark, a reminder of the world's indifference to personal grief and turmoil.

The shop, once a beacon of hope and dreams built together with Brody, now stood as a monument to all that had been lost. The silence of the early morning, broken only by the occasional distant sound of a waking world, served as a backdrop to the tumult of emotions that coursed through me. The decision to stand here, in the shadow of our shared past, was one I couldn't fully explain, driven by a mixture of longing, regret, and a desperate need for closure.

My heart raced, a steady drumbeat echoing the turmoil within as I approached the front door of what was once our dream. The glass fogged under the warmth of my cupped hands, my breath a ghostly whisper against its cold surface. I leaned in, trying to pierce the darkness that enveloped the interior of our old antique store, searching for a glimpse of the past, for some sign of the life we had built. But the shadows remained impenetrable, a solid wall of darkness that my eyes couldn't breach. Pulling away, a sigh escaped me, laden with the disappointment of the unseen and the unattainable.

The cold began to seep through the soles of my feet, a chilling reminder of the early dawn's unwelcoming embrace. I navigated my way down the dark alley, the narrow passage sandwiched between the solemn old stone of the church—our antique store in its previous life—and the newer, smooth brick of the flower shop next door. The contrast between them, one bearing the weight of history and the other the promise of the present, mirrored the conflict raging within me.

Reaching the back door, a flicker of hope ignited as I retrieved the spare key from my purse. This key, a small piece of metal imbued with so much significance, was a secret kept from the clutches of the law by Detective Karl Jenkins. In an act that blurred the lines between duty and compassion, he had chosen not to turn it into evidence but instead handed it discreetly to me. My breath formed a thick puff of warm air in the cold night as I approached the door, the anticipation building with each step.

But my hopes were quickly dashed by the sight of the new padlock that barred entry, its presence a haunting symbol of the barriers that stood between me and the remnants of our past. The chains rattled loudly, a jarring sound in the quiet of the alley, as I shook the padlock in a mix of frustration and desperation. The noise seemed to echo off the walls, a tangible manifestation of my inner turmoil.

Standing there, the cold biting at my flesh and the reality of my situation setting in, I realised the futility of my actions. The padlock, cold and unyielding under my fingers, was more than just a physical barrier; it was a representation of the closure I had yet to find, of the doors to the past that remained firmly shut, no matter how desperately I sought to open them. The realisation weighed heavily on me, a solemn reminder of the journey still ahead, of the need to find a way forward, even as the ghosts of what once was clung tightly, refusing to let go.

"Beatrix," the soft call sent a jolt of surprise through me, my heart skipping as the chain slipped from my grasp. The sound of the large padlock hitting the door reverberated through the stillness of the alley, a harsh clang that seemed to echo the sudden spike of my pulse. Whirling around, I was met with the sight of Leigh's tall figure, his silhouette framed against the brick wall by a dim light that cast a gentle glow around him, giving him an almost ethereal presence.

"What are you doing here?" I whispered back, a mix of surprise and a burgeoning sense of relief threading through the sharpness of my words. My brow furrowed, not just from the cold but from the swirling confusion at his unexpected appearance.

Leigh's smile was a warm beacon in the cold, dark alley. "I told you I'd find you, didn't I?" he said, his voice carrying a hint of something unspoken, a promise that extended beyond the words themselves.

"I guess," I managed, my response a reflection of the turmoil within, a storm of emotions that Leigh's presence both calmed and stirred anew.

"Here, you're shivering," he observed, his actions speaking louder than his words as he draped his long jacket around my shoulders. The fabric enveloped me, a shield against the chill that had seeped into my bones. "And what the hell are you doing walking around barefoot?" he added, a note of concern lacing his question.

I could only offer a shrug, an inadequate response to his valid query. My mind was a whirlpool of thoughts and emotions, making it difficult to articulate the confusion that fogged my brain.

Leigh's gaze upon me was intense, searching, as if he were trying to read the chapters of the night that even I couldn't fully understand. "Isn't that the dress you wore to the function last night? Have you even been home?" he probed further, his voice gentle yet insistent.

Slowly, I shook my head, the gesture a silent admission of my aimless wandering, of the night spent in a limbo of grief and memories. Hesitating to respond, I was acutely aware of the reality that I wasn't entirely sure of my own movements after leaving the memorial of Joel. The fragments of the evening were disjointed in my mind, a puzzle whose pieces refused to fit neatly together. The car, the drive, the decision to stand outside our old shop—all seemed like actions taken by someone else, or perhaps by a version of myself driven by an unseen force.

And yet, here I was, wrapped in Leigh's jacket, confronted by his concern and the undeniable fact that, despite my confusion and the chaos of my emotions, I wasn't alone. Leigh's presence, unexpected as it was, offered a glimmer of comfort, a steadying hand in the tumultuous sea of my thoughts. The realisation that, in the midst of my aimless drifting, someone had come looking for me, someone cared enough to find me, was both humbling and heartening.

"Let me take you home," Leigh's voice was a blend of command and concern as he reached for my arm, his intent clear in the firm, yet gentle grip.

"No," I resisted, pulling my arm away with a force that mirrored the turmoil inside. "Not yet." There was something unresolved, a need that tethered me to this spot, to the shadow of the shop that once held dreams and memories.

"What is it?" Leigh's inquiry came with a furrow of his eyebrows. His gaze searched mine, looking for answers.

"I need to get inside," I confessed, the words a whisper of desperation. The shop, my shop, held more than just antiques; it was a repository of my past, of hopes and losses intermingled.

"So, go inside," Leigh offered, his shrug meant to be encouraging, but the simplicity of his suggestion belied the complexity of the situation.

"They've chained and padlocked it," I hissed, a mix of anger and helplessness fuelling my actions as I turned back to rattle the padlocked chains in futile frustration. "This is my shop. They had no right to do this." The injustice of it, the violation of what had once been a sanctuary of sorts, ignited a fire within me.

A wide smile unexpectedly crossed Leigh's face, an incongruous reaction that caught me off guard.

"What?" My demand was sharp, a reflection of the confusion and growing irritation at his seemingly inappropriate mirth.

"Wait for me. I won't be long," he said, a mysterious edge to his voice. A cautious glance around preceded his next action, one that had become less shocking to me over time yet never failed to captivate.

The nearby wall erupted into a spectacle of technicolor, a vibrant display that cast a surreal glow against the dark morning air. The buzzing, swirling colours, though no longer a surprise after having witnessed Luke's demonstration, still held a certain mesmerism, a captivating beauty that momentarily lifted the weight from my shoulders.

As Leigh stepped into the chromatic spectrum and vanished, a part of me wanted to follow, to step into that unknown and escape the cold, harsh reality. The wall returned to darkness, a brief interlude before bursting back into colour less than five minutes later, heralding his return.

"These ought to take care of it," Leigh announced, stepping back into the realm of the ordinary from wherever his abilities had taken him, brandishing a pair of bolt cutters with a flourish that seemed almost theatrical under the circumstances.

"I'll take those," I responded, reaching out to take the offered tool from him. The weight of the bolt cutters felt reassuring in my hands, a tangible solution to the barrier that stood before us. Positioning the padlock between the cutters' jaws, I squeezed with a determination fuelled by the night's frustrations and the symbolic act of reclaiming what was mine. With a sharp movement, the resistance of the metal gave way, the snap of the lock breaking through the silence, a sound of victory against the small injustices of the world.

"Don't look so surprised," I chided Leigh, catching a glimpse of his reaction out of the corner of my eye. He stepped in to remove the remnants of the broken lock, his actions swift and sure.

"I'm... I'm not surprised at all," he countered, the grin that spread across his face betraying a mixture of amusement and admiration. "I know you're more than capable of doing such things."

"Good," I affirmed, feeling a surge of satisfaction at the acknowledgment. The chains fell away with a clatter as Leigh removed them, clearing the path to what lay beyond. Sliding the key into the door, a small part of me revelled in the act of physically unlocking a door that had been metaphorically closed to me. The action was a reclaiming of power, a small defiance against the forces that had sought to keep me out.

The door's loud creak seemed to echo through time, a herald to the past as I crossed the threshold into a space that had once been so familiar. Instinctively, my hand moved to swipe away a dusty cobweb, its sticky silk a testament to the long span of neglect that had befallen my once cherished shop. Despite the layer of dust and the passage of time, the hardwood floor beneath my bare feet felt oddly warm, a silent reminder of the life that once pulsed through this space.

The air, thick with mustiness, enveloped me like an old blanket, its scent a powerful trigger transporting me back to days gone by. It was remarkable how, even in its prime, this place had held onto its unique aroma, a blend that spoke of history and stories embedded in every nook and cranny. To me, this scent was not just the mustiness of age but the essence of the shop's character, an aromatic tapestry woven from the countless antiques that had passed through these doors.

"What is that smell?" Leigh's question pulled me back from my reverie, his voice a note of curiosity amidst the silent dialogue between me and the shop's memories.

"Probably a dead mouse," I answered, half-distracted. My response was automatic, a guess rooted in the reality of old buildings and their inevitable cohabitants. Yet, as I spoke, my focus wasn't on the present but lost in the past, in the countless days spent in the company of relics that whispered of yesteryears.

As Leigh stepped closer, I found myself beside a large chair, its familiar contours inviting my touch. My fingers trailed along its ridge, each curve and crevice a memory, a story waiting to be retold. The present seemed to blur, the boundaries between then and now fading as I allowed myself to be swept into the currents of memory, each artefact a beacon guiding me through the shop's once vibrant life.

The small porcelain doll ornaments scattered across the floor, their shattered pieces a disheartening reminder of the tumultuous day when I had knocked them over in a fit of desperation and anger, stood as silent witnesses to the chaos that had once unfolded within these walls. That day, which remained vivid in my memory as if it had occurred only yesterday, marked the beginning of the end for the shop, a day when the culmination of unpaid bills and relentless pressure from the bank had finally resulted in the loss of what Brody and I had worked so hard to build. The shop's closure felt like a personal failure, a dream snuffed out too soon, leaving behind a trail of broken promises and broken dreams.

The local New Norfolk police, who had been summoned to enforce the bank's claim on the property, had met my stubborn refusal to leave with equal determination. The stand-off that ensued, my parents at my side, trying to coax me into surrendering without further incident, was a blur of shouting and heated pleas. It was then, amidst the turmoil, that Officer Karl Jenkins had made his unexpected appearance. His actions that day, slipping me the spare key and whispering assurances that he'd help rectify my dire situation, were a lifeline thrown in the midst of a storm. Karl's intervention, though unexpected, was not entirely surprising given the complex relationship we had developed over the years.

That relationship with Karl Jenkins had been a reluctant partnership born out of necessity rather than choice. After being caught red-handed with my purse full of casino chips, spoils from my not-so-proud ventures of relieving inebriated casino-goers of their winnings, I had found myself in a precarious position. To avoid legal repercussions, I had resorted to paying off Officer Jenkins, a decision that had led to several more such transactions over the years. It was a secret I had kept even from Jarod, a part of my life I had hoped to leave in the shadows.

Standing amidst the remnants of the past, the broken porcelain dolls beneath my feet serving as a grim metaphor for the shattered dreams and compromises I had made, I was reminded of the heavy price of survival. The spare key, once a symbol of hope, now felt like a weight, a reminder of the choices and secrets that had defined my path. As I navigated through the dusty remains of the shop, each step was a confrontation with my own past, a past filled with moments of desperation, of moral ambiguity, and the lengths to which I had gone to keep afloat in a sea of challenges.

Navigating the cluttered aisles felt like traversing through layers of time, each object a marker of a past both cherished and mourned. My hands moved almost of their own accord, brushing away layers of dust from items that once gleamed with the promise of history and stories untold. Despite knowing that my efforts were but a drop in the ocean of neglect that had claimed the shop, I couldn't help but try, driven by a heart that yearned to see a glimmer of the past, however fleeting.

"You've never told me what happened," Leigh's voice broke through my reverie, pulling me back to the present. He held an old teapot, its surface a canvas of time, as he gently brushed away the grime that had settled on its sides.

"You've never asked before," I found myself responding, my voice a mix of resignation and a faint hint of surprise. It was true; despite the years and the closeness that had developed between us, some chapters of my past remained closed, untouched by questions or confessions.

"Would you have told me if I had?" His question hung in the air between us, a bridge to conversations never had, to secrets kept closely guarded.

I shrugged, a non-committal gesture that belied the turmoil of thoughts swirling within me. I understood Leigh's tentative approach, his sensitivity to the scars that the past had etched deep into my being. Yet, his reluctance to probe further, to peel back the layers of my history, spoke volumes. If he couldn't muster the courage to ask, to dive into the depths of my past sorrows and sins, then perhaps he wasn't ready to bear the weight of the truths that lay hidden there.

The memory of that night in the casino carpark, stark and vivid against the backdrop of time, remained etched in my mind with unwavering clarity. The thin, pale man, a stranger whose name I never knew, had emerged from the shadows like a spectre, his presence heralding the unravelling of the life I had so carefully constructed. The yellow envelope he produced from his briefcase, the photos it contained of Jarod and me in the midst of our carefully orchestrated deceit on the casino floor, was like a grenade tossed casually into the normality of my existence.

One photo in particular, that of a wealthy patron we had targeted over the years, served as a chilling reminder of the consequences of our actions. The threat of exposure, of our carefully curated world crashing down around us, was palpable in the air between us. Yet, despite the fear that gnawed at the edges of my composure, I clung to the belief that my clandestine arrangement with Officer Jenkins would shield me from the fallout.

"I don't have the money," I stated, a mix of defiance and resignation in my voice. The money, long since funnelled into the dream of the antique store, was beyond retrieval, a fact that left me standing on the precipice of an unknown and terrifying future.

The man's reaction, a simple shrug as he returned the photos to their envelope and snapped his briefcase shut, seemed almost anticlimactic. As he turned to leave, a part of me dared to believe that I had navigated the threat, that his bluff had been called and dismissed. The relief that washed over me was tinged with a smug sense of victory. *I work the casino floor for easy pickings. I know how to call a bluff,* I reassured myself, a grin pulling at the corner of my mouth.

But that sense of security was shattered in an instant. The man's sudden pivot, the glint of a blade catching the overhead light and casting bright, menacing streaks across my vision, froze me in place. My attempt to gasp for air faltered, choked by the sudden grip of fear. My eyes, wide and searching, found the nearest security camera, a lifeline in the desperate hope for intervention.

"The money or Brody's life. You have until midday tomorrow. I'll be waiting right here," his words sliced through the night, a cold, hard ultimatum that left no room for doubt or negotiation.

Standing in front of the counter, the stillness of the shop enveloping me, I felt an overwhelming surge of emotion. Tears, unbidden, began to well up in my eyes as I gazed towards the front door. Its dark, silent form stood as a grim reminder of the shop's long disuse, yet my memories of that fateful day remained as vivid and piercing as ever.

I had been determined to call the man's bluff, to stand firm against the threat that loomed over Brody and me. The anxiety that had gripped me in the early hours of that morning had gradually dissipated as I threw myself into the day's work, seeking refuge in the mundane tasks that demanded my attention. As midday passed without any sign of the man or the fulfilment of his ominous threat, my confidence swelled. I had convinced myself that I had made the right decision, that my gamble would not have dire consequences.

But the false sense of security was short-lived. I remember rubbing my arms, just as I did now, as a sudden chill ran through me, a precursor to the dread that would soon engulf me. It was one-fifteen in the afternoon when the realisation hit me with the force of a tidal wave: I had made a grave mistake. The darkness that descended upon my mind in that moment was suffocating, a visceral fear that clutched at my heart and sent it plummeting into the depths of despair.

The gamble with my love's life, a risk I had taken with a bravado I did not truly feel, had been a miscalculation of catastrophic proportions. The clarity of hindsight laid bare the folly of my actions, the hubris that had led me to believe I could outmanoeuvre the consequences of our deeds. Standing in the quiet of the shop, the weight of that realisation pressed down on me with unbearable heaviness, a burden of guilt and regret that time had not eased.

"Why don't you take it all back?" Leigh's question, gentle yet laden with implication, cut through the fog of my reminiscence, drawing me back to the present.

"What do you mean?" My response was automatic, my attention shifting from the past to Leigh, who stood beside the table that bore the weight of a dusty collection of teaspoons, symbols of a life paused.

With a deliberate motion, Leigh reached into his shirt and revealed a thin, silver chain I had never noticed him wear before. The surprise must have been evident on my face, for he met my gaze with an expression that hinted at revelations yet to come.

"I was the one who gave Luke his Portal Key, you know." His voice held a note of casual revelation, as if unveiling a secret he knew I had already guessed at.

"I suspected as much," I admitted, the pieces of the puzzle aligning with a clarity that brought both comfort and unease.

"I still have four devices to help Luke form his team of Guardians," Leigh continued, his fingers deftly removing the chain from around his neck. The significance of his words, of the responsibility and power entwined within the small Portal Key that now dangled from the chain, was not lost on me.

As he held out the device, the symbol of a doorway to Clivilius and to possibilities beyond my current understanding, a myriad of emotions coursed through me. "You should join him. Reclaim what is rightfully yours. Take all of this to Clivilius with you," Leigh urged, his arms encompassing the space around us, the shop that was a mausoleum of dreams and memories. Gently, he placed the device and its chain into my hand, the cool metal a tangible invitation to a path untravelled.

My pulse raced at the prospect, a torrent of thoughts urging me to seize the opportunity, to embrace the power to alter my destiny, to do it for Brody, for myself. The idea of reclaiming what had been lost, of stepping into a role that could transcend the confines of this reality, was intoxicating.

Yet, as I held the key, the weight of the decision pressed heavily upon me. The emotion that threatened to surface was kept at bay, my resolve firm as I handed the device back to Leigh. "Not today," I whispered, the words a gentle refusal of the call to adventure. The idea of joining Clivilius, of becoming a Guardian, held an allure that was undeniable, yet I knew within my heart that I was not ready to step into that world, to bear the responsibilities it entailed.

The decision to refuse Leigh's offer was not made lightly. It stemmed from a deep understanding of my own readiness, of the journey I still needed to undertake before I could embrace such a role. The shop, with its layers of personal history, its connection to Brody and the life we had envisioned, remained a tether to this world, a reminder of the paths yet to be walked, the healing yet to be done.

In that moment of refusal, I acknowledged not only the loss and the love that had shaped me but also the strength that lay in knowing one's own limitations. The future, with its boundless possibilities, remained open, but for now, I chose the path of introspection, of healing, of preparing for whatever lay ahead, on my own terms.

# 4338.208

## (27 July 2018)

# GAMBLE

## 1338.208.1

    Staring at the revolving glass door, its surface a mirror to the mundanity of the world outside, I felt a shift within me. The outlines of passing people blurred into ghostly apparitions, their forms fleeting and insignificant against the backdrop of my own focused intent. The restless feelings of anticipation that had plagued me all day, the nagging doubts and the whispers of excitement, quickly subsided as if quelled by the gravity of the moment. My pulse accelerated, not from fear but from an electrifying sense of purpose, as I stepped through the doors, allowing them to sweep me into the belly of the beast – Wrest Point Casino.

    The air inside was charged, a palpable current of energy, excitement, and desperation. It was a world unto itself, pulsating with the vibrant lights, and a symphony of greed and hope. Small groups of people congregated around the concierge, their voices a cacophony of excitement and impatience, chatting loudly while they waited for their turn to check into the hotel. It was a scene of eager anticipation, a prelude to the night's adventures, or misadventures, as fate would have it.

    Turning back for a brief moment, a flash of irritation pierced through me as I glared at the young twenty-something-year-old that carelessly bumped into me. She, along with her nightclub-dressed, already slightly intoxicated entourage, bustled through the revolving door with a carelessness that grated on my nerves. They headed straight for the eccentric Birdcage Bar, a beacon of artificial glamour in this temple of chance and fortune. There, they would, no doubt, indulge in more than one cocktail, their laughter too loud, their conversations sprinkled with the self-assuredness of those who are blissfully unaware of the deeper currents beneath the surface of this gilded world. They congratulated themselves on their own faux-sophistication, a display that was as transparent as it was pitiable.

They didn't compare, not really. Not to my own carefully chosen attire, a short, red dress that spoke volumes in its understated elegance. Its subtle yet seductive plunge hinted at mysteries untold, while the thin silver belt cinched at my waist served as a delicate demarcation between confidence and the promise of allure. In this ensemble, I felt like a predator among sheep, my intentions sharp and clear, my resolve steeled.

Despite my contempt for the youthful crowd, their laughter and carefree spirits acted like a contagion. I found myself inadvertently siphoning some of their lively energy, a feeling foreign yet invigorating, as it spurted through my veins, igniting a flame of ambition for the night ahead. The excitement bubbling inside me felt almost rebellious. *But Brody is dead, and the antique shop is gone. What more do I have to lose?* The thought echoed in my mind, a haunting reminder of my current state of desolation.

Walking through the casino, every step felt like a defiance of my reality, a reality where everything I cherished had been stripped away, leaving behind a void that hungered for purpose, for revenge. As tempting as Leigh's proposal had been yesterday, dangling before me like a lifeline in my sea of despair, I wasn't yet convinced that it was the right solution. It seemed too easy, too convenient. Opting for Leigh's plan meant letting all those who wronged me, who dismantled my life piece by piece, off without facing any real consequences.

It was an injustice I couldn't stomach, a betrayal of everything Brody and I had stood for.

The dimly lit corridors of the casino, filled with the clinks of chips and the murmurs of hopeful gamblers, mirrored the turmoil within me. But then, amidst the clutter of my thoughts, an idea began to crystallise. *Maybe, just maybe, if my skills hadn't yet completely abandoned me, I could use Jarod to help steal enough money to reclaim the antique store.* The notion was risky, fraught with peril, but it ignited a spark of hope, a flicker of excitement at the challenge it presented.

*Leigh was right about that part – it is rightfully mine!* The conviction in Leigh's voice when he spoke of the antique shop resonated with me now more than ever. It wasn't just about reclaiming a property; it was about reclaiming a piece of myself, a testament to the resilience that Brody always believed I possessed.

As I navigated through the crowd, my mind raced with possibilities, strategies forming and reforming with each step I took. The idea of leveraging Jarod, of orchestrating a heist so bold, it would not only restore what was unjustly taken from me but also serve as a fitting tribute to Brody's memory, was exhilarating. It was a gamble, yes, but wasn't life in itself the biggest gamble of all?

My resolve hardened with every thought of the injustice I had endured, the loss of Brody, the loss of our dream. The casino's vibrant energy, its cacophony of hope and despair, suddenly felt like an anthem to my own brewing storm. Tonight, the stakes were more personal than ever, and I was ready to bet it all, to reclaim what was rightfully mine, to honour Brody's memory, and to prove to myself that the fire within me hadn't been extinguished by the tragedies I had faced.

In the grand scheme of the casino, with its bright lights and shadowed corners, I found a reflection of my own journey—brilliant yet dark, hopeful yet filled with uncertainty. But above all, it was a journey of reclaiming control, one daring move at a time.

❖

With the cloak of the late evening wrapping around the casino, the table game floor transformed into a vibrant tapestry of human endeavour. It was bustling, alive with a crowd whose attire spanned the spectrum from the barely passable remnants of a day's work to the unapologetic display of high-class money, their fabrics whispering tales of affluence and ambition. The air was thick with chatter and loud laughter, each sound a testament to the myriad hopes and dreams packed into this space. It was a symphony of human emotion, and amid this cacophony, I found myself a solitary note, lingering on the edge of harmony and discord.

Steering myself through the clustered bodies, I moved with a purpose, my gaze sharp and calculating. I surveyed the gamers as I passed by each table—blackjack, pontoon, and roulette, a parade of chance and skill. Taking mental note of what could be our first easy pickings, I evaluated the players, searching for weakness, for that telltale sign of vulnerability that could be exploited. This wasn't just a game; it was a battlefield, and every piece of information was a weapon.

As the several poker tables came into view, located in the far back corner, the scene shifted subtly. The lights seemed to dim, the chatter to soften, as if the very atmosphere acknowledged the gravity of the stakes here. Jarod, dressed in a fine dark navy suit that spoke of quiet confidence, was a beacon amidst the shadows. Seated at the higher buy-in table, he held a glass of whiskey poised mid-air, a picture of contemplation and control.

Our eyes met briefly, a fleeting connection in the sea of faces. It was just long enough for me to signal my arrival and to let Jarod know that I'd seen him. In that glance, a myriad of unspoken understandings passed between us, a reaffirmation of the plan that had brought us to this point. With the connection made, I turned away, allowing the currents of the crowd to carry me to the closest bar.

Ordering myself a gin and tonic, my beverage of choice, I took a moment to steady myself. The cold, crisp liquid was a welcome balm, grounding me in the here and now. As I sipped my drink, my mind raced, not just with the details of the plan, but with the weight of everything that rested upon its success. It wasn't just about the money or reclaiming what was lost; it was about proving to myself that I could navigate this world of shadows and light, of risk and reward.

In that bustling casino, amid the throngs of hopefuls and dreamers, I found a strange solace in the knowledge that, for tonight at least, I was not just a passive participant in the game of life. I was an active player, with stakes that went far beyond the green felt of the poker tables. This was more than a gamble; it was a statement, a declaration of my unwillingness to be swept away by the tides of fate. Tonight, I would be the one setting the course, come what may.

Jarod was still in his seat, a picture of calm amidst the storm, when I arrived to stand amongst the onlookers. The timing was impeccable, or perhaps fate had a sense of irony, for just as I melded into the crowd, I witnessed a young gentleman throw his cards onto the table in defeat. His face was a canvas of frustration, painted with the broad strokes of a lost gambler. He rose from his chair in a huff, the very image of dashed hopes. A small smile involuntarily crossed my face as I watched the pile of chips in the centre of the table being pushed in Jarod's direction. It was a small victory, perhaps, but in our line of work, every little bit helped.

"Beatrix Cramer?" the employee called out, her voice slicing through the din of the casino. She looked into the crowd, her gaze searching for the owner of the name. The call felt like a spotlight suddenly trained on me, exposing me to the curious eyes of the onlookers.

I sighed lightly, a mixture of annoyance and resignation fluttering in my chest. Poker had never been my game of choice. It demanded a patience I didn't possess, especially not tonight. It was my least favourite table game, a sentiment that had only deepened over time. The game was a labyrinth of strategy and deceit, a time-consuming dance around the table that required not only an understanding of the official rules but also the countless covert signals Jarod and I had developed over time. These secret signs and signals were our language on the felt, a way to communicate our cards and intentions without uttering a single word. Yet, despite its utility, the complexity of it all was a constant thorn in my side. Jarod, of all people, should have known better than to put my name on the waitlist without consulting me first.

"Beatrix Cramer?" the young woman repeated, her tone a blend of impatience and obligation as her eyes darted between the faces in the gathering crowd, seeking mine.

"Excuse me," I murmured, my voice barely above a whisper as I navigated through the tipsy gentlemen beside me. Their laughter and slurred words were a stark contrast to the tension coiling within me. With each step towards the table, the weight of the night's stakes pressed heavier on my shoulders. I took my seat in the one freshly vacated, a silent battlefield awaiting its next contender.

Refusing to allow even the quickest of glances at Jarod, I focused my attention on the table before me. This was a deliberate choice, a way to shield my turbulent emotions from those keen enough to look. Jarod and I had always been a formidable team, but tonight, the blend of personal stakes and the intricacies of my lofty goal made everything feel more acute, more dangerous. In the mirrored surfaces of the casino, amidst the clinking chips and shuffled cards, I found a reflection not just of the gambler I had become, but of the person I was outside this gilded cage. Tonight, every move was a gamble, not just with the chips on the table, but with the very fabric of our futures.

My heart skipped erratically, like a novice dancer tripping over an unseen obstacle, as the dealer's hands moved with practiced ease, distributing destiny in the form of cards. The shuffle and snap of the cards against the green felt was a familiar cadence in this cathedral of chance, yet it did little to soothe the quickening of my pulse. I stared down at my cards, the symbols seemingly mocking me with their simplicity. It had been ages since I last played, and the rules felt like distant memories, obscured by the fog of time. *It's been a while,* I chastised myself silently, feeling the weight of the moment press down on me.

"Graeme," the young man beside me, introduced himself with a casual ease, his half-grin carrying a hint of camaraderie, or perhaps it was the beginnings of a competitive jest. He finished his introduction with a slight nod of his head, a gesture of acknowledgment or perhaps challenge, before he downed the last of the clear liquid in his glass in a single, confident gulp. The action, so full of certainty, contrasted sharply with the turmoil churning within me.

I managed to give Graeme the faintest of smiles in return, a gesture so slight it could easily be missed. My mind was a whirlwind of calculations and doubts, leaving little room for social niceties. I quickly turned my attention back to the two cards that lay face down before me – the four and nine of spades. *Getting the shit hands already,* I thought grimly, the cards a poor omen of the evening's fortunes.

As my turn approached, the weight of decision pressing down on me, I felt the eyes of the table boring into me. *To call or to fold?* It was a decision wrapped in strategy and chance, a gamble on the unknown. With a heavy sigh, born of frustration and resignation, I tossed the cards towards the dealer, signalling my retreat from this round. My action was met with Jarod's narrowed eyes, a silent questioning of my choice. His look was a mixture of concern and confusion, an unspoken dialogue between us. *It's his fault, anyway,* I retorted silently, deflecting the blame for my current state of agitation. Jarod's insistence on my participation, his strategic positioning of me in this game, felt like an anchor dragging me down into waters I had no desire to navigate.

In that moment, surrounded by the focused intensity of the game and the casual indifference of my fellow players, I felt a profound sense of isolation. It wasn't just the game that was against me; it was the realisation that in this endeavour, I was truly out of my element, thrust into a scenario where my usual confidence and control were replaced by uncertainty and improvisation. The casino's bright lights and the clatter of chips against the backdrop of murmured conversations seemed to underscore my discomfort, a vivid reminder of the high stakes and personal vulnerabilities involved in this game of chance and deception.

"You're already not enjoying it?" Graeme's voice was a soft intrusion, his body leaning in closer than comfort would dictate, breaching the invisible boundary of personal space. His inquiry, laced with a hint of genuine concern and curiosity, brushed against my ear in the crowded din of the casino.

"Not particularly," I replied, my voice a mix of resignation and mild irritation, as my eyes finally found Jarod's across the felt battlefield that lay between us. In that moment of eye contact, a silent battle of wills ensued, an exchange of unspoken grievances and challenges.

"You friends?" Graeme's question, simple on the surface, was loaded with implications, and it sent a jolt of alarm through me. He nodded subtly in Jarod's direction, his inquiry seemingly innocent but fraught with potential peril for our carefully constructed façade.

*Shit!* The thought erupted in my mind, a silent curse as I felt the precarious balance of our ruse threaten to topple. Biting the corner of my lower lip, a gesture of nervous contemplation, I knew that any misstep now could unravel the delicate tapestry of deception we had woven. "Old acquaintances," I answered, offering a wide smile that I hoped would deflect further scrutiny. It was a response designed to straddle the line between truth and necessity, a verbal sidestep.

Graeme's face flushed pink at the response, an intriguing mix of embarrassment and something else—perhaps intrigue. It was an unexpected reaction, one that briefly shifted the dynamics of our interaction, casting him in a more vulnerable light.

"Graeme!" The sharp reprimand came from the older gentleman seated on his other side, a sudden interruption that thankfully diverted Jarod's penetrating gaze away from us. The moment of tension dissipated, replaced by a return to the game at hand.

"Call," Graeme announced, his voice steadier now as he tossed several chips into the centre of the table, the clinking sound melding with the ambient cacophony of the casino.

I watched the interplay between Graeme and Jarod carefully, noting the subtle shifts in their expressions, the calculated casualness of their movements. It was a high-stakes dance of bluffs and reveals, each participant carefully cloaked in their own armour of composure.

"Check," Jarod finally broke the silence, his voice carrying a weight of finality, of decisions made and strategies set in motion.

"Two pair. Queens and jacks," declared the third man, the only other player still in the game, his tone cheerful, almost triumphant, as he revealed his hand.

"Sorry mate. Three of a kind – aces," Graeme countered, his voice even, his face a mask of controlled nonchalance as he reached for the chips, a gesture of victory devoid of gloating.

"Straight, ace high," Jarod's voice cut through the tension, his cards flipping over to reveal the winning hand. It was a moment of revelation, a turn of fortune that shifted the tide in his favour.

I couldn't help but grin inwardly at the turn of events. *At least one of us was having a bit of luck.* It was a small consolation in the grand scheme of things, a fleeting victory in the face of the night's larger battles.

The next quarter of an hour felt like an eternity, each minute stretching and warping in the dim, buzzing atmosphere of the casino. I remained a spectator in this game, my cards consistently lacking the promise of victory or even a fighting chance. My participation was purely theoretical, a series of folds that left me itching for action, for a hand that spoke of possibility. I estimated Jarod's performance from the corner of my eye, noting the slight increase in his chip stack. It seemed he was maintaining a steady course, hovering just above the starting line in this financial race. Meanwhile, my glass, once a comforting companion in this tableau of tension and strategy, now sat empty, its contents a distant memory.

Ignoring Jarod's questioning look, a silent inquiry into my next move, I gathered my chips with a sense of finality. The weight of the cold, hard tokens in my hand felt oddly satisfying, a tangible reminder of the stakes I was playing for. I rose to my feet, the action a declaration of my departure from this stage of uncertainty and patience-tested endurance.

"Leaving already?" Graeme's voice held a note of surprise, maybe a hint of disappointment. It was clear that my sudden exit disrupted the delicate balance of the game, an unexpected variable in the evening's equation.

"Sorry guys. The table's boring tonight," I said, my voice carrying a blunt honesty that left no room for negotiation. The words felt heavy as they left my lips, a mixture of frustration and strategic retreat. It wasn't just the lack of engaging hands that spurred my departure; it was the gnawing realisation that this game, this entire scenario, was a far cry from the action and direct confrontation I craved.

With that, I walked off, leaving the table and its occupants behind. The sounds of the casino enveloped me once again, a cacophony of hopes and dreams being wagered in real-time. My steps were deliberate, each one taking me further away from the felt battleground and into the labyrinth of the casino floor. I felt a strange mixture of relief and anticipation coursing through me. Relief at stepping away from the stifling atmosphere of a game that offered no satisfaction, and anticipation for what was to come next. This night was far from over, and my plans, my real gambit, lay ahead, waiting to be set into motion.

❖

With a renewed drink in hand, its contents shimmering under the casino's bright lights, I found myself wandering with a feigned casualness between the blackjack tables. The clatter of chips and the murmur of hushed strategies provided a backdrop to my aimless saunter. Despite the pretence of interest in the games unfolding before me, my true focus lay elsewhere. From the corner of my eye, I could see Jarod, a steadfast figure amidst the fluctuating fortunes of the poker table. His concentration was unwavering, a testament to the gravity of our undertaking, and it anchored me amidst the swirling bustle of the casino floor.

"Sorry," I mumbled almost reflexively as my distraction led me to collide with a passer-by. It was a minor incident, the kind that occurred a dozen times a night in a place like this, but the moment I glanced up at the man, the word "Security" emblazoned on his shirt sent a jolt of alarm through me. My eyes widened in shock, not so much at the title but at the recognition of the man it was attached to.

"Shit!" The expletive slipped from my lips, a whisper drowned out by the cacophony of the casino yet thunderous in its implications. I quickly turned away from the man's gaze, hoping to blend back into the anonymity of the crowd. He did a double take, his movements momentarily pausing as if he sensed the significance of the encounter before he resumed his march across the casino floor. His presence here, in this role, was an unexpected and unsettling revelation.

I grabbed hold of the edge of the nearest blackjack table to steady myself, the cold metal a sharp contrast to the sudden warmth flooding my body. My mind raced, teetering on the edge of panic. *The blade-wielding man. He works here!?* The realisation was like a puzzle piece clicking into place, but it was a piece that I hadn't known was missing, revealing a picture far more complex and dangerous than I had anticipated.

The implications were immediate and troubling. *If he recognised me, if he connected me back to...* No, I couldn't afford to spiral down that line of thought. Not here, not now. I took a deep breath, attempting to quell the rising tide of panic, to regain the composure necessary to navigate this unforeseen obstacle. My grip on the table loosened as I forced myself to take a step back, to blend into the flow of casino patrons once more.

This encounter, brief as it was, served as a stark reminder of the stakes I was playing for, far beyond the chips and cards of the casino's games. Our presence here, the roles Jarod and I had assumed, were part of a larger game, one with real dangers and consequences. As I moved away from the blackjack table, my mind was already racing through scenarios, planning countermeasures, and contingencies. The night had just taken on a new level of complexity, and I needed to be ready for whatever came next.

"Still bored?" The voice, distinct and unmistakably familiar, cut through the noise of the casino, a soft inquiry laced with an undertone of suggestion. As the man stepped closer, his presence immediately behind me was invasive, his breath warm against the cool skin of my neck. The subtle pressure of his proximity, an unwelcome intrusion, sent a ripple of discomfort through me.

I turned to face Graeme, forcing a flirty smile onto my lips in an attempt to mask the sudden surge of unease. It was a reflex, a defence mechanism honed from years of navigating unwanted advances. Graeme, seemingly oblivious to the discomfort he had just imposed, grinned back at me, his expression one of anticipation, as if my smile was an invitation rather than a façade.

My smile vanished as quickly as it had appeared. "Fuck off. I'm not interested," I said, my voice carrying a sharp edge, a clear boundary being drawn. With deliberate force, I pushed past him, my movement through the crowd a blend of escape and assertion. As I walked, I finished the drink in my hand in three large gulps, each swallow an attempt to wash away the bitterness of the encounter. The glass hit the bar harder than I intended, a physical manifestation of the turmoil swirling within me. My heart was thumping in my chest, each beat a loud echo of my growing frustration and confusion. *What the fuck am I doing here tonight?*

The question hung heavily in my mind as I stood at the bar, the noise and lights of the casino blending into a dissonant blur around me. This night, supposed to be a carefully orchestrated play within the grand scheme of our plans, was unravelling at the seams. Encounters with security personnel from a past I wished to forget, unwelcome advances from Graeme, and the ever-present weight of my focus on winning my antique shop back—it all coalesced into a suffocating fog of doubt and disorientation.

"Rum and coke," Leigh's voice cut through the ambient noise of the bar, clear and composed, as he stepped beside me. His presence was unexpected, a sudden variable in the already complex equation of the night. With a casual sideways glance, he acknowledged me, his demeanour as nonchalant as if we were crossing paths in the most mundane of settings, not the charged atmosphere of the casino's bar.

"What are you doing here?" The words slipped from my lips, a hiss borne of surprise and suspicion. In the tangled web of our current endeavour, Leigh's sudden appearance felt less like a coincidence and more like a calculated move. "You spying on me?" The question was pointed, my gaze sharp as I searched his face for any telltale sign of his true intentions.

"It's not always about you," Leigh scoffed, his response a blend of dismissal and irritation as he collected his drink from the bartender. His words stung, a reminder of the broader machinations at play, of which we were both a part, willingly or not.

"What can I get you?" The bartender's voice, professional and oblivious to the undercurrents swirling between Leigh and me, broke through the moment of tension.

"Shut up," the words tumbled out, a reflexive response to the irritation simmering within me, not intended for the bartender but as an outburst of my fraying patience. Realising my poor choice in words and their unfortunate timing, I quickly redirected my frustration. "Sorry, not you," I amended, my voice softening as I addressed the bartender, a flush of embarrassment colouring my cheeks at the unintended rudeness.

A soft chuckle slipped from Leigh's lips, a sound that under different circumstances might have been infectious, lightening the mood. Yet, in the moment, it only served to underscore the complexity of our interactions, a mix of camaraderie and contention.

"Gin and tonic, thank you," I ordered, my voice steadier now, an attempt to reclaim some semblance of control over the situation. The request was a lifeline back to normality, a simple transaction devoid of the layers of intrigue and emotion that Leigh's presence had stirred.

Leigh spun himself around with a fluid motion that spoke of his constant vigilance, even in such a casual gesture, and leaned against the bar. His stance was relaxed, but his eyes, sharp and calculating, missed nothing. "Actually, I'm here keeping an eye on Charlie," he confessed, as if revealing a piece of a puzzle I hadn't realised was missing.

"The Sergeant?" My voice spiked with surprise, the name 'Charlie' tethered to a context far removed from the glittering casino lights and the clinking of glasses.

"Yes." The confirmation was succinct, a verbal nod that added weight to the already tense atmosphere between us.

"The Sergeant is here?" I repeated, my mind racing to connect the dots, to understand the implications of this revelation. "Yes," Leigh affirmed once more, his patience with my shock evident but wearing thin.

"Shit! What the hell is Charlie—" My question was cut short, a jumble of confusion and concern that threatened to rise in volume. Leigh's sharp "Shh, keep your voice down," came as a hiss, a command delivered with an urgency that made me snap my mouth shut. He broke eye contact, his gaze darting nervously around the bar, an unspoken reminder of the stakes involved and the importance of discretion.

The bartender placed the gin and tonic in front of me, a silent exchange that momentarily grounded me as I searched my purse for a bank card. The action was mechanical, a distraction from the whirlwind of questions and fears swirling in my mind. Leigh's presence, initially a source of irritation, had morphed into a crucial link to a larger, more dangerous game being played just beyond our immediate sight.

"I got this one," Jarod's voice, unexpected and close, startled me from my thoughts. His presence, appearing suddenly from behind, was both a reassurance and a reminder of the complexities of our night. "And her friend's," he added, a gesture of camaraderie or perhaps strategy, motioning for Leigh to put his cash away. It was a move that blended seamlessly into the tableau of the casino night, yet carried with it an undercurrent of our shared, unspoken agendas.

"Sure," the bartender responded, a neutral participant in the night's unfolding drama, his attention momentarily ours before it drifted to the next customer, the next order.

"Oh, and I'll have another whiskey, thanks," Jarod announced, pushing his empty glass across the bar with a casualness that belied the tension simmering beneath our trio's calm exteriors. "Gotcha," came the bartender's easy acknowledgment, the exchange a familiar dance in this place of escape and excess.

While Jarod and Leigh made their introductions, a veneer of normality in an evening anything but, I couldn't shake a growing sense of unease. My gaze drifted across the casino floor, a minefield of potential complications. Between the security guard whose path I'd crossed earlier and the young poker player Graeme, the evening seemed destined to be a series of navigating unwanted glances and the implications they carried. It was a tightrope walk of visibility and anonymity, each step measured, each breath calculated.

"I think we should go," the words tumbled out, almost of their own accord, as I raised the glass to my lips. The statement was more an instinctive response to the night's escalating unpredictability than a calculated decision.

"Go?" Jarod echoed, the single word a query loaded with surprise.

"Probably a good idea," Leigh concurred, his agreement swift, his eyes narrowing as he assessed the situation with a strategist's mind.

I followed Leigh's gaze, his attention sharply focused on a figure across the room. Charlie, the sergeant whose presence added a volatile element to the night's equation, stood half-slumped against the far wall. The sight of him, counting what appeared to be a considerable wad of cash in his hands, was a jarring juxtaposition against the backdrop of casual gambling and leisure. It was a visual reminder of the layers of intrigue and danger that lay just beneath the surface of our gathering.

"Excuse me," Leigh said, pushing himself away from the bar. "Thanks for the drink." His words were polite, a façade of civility that barely masked the urgency of his departure.

"My pleasure," Jarod replied, his grin wide and genuine.

The frequent glances of the security guard had woven a thread of unease through the evening, a persistent reminder of the precariousness of our situation. "I'm going home," I declared with a finality that felt like a lifeline, placing my glass on the bar as if sealing the decision. The cool surface of the counter under my fingertips felt grounding, a stark contrast to the anxiety churning within me.

"Oh, come on, Beatrix," Jarod's voice, tinged with a mix of persuasion and disappointment, reached out to me. His hand clasped my bare arm, a touch meant to reassure, to persuade. Yet, it only served to heighten the sense of entrapment I felt.

I spun to face him, ready to unleash a barrage of excuses and reasons why his suggestion was untenable. The space between us was charged with unspoken tensions and unresolved conflicts, a battlefield of wills.

"Just for an hour," he implored softly, his gaze locking onto mine with an intensity that seemed designed to dismantle my defences. "Then we can go home. I promise."

"We?" The word escaped me, laced with incredulity and a rising ire. The presumption that he could weave a 'we' into the fabric of the evening, after everything, felt like a breach of understanding, a step too far. "No," I affirmed, my head shaking in both disbelief and determination. "We're not having another repeat of last time." The memory of 'last time' hovered between us, a spectre of past entanglements and consequences, a line I was not willing to cross again. With a force born of clarity and resolve, I extricated myself from his grasp, the heels of my silver stilettos sinking into the carpet as I turned away, each step a declaration of my intent to distance myself from the situation, from him.

"I didn't mean it like that," Jarod's protestation reached me, his words chasing after me as he hurried to catch up. His insistence did little to quell the storm of emotions brewing within me, the sting of tears threatening to breach my composure.

"Like hell you didn't," I retorted, the anger and hurt intermingling, creating a volatile mix that threatened to spill over. The tears, unbidden yet unmistakable, began to form, blurring my vision.

"Beatrix, please." His plea was a soft echo in the tumult of the casino, a last-ditch attempt to bridge the chasm that had opened between us.

"No, Jarod." The finality in my voice was a closing door, a boundary set against the backdrop of the night's complexities. The decision to walk away, to sever this conversation, was not just a physical act of leaving but a stand against the repetition of past mistakes, a declaration of my need for autonomy and respect.

A raucous cheer erupted from the roulette table beside me, a sudden burst of energy that shattered the tense atmosphere I had been wading through. In the midst of the excited commotion, an inadvertent jostle from the crowd caused me to lose my footing momentarily, sending me stumbling sideways into an unforeseen and uncomfortable collision. My arm brushed firmly against a man's excited crotch, a contact that made my skin crawl with revulsion. I grimaced, the involuntary physical reaction a stark reminder of the unpredictability and often unsavoury encounters within the casino's bustling environment.

"Changed your mind, have you?" Graeme's voice cut through the clamour, his tone dripping with unwarranted amusement and suggestion. A wild grin swept across his face as he spoke, his eyes lingering with inappropriate interest below my neck. His leering gaze felt like a violation, igniting a fierce indignation within me.

"Fuck off!" My response was a yell, a release of pent-up frustration and anger, as I slapped the young man's cheek with a force born of self-defence and sheer disgust. My action caught him completely off guard, sending him stumbling back into the unsuspecting crowd behind him. The momentary calamity of our confrontation drew the attention of those nearby, ensuring that all eyes were momentarily diverted from anything but the spectacle we created.

In the brief window of distraction, my other hand acted of its own accord, instinctively sweeping across the rim of the table to collect several unsupervised chips. It was an impulsive move, driven by the chaos of the moment and the knowledge that the attention of the crowd was fixated elsewhere, on the dramatic altercation rather than the sleight of hand unfolding at the edge of their vision.

"Bitch!" Graeme hissed, venom lacing his voice as he regained his balance, the sting of the slap and the humiliation of the public scene fuelling his anger. His insult hung in the air, a bitter testament to the encounter's escalation from an uncomfortable bump to an outright confrontation.

As I turned away from Graeme and the scene we had inadvertently created, Jarod approached from the side, his presence a silent support in the aftermath of the commotion. Without a word, I slipped the chips into his waiting palm, a seamless transfer that went unnoticed by the surrounding crowd, still absorbed in the aftermath of our altercation. Jarod's arrival felt like a timely intervention, a reminder that despite the night's upheavals, I wasn't navigating these turbulent waters alone.

"You got a problem there, mate?" Jarod's voice, firm and challenging, sliced through the tense air, as he positioned himself between Graeme and me. His intervention was a physical barrier, a declaration of allegiance and protection that momentarily shifted the dynamics of the confrontation.

My pulse skyrocketed, a visceral reaction to the escalating situation. With sharp eyes, I scanned our surroundings, hyper-aware. The tables were laden with chips, their guardians momentarily distracted by the drama unfolding. I gulped for air, the abundance of unguarded stakes fuelling a temptation that was both suffocating and irresistibly intoxicating. The ease with which I could capitalise on the situation was overwhelming, a siren call to my baser instincts.

"Your bitch here just hit—" Graeme's accusation was cut short by my actions. Another swift hand glide across the table's edge, my movements precise and covert under the guise of the commotion. A strategic hip bump sent another young man's efforts to secure his winnings into disarray, his chips scattering in a testament to the tumult of the moment.

The crowd gasped loudly, a collective intake of breath, as Jarod's fist connected solidly with Graeme's face. The impact was visceral, a release of pent-up tensions that had been simmering beneath the surface. Blood began to gush from his broken nose, a stark, crimson testament to the violence of the encounter.

A rush of exhilaration surged through me as I seized the momentary distraction to pocket several more chips, each one a tangible reminder of the stakes at play this evening. The thrill of the act, the rush of defiance against the unfolding drama, was electrifying.

But then, wildfire ignited in Graeme's eyes as he rose to his full height, the ferocity of his gaze cutting through the chaos. "You're assaulting a police officer," he announced sharply, his words slicing through the noise and halting Jarod's raised fist in mid-air. The revelation was a cold splash of reality, a stark warning of the precipice on which we teetered.

"Shit!" The expletive slipped from my lips, a reflexive response to the sudden and dangerous shift in our circumstances. My eyes widened in shock, the gravity of the situation crashing down on me. In a moment of clarity, I released the remaining chips from my grasp, letting them clatter to the floor, their sound a final note in the cacophony of the night's events.

*Time to go!* The thought was a clarion call, an imperative that brooked no hesitation. My legs, fuelled by adrenaline and the instinctual drive to evade the rapidly closing net of consequences, sprang into action. The casino, once a labyrinth of opportunity and danger, had become a trap, one that Jarod and I needed to escape before the repercussions of our actions could fully manifest.

"Can I see your bag, please, miss," the stern voice rooted me to the spot, a cold hand of dread closing around my heart. The authority in the tone, unmistakable and commanding, left no room for refusal.

"Argh! Get the fuck off me!" Jarod's yell sliced through the tension, a raw sound of resistance and defiance. His outburst was a stark contrast to the icy fear that had ensnared me.

"They're mine," I said, my voice a calm façade over the roiling storm of emotions within. Turning to face the security guard, my eyes locked onto his name tag. *Blake*. The name seared into my consciousness, a label for the fury and disbelief churning inside me. *So, the blade-wielding, murdering son-of-a-hitch is named Blake.* The realisation was like venom, a bitter acknowledgment of the adversary now standing before me.

"I'm sure the cameras will tell us a different story," Blake retorted smugly, his confidence bolstered by the silent sentinel of the security camera he pointed towards. His assurance was a cold calculation that our actions had not gone unnoticed.

"Shit!" The curse was a whisper, a quiet admission of the precariousness of our situation, the reality of the trap snapping shut around us.

"Hands out in front of you, Ms. Cramer. You're coming with me." The directive was final, a command that spelled out the end of this high-stakes game we had been playing.

Feeling like a cornered animal with no avenue for escape, I complied reluctantly, a sense of defeat washing over me as my hands were yanked together harshly and secured with flex-cuffs. The physical restraint was a tangible manifestation of the loss of control, a binding symbol of our capture.

Glancing across at Jarod, I saw the tangible marks of his own struggle—a bruised eye and a small cut above his brow, trophies of resistance in a battle that had swiftly turned against us.

Before either of us could exchange a word or share a glance that might communicate a thousand unsaid things, rough hands seized us, their impersonal grip guiding us forcibly in the same direction. The abruptness of our capture, the swift transition from players to pawns, was disorienting.

As we were prodded forward, every step away from the casino floor felt like moving through a dense fog of disbelief and shock. The realisation that our night had taken a disastrous turn was overwhelming, a bitter pill coated in the harsh reality of our situation. The complex web of actions and reactions that had led to this moment played back in my mind, a series of choices and chances that had spiralled far beyond my control.

*What the fuck?* The thought ricocheted through my mind as Leigh, in a performance of drunkenness, staggered toward us, his glass of rum and coke carelessly sloshing over its edges. It was a scene so surreal, unfolding amidst the tense backdrop of our apprehension, that it felt as though it were momentarily suspending time itself.

"Move aside," Blake barked, his authoritative tone cutting through the thick air of curiosity that had enveloped the onlookers. His demeanour was unyielding, a forceful push against the tide of bodies that had gathered to witness the drama.

Leigh, with a determination that seemed at odds with his feigned inebriation, made no effort to deviate from his collision course. It was a deliberate act, a planned intervention cloaked in the guise of an accidental encounter.

"Watch it," Blake warned, pushing Leigh aside as their shoulders collided. The contact, a physical assertion of dominance, was meant to sideline Leigh, to remove him from the equation.

"Sorry," slurred Leigh, executing a pivot on his heel that was too precise for his supposed state. He continued his trajectory, now aimed directly at me. The deliberate nature of his actions, hidden beneath the veneer of drunken missteps, was becoming increasingly clear.

"Shit!" I couldn't contain my exclamation, my instinct to retreat hindered by the restraints binding my hands and the bodies pressing in around us. Leigh's stumble into my side, the cold splash of his drink soaking my front, was a chaotic intrusion, a physical manifestation of the night's unpredictability.

Leigh's grip on my shoulder was firm, incongruous with his earlier display of instability. He leaned closer, his voice a stark contrast to his earlier slurred apologies. "Remember, you need a flat surface," he hissed, his words a clandestine message delivered with urgent clarity. The small, metallic object he pressed into my flex-cuffed hands was unmistakable—a Portal Key. My eyes bulged in disbelief. *What the fuck is he doing?* The question was a whirlwind of confusion and sudden hope, a lifeline offered in the guise of an accidental encounter.

"Get rid of him," Blake's voice commanded, breaking through the moment of secret exchange. His order was a dismissal, an attempt to regain control over the situation that Leigh's intervention had momentarily disrupted.

"Sorry, so sorry," Leigh continued, his apology waved off with a hand that belied the precision and purpose of his actions. His feigned drunkenness, a carefully crafted ruse, had provided the perfect cover for delivering the Portal Key, a move that shifted the dynamics of my capture.

As Leigh was ushered away, his act of stumbling drunkenness never faltering, I was left with the weight of the Portal Key in my hands and the realisation that our situation had just taken a turn toward the unfathomable. Leigh's intervention, so unexpected yet meticulously executed, opened a realm of possibilities that had seemed shut mere moments before. Amidst the chaos, a glimmer of hope flickered, a sign that the night's dark turn might yet hold paths to escape I hadn't dared to imagine.

Jarod's bewildered gaze pierced through the turmoil swirling inside me. "You okay?" His question, soft and laced with concern, felt like an anchor in the whirlwind that had enveloped us. Unable to muster the coherence for speech, I nodded silently, my acknowledgment a fragile thread of communication in the escalating situation.

"I'll take them from here," came a deep, authoritative voice, booming with a command that brooked no dissent. My body tensed instantaneously, a visceral reaction to the recognition of who stood behind us. *Charlie!* The name was a storm cloud in my mind, darkening the already fraught situation with its ominous implications.

"Bring them with me," Charlie ordered, his voice a decisive crack of thunder that set us in motion. I felt an involuntary lunge forward, propelled by the firm push of the officer behind me, a physical manifestation of Charlie's command. My legs moved mechanically, forced into action by the situation's gravity, as I struggled to maintain a semblance of composure amidst the whirlwind of emotions and questions battering my thoughts. *Am I in danger? Why isn't Leigh doing anything?* The queries circled like vultures, preying on the uncertainty that gripped me.

The brief conversation from the other night flashed through my mind with startling clarity. "Charlie is connected to it all, I just haven't figured out how yet." The words, once spoken in the realm of speculation, now seemed to hover at the edges of reality, gaining weight and significance with each step I took. The puzzle of Charlie's involvement, a mystery that Leigh had been piecing together, suddenly felt like a missing key in understanding the labyrinth I found myself ensnared within.

Had Leigh worked out the connection now? The question lingered, a flicker of hope amidst the dread. Leigh's actions, his calculated intervention, and the delivery of the Portal Key, suggested a deeper strategy at play, a plan that was unfolding even as we were led away. The realisation that there might be layers to our predicament yet unseen, plans within plans that could alter the course of events, provided a glimmer of hope in the darkness.

"You can't go in there," the woman's voice was firm, a barrier to the unfolding events, her hand outstretched as if her physical presence could halt the momentum of authority that Charlie wielded.

"I'm Sergeant Charlie Claiborne from the Hobart Police Department," he stated with a confidence that brooked no argument. The flash of his badge was not just a display of identity but of power, a symbol that demanded compliance and respect. The woman, recognising the authority imbued in that small metallic emblem, moved aside without further protest.

As Charlie placed one hand on the door, a deliberate pause held the air, thick with anticipation. He turned to us, his gaze sweeping over Jarod and myself with a scrutiny that felt both invasive and calculating. It was as if in that brief moment, he was assessing us, weighing his decisions based on what he saw in our faces, in our stances.

"Sergeant?" The security guard's voice broke the heavy silence, his question hanging between us, seeking direction in the midst of uncertainty.

Claiborne's response was immediate, his eyes narrowing, the lines of his face hardening with resolve. "Separate them." The command was sharp, an unwelcome decree that sent a ripple of dread through me.

"Watch it!" My protest was a reflex, a cry of alarm as my balance was compromised, my foot twisting beneath me. The yank backwards was sudden, a firm grip on my arm preventing any escape. The physicality of the moment, the sensation of being physically controlled, ignited a primal fear within me.

"I've got this one," Charlie declared, his grip tightening as he pulled me toward the door. His assertion was a clear claim, separating me from Jarod, from any semblance of safety or familiarity.

"Beatrix!" Jarod's call was a mix of desperation and determination, his attempt to reach me halted by the guards. The terror in his eyes mirrored the fear coursing through my own veins, a silent scream that enveloped us.

The sight of Blake's creepy grin as he reached for Jarod was a vision that would haunt me, a symbol of the threat we faced. In that moment, the danger we were in became tangibly real, a shadow that loomed large over us.

Seizing the sliver of opportunity before me, I lunged in their direction, my whispered promise to Jarod a vow in the face of despair. "I'll come back for you, I promise." Our brief connection, a fleeting touch of foreheads, was a moment of solidarity in the eye of the storm.

Then, with a forceful pull, I was dragged into the restricted room by Charlie, the door slamming shut behind us.

*4338.209*

*(28 July 2018)*

# FRIEND OR FOE?

## 1338.209.1

"What the hell do you think you're doing, Beatrix?" The words thundered from Sergeant Claiborne, his voice a tempest of fury and disbelief. The sudden slam of his fist against the wall reverberated through the room, a physical manifestation of his anger that made me flinch. My heart raced, adrenaline flooding my system, a primal response to the unexpected violence of the gesture.

My blood warmed, a fiery cocktail of fear and defiance coursing through my veins. My lips pressed together tightly, a physical barrier to the retort that danced on the tip of my tongue. My eyes, however, met his with a steely resolve, refusing to back down even as they screamed a thousand questions. *What had I done to warrant such rage? Was it fear or frustration that painted his features so vividly?*

The intensity of his gaze was palpable, a force that seemed to press against me with the weight of the unsaid. Time stretched thin between us, a fragile thread straining under the weight of our silent confrontation. Finally, Charlie broke contact, turning away with a loud huff that filled the tense silence. His body language shifted, a subtle but clear retreat from the brink of whatever precipice we had found ourselves teetering on.

Seizing the moment, my eyes darted around, taking in the details of our surroundings with practiced precision. The room was awash with the harsh glare of overhead lights, casting stark shadows that played across the surfaces of the furniture stacked neatly along the wall. My gaze flickered to the corner where several poker machines stood silent, their usual cacophony of lights and sounds eerily absent.

And then, my attention snapped to the object of my immediate interest—a large, moveable whiteboard positioned strategically to my right. Can't be more than three metres away, I estimated, a plan beginning to form in the depths of my mind. The small device, previously concealed, wedged between my flex-cuffed hands, suddenly felt like a lifeline. With a subtle shift, I nudged the Portal Key into my palms, its presence a reminder of the possibilities that lay within reach.

"I can't help you if you run," Charlie's voice tethered me back to the present, pulling me from the swirling vortex of my thoughts.

My eyes narrowed at him, skepticism and wariness etching deep lines into my gaze. My lips, however, remained a sealed vault, holding back the flood of questions and accusations threatening to spill out. *Does he really want to help me?* The question echoed in my mind, bouncing off the walls of my skepticism. *What does he know? Why was Leigh watching him so closely? Would Leigh approve if I ran? Of course, Leigh would approve, he gave me the fucking device!*

"Beatrix, I can help you," Charlie persisted, his eyes not just looking at me but focusing intently on the device cradled in my hands. His gesture of surrender, hands raised yet stepping closer, was a paradox that did little to ease the tightening knot of anxiety in my chest. "I can help you protect Luke."

His words cut through the air, sharp and unexpected. A soft gasp betrayed my shock. *Does he know Luke's a Guardian?* The question surged forward, pressing against my lips, desperate for release. And then, the deeper fear—*Does he know who is trying to kill him?* The image of a bloodied body, lifeless in the grim confines of a delivery truck's back, flashed before my eyes, a chilling reminder of the stakes at play. I swallowed hard, stifling another gasp. *Does Charlie know about Joel? Does he know what I did?*

"I'm on your side, Beatrix," Charlie said, inching closer with each word, his steps cautious yet determined.

With every advance he made, I retreated, a dance of distrust and fear. My mind screamed warnings at me, a cacophony of doubts and suspicions. *No*, it hissed. *If Leigh was watching him, then Charlie isn't to be trusted*. This mantra became my anchor, a steadfast hold in the swirling sea of uncertainty.

My heart hammered against my ribcage, a relentless drum echoing the rhythm of my escalating fears. The room seemed to close in around us, the air thick with unspoken tension and the weight of decisions yet to be made. The device in my hands felt heavier, a symbol of the complex web of alliances and betrayals that I found myself entangled in.

A sharp rap on the door shattered the tense atmosphere, a sound so unexpected it momentarily diverted Charlie's focus —and mine. Seizing this fleeting window of opportunity, my fingers fumbled with the device Leigh had entrusted to me, pressing the small, inconspicuous button at its end. A sting bit at my finger, a minor sacrifice as a tiny orb of bright energy burst forth, racing towards the whiteboard. The moment it made contact, an explosion of pulsating colours erupted, painting an impromptu barrier between reality and the unknown.

Charlie, caught in a moment of indecision, seemed torn between halting my escape and addressing the intrusion at the door. Fortune, it seemed, tipped in my favour as he opted to investigate the latter. A parting glance was all I could afford him, a silent acknowledgment of the game's new turn, before my body propelled forward, my feet barely touching the carpet as I dove into the vibrant spectacle before me.

The transition was surreal, a sensation unlike any I had experienced. As I pierced the veil of colours, a voice greeted me—not through the air or as a sound that my ears could detect, but as a resonance within my very mind. "Welcome to Clivilius, Beatrix Cramer," it intoned, a greeting both ominous and awe-inspiring. The voice, imbued with an unknown power, seemed to echo from the very essence of this new realm, wrapping around me like a cloak.

I landed with a jarring thud on the other side, the soft dust doing little to cushion my fall. My hands, still encased in the unforgiving grip of the cuffs, provided inadequate support, sending a jolt of pain through my wrists and up my arms. A gust of wind, alien yet strangely comforting, caressed my face as I struggled to orient myself.

Raising my head, the sight that greeted me was one of stark contrasts. Behind me, the Portal—a giant canvas of swirling colours—cast its ethereal glow over the landscape, painting the barren hills in hues of an otherworldly palette. The beauty of it was breathtaking, a spectacle of light against the desolation that stretched out before me.

And then, as if someone had flipped a switch, darkness enveloped everything.

# LOSE-LOSE

## 1338.209.2

The sudden transition from the brilliance of the Portal's light to the absolute absence of visibility was disorienting. My heart pounded in my chest, a lone sentinel in the vast silence that now surrounded me.

The wind whipped around me, its breath laden with a thousand minuscule grains of dust that found their way into every crevice of my skin. I grimaced as the tasteless particles of Clivilius dust invaded my mouth, an unwelcome reminder of the reality of this new and uncharted world.

Fumbling in my bag, I retrieved my phone, its torch a beacon of hope in the oppressive darkness. The light, though feeble against the blackness of the night, illuminated the ground directly in front of me. On hands and knees, I began a cautious advance toward where I believed my missing shoe lay discarded, a minor but grounding mission in the face of overwhelming uncertainty.

Then, without warning, I halted, my body tensing instinctively. The hairs on the back of my neck stood on end, a primal alarm system alerting me to an unseen presence. A shiver cascaded down my spine, a physical manifestation of the sudden spike of fear that pierced my initial curiosity. Was this sensation merely a reaction to the dust-laden wind, or was it something far more ominous—a presence, perhaps, lurking just beyond the reach of my light?

The darkness around me felt alive, charged with an energy I couldn't explain. Every rational fibre of my being told me it was just the unfamiliarity of Clivilius playing tricks on my senses, yet a deeper, more instinctual part of me whispered warnings of caution. The light from my phone cast long shadows, transforming ordinary shapes into spectres of doubt and fear.

A low growl, primal and unsettling, cut through the silence, reverberating in the darkness that enveloped me. "Duke?" My voice was a whisper, a mix of hope and dread, as I sank down, instinctively making myself smaller. The name slipped out, a futile attempt to attach familiarity to the unknown. My hand, gripping the phone, moved in wide, erratic arcs, the beam of light a desperate, flailing attempt at defence.

The brief illumination revealed a silhouette—a creature of considerable size, its form outlined against the lesser darkness. It was a fleeting glimpse, but enough to confirm my fears; this was no small domestic pet, no Shih Tzu lost and wandering. The creature snarled, a sound that seemed to scrape against my nerves, raw and terrifying.

My scream, loud and sharp, pierced the night as the creature lunged from the shadows. The light from my phone, a transient shield, flashed across its face—an expanse of black fur, eyes reflecting a momentary glint of surprise or pain. A claw, sharp and unyielding, raked across my arm, leaving a trail of fire in its wake as the beast bounded away, propelled by the same light that had revealed it.

The wind, as if encouraged by the encounter, picked up with renewed vigour. It whipped around me, a cyclone of dust obliterating any remaining visibility. The shoe, that mundane objective, was forgotten in an instant, its importance lost to more pressing survival instincts.

Pulling myself upright, I ran. The direction was guided by instinct more than sight, a desperate dash towards the safety I hoped the Portal represented. Another growl, deeper, closer, fuelled my flight, each step driven by adrenaline and the sheer will to escape.

The wind bit at my face, carrying with it not just the physical sting of sand and dust but the sharper sting of fear. My heart, a relentless drum, echoed the turmoil of my thoughts. The dark creature, whatever it was, had marked me with its claw, a tangible reminder of the dangers lurking in Clivilius.

As the Portal loomed before me, its surface came alive with a dizzying array of destinations. The giant screen, a gateway to numerous destinations, flickered with the promise of escape or peril.

*Select your location, Beatrix Cramer,* the voice of Clivilius, now familiar yet still unnervingly intimate, echoed within the confines of my mind.

The casino room, the scene of my recent ordeal, flashed before my eyes on the screen. A visceral reaction coursed through me—a wave of panic, repulsion, and an urgent desire to flee from what had become a place of danger and betrayal. "Not that one!" My voice was a mix of fear and defiance, an audible rejection of the path that would lead me back into the lion's den.

*Select your location, Beatrix Cramer,* the voice insisted, unyielding, as if oblivious to the chaos that surrounded me and the terror that gripped my heart.

My pulse thundered in my ears, a relentless drumbeat that mirrored my frantic state. Another growl, closer this time, punctuated the night, a reminder of the immediate threat that hunted me. *Focus!* The command was a desperate attempt to marshal my thoughts, to cling to the sliver of hope that Luke's study room represented. The image of that safe haven flickered on the screen, a visual anchor amidst the storm.

The creature, a nightmare made flesh, launched itself at me in a blur of motion. A scream tore from my lips as my phone, my last source of light, was flung from my grasp. It skittered across the ground, its light dimming as it settled far beyond my reach. *It's too far!* Desperation clawed at me, a visceral fear that I might not make it, that the darkness and the creature would claim me.

In a wild, instinctive gesture, I pulled off my remaining stiletto, wielding it as a makeshift weapon. I swung it through the air, a futile defence against an unseen assailant. The only resistance was the bite of dust-laden wind against my skin.

With the image of Luke's study room fixed in my mind's eye, I made a desperate leap towards the Portal. The action was a leap of faith, a physical manifestation of my hope and will to survive. Yet, as I hurled myself towards salvation, pain lacerated my leg—a cruel parting gift from the creature as its claw found me once more.

We crashed into the reality of Luke's study, an unceremonious entrance marked by chaos. Books, those silent witnesses to countless hours of study and contemplation, rained down upon us, a storm of paper and leather. The impact was disorienting, a cacophony of sound and sensation as I found myself entangled with my pursuer amidst the ruins of what should have been a sanctuary.

The creature's retreat was brief, a momentary pause in the relentless dance of predator and prey. As the Portal's light flickered out, the room was plunged into an oppressive darkness, a tangible cloak of fear and uncertainty. My breaths came in short, ragged gasps as I scrambled along the carpet, seeking the cold comfort of the doorframe. Pressing my back against its solid form, I tried to ground myself in the reality of the room, even as my heart raced with the terror of the unseen.

The growl that broke the silence was menacing, a sound that seemed to vibrate through the very air. In the dim light trickling in from the bedroom up the hallway, the creature's sharp teeth gleamed—a sinister smile in the shadows. My gaze locked onto the black eyes of my attacker, a connection fraught with primal fear and the instinctive knowledge of the life-and-death stakes between us.

With my back pressed against the doorframe, I slowly rose, every muscle tensed for action, my eyes never straying from those malevolent orbs. The light switch, a mere arm's length away, became the focal point of my desperate plan. Timing my move with care, I stretched out and flicked the switch, a flicker of hope igniting alongside the sudden illumination.

The creature's reaction was immediate and visceral. It howled, a sound of pain and rage, as the light assaulted its senses. The dead eyes, moments ago filled with predatory intent, now reflected only agony. But the triumph was short-lived. A loud pop heralded the bulb's demise, plunging the room back into darkness, and with it, my fleeting sense of control evaporated.

"Shit!" The expletive was a burst of frustration and fear, a vocal release of the tension that had built up. Blood, warm and sticky, trickled down my arm from the gash left by the creature's claw.

In that moment, a decision was made—not through logic, but through the sheer, unthinking instinct to survive. My legs propelled me forward, fuelled by adrenaline and the visceral need to escape the immediate danger. The familiar environment of the casino, where reflexes and quick decisions were part of the game, now seemed like a distant memory. Here, in this real and deadly game of survival, every choice, every movement, was imbued with a weight far greater than any wager I had ever placed.

The cacophony of growls and gnarls chasing me, a terrifying symphony that spurred my desperate flight, filled the air. I hurled myself into the hallway, a frantic, almost blind rush for safety. My cuffed hands became unwilling allies in my escape, thumping against the walls for support as my body waged a war against the limits of its own speed. The imbalance was sharp; my upper body surged ahead in urgency, while my legs scrambled to keep pace.

The living room materialised as an unexpected battlefield as I stumbled upon a scene as absurd as it was chaotic—a bright red kayak, incongruously placed, became both obstacle and marker of the surreal turn my life had taken. My fall over it was graceless, a tumble that embodied the disarray of my situation.

"Fuck off!" The shout was more than a command; it was a defiance, a refusal to succumb to the fear that the black beast, with its dripping saliva and careless destruction, embodied. My hands, restricted yet determined, grasped at small boxes—feeble weapons in this uneven contest. I threw them with all the force my constrained circumstances allowed, a futile attempt to ward off the looming threat that prowled the room, indifferent to the disarray it wrought among the scattered camping gear.

In my frantic search for anything that might offer a semblance of defence, my fingers stumbled upon a small camping lamp. Time was a luxury I didn't possess, leaving me no moment to test its functionality. Driven by instinct more than hope, I hurled the lamp towards the beast, watching as it struck its head and bounced away, an ineffectual gesture against the relentless advance of my attacker.

My scream tore through the silence. It was more than a reaction; it was a declaration of my refusal to succumb without a fight. Harnessing a final reserve of energy, born of desperation and determination, I hurled myself towards the salvation of the doorway in the far corner of the living room. My hand slapped against the light switch, an instinctive search for safety in illumination, as I collided with the wooden doorframe. The light heralded my descent down the carpeted staircase, each step a leap of faith in the face of unseen terror.

The animal's response was immediate—a howl that was both haunting and harrowing, a sound that seemed to chase me into the depths of my own fear. I couldn't tell if the creature braved the light to follow, but I couldn't afford to slow down to find out. My movements were less about thought and more about instinct, an intuitive understanding that light was my only ally in this nightmare. Flicking on the light of the large room downstairs, I propelled myself towards the perceived safety of the outdoors.

My hands met the glass sliding door with an inelegant thud. My fingers, trembling uncontrollably, struggled with the lock. Finally, the door yielded, and I stumbled out into the night, the sensor light snapping to life and casting my shadow across the cold grass.

Then, unexpectedly, the creature—a mass of black fur and primal energy—brushed against my leg as it sprinted past, its howl slicing through the night. The encounter, fleeting yet terrifying, rooted me to the spot. The decision not to follow the panther-like beast as it vanished into the shadows was instinctive, a deep-seated recognition of the boundary between its world and mine.

As it moved along the back fence, the creature's snarls and growls filled the air, a stark reminder of the wildness that had invaded this space. Our eyes met—mine wide with fear, its black and lifeless—and in that moment, a chilling understanding passed between us. This was no random encounter; it was a crossing of paths that left an indelible mark on my psyche.

Retreating, I felt the chill of the night seep into my bones, each step backwards a cautious withdrawal from the confrontation. My back eventually met the cold, metal doorframe, a barrier between the safety of the house and the untamed danger that lurked just beyond its threshold.

The beast's repeated lunges, each a study in restrained aggression, tested the limits of my resolve. It danced at the edge of the light, a predator gauging its prey, retreating into darkness only to edge closer with each attempt. The tension was a palpable thing, a tightrope I walked between panic and determination.

Then, abruptly, the night was pierced by the blare of a car horn from the main road beyond the fence. The sound, unexpected and jarring, startled the beast, driving it into the shadows. It was a reprieve, however brief, and I seized it with a desperation born of raw survival instinct.

I bolted inside, taking the stairs two at a time, my actions fuelled by adrenaline. Lights came on in my wake—bedrooms, toilet, bathroom, and, finally, the kitchen. Each flick of a switch was a plea for safety, a barrier against the darkness that pursued me.

In the kitchen, my hands, still awkwardly bound, grasped the largest knife from the block. Its weight was both a comfort and a reminder of the danger I faced.

A thump echoed through the house, a sound out of place in the silence. My mind, already stretched to its limit, whirled with possibilities, unable to pinpoint the source. Fear and uncertainty gripped me, a vice that tightened with every unknown noise.

Gripping the knife tightly in my bound hands, I took refuge behind the large island bench, the cold tiles slick beneath my feet with blood—my own, I realised with a shock. The trail I'd left was a stark, grim map of my passage through the house.

Then, soft but unmistakable, footsteps approached. Each one a measured beat that drew closer, winding its way down the hallway towards my makeshift sanctuary. My stomach clenched, a knot of dread and anticipation as the footsteps continued, their destination unknown.

Hidden behind the bench, my heart hammered against my ribs, a frantic rhythm that matched my laboured breaths. Peering out from my concealment, the relief that washed over me was palpable, overwhelming. *It's Luke!* Relief mingled with a flood of emotions—fear, confusion, gratitude—each vying for dominance as I took in the familiar figure moving through the living room.

"Luke!" The urgency to warn him clawed at my insides, but my voice betrayed me, a mere whisper lost in the void of my dry throat. I could only watch, a silent sentinel gripped by fear, as he moved through the living room, unaware of the lurking danger. His footsteps, a fading echo as he descended the stairs, ignited a frantic worry within me. My mind screamed a silent alarm: *Fuck! It's going to get him!*

The anticipation of his scream—a sound I dreaded yet expected—tightened the knot of anxiety in my stomach. The first tear, a symbol of my helplessness, trailed down my cheek. Yet, the house remained eerily silent, no sounds of a struggle, only the distinct noise of the downstairs glass door shutting with a conclusive thud. It was a sound both terrifying and confusing, defying my worst fears yet amplifying the uncertainty.

Forcing myself to stand, the effort sent a fresh wave of pain through my arm, as blood continued its slow descent, marking my path with droplets on the cold tiles.

Then, Luke reappeared, stepping back into the living room. His voice, laden with shock and concern, broke the tense silence. "Beatrix! What the fuck happened?" His eyes, wide with disbelief, took in my condition—bloodied, bruised, and shaken.

As Luke drew nearer, my grip on the knife became a vice, turning my knuckles an eerie shade of white. Every breath felt like a battle, my chest rising and falling with effort. "Don't turn off the lights," came my warning, strained through clenched teeth, a plea wrapped in fear.

Luke gently pried the knife from my tense grip. Then, with purpose, he retrieved a pair of scissors from the top drawer, aiming their blades at the flex-cuffs that imprisoned my wrists. The cuffs, once merely tight, now felt like iron bands, squeezing with a merciless finality.

I watched, frustration knitting my brow as Luke's efforts to cut through the bindings proved futile. The scissors, despite his determination, barely made a dent. The situation, already dire, seemed to mock us with its complexity.

"Use a lighter," I whispered, the suggestion borne of desperation. The idea of remaining trapped, vulnerable to another attack, was unbearable. "It's easier if you melt them." My voice, though soft, carried the weight of urgency, a solution within reach yet fraught with its own risks.

Luke hesitated for only a moment before he acted on my advice, fetching the gas lighter from the drawer. The flicker of flame that followed was a beacon of hope, a potential end to my physical constraints. Yet, as he moved to apply the flame to the plastic cuffs, the tension between relief and apprehension was palpable.

"You came from the casino, didn't you?" Luke's question cut through the tension as he snapped the last of the flex-cuffs, discarding them onto the kitchen bench like remnants of a nightmare.

I could only nod, slowly, the motion laborious, as if my body bore the weight of the night's terrors. My muscles trembled uncontrollably, while my gaze remained fixed, unblinking, as though afraid to break contact with reality.

"I'm just going to lock the stair door," Luke announced, his back turning to me. That simple act, meant for our protection, sent a wave of panic through me. The thought of being alone again, even for a moment, was unbearable.

My body reacted with a full shudder, a visceral response that seemed to echo in the empty spaces of the room. Luke's figure started to blur, my vision clouding as if to shield me from the reality of my solitude. "Don't leave me," slipped from my lips, a whisper barely audible, a plea born of raw vulnerability.

Luke's return was swift, his concern evident as he repeated his earlier question, "Beatrix, what the fuck happened to you?" There was an urgency in his voice, a need to understand, to piece together the events that had left me in such a state.

"I'm cursed," I confessed, the words heavy with the weight of my newfound belief. Reaching into the protective confines of my clothing, I retrieved the small Portal Key, its mere presence a harbinger of chaos. Placing it on my open palm, I offered it up to Luke as both evidence and explanation.

His gasp was sharp, a reaction to the unexpected sight. "Where did you get that?" The question hung between us, laden with implications and unspoken fears.

Tears blurred my vision as I collapsed onto the cold, unyielding floor, the reality of the situation crashing down on me. "It's all my fault!" The words burst from me, a confession of guilt and despair.

"What's your fault?" Luke's voice was laced with concern as he crouched to my level, trying to meet my gaze.

"They have Jarod!" The admission felt like a betrayal, voicing the fear made it all too real.

Luke's reaction was instant, his eyes widening as the pieces fell into place. "You both got caught stealing casino chips, didn't you?"

"Yes," I sobbed, the word a mere whisper, a confirmation of our folly.

Luke inhaled deeply, seeking patience or perhaps clarity. "But where did the Portal Key come from?" His question, so direct, demanded an answer I wasn't sure I had the courage to give.

I raised my eyes to meet his, aware of the streaks of mascara marking my face. *How much should I reveal? Do I mention Leigh's name?* "From the same person who gave you yours," I said, choosing my words with care, hinting at a connection I hoped he would understand.

"You know who gave me mine?" His surprise was evident, his eyes widening further.

I nodded silently.

"Who?"

I shook my head.

"Beatrix, I need to know."

"No!" The word snapped out. "I can't tell you. It's too dangerous, Luke." My voice, firm yet fraught with emotion, held a warning.

Luke retrieved a tea towel from the drawer, his movements deliberate as he began to address the wounds that marred my skin. The touch of the fabric against my cuts was a minor discomfort compared to the turmoil churning within me.

"Were you wounded at the casino?" His inquiry, simple and direct, hinted at an attempt to unravel the night's events.

The question triggered an immediate physical response, a surge of fear that stiffened my muscles and sent a shiver down my spine. The sensation of black fur against my skin flashed through my memory, a vivid reminder of the terror I had faced. "No," I managed to say, the word a whisper of defiance against the recollection of my ordeal.

"Then what happened?" Luke persisted.

"It first attacked me in... in Clivilius," I admitted, the name of that otherworldly place feeling alien on my tongue, its mention a reluctant confession of the nightmare I had encountered.

"First attack?" Luke echoed, his voice laced with increasing worry. "It attacked you again? Here?" His questions painted a picture of the reality we now faced, one where the boundaries between worlds had been breached.

"Yes," was all I could muster, an acknowledgment of the horror that had followed me back, a shadow from a place I wished I could forget.

"But how?" Luke's question was soft, reflective, as if he was piecing together a puzzle whose edges were blurred and indistinct.

"I think it followed me through the Portal," I explained, the words tasting of fear and disbelief. The admission was not just for Luke's benefit but a confrontation of my own harrowing experience. "It looked like some sort of wild animal. It was black and it moved fast. I didn't get a good look. And it doesn't like the light."

"That explains all the lights on, then," Luke observed, his gaze sweeping the room, noting the artificial daylight I'd created in my bid for safety.

"Its eyes looked so dead," I murmured, the memory haunting me. I lowered my gaze, attempting to dispel the vivid image of those soulless black orbs that seemed to pierce through the darkness directly into my psyche.

Luke's hands were firm yet gentle as he helped me to my feet. "We need to get your wounds dressed properly."

"I don't want to go home," the words tumbled out of me, laced with apprehension. The thought of facing my parents in this state, of trying to concoct a story they might believe, was overwhelming. There was no version of this night's events that could be neatly explained away.

"I'm not taking you home," Luke assured me, his actions speaking louder than his words as he activated the Portal on the living room wall. My heart skipped a beat at the sight, fear mingling with the realisation of what this meant. Despite my gasp of fear at the possibility of facing another monstrous entity, Luke's decision was made.

The memory of my promise to Jarod surged to the forefront of my mind, anchoring me to my resolve. "I can't," I insisted. "Jarod's in trouble. I need to find Leigh."

"Leigh?" Luke echoed, his movement halting as he processed the information. "He gave you the Portal Key, didn't he?" There was a new understanding in his voice, a piece of the puzzle clicking into place.

I bit my lip in a futile attempt to guard my secrets, but the truth spilled out regardless. "Yes." My admission hung between us, heavy with implications.

"Do you know how to contact him?" Luke's skepticism was evident, his mind likely racing through the implications of my association with Leigh.

"Yes," I affirmed, a simple truth amidst the complex web of lies and half-truths that had defined the night.

"And you trust him?" The question was loaded, probing not just my judgment but the nature of my relationship with Leigh.

"I do." My response was firm, a declaration of faith in the face of uncertainty. Trusting Leigh was not just a matter of choice but of necessity. In the shadowed world we were navigating, allies were as valuable as the truths they held, and I believed in Leigh's role in this twisted narrative I was living.

"Then find Leigh. Make sure you are somewhere safe where you can get yourself cleaned up and tell me when you get there. I'll meet you and help you get Jarod." Luke's instructions came with a sense of urgency, yet his pause as he surveyed the camping supplies cluttering the living room spoke of other responsibilities he bore. "I need to get these to the settlement first. I won't be long."

I nodded. The prospect of being alone was daunting, yet the thought of Luke venturing out again, possibly facing unknown dangers, was equally troubling. The beast's aversion to light offered a sliver of comfort, a strategy to keep the darkness at bay. Still, the soft gasp escaped me before I could hold it in, a reflexive response to the growing knot of anxiety within me.

"Luke," I called out, a last-minute thought catching him just as he was about to step into Clivilius once more, the unlit camping light in his grasp. He stopped, turning back with a look of readiness for yet another concern. "I lost my phone in Clivilius."

"Shit," he muttered, the frustration clear in his voice. The loss of the phone wasn't just about the device itself but what it represented—our link to each other and to safety. "I'll see if I can find it." Then, holding up the camping lantern, he posed a question that mirrored my earlier dilemma. "Any idea how to get this working?"

I could only shrug, my earlier attempt to use the lantern as a weapon against the beast leaving no room for technical troubleshooting. It was a moment of desperation, one that now left us with more questions than answers.

"Shit," Luke said again, the word echoing his initial reaction, a succinct summary of our predicament.

The ominous growl that resonated from the other side of the front door halted time itself, binding Luke and me in a shared moment of dread. Our gazes snapped to the door as if drawn by strings, hearts hammering against our ribcages in a frantic rhythm. A silent exchange passed between us, a tangible wave of fear that momentarily rooted us to the spot. The world outside our sanctuary, now a source of palpable terror, seemed to press against the barriers of the house with a malevolent intent.

"What the fuck are you doing, Luke?" The whisper tore from my lips, harsh and laced with panic, as I found myself retreating until my back met the cold, unyielding surface of the pantry. Every instinct screamed for silence, for invisibility against the threat that lurked outside.

Luke's response was a silent symphony of caution—a finger pressed to his lips followed by a pointed gesture towards his eyes and then the door. His silent message was clear: he needed to see, to confirm the danger that our ears had already acknowledged. My head shook in disbelief that bordered on desperation. *Was the need to visually confirm the beast's presence worth the risk?*

Another growl, deeper, closer, sent a jolt of fear through me, a physical manifestation of the terror that clawed at my insides. Luke's cautious advance towards the door was a study in bravery—or folly—I couldn't decide which. My heart, a traitorous drum, beat a staccato rhythm of impending doom.

Bloodied hand pressed to my chest, I fought to quell the rising tide of panic that threatened to overwhelm me. The act of breathing, normally so automatic, now required a conscious effort, each inhalation a battle against the fear that constricted my lungs.

Luke, now at the door, placed his palms against it as if to steady himself. Leaning forward, he dared to peek through the peephole, a scout surveying the unknown. His sharp intake of breath, a sound laced with fear, sent a wave of acid surging up my throat. My eyes clamped shut, a feeble defence against the reality we faced. The beast, our unseen tormentor, was no longer a shadowy threat relegated to the darkness of Clivilius—it was here, on our doorstep.

The cacophony of Luke's body colliding with the wall merged with the thud of the beast against the door in a symphony of chaos and fear. "Luke!" My voice tore from my throat, a scream fuelled by terror. Instinctively, my hand flew to the knife left abandoned on the kitchen bench, a flimsy talisman against the nightmare at our door.

Luke, propelled by a mix of adrenaline and determination, rebounded from the wall in a single, fluid motion. He lunged towards the door, his hand desperately flicking the porch light switch in a bid for salvation.

The animal's response was immediate and visceral—a howl of pain that cut through the tension, followed by the sound of claws scraping against concrete. That sound, a harrowing reminder of the creature's physicality, sent an icy shiver racing down my spine, a primal fear that whispered of danger too close, too real.

"It's gone," Luke's voice, barely above a whisper, cut through the aftermath. His quick grasp on my arm was both a reassurance and a command, a silent agreement that our only option was flight. "Come on, we need to get out of here."

"Luke," my reply was a whisper, a mixture of disbelief and dawning realisation. The tears threatened to break through my resolve. "What the fuck have we done?" The question hung between us, heavy with implications we were only beginning to understand.

Exhausted, my body ached from the night's ordeals, and fear clung to me like a second skin. We collapsed together on the cold kitchen tiles, a silent pact forming in our mutual exhaustion. Words were unnecessary, the shared experience speaking volumes more than any conversation could. There, in the dim light of the kitchen, we sat side by side, waiting for the first light of dawn to signal the end of the nightmare.

❖

Luke's abrupt movement jerked me awake, breaking the uneasy slumber that had claimed me in the aftermath of our ordeal. My neck ached from the awkward angle at which I had rested against him, a small discomfort compared to the night's terrors.

As our eyes met, a familiar sense of dread welled up inside me, magnified by the alarm I saw reflected in his gaze. "You said this creature followed you from Clivilius?" His question, weighted with implications, reignited the fear I had managed to momentarily quell.

"Yes," I answered, my voice barely a whisper, heavy with the realisation of what this meant. The thought that had been gnawing at the edges of my mind was now spoken aloud, confirming my worst fears: *if the beast had followed me from Clivilius, was anyone truly safe there?*

"Fuck!" Luke's exclamation was a sharp punctuation to the silence that had fallen between us. With a speed born of sudden resolve, he leapt to his feet, igniting the Portal with a burst of technicolour brilliance before stepping through it, leaving me alone in the wake of his departure.

For a moment, I contemplated following him, but the sight of my own battered reflection in the pantry door halted me. Instead, I moved to the windows, cautiously scanning the surroundings for any sign of the black beast. Relief washed over me as I found nothing amiss; the creature had not returned since its retreat into the night.

Allowing myself a brief moment of gratitude for the silence and safety of the house, I gathered a towel and made my way to the bathroom. The warmth from the lights was a balm to my chilled skin, casting a stark light on the bruises and cuts that marred my flesh—a map of the night's harrowing journey.

With a sense of finality, I locked the bathroom door behind me and started the shower. The sound of water was a comforting background noise as I began the slow process of disentangling myself from the remnants of the night. The steam filled the room, offering a shroud of privacy as I let the red dress, now a symbol of my terror, drop to the floor. The act of shedding the dress was more than physical; it was a symbolic gesture of washing away the fear, the pain, and the memories of a night that had changed everything.

# STILLNESS

## 1338.209.3

"Why on earth did I think this was a good idea?" I mumbled under my breath, my voice barely rising above a whisper as I dragged the cumbersome red kayak through the thick, ochre dust. The barren landscape stretched endlessly around me, a sea of red and orange, under a sky that was a perfect shade of blue. Ahead, a haphazard collection of assorted goods lay scattered, encircled by a makeshift boundary of small, meticulously placed rock piles, their arrangement suggesting some attempt at organisation in this otherwise bland wilderness.

The kayak's bright hue was oddly reminiscent of the torn dress I was wearing. It clung to my body, its fabric tattered, a testament to the night's earlier ordeals. After a fruitless search through Luke's sparsely furnished bedroom, I was forced to put this dress back on, its colour now mirroring the kayak, as if fate was mocking my predicament.

Despite my lack of experience with kayaks, a surge of instinctual confidence had compelled me to choose it as my first object to bring to Clivilius. But now, the weight of my decision bore down on me, literally and figuratively, as the kayak's heft strained my unscathed arm, igniting a dull ache that crescendoed with each step I took. The realisation dawned on me – bringing this kayak through the Portal might have been foolish after all.

"Beatrix?" The voice sliced through my tumultuous thoughts, causing me to halt mid-stride. I turned, my weary gaze falling upon the approaching figure. It was Paul, Luke's brother. My expression softened involuntarily, a semblance of relief washing over me. I had always harboured a fondness for Paul, with his quick wit and keen intellect, qualities that shone through even in our brief encounters. Despite the direness of my situation, his presence brought a flicker of comfort, a momentary respite from the relentless tide of uncertainty and fear.

"You look like shit," Paul declared, halting a few feet away from me, his eyes scrutinising me from head to toe with an unsettling intensity.

"Like you look any better," I retorted, feeling a half-smile flicker on my lips before it quickly vanished. Despite the attempt at humour, the words felt hollow, echoing the weariness and turmoil churning inside me.

"Here, let me take that," Paul offered, reaching out for the kayak with a kind of brisk efficiency that belied the concern etched in his features. His hands, firm and sure, relieved me of the burden, and I felt a weight lift off my shoulders, both literally and metaphorically.

And without any further instruction, Paul subtly changed our direction, guiding me with an unspoken understanding that I was in no state to lead. I followed him, the two of us trudging through the thick, dry dust that seemed intent on claiming us as its own. Walking beside Paul, a man whose height I'd always found comforting, a semblance of security enveloped me in the vast, desolate landscape.

The early morning sun, a fiery orb in the sky, cast a warm glow on my exposed arms, its rays a stark contrast to the chilly ambiance of the kitchen where I had spent the latter hours of the night, lost in a tumult of thoughts and fears.

"Luke brought you in?" Paul's voice broke the silence, his tone casual yet laden with an undercurrent of curiosity.

"No," I replied tersely, my voice barely above a whisper. I wasn't ready to unravel the threads of the past twenty-four hours, not ready to relive the cascade of events that had led me to this moment. The simple response was a shield, guarding the turmoil that roiled beneath the surface, the memories of the night still too raw, too vivid to dissect.

After a moment of heavy silence, filled with the unsaid and the echoes of our previous conversation, Paul threw me a sideways glance. It was a look that seemed to probe, to question, not just my state but the undercurrents of the situation we found ourselves in.

I took a deep, steadying breath, feeling the weight of the Portal Key in my hand. It felt cold, its metallic surface contrasting with the warm, dry air surrounding us. With a deliberate motion, I extended my arm, holding the key out for Paul to see.

"From Cody?" he asked, his voice steady but I detected a flicker of recognition in his eyes, a hint of curiosity that went beyond casual inquiry.

"No," I replied, my voice firm yet tinged with surprise at his familiarity with the name.

"Oh, then who?" Paul pressed, his gaze shifting from the device back to my face, searching for answers I wasn't fully prepared to divulge.

Rather than answering, I found myself deflecting, driven by a sudden urge to understand the extent of Cody's reach and reputation. "What do you know about Cody?" I asked, my tone sharper than intended, eyes locked on Paul's, searching for any flicker of insight or recognition.

"Nothing, really," Paul admitted after a brief pause, his expression open and somewhat perplexed. "Luke mentioned the name when Joel arrived. But I haven't..." His voice trailed off, an unspoken acknowledgment that his involvement or knowledge was limited.

"Joel? Jamie's son, Joel?" The words tumbled out of me, a torrent of surprise and concern that I couldn't suppress. The notion that Joel was here, was both startling and alarming.

"Yeah. You knew?" Paul's question, filled with confusion, mirrored my own tumult of emotions. The layers of our predicament seemed to deepen with each shared piece of information, weaving a tapestry of complexity that was both intriguing and daunting.

"Joel is here?" The question escaped my lips again, a reflection of my jumbled thoughts, echoing louder in my mind than in the open air. I ignored Paul's previous question, my focus narrowing on this new, unexpected piece of information. "I thought Luke wasn't going to bring him here," I murmured, half to Paul, half to myself, my voice a mix of disbelief and concern. The words slipped out before I had a chance to weigh them, to decide whether I wanted to voice my internal dialogue or keep it locked away.

"He didn't, apparently," Paul replied, his tone neutral, yet I sensed an undercurrent of uncertainty, a hint that he, too, was trying to make sense of the situation. His response did little to ease the swirling pool of confusion inside me.

*Why would Luke bring him here?* The question replayed in my mind, a persistent echo that refused to be silenced. My eyes scanned the barren landscape around us, the stark, unforgiving terrain of our surroundings magnifying my sense of isolation and vulnerability. The emptiness seemed to mirror the growing void of unanswered questions within me.

"We think he came down the river," Paul offered, his voice pulling me back from my thoughts. His speculation seemed plausible, yet it did little to dampen the storm of questions and concerns still churning inside me.

*Jamie must be devastated.* The thought struck me, adding a new layer of emotional turmoil to the already heavy burden weighing on my mind.

"Did Luke say what happened to him?" The question lingered in the air, tinged with a mix of concern and a hidden layer of self-preservation. I couldn't help but hope that my own involvement, my presence in this tangled web, hadn't been highlighted in the recounting of events.

"He told us about the blood and the truck," Paul replied, his voice steady but the content of his words sending an involuntary shiver through me. The vivid imagery of blood and violence painted a grim picture, and the realisation that Luke had divulged details of the ordeal added a weighty layer of anxiety. My mind raced with the implications, with the fear that my name might be entangled in the narrative of Joel's harrowing experience.

The thought of Jamie's reaction loomed large in my mind. *Would he ever look at me the same way again, knowing I was a part of this tragedy?* The possibility of our relationship being irrevocably altered, of a shadow being cast over our future interactions, was a bitter pill to swallow.

"But Glenda stitched his throat and he seems to be making a remarkable recovery."

"Glenda?" The name was unfamiliar, a new character in the unfolding drama. "And Joel's alive?" I echoed, seeking confirmation, utterly bewildered that the young man could have survived his severed throat.

"Yeah," Paul affirmed. "And Glenda is the camp's doctor."

"Can I see him?" The words tumbled out, driven by a surge of relief mixed with a deep-seated need to confront the reality of Joel's condition, to see with my own eyes that he was indeed alive, to perhaps alleviate the guilt that gnawed at me.

"I'm sure you'll see him soon enough." Paul's response was noncommittal, lacking the certainty I craved. His words did little to quench my growing thirst for closure, for tangible proof that Joel was alive.

Our walk continued in silence, the kind of silence that's so heavy, so thick, you feel like you could reach out and touch it. Neither of us seemed ready, or perhaps able, to break it. I noticed Paul's pace begin to slow, his previously assured steps faltering. His shoulders, once square, now seemed to curve inward, as if he was carrying a weight much heavier than the physical world could impose. His eyes, when they met mine, were pools of unspoken anguish, telling stories of pain and fear that his lips had yet to confess.

"A... a shadow panther?" The words stumbled out of Paul's mouth, fragile as glass and laden with a dread that seemed to suck the air from our surroundings.

"Huh?" My response was automatic, a knee-jerk reaction to the unexpected turn in our conversation.

"Your dress and cuts. Were they from a shadow panther?" His voice held a desperation now, a palpable need for confirmation that seemed to stretch far beyond simple curiosity.

My response was a silent stare, a momentary pause where time seemed to stand still as I wrestled with the reality of my encounter. The memory of the shadow panther, its terrifying form and lethal grace, flashed vividly in my mind's eye.

"A panther-like creature?" Paul pressed, his voice sharpening with urgency, as if sensing my hesitation to dive back into the harrowing memory.

"Yeah," I admitted quietly, the word barely more than a whisper, yet heavy with significance. Acknowledging the encounter felt like unravelling a thread from a tightly wound spool of experiences, exposing a vulnerability I wasn't ready to confront. The memory of the creature's assault was not just fresh; it was raw, a vivid recollection of a nightmare that had leapt from the shadows into stark, terrifying reality.

Paul swallowed hard, the action echoing the turmoil that seemed to churn within him. His reaction was a complex tapestry of fear and realisation, emotions that danced across his face, fleeting yet unmistakable. "It was you who screamed last night, then?" His voice, though steady, carried an undercurrent of something I couldn't quite place—was it guilt, concern, or perhaps a hint of fear?

"I guess," I replied, my tone nonchalant, an attempt to mask the storm of emotions raging inside me. Accompanied by a shrug, my response was an effort to downplay the raw, primal fear that had prompted the scream—a visceral, uncontrollable reaction to the terror I had faced.

Paul's actions spoke louder than words could. A simple gulp, a motion of wiping his eyes, each a subtle yet powerful testament to the emotions he was grappling with. It was clear that the echo of my scream had reached more than just the barren, silent landscape around us; it had touched something in Paul, stirring a whirlwind of thoughts and feelings.

"Everything okay here?" I ventured, my voice a mere whisper, almost lost amidst the vast, empty expanse that surrounded us.

"We had an incident here last–" Paul began, his words trailing off as if the act of voicing the events would make them all the more real, all the more terrifying.

The sharp intake of breath was involuntary as we crested the final hill, the small camp coming into full view below us. My eyes widened at the sight of the campfire, its flickering flames a stark contrast to the row of large, almost military-like tents that stood in an orderly fashion behind it.

My voice faltered, catching in my throat as I watched Luke's figure storm past us. His back was a rigid line of tension, his movements brusque and hurried, betraying a turmoil that seemed to radiate from him. I could see him furiously wiping at his eyes, a clear indication of the emotional storm brewing within him.

"Luke!" The name finally broke free from my lips, a desperate attempt to bridge the distance, to understand the cascade of events that had unfolded. But before I could take a step, Paul's hand clasped firmly around my arm, his grip urging me to hold back. A tight knot of apprehension formed in the pit of my stomach, a gnawing sense of dread that begged the question: *What the hell happened last night?*

My gaze drifted to the gash on my arm, a painful reminder of my own recent brush with danger. The thought that talk of shadow panthers might be spreading through the camp sent a ripple of unease through me.

As we walked into the camp, a shudder coursed through my body, an involuntary response to the scene that greeted us. There, lying lifeless by the campfire, was a shadow panther, its presence a chilling testament to the night's events. The dried blood, a dark, almost black hue, had oozed from a slice in its belly, seeping into the surrounding dust, staining the earth with its final moments.

As the oppressive mood of the camp enveloped me, a dreadful thought clawed its way into my mind: *Who's dead?* The heaviness in the air, the sombre faces I glimpsed as I passed, all pointed to a loss, a void that had suddenly been ripped open in their tight-knit community. Turning to Paul, a knot of anxiety tightening in my stomach, I asked, "Where's Jamie?" The fear that Jamie might have been the one to succumb to some dire fate was overwhelming, a possibility I could barely entertain.

"Probably still in the river behind the tents," Paul's voice was soft, carrying a hint of sorrow that did little to ease my growing dread. He halted, his steps ceasing as if the weight of the situation anchored him to the spot.

Compelled by a mixture of fear and a desperate need for clarity, I pressed on alone, my heart pounding in my chest as I navigated the path between the tents. There, along the riverbank, sat Jamie, his figure solitary against the backdrop of the flowing water. His legs dangled in the water, but it was what he cradled in his arms that drew my focus. With his back to me, the details were obscured, shrouded in the same uncertainty that cloaked my heart.

With each step closer, the scene before me became heartbreakingly clear. I gasped, my eyes stinging with the onset of tears, as I approached Jamie. "Is he–?" My voice broke, the question dissolving into the heavy air, unfinished yet laden with meaning.

Jamie's gaze met mine, his eyes a mirror of the pain I felt, red and swollen from crying. Wordlessly, he continued to stroke Duke's fur, the gentle motion a heartbreaking contrast to the stillness that enveloped the once vibrant dog. The silence was deafening, a void where Duke's lively presence should have been, now filled only with the palpable grief shared between us.

In that heartrending moment, the world seemed to narrow to the space where Jamie sat. I knelt beside Jamie, an instinctual need to offer comfort, to share in the mourning of our lost companion. My arms wrapped around him, gripping his shoulder tightly, a physical anchor in the torrent of our shared sorrow. And there, beside the river, our tears merged with the flowing water.

❖

Clasping Jamie in an embrace that felt like a lifeline amidst the storm of our grief, I felt a surge of emotions I had been holding back, a torrent unleashed by the recent cascade of events that seemed hell-bent on tearing through the fragile fabric of our existence. In the silence of our shared sorrow, I found myself silently pleading, *Please, don't let me go, Jamie. Not yet.* The intimacy of the moment, the shared space of our mourning, felt like a temporary refuge from the darkness that loomed just beyond.

As the moments stretched, each second feeling more precious than the last, I eventually and reluctantly pulled back. Remaining hunched on my knees, I extended a trembling hand towards Duke, allowing my fingers to brush gently against his fur. The once vibrant and lively companion now lay motionless, his stillness an unsettling reminder of the cruel reality we faced.

Jamie's gaze, heavy with loss and rimmed with red, met mine as he uttered a vow of retribution, "I'm going to get whatever did this." The resolve in his voice, the rekindling of a fire in his eyes, spoke of a determination forged in the depths of his anguish.

I nodded, understanding the need for action, for some semblance of control in the midst of our powerlessness. "Do you think it was a shadow panther?" The question emerged from my own fears, from the harrowing encounter that still haunted my thoughts.

"A what?" Jamie's confusion was palpable, his brow creasing in a mix of curiosity and bewilderment.

"A shadow panther," I clarified, my hand subconsciously moving to the scratches on my arm, a physical testament to my own brush with death. "It's the creature that attacked me last night." The words hung between us, a new layer of terror for Jamie to absorb.

"It wasn't a shadow panther," the unexpected voice cut through the heavy air, startling me from my thoughts and turning our attention away from our grief, if only for a moment.

Simultaneously, Jamie and I twisted around to face the source of the interruption. A woman stood there, her presence as sudden as her announcement. "I'm Charity," she stated plainly, her demeanour lacking the usual formalities of a first encounter. No handshake extended, no smile offered—just a straightforward introduction.

My eyes scanned Charity, taking in her appearance with a mix of curiosity and caution. It was clear she wasn't from Earth, her attire—or the lack thereof—speaking volumes of a background far removed from our own. Her outfit, if it could be called that, consisted of hard metal coverings strategically placed over vital areas, leaving much of her skin exposed to the elements. With a bow in her hand and a quiver slung across her back, she looked like she had stepped out of a scene from a warrior princess movie.

"How do you know that it wasn't a shadow panther?" Jamie's voice broke through my observations, his tone a mix of curiosity and a faint trace of skepticism.

Charity, without missing a beat, motioned toward Duke's lifeless form. "May I?" she requested, her eyes locking with Jamie's, seeking permission to approach. There was a certain respect in her stance, an understanding of our loss, yet she exuded a confidence that suggested she was well-versed in matters far beyond our comprehension.

Jamie's pause was palpable, a brief moment where the weight of his decision seemed to rest heavily upon his shoulders. Yet, there was an unspoken acknowledgment in his nod, a relinquishment of control to this stranger who had appeared so unexpectedly in our midst.

Henri's low growl cut through the tension like a knife, snapping my focus to the small, stout dog that I hadn't noticed beside Jamie until that moment. A wave of self-reproach washed over me—*how could I have been so absorbed in my own emotions that I overlooked Henri, Duke's loyal brother?* The question gnawed at me, reminding me how the whirlwind of recent events had frayed my usual attentiveness.

As Charity moved closer, Henri's growl morphed into a bark, a clear sign of his unease or perhaps his protective instincts kicking in. But his attention was quickly diverted by the loud clattering of pots near the campfire, a sound that seemed to momentarily erase his apprehension. With a sudden burst of energy, Henri's short, stubby legs propelled him toward the noise, kicking up small clouds of dust in his wake.

I watched him pause near the back of the tent, his body tensing as he glanced back at us. His expression was pitiful, imbued with a sadness that tugged at my heart. His gaze seemed to search for his brother, a silent question in his eyes that spoke volumes of his confusion and sorrow.

A lump of emotion clogged my throat as I witnessed his distress. *Poor Henri.* The question of whether he could comprehend the loss of Duke lingered in my mind, adding a layer of poignancy to the already heavy atmosphere. And then, just as suddenly as he had captured our attention, Henri scampered around the side of the tent, disappearing from view, leaving a palpable void where his small, mournful presence had been.

As Henri scurried away, his absence was quickly filled by Charity, who assumed his position with a sense of purpose that was both intriguing and unsettling. Squatting beside Jamie, she leaned in with a hesitancy that swiftly shifted to determination, her hands reaching for Duke with a delicacy that belied her unfamiliarity.

I watched, drawn in by her actions, as she carefully brushed aside Duke's fur to reveal the wound. "See the edges around the wound?" she inquired, her tone inviting scrutiny. Curiosity piqued, I leaned in closer, my eyes tracing the contours she pointed out, noticing the unnatural precision of the wound's edges.

"It's too clean to have been caused by any claw or tooth," she explained, her confidence in her assessment evident. Her words hung in the air, heavy with implications that twisted my stomach into knots.

"Then what was it?" My voice barely rose above a whisper, echoing the mix of fascination and dread that gripped me.

Charity's response was clinical, devoid of the emotion that clouded my own thoughts. "Looking at the discolouration of the skin, my best guess is that it was an Okaledian dagger that killed the creature," she declared, introducing a term so foreign, it seemed to widen the chasm between her world and ours.

*Okaledian dagger?* The term echoed in my mind, a puzzle piece so alien it seemed to warp the fabric of my new reality. *What the hell is that?* I wondered, the question ricocheting through my thoughts, unanswered.

"Creature?" Jamie's voice cut through my reverie, sharp with indignation. "His name is Duke." The simple statement was a defence, a testament to Duke's significance, far beyond that of a mere creature.

Compelled to support Jamie, I found my own voice. "You do know he is a dog, don't you?" The question was directed at Charity, though it was tinged with my own rising uncertainty. *Did she understand? Could she comprehend the bond, the essence of what Duke meant to us?*

Charity's focus remained unbroken as she scrutinised Duke, her eyes narrowing in concentration. "I've seen similar creatures... dogs, like yours, but nothing quite like it. Creatures like this aren't so common in Chewbathia." Her words, meant to clarify, only added layers to the mystery enveloping her. *Chewbathia?* Another term, another piece of the puzzle that was Charity, hinting at origins and knowledge far removed from the immediate, painful reality we faced.

*Why not?* The question pulsed in my mind, demanding attention, yet I found myself voicing a different, more tangible thought. "I feel like my brain suddenly has another dozen questions after that." The words left my lips as I rose, my body echoing the fatigue and stress that had settled into my mind, manifesting as a dull ache at my temple.

"So do I," Jamie echoed, his voice laden with a mix of confusion and burgeoning anger. I watched him rub a bloody finger across his forehead. His gaze met mine, seeking a shared understanding before he directed his next words to Charity. "But if Duke was killed by a dagger," he began, the pause that followed heavy with the gravity of his realisation. Then, turning to Charity with an intensity that matched the seriousness of his query, he demanded, "then who the fuck was wielding the dagger?"

His words struck a chord, igniting a surge of fresh adrenaline that raced through my veins. Crouching beside Jamie, I lowered my voice to a whisper, the urgency of my thoughts spilling out. "Do you think somebody in the camp killed Duke?" The possibility was chilling, introducing a layer of mistrust and fear that we could ill afford.

"Nobody that you know," Charity interjected, her voice carrying a certainty that was both reassuring and terrifying in its implications.

Jamie and I simultaneously turned to her. "What do you mean?" we demanded together, our voices intertwining in a chorus of confusion and concern.

"There's someone here that we don't know?" Jamie's question trembled through the air, his composure giving way to a hint of panic. The implication that an unknown threat lurked among us, possibly harbouring ill intentions, was a terrifying prospect.

"A Portal Pirate," Paul's words sliced through the tension, his presence suddenly manifesting alongside a title that sounded like something conjured from a dystopian novel. His tone, laden with the self-assurance of someone who had perhaps found a piece of the puzzle, did little to alleviate the growing knot of anxiety in my stomach.

"What the actual fuck?" Jamie's whispered exclamation, though intended to be under his breath, resonated with the shock rippling through me. His eyes, wide with a mix of fear and incredulity, met mine, seeking some semblance of understanding in a situation that was rapidly spiralling beyond our comprehension.

Before the silence could settle, Charity interjected, her voice steady, painting a picture of the threat that loomed unseen yet palpably close. "He's likely lost and been separated from his partner. Some danger must have befallen one of them before they could execute the location registration. They're always in pairs. Never work alone. Cunning and violent bastards they are together. But alone, they can be brute savages. Their instinct for hunting and survival runs deep." Her words, meant to inform, felt like cold fingers tracing my spine, introducing a new fear to wrestle with—the idea of a Portal Pirate, desperate and dangerous, lurking among us.

Paul's next words were directed at Jamie, a misguided attempt to impress or perhaps reassure, "Charity managed to kill one of the beasts last night. It's at the camp if you want to see it." The pride in his voice, the slight lift in his demeanour at the mention of the slain beast, struck a dissonant chord within me. The gravity of our loss, the fresh wound of Duke's death, seemed momentarily eclipsed by Paul's fascination with the creature's demise.

As Paul's excitement bubbled over, revealing yet another layer to the night's events, I felt a wave of frustration. "She wounded another and it appears, somehow, that a third shadow panther managed to follow Beatrix through the Portal to earth," he said, turning his gaze towards me.

Reluctantly, and with a keen awareness of Jamie's grief-stricken state, I offered a nod—a silent confirmation of Paul's words.

Jamie's eyes, momentarily ignited with a flicker of hope, prompted a surge of curiosity within me. *What was he thinking?* The possibility that he might see a way back to Earth seemed to dance in his gaze. Yet, as quickly as it appeared, Charity's words quashed it with the blunt reality of our circumstances.

"It doesn't change anything for you," she stated, her hand on Jamie's shoulder not so much a gesture of comfort as it was a grounding reminder. "You'll never leave Clivilius alive." The finality in her tone was chilling, a cold splash of truth on the fleeting spark of Jamie's hope.

Paul's interjection, seemingly well-intentioned but profoundly misguided, only added to the surreal nature of the discussion. "But I think Duke can leave. You could have Luke take him to be buried on Earth?" The suggestion seemed to echo bizarrely in the charged atmosphere, out of touch with the weight of Jamie's grief.

My reaction mirrored Jamie's—astonishment, disbelief, then a rising tide of indignation. *Duke was not just a pet; he was family*. The thought of sending him away, even in death, felt like a violation of the bond he and Jamie shared.

"Fuck no!" Jamie's response was visceral, a raw outpouring of his resolve to keep Duke's memory close, even in the face of such otherworldly circumstances. His words resonated with me, affirming the conviction I sensed in his heart. "It's not fair on Henri. Duke belongs here now. We'll find a suitable place to bury him here today." His declaration was a testament to his love for Duke, an unbreakable bond that not even death or the bizarre reality of Clivilius could sever.

Paul's silence, marked by a subdued nod, signalled the end of the conversation.

"It's not possible to bury him," said Charity, her voice cutting through the heavy air, shattering the fragile veil of silence that had cloaked our small, grief-stricken group. "You have no walls, no protection, burying him will only attract creatures much worse than shadow panthers and Portal Pirates."

My stomach plummeted to the cold, unforgiving ground beneath us. A chilling breeze whispered across the river, carrying with it the weight of our grim reality. *What the hell could be worse than those nightmarish beasts we had already encountered?* My mind raced, imagining all manner of grotesque creatures lurking just beyond our sight, drawn by the scent of death.

"What then?" asked Paul, his voice tinged with a hesitancy that mirrored the fear and uncertainty that clutched at my own heart.

"You'll need to cremate his body," Charity directed, her tone devoid of the warmth or comfort one might crave in such a bleak moment.

"Like fuck we will!" The vehement protest erupted from Jamie, his voice cracking under the strain of his raw, palpable grief. He rose to his feet, his movements jerky and uncontrolled, as if every fibre of his being rejected the very notion of what Charity proposed. Duke, the loyal companion now forever still in Jamie's arms, was clutched against his blood-soaked chest.

"Don't worry, Duke," Jamie leaned in, his voice now imbued with a heartbreaking softness. "I won't let them destroy any trace that you ever existed."

"Jamie," Paul interjected, his voice a gentle attempt to bridge the chasm of Jamie's despair. He cautiously took a few steps toward the man and his deceased dog. "We don't have a lot of options here."

My shoulders slumped, the weight of our situation pressing down like a physical burden. Despite the turmoil swirling within me, a part of me—the logical, detached part—knew that Paul was right. The pragmatic corner of my mind whispered harsh truths: unless Jamie could accept the grim necessity of our situation, he might unwittingly invite even greater horrors upon us.

"No!" The word was a defiant roar from Jamie, a resolute stand against a reality too cruel to accept. "We're not burning Duke."

Paul, Charity, and I launched into a concerted effort to break through Jamie's wall of resistance, our voices intertwining, each of us desperate to inject a dose of reality into the cloud of grief that enveloped him. Yet, our earnest persuasions were abruptly sliced through by an intrusion from the periphery of our taut bubble of tension.

"Has anyone seen Joel this morning?" The question came from an unfamiliar woman, her presence almost ghostlike until this moment. Her voice, laced with a tremor of anxiety, cut through the air, her words imbued with an urgency that momentarily redirected our collective focus from Jamie's despair to another brewing storm of worry.

"I've been with Jamie since I arrived," I found myself responding, the realisation hitting me with a cold jolt. In the trauma of our survival, the truth was stark—I had never actually laid eyes on Joel, at least not beyond the lifeless form that I had already memorialised.

"I've not seen him at all this morning. I just assumed he was still resting in his tent. Is he not there?" Paul's query hung in the air, his voice a mix of concern and bewilderment, reflecting the sudden shift in our group's attention.

"No," the woman's reply was succinct, yet it reverberated with a weight that seemed to push the air out of our lungs.

In an instant, as if the news had physically struck him, Jamie's knees gave way, his form collapsing with an almost cinematic slow-motion quality. The thud of his elbows hitting the ground punctuated his descent, his grip on Duke unyielding even in his own collapse.

"Jamie!" Our voices overlapped in a chorus of concern as we instinctively moved toward him, our previous contention momentarily forgotten in the face of his evident distress.

The woman, her role shifting seamlessly from inquirer to caretaker, squatted beside Jamie with an efficiency that spoke of experience. Her hands moved with purpose, assessing his condition with a practiced eye before she paused, her gaze lifting to meet Paul's.

"Gather everyone to the campfire," she directed, her voice steady, commanding attention amidst the swirling eddy of emotions and unfolding crises.

Paul nodded once—a silent acknowledgment—before turning on his heel to execute her command.

I eyed cautiously the woman who I could only assume to be the camp's doctor that Paul had mentioned earlier in the morning. "You must be Glenda," I ventured, my voice tinged with a mix of curiosity and respect.

"I am," she replied, her voice steady, as she brushed dust from her clothes with a pragmatic hand, rising to her full stature. "I'm going to find something suitable to wrap Duke in. Please help Jamie get himself cleaned up. I'll meet you back here before we take the dog to the campfire."

"Yes, doctor," I replied dutifully, my response automatic, influenced by the immediate authority that emanated from her, her Northern European accent reinforcing her commanding presence.

With Glenda and Charity disappearing from sight, I turned my attention to Jamie, who seemed lost in a haze of grief and shock. I leaned in close to him, my voice soft yet insistent. "Come on, let's get you clean," I coaxed, my hand gently tugging at his dirt-encrusted arm, offering a sliver of comfort in the tangible action of care.

It required a gentle, persistent effort, but I finally persuaded Jamie to lay Duke gently beside the river, a place where he could maintain a vigilant watch over his fallen companion. As Jamie rose, my gaze lingered on the amount of dried blood that adorned his chest, a gruesome testament to the tragedy he had endured, painting him in the brutal hues of death and survival.

His trousers, too, told a tale of the ordeal, stained and soiled, a fabric chronicle of the night's horrors. With a resigned motion, Jamie shed the bloodied garments, letting them fall in a heavy, sodden heap onto the ground. Then, with a deep, almost imperceptible sigh, he stepped into the river.

The water, a silent witness to our collective sorrow, embraced him. I watched, a silent sentinel, as Jamie surrendered momentarily to the cleansing embrace of the river, each ripple carrying away fragments of his agony, though the stains it could wash from his soul were far less tangible.

"I'll go and get you some fresh clothes," I assured Jamie, my voice laced with a quiet resolve. In the back of my mind, I harboured no illusions about the fate of his old clothes—soon, they would likely be surrendered to the flames, erased without a trace as we sought to cleanse the reminders of our trauma.

"Paul or Glenda can direct you to the right tent," Jamie responded, his voice low, tinged with the raw edge of his grief. Then, without another word, he turned his back to me, his posture a silent testament to the weight of his sorrow.

With a heavy heart, I crouched beside Duke, the stillness of his form a mournful contrast to the vibrant spirit he once embodied. My fingers gently brushed his unmoving head, an action so simple yet laden with the sadness of our loss. As I touched him, a cascade of memories flooded through me—images, sounds, and sensations that danced across my consciousness, vivid and poignant.

There was laughter, a bright, joyful sound that seemed to echo around me, a reminder of the days when Duke's energy was a boundless force of happiness. I remembered how he would clamber over me, a whirlwind of affection and playfulness, his kisses dispensed generously, his commitment to our shared moments of joy unwavering.

"It's not fair," I murmured, my voice barely a whisper, a tender lament for a soul taken too soon. The words slipped out amidst the silent tears that traced paths down my cheeks. "You didn't deserve this, dear, sweet Duke."

# DISARRAY

## 1338.209.1

"Which tent?" I mumbled, my voice barely a whisper, as I dragged my feet through the dust. Each step felt heavier than the last, Duke's absence a silent weight upon my shoulders. *He can't really be gone, can he?* The question echoed in my mind, a relentless whisper.

"Beatrix!" Paul's voice pierced my reverie, a sharp contrast to the soft, haunting questions swirling in my thoughts. I saw him rushing toward me, his expression a mixture of urgency and concern.

"What do you want?" The words escaped my lips more harshly than intended. But the moment I spoke, I realised that my needs and his purpose might just align, despite my brusque demeanour.

"I've sent Karen to the lagoon to fetch Chris and Kain. Hopefully, Joel found his way there, too. You've still not seen him?" Paul's words tumbled out.

"No," I said simply.

Paul's reaction was immediate, his brow furrowing, a physical manifestation of his growing concern and frustration.

"Which tent is Jamie's?" I interjected, seizing a moment to steer the conversation toward the practical concern at hand. "He needs clean clothes."

"Follow me," Paul replied, a hint of resignation in his voice as he gestured toward the tent on the far left.

A soft sigh escaped me as I trailed behind him, my mind grappling with the unfolding events around us. "You could have just pointed the tent out to me," I grumbled under my breath, a quiet protest against the unspoken expectation of companionship in this moment of shared adversity. Yet, as I followed Paul, I couldn't help but feel a twinge of gratitude for the presence of someone who, despite everything, remained steadfast in the face of our collective challenges.

Paul held back the front flap of the tent, and I hesitantly stepped inside, my eyes widening as I took in the expanse before me. "Impressive," I whispered, my voice barely carrying in the spacious interior. The large central living area branched off into additional rooms on either side, each inviting a sense of wonder and curiosity about their contents. "It looked big on the outside, but the inside is even—"

"They're ten-man tents," Paul cut in, his voice pulling me back from my awe. "Almost military-grade quality."

I scoffed lightly, a mix of admiration and skepticism swirling within me. *Where the hell did Luke get these from?*

Our attention was abruptly diverted by a loud grunt emanating from the floor. Turning, I saw Henri, his furry face tilted upwards, eyes locking onto mine with an expression that tugged at the heartstrings.

"He looks so sad," Paul observed, his voice tinged with a gentle empathy as he squatted beside the chubby dog.

"He's hungry," I corrected, a wry smile tugging at the corners of my mouth despite the sombre mood. "Don't mistake that resting bitch face for sadness. I've seen that gluttonous look in his eyes many times." My familiarity with Henri allowed me to read beyond the superficial cues, to the more mundane, yet endearing, aspects of his personality.

At my words, Henri let out a yap, his tail swishing against the tent floor, as if in agreement or perhaps just in anticipation of what was to come.

"Come on, Henri," Paul said, a hint of affection in his voice as he rose to his feet and headed toward the collection of bags along the wall of the right wing.

"I'll feed him," I interjected quickly, the words leaping from my lips before I fully registered them. My affection for animals, particularly in these trying times, seemed to amplify, and Henri's recent loss of his older brother tugged sharply at my heartstrings. I caught a tear that dared escape.

Henri, with a sense of understanding or perhaps just a response to the routine, followed me to his bowl, his steps echoing softly in the vast tent.

"Here, catch," Paul's voice broke through my thoughts, a tin of food arcing through the air toward me.

Catching it deftly, I paused to inspect the label, my fingers tracing the outlines of the text. Henri, clearly unimpressed with the delay, voiced his impatience with a sharp yap, urging me to hasten.

With a slight smile, I pulled the ring, the tin yielding with a satisfying hiss. The rich scent of beef and gravy wafted out, surprisingly appetising given its canned origin.

"That almost smells good," Paul remarked, a hint of humour in his tone, his chuckle resonating softly in the spacious tent.

As I scooped the food into Henri's bowl, his eager eyes and wagging tail animated by the prospect of his meal, I couldn't help but respond to Paul's comment. "And people say that I'm the odd one," I said, directing a playful look at Henri, as if including him in the joke.

Henri, for his part, offered a snort in response, his focus shifting immediately to the meal before him, his tongue eagerly lapping at the air, anticipating the taste of his breakfast.

"Hey, Beatrix!" Paul's voice echoed from the left wing, drawing my attention away from Henri and the momentary solace of our interaction.

"Enjoy, little fella," I murmured to Henri, giving his head a gentle scratch, feeling the soft fur under my fingers before reluctantly pulling myself away.

"Come take a look at this," Paul's voice carried a note of urgency that piqued my curiosity despite the lingering scent of the tin in my hands.

With no bin in sight to dispose of the offensive container, I carried it with me, navigating through the tent's spacious interior to where Paul had stationed himself. "What am I looking at?" I asked, my gaze following his to the canvas floor.

Paul was crouched, his finger pointing at several small, dark droplets that marred the otherwise pristine surface. "Does this look like blood to you?" he asked, his tone serious, his focus intense.

Squatting beside him, I peered closer at the droplets, the familiarity of the scene unsettling. "I guess it could be," I conceded, the ambiguity of my response reflecting the churn of thoughts in my mind.

Paul's eyes met mine, laden with a mixture of frustration and expectation. "I would have thought you'd be able to give a more certain answer given how much blood you've seen recently," he remarked, a hint of accusation threading through his words.

I felt a flicker of annoyance at his comment, a surge of defensiveness rising within me. But rather than engage in a pointless spat, I rolled my eyes and turned away.

Pushing Paul's remark to the back of my mind, I made my way to the small assortment of bags and suitcases clustered in a corner, rummaging through them in search of clean clothes for Jamie. The task provided a welcome distraction, allowing me to momentarily set aside the weight of Paul's words and the foreboding implications of the mysterious droplets.

"I'm sorry, Beatrix, I didn't mean it like that," Paul's apology cut through the tense air, his tone attempting to mend the rift his earlier words had caused.

"It's fine," I snapped back, more sharply than I had intended. The simmering ache in my head was now a pounding drum, threatening to split my skull open, and my patience was wearing thin.

"I think Joel's in real trouble," Paul continued, his attention returning to the suspicious stains and the dishevelled bed sheets, his voice laced with concern. "We're just not equipped to survive out here."

His words pulled me from my focused search through the luggage. "There's a bunch of camping gear and related shit piled in Luke's living room," I pointed out, a hint of frustration in my voice at the oversight.

"Really?" Paul's interest was piqued, a note of hope threading through his tone.

"It's where that kayak came from," I reminded him, trying to anchor his understanding to something tangible. "I think some of it may have got a bit damaged during the shadow panther attack last night, but I can bring you everything that's there anyway."

"That'd be great," he agreed, a flicker of relief crossing his features. "We'll sort that out once we've decided what to do about Joel."

"And Duke," I couldn't help but add, the unresolved tension around Duke's fate hanging heavy between us.

Paul's expression softened, a shadow of sorrow passing over his face. "It's really sad that we can't give Duke a proper burial."

That statement hit a nerve, and a wave of anger washed over me. My hand clenched around a handful of clothes, the fabric wrinkling under my grip.

Pausing in the archway that led back to the main area, I turned back to Paul. "Jamie won't let you cremate him," I stated flatly, the finality in my voice a clear signal that I was done with this conversation.

With that, I hurried out of the tent, leaving Paul behind. I needed to escape, to breathe, to not be suffocated by the heavy air of grief and impending decisions that loomed over us.

Head down, absorbed in her thoughts, Glenda rushed toward me, her urgency palpable. I let out a startled gasp as our paths crossed, narrowly avoiding a collision. Her presence was like a sudden storm, unexpected yet unmistakably charged with purpose.

"Please take this with you and give it to Jamie. He can wrap Duke in it until we can organise more suitable arrangements," Glenda implored, her voice a mix of haste and compassion. She extended a clean, neatly folded sheet toward me.

With a silent nod, I took the bedsheet from her hands, the fabric cool and smooth against my skin. The weight of the sheet felt heavier than it should, laden with the sombre task it was destined to fulfil.

"Charity is right, Beatrix," Paul's voice came from behind me, pulling my attention away as he exited the tent.

"You take charge of it then," I huffed, my frustration bubbling to the surface. My head throbbed in time with my beating heart, a physical manifestation of the emotional turmoil that churned within me. Determined to distance myself from the matter and the mounting pressure, I turned sharply on my heels and walked away.

Each step I took was a bid for escape, an attempt to put some physical space between me and the weight of decisions, arguments, and grief that clung to the air like a persistent fog. I needed a moment—a breath of fresh air, a sliver of solace in a world that seemed determined to deny me any peace.

❖

Approaching the river, I consciously inhaled several deep breaths, each one a deliberate attempt to don a veneer of calm and sympathy for Jamie's sake. The cool air filled my lungs, a temporary balm to the burden of my thoughts and the throbbing pain in my head.

"Is it cold?" I ventured, pausing beside Duke, who lay still and peaceful by the water's edge.

My voice seemed to startle Jamie; he turned abruptly, sending small droplets flying into the air like miniature crystals, catching the sunlight. His surprise was palpable, yet his face remained an impassive mask.

A vacant shrug was his only response, words seemingly too heavy to muster.

"I've brought you a towel and change of clothes," I announced, setting the items down on the ground. The towel unfurled slightly, touching the earth, and I carefully placed the clothes atop it, a makeshift altar of fabric and necessity.

"Thanks," Jamie's voice was a low murmur, almost lost amidst the gentle sounds of the river. He splashed water onto his chest, his movements deliberate, methodical, as if each gesture was an effort to wash away more than just the physical remnants of the night's events.

"I... I've also brought a bedsheet to wrap Duke in," I added hesitantly, my voice trembling slightly with the weight of the words. "To keep him safe," I quickly said, hoping to cushion the impact of the reminder of Duke's fate.

Jamie's reaction was a void, his silence a chasm that seemed to stretch between us. He continued his ritual of cleansing, each stroke of his hands an attempt to scrub away the pain, the loss, the dark reality that clung to him as stubbornly as the dried blood he sought to remove.

I bit my lower lip, feeling it tremble uncontrollably. The saline behind my eyes threatened to breach their barriers, stinging with the promise of tears not yet shed. Torn between the impulse to provide solace and the respect for privacy, I chose the latter, positioning myself near Duke but with my back to Jamie. *He deserves at least a little privacy*, I reassured myself, trying to find solace in the decision.

There, beside Duke, I sat enveloped in silence, my mind wandering through the labyrinth of recent events. The world around me seemed to fade into the background as I delved into introspection. *What would life be like now if I had never answered that phone call from Gladys?* The question echoed in my mind, a haunting refrain that offered no comfort. Even as I pondered alternate realities, I understood a harsh truth: my ignorance of Clivilius would not have altered Duke's fate. His tragic death was a cruel stroke of destiny, one that perhaps no foresight or precaution could have averted.

*Stop it, Beatrix!* I chastised myself, an internal rebuke aimed at curbing the spiralling thoughts that threatened to overwhelm me. Yet, despite my efforts to steer clear of despair, my gaze inevitably drifted back to Duke. Each time I looked at him, lying so still and serene, a fresh wave of sorrow clenched my heart, tightening its grip with merciless persistence. *You're going to give yourself a stroke*, I silently warned, recognising the futility of my emotional turmoil but feeling powerless to quell it.

"Do you mind if I do it alone?" Jamie's voice, tinged with a quiet resolve, caught me off guard from behind.

I turned to face him, noticing how the droplets of river water clung to his skin, reflecting the bright sunlight. His eyes, laden with a depth of sorrow, met mine as he gestured toward the bedsheet cradled in my lap.

"Of course," I managed to reply, my voice a whisper, betraying my internal conflict. I wished he hadn't felt the need to take on this burden solo. Wrapping Duke was a final act of farewell, one that seemed too heavy for any one person to bear in isolation.

"Thank you, Beatrix," Jamie said, a hint of gratitude piercing through the dense fog of his grief. With a measured movement, he grabbed the towel, pulling himself from the river's embrace to wrap the fabric around his damp form.

I nodded silently, my heart heavy with empathy for his solitary struggle. Gently placing the sheet beside Duke, I allowed my fingers to linger on the fabric, an unspoken goodbye. Casting one last glance at the dog who had been more than a mere pet but a source of joy and comfort, I blew Duke a soft, tender kiss, a final gesture of affection.

Reluctant to return to the others, yet unwilling to intrude on Jamie's moment of private mourning, I found a compromise in the shade at the back of the tents. There, amidst the dappled light and the soft rustling of the fabric, I stood in liminal space—close enough to offer support if needed, yet far enough to respect Jamie's request for solitude.

❖

The lively chatter that had been permeating the air tapered into a hushed silence as Jamie and I emerged from behind the tent, stepping into the collective gaze of the group gathered around the campfire. A thick, uncomfortable lump of bile lodged in my throat, making it difficult to swallow, as my anxiety surged to new heights. I could feel the weight of everyone's eyes upon us, a collective scrutiny that sent a shiver skittering across my shoulders. Deep down, I recognised that their focus wasn't truly on me; it was Jamie, bearing the weight of Duke, now shrouded in the bedsheet, who commanded their attention.

"Jamie," Paul initiated, his voice betraying a tremor of emotion as he addressed him. There was a brief pause as Paul's eyes flitted across the faces surrounding the fire, seemingly seeking a silent solidarity before he pressed on. "I know things are a bit painful right now, but we need to know when you last saw Joel."

Jamie halted in his tracks, the gravity of the question anchoring him momentarily. After a contemplative pause, he responded, "It was just before the attack last night. He was in his bed in the tent when I took off after Duke."

The air seemed to thicken with tension as Paul continued, treading lightly, "And when you returned?"

A visible shadow passed over Jamie's features, his expression dimming as he offered a simple, yet heavy shrug in response.

"Then it's settled," Glenda interjected, her arms wrapping around herself in a self-comforting gesture, her nerves palpable even in her posture. "Joel is missing."

As Glenda's words hung heavy in the air, my eyes shut instinctively, an involuntary response to the mounting cascade of grim tidings. My fingers found their way to my temples, massaging gently in a futile attempt to stave off the throbbing ache that seemed to pulse in sync with the escalating tension around us. *Could this day possibly get any worse?*

Amidst the sombre assembly, Charity, who until now had remained a somewhat enigmatic presence at the periphery, stepped forward. An aura of confidence and authority seemed to radiate from her, casting a stark contrast to the prevailing mood of despair and uncertainty. "I am certain Joel has been taken by the Portal Pirate. I will hunt him down and bring Joel back," she declared, her voice imbued with a resolve that seemed to pierce the fog of our collective despondency.

My eyes opened wider, my gaze locking onto Charity as her words registered. *Come again? Did you just say that Joel was taken by a Portal pirate?* The notion, while not entirely new, struck me with renewed force. I recalled Charity's earlier mention of such a being, a detail I had dismissed too hastily amidst the shock of grief, now surfacing with jarring clarity.

Before I could fully process the implications, Jamie's voice cut through the air, decisive and devoid of any doubt. "I'm coming with you," he stated, his resolve starkly evident.

My gaze shifted to Jamie, a maelstrom of emotions swirling within me. A grave shadow of concern enveloped my heart. *Don't be a bloody fool, Jamie,* I implored silently, wishing my thoughts could reach him, steer him away from this perilous path. *You're not equipped to take on a freakin' Portal pirate!*

Charity's nod was like a gavel striking, her decision final. "Prepare your things. We leave immediately." Her command sliced through the heavy air, leaving a trail of incredulity in its wake. *Seriously!? She can't be serious... is she?* My mind raced, teetering between disbelief and a creeping sense of urgency.

Jamie's reaction was visceral, his eyes wide with a terror that mirrored my internal turmoil. He looked down at Duke, the bond between them palpable even in the silent, heavy air.

Charity's presence was commanding as she closed the distance between her and Jamie, her stride purposeful. With a gesture that brooked no refusal, she gently but firmly lifted his chin, compelling him to meet her gaze. "If you want any chance of finding Joel alive, we must leave immediately." Her voice, while steady, carried an undercurrent of unspoken urgency that tugged at my consciousness.

*Hell no!* The silent protest screamed within me, echoing my deep-seated dread and resistance to the unfolding scenario.

Jamie's voice broke through the tension, "I need to say farewell to Duke first," his vulnerability laid bare in his quivering lip and trembling arms.

Charity's eyes remained locked on Jamie's, unwavering in their intensity. "Life is full of decisions and consequences, Jamie. You need to make a choice: Joel or Duke." Her words, haunting and unyielding, cut through the air like a cold blade.

*This hunter bitch is a freakin' psychopath,* I couldn't help but think, my gaze fixed on her with a mix of horror and disbelief. Her blunt, unsparing approach to the situation struck me as brutally insensitive, her ultimatum laying bare the harsh realities of our existence in this new, unforgiving world.

The camp was enveloped in a palpable, uncomfortable silence following Charity's ultimatum. It was as if the air itself had thickened, laden with the weight of impending decisions. Finally, Jamie's gaze shifted toward me, his eyes conveying a storm of emotions, and he gave a gentle nod. *Fuck no!* the protest screamed inside my head, yet my face remained a mask of empathy and understanding, a façade honed by necessity.

With reluctant steps, I moved toward Jamie, my heart pounding against my chest as if trying to escape the unbearable situation I found myself in. As I reached out to take Duke from Jamie's arms, my hands were steady, belying the turmoil that raged within. Jamie's grip loosened with a hesitance that spoke volumes, and as Duke's weight transferred to me, a tear broke free from my eye, a silent witness to the internal storm I fought to contain.

"Duke knows you love him, Jamie. He won't ever forget that," I managed to utter, my voice laced with an involuntary sniffle that punctuated the emotional weight of the moment.

Jamie's response was a raw, visible cascade of grief as tears streamed down his face, each one a testament to the depth of his bond with Duke. He leaned in, his lips gently brushing Duke's bedsheet-clad form. "I'm so sorry, Duke," he whispered, his voice breaking with the weight of his remorse and love.

I fought to control my own rising emotions, the threat of tears and sobs wrestling for release as I tried to maintain a semblance of composure.

Taking a moment to compose himself, Jamie inhaled deeply, as if drawing strength from the air itself. When he spoke again, his voice carried a new resolve. "I'll grab my things," he announced, his gaze meeting Charity's, signalling his readiness to face whatever dangers lay ahead in their quest to find Joel.

Disbelief clung to me, thick and unyielding, as I watched Jamie stride towards his tent. The world seemed to tilt, reality skewing at the edges as I grappled with the rapid unravelling of our group's cohesion. Then, unexpectedly, Jamie paused, casting a look back over his shoulder. "Take good care of Henri for me," he implored, his voice carrying a blend of resolve and underlying sorrow.

Henri, upon hearing his name, perked up, his tail wagging briefly before his attention was diverted by some intriguing scent near a log by the campfire. His nose twitched, exploring the invisible trails left by cooking, oblivious to the emotion of the moment.

Paul stepped in, lifting Henri into his arms. "We'll keep him safe, Jamie. You have my word," he promised, his voice firm.

Jamie, without a further glance, resumed his march to the tent, with Charity's silent, determined figure shadowing him. I watched, a lump forming in my throat, as the reality of our situation sank in.

"Oh, Henri," I murmured under my breath, my gaze lingering on the dog now nestled in Paul's embrace. My thoughts spiralled, considering Henri's simple, joyous nature, how he found delight in the smallest things, like a hearty meal or a new scent. The pang of sadness hit anew, realising he wouldn't understand why Jamie, his constant companion, had disappeared or why Duke wouldn't be bounding around camp anymore.

My introspection was shattered by Glenda's sudden outburst. She collapsed to her knees, her voice tearing through the air. "Clivilius!" she cried out, her fists pounding the earth, her despair manifesting in a raw, physical display.

*Oh my God, I can't take any more of this stupidity,* I internally raged, feeling a surge of exasperation so intense it threatened to consume me. My eyes glazed over, a deliberate shield against the pandemonium that unfolded around me. Without a word, I began to walk away, distancing myself from the turmoil that had engulfed the group beside the campfire.

I hadn't gone far when Paul's voice pierced the veil of my retreat. "Beatrix, where are you going?" he called out, his tone laced with a mix of concern and confusion.

"Home," I shouted back, the word echoing with a mix of defiance and despair. The concept of 'home' felt abstract, almost mocking in our current predicament, yet it was the only refuge my mind could seek in that moment.

"What? Now? What?" Paul's bewildered response floated towards me.

My head throbbed mercilessly, a relentless reminder of the physical and emotional toll the past days had exacted. Scratches and bruises adorned my body, souvenirs from a brutal encounter with a shadow panther. Sleep had been elusive, a fleeting luxury. Even the ground beneath my feet seemed hostile, the fine dust irritating my bare skin with every step I took.

With no hand free to dismiss Paul's inquiry – not that a dismissive gesture would encapsulate the whirlwind of frustration and fatigue that engulfed me – I continued forward. My silence was my shield, my solitude my salvation, as I walked away from the campfire's flickering light and toward the familiar embrace of the Portal.

# ABSENTMINDED

## *1338.209.5*

The soft carpet, a plush sea of comfort, offered a gentle reprieve to my aching feet. Leaving the sanctuary of my room, I embarked on the familiar yet heavy trek down the passageway toward the bathroom. My day had commenced with a desperate attempt to cleanse myself of the morning's horrors—scrubbing away the blood and the vile residue of shadow panther saliva. Yet, the brief and tumultuous sojourn in Clivilius had marred me once more, layering new stains over the old.

*Why did I activate that cursed Portal Key?* The question ricocheted through my mind, sparking a blush of foolishness across my cheeks—a vivid reminder of my vulnerability. "Oh, that's right, I had no choice," I muttered, the words barely escaping my lips as I trudged forward, each step a reminder of the relentless cascade of events at the casino. The memories clung to me as tenaciously as the dirt and blood I was desperate to wash away. *There hadn't been another way out, had there?*

The bathroom door loomed before me, a barrier to the solace I sought. A sudden halt—my hands, occupied with the weight of Duke's wrapped body, denied me the simple act of turning the knob. "Shit!" The curse slipped out in a hushed exhale, a whisper to the stillness of my home, now breached by the savagery of Clivilius. And not just breached, but invaded—Duke's lifeless form a tortured testament to the violence that had followed me home.

"Oh, Duke," I whispered, my voice cracking, laden with a sorrow too heavy to bear. The weight of his small, brave body in my arms was a cruel reminder of his fearless nature—the very trait that had endeared him to me, now the cause of my heartache. I turned, the burden of guilt and grief pointing me back toward the solitude of my room. "Why did you always have to be so fearless? You know how that always got you into trouble." My words, a mix of lament and love, filled the air as I spoke to him, to the memory of his spirited little soul. "And now look at you—" The sentence trailed off, unfinished, much like the fate that had befallen my dear, daring Duke.

"Beatrix!" The sharp, piercing call of my mother's voice sliced through the silence, jolting me from my sorrowful reverie. The familiar creak of the stairs under her hurried steps was like a countdown, each groan of the wood a second ticking away.

My heart raced, skipping a beat as panic set in. "I don't think we can make it back, Duke," I whispered to the lifeless form in my arms, my gaze frantically sweeping from the top of the stairs to the sanctuary of my bedroom at the corridor's end. My mind raced, weighing the scant options, calculating the slim chances of evading my mother's imminent intrusion.

"Are you home?" Her voice, now alarmingly closer, clawed its way up the staircase, each syllable heavy with the weight of impending confrontation.

I faced the bathroom door, a makeshift barrier between my current exposure and the need for concealment. My elbow, guided by desperation, collided with the cold chrome of the door handle with more force than intended. Clumsily balancing Duke's wrapped form, I pushed down, feeling the cool metal slide under my skin as the latch yielded with a click. "I'm having a shower!" The words erupted from me, a desperate declaration thrown towards the encroaching presence of my mother.

In the nick of time, my heel struck the door, ushering it shut with a decisive movement. My back hit the door with a solid thump, a physical full stop to the motion of the moment. I slid down, the coolness of the door seeping through my shirt, grounding me as I clutched Duke close.

"That was close, Duke," I murmured into the silence, my breaths deep and quivering. The tension hung thick in the air, a tangible cloud of unspoken fears and close calls.

Then, a sharp knock on the door shattered the fragile peace, a sudden reminder that questions remained just outside, as relentless and probing as ever.

"Beatrix, is everything alright?" The concern in my mother's voice seeped through the door, its undercurrent of tension striking a dissonant chord within me.

"Yeah," I called back, attempting to infuse a semblance of normality into my voice, even as my heart waged a relentless battle against my chest, each beat a loud echo in the confined space.

Mother's voice pierced the veil of my feigned calm once more. "Can you come downstairs when you're finished in there? Your father and I need to speak with you about something important." The gravity in her tone, an unusual intrusion into my private turmoil, sent a ripple of anxiety coursing through me.

"Can't it—" My words faltered, my throat constricting, transforming my inquiry into a strained croak. The sudden realisation dawned on me—it must be something of significant weight to warrant such an interruption, especially here, now. My heart rate escalated, the beats now thunderous in their rapid succession.

"Sure thing, Mum," I managed to muster a more composed response, masking the whirlwind of thoughts and fears churning within me.

A peculiar hush followed, stretching out like a taut thread, leaving me to wonder if she had departed. In a bid to ensure a semblance of privacy, I gingerly placed Duke's still form in front of the washing basket nestled in the nook between the bathtub and the vanity. The urgency to shield myself from an unexpected entry spurred me to twist the shower taps, coaxing a cascade of cold water to erupt with a sputter, its sound a temporary barrier against the world outside.

"Thanks, Beatrix," her voice reached me again, a distant anchor as I grappled with the maelstrom of emotions inside me.

With a heavy heart, I cast one more glance at Duke, the once-white sheet marred by the stark, accusing red of blood—a visceral testament to the day's horrors. A grimace etched itself onto my face, a silent acknowledgment of the pain and loss that lay so lamentably before me. With cautious steps on the cold, hard tiles, I moved to lock the bathroom door, securing myself, for a fleeting moment, from the impending confrontations and the relentless tide of reality awaiting me beyond its barrier.

# LEIGH'S CHECK-IN

## 1338.209.6

One large turquoise towel hugged my frame tightly, its plush fabric cocooning my skin as droplets of water trickled down my legs. A smaller cream towel, twisted into a makeshift turban, ensnared the damp tendrils of my hair, my fingers meticulously wringing out the stubborn droplets from a few stray strands that had audaciously clung to my cheek. The sensation was oddly comforting, a fleeting moment of solitude in the whirlwind of my day.

With each step down the hallway, the carpet squelched softly under my damp feet, leaving behind a trail of wet footprints like breadcrumbs. I barely noticed, my mind preoccupied with the warmth seeping back into my skin, the fabric of the towels absorbing the lingering moisture. The hallway felt longer today, each step echoing in the silence, as if the house itself held its breath.

My sanctuary, my bedroom, loomed at the end of the corridor, a beacon of privacy and personal space. But as I approached, my heart skipped a beat. There, in my sacred space, was Leigh, an unexpected shadow against the familiarity of my room.

"Shit, Leigh! What the hell are you doing here?" The words erupted from me, a cascade louder than I had anticipated, reverberating against the walls. My pulse quickened, a surge of adrenaline tingling through my veins as I leaped in surprise at his unforeseen presence.

Without missing a beat, I darted into the room, my actions swift, fuelled by a sudden urge to shield this intrusion from my mother's prying eyes. The door clicked shut behind me, a barrier between us and the outside world.

"Sorry," he uttered, his voice laced with a sincerity that tugged at my defences. His face bore the weight of his apology, eyes reflecting a turmoil that piqued my curiosity despite my initial shock. "I thought you were out."

"What, so you thought you'd lurk about in my room?" My voice, tinged with disbelief, cut through the tension, a sharp note that seemed almost foreign in the usually tranquil haven of my bedroom. I could feel my eyebrows knitting together, my eyes narrowing into a glare that I hoped would convey my irritation. *Today of all days*, I thought, my mind a silent snarl, I didn't need this—this invasion, this disruption.

"No. I just meant that I didn't realise you were in the shower. If I knew, I would have left and come back later," Leigh stammered, his words tumbling out in a clumsy attempt to shield himself from my growing frustration. His defence, earnest yet feeble, hovered in the air, an unsatisfactory explanation that did little to quell the storm brewing inside me.

"Unlikely," I muttered under my breath, my tone softer now but laced with a cynicism I couldn't suppress. Turning my back on Leigh, I sought refuge in the ritual of selecting my attire, allowing the familiarity of the action to soothe my frayed nerves.

My fingers trailed over the fabrics in the closet, the smooth textures and familiar contours grounding me as I sifted through my belongings. The metallic whisper of coat hangers gliding along the rail punctuated the silence, a soundtrack to my indecision. After a moment's hesitation, I extracted a pair of jeans and a top, the fabric cool against my skin as I balanced them on my shoulder.

Yet, as I reached for a hooded sweater, a more forgiving garment, I paused. The fabric brushed against the recent scratches on my arms, a stark reminder of the turmoil that lay just beneath the surface. *It's still winter*, I reminded myself, a justification that felt as much for the sweater as it was for the need to conceal my vulnerabilities. In that moment, the weight of the garment felt like a shield, a barrier between myself and the world, even as Leigh's presence behind me loomed like a question mark, persistent and unresolved.

My gaze hardened, a fusion of anger and disbelief, as I swivelled to confront Leigh. There he stood, awkwardly clutching the remnants of what once was a dress I cherished – now nothing more than a crumpled, torn fabric stained with blood. The sight of it, dangling limply in his grasp, was like a visual echo of pain, reigniting memories I wished to bury.

Leigh's face was a canvas of concern, his usual carefree expression marred by deep furrows of worry. "Care to explain?" he questioned, his voice steady yet laden with an unspoken gravity, his eyes flicking between me and the tattered red dress.

"What the fuck is your problem today!" I couldn't hold back the surge of anger, my voice a growl of frustration as I snatched the dress from his hands. It felt like an invasion, a violation of my private turmoil. "First you lurk in my room and now you demand an explanation."

"I'm concerned for you, Beatrix," he countered, his tone shifting to a gentle cadence. His words, meant to soothe, only fanned the flames of my indignation.

"Perhaps you should have been more concerned about me when you gave me that stupid device," I retorted, the words spilling out with a venom I barely recognised in myself.

"You mean the Portal Key?" His inquiry was tentative, as if he were now treading on broken glass.

"You didn't give me any other device," I shot back, my voice laced with a bitterness that tasted foreign on my tongue. As I spoke, a tremor began to weave through my hands.

As Leigh advanced towards me, my eyes bore into him with such intensity that he halted abruptly, as if struck by an invisible barrier. The air between us crackled with tension, a palpable force that seemed to ignite the familiar, unwelcome sensation of burning within me.

"Now, get out so I can get dressed," I commanded, striving for authority. Yet, despite my efforts to cloak myself in a veneer of strength, my voice betrayed me, fracturing on the final word, revealing the turmoil beneath my stern exterior.

A heavy silence enveloped us, thick with unspoken words and tension that you could almost reach out and touch. Leigh then broke the silence, his voice carrying a decisive edge that contrasted with the tumult churning within me. "I'll return in ten," he declared, leaving no room for argument.

Leigh possessed the ability to conjure his Portal effortlessly within the confines of my room, yet he refrained, his intention—to shield me from its mesmerising draw. He was well aware of the Portal's seductive call, an allure so potent that a mere touch from me could result in my inadvertent exile to Clivilius—a fate he seemed keen to prevent. With this resolve, he stepped out, the door's closure echoing his departure. Moments after, a distinct shiver coursed through my arms—a sensation now eerily familiar. Simultaneously, the room's light offered a subtle yet unmistakable dance, a silent herald of the Portal's activation somewhere beyond my immediate view.

The moment I was alone, a torrent of emotions erupted. With a swift, almost violent motion, I yanked the clean clothes off my shoulders, the garments cascading onto the bed in a tumultuous heap, a physical manifestation of my swirling frustration, anger, and the ache that clung to my bones.

"Fucking shadow panther," I muttered venomously, my voice a low growl as I seized the dishevelled dress, a reminder of the ordeal, from where Leigh had carelessly discarded it. My movements were brisk, fuelled by a storm of emotions, as I hurled the dress into the wastebasket beside my desk, eager to banish it from my sight.

In a rush, I slipped into the fresh clothes, my actions quick and mechanical. I was acutely aware of the time, the ticking clock a reminder of Leigh's impending return, and the last thing I wanted was for him to intrude upon my privacy once again.

A sharp pang throbbed at my temple, a physical echo of the turmoil within. My fingers pressed against the tender skin, massaging in vain as I sought a momentary respite from the relentless pounding. My eyes closed, heart stuttering in my chest when a soft yet insistent knock broke the silence.

Cautiously, I inched towards the door, my mind racing with the possibility of facing my mother, a confrontation I was not prepared for. But it was Leigh's voice that filtered through, a soft whisper carrying a sharp edge, "Beatrix."

With a deep breath to steel myself, I pulled open the door, allowing Leigh to step inside. The door shut swiftly behind him, a barrier once more erected between us and the world, sealing us within the confines of my room

"You're really not going to leave me alone, are you?" The words slipped out, tinged with a complex mix of emotions. My sigh mingled frustration and annoyance, yet beneath it all lay an undercurrent of relief, a reluctant acknowledgment of not facing the madness alone.

"Of course not," Leigh responded, his voice firm, imbued with an unwavering resolve. He casually positioned himself against the desk, a casual stance that contrasted sharply with the intensity of our conversation.

My gaze inadvertently flickered to the wastebasket beside Leigh, the discarded dress peeking out like a ghost of recent turmoil. *I can't really leave that*—my thoughts fractured as Leigh's voice sliced through the silence, his questions rapid and probing.

"What happened to you? How did you manage to get yourself all scratched up? Is Luke's settlement that dangerous?" The inquiries poured out, each one laden with concern and a desire to understand, to peel back the layers of the mystery shrouding my recent ordeal.

My lips pressed tightly together, a barrier holding back the flood of explanations and emotions threatening to spill. "You could say that," I offered, a terse reply that held volumes, my voice a mix of weariness and defiance.

"Say what?" Leigh's inquiry was gentle, yet persistent, his head tilting in a silent prompt for more, his eyes a mirror of his concern, reflecting a genuine desire to delve deeper.

"That Luke's settlement is dangerous," I exhaled, the words leaving me in a huff, a simplistic summary of a complex, harrowing reality.

Leigh's body language shifted as he encouraged me to elaborate, his shoulders lifting in a silent gesture of readiness, hands raised slightly in anticipation of what I was about to reveal. The room seemed to hold its breath, waiting for my words.

"I was attacked by a freaking shadow panther!" The words burst from me, a torrent of pent-up frustration and fear. The memory of the attack, so vivid and terrifying, reignited a fresh wave of anger within me, especially as I thought of Duke's tragic fate.

Leigh's reaction was immediate, his face morphing into an expression of sorrow, an unmistakable shadow of sadness darkening his features. "Oh," he uttered, the simplicity of the word laden with a profound depth of understanding and empathy.

"You're familiar with the creatures, I gather?" My question was pointed, a mixture of accusation and a desperate search for answers.

Leigh's nod was gentle, almost reluctant. "Unfortunately, I am," he confirmed, his voice carrying the weight of his regret.

"And you didn't think to warn me?" The accusation snapped from me sharply, my patience frayed, my trust wobbling on an unsteady axis.

A heavy silence enveloped us, thick with tension and unspoken recriminations. Leigh's face became a canvas of conflicting emotions, each one flitting across his features in a rapid, almost indecipherable dance. After what seemed like an eternity, he found his voice again.

"Beatrix," he began, his tone soft, infused with a sincerity that reached out, attempting to bridge the gap my anger had forged. "Attacks on new settlements are rare. If I thought you were in any immediate danger, I would have said so." His words hung in the air, a plea for understanding, a bid to temper my indignation with his perspective, offering a glimpse into his rationale, flawed or not, in the face of the unpredictable wilderness I was navigating.

My gaze sharpened, slicing through the space between us as I weighed Leigh's explanation. His hesitation, the careful construction of his response, all while omitting any mention of Portal pirates or other perils he deemed unworthy of disclosure, eroded my trust. *How could I believe he'd truly warn me of dangers when his silence had already spoken volumes?* A wave of suspicion washed over me, cold and unsettling, sparking a cascade of doubts about what other secrets Leigh might be harbouring. The thought sent a shiver through me, an involuntary reaction that I hastily masked with a hand to my mouth, stifling the gasp that threatened to escape.

"I need to find Jarod," I declared abruptly, the words tumbling out in a rush. The urgency to divert our conversation and propel myself into action was overwhelming; standing idle was fuelling my restlessness, my mind racing with the implications of Leigh's admissions and omissions.

Leigh's movement was sudden, a slight miscalculation causing him to knock over the wastebasket as he slid off the desk. Papers and discarded items cascaded onto the floor in a silent testament to the turmoil that seemed to follow me. "I've already taken care of that," he announced, bending down to collect the scattered debris, his actions meticulous yet oddly grounding in the heat of our exchange.

"What does that mean... you took care of it?" My voice wavered slightly, betraying a surge of apprehension. Leigh's enigmatic demeanour only amplified my fears, conjuring images of grim outcomes far beyond what I felt equipped to handle at the moment.

"Don't look so worried," Leigh attempted to reassure me, his chuckle light, yet it failed to dispel the growing tension. The waste basket's metal rim echoed a clang against the desk as he set it upright, a minor distraction from the weight of our conversation.

I couldn't help but respond with a skeptical shrug, my eyes widening into a glare that silently demanded he shed more light on the matter.

Leigh seemed to understand the urgency in my silent plea, elaborating, "I followed the events of the night very closely after I purposely bumped into you."

"And?" I couldn't contain the impatience in my voice, my need for answers pressing. "What happened when he and I were separated? Did they hurt him?" The questions spilled out, each one laced with concern for Jarod's well-being.

"Jarod did get arrested—" Leigh started, his words sending a jolt of alarm through me.

Instinctively, I lunged for my handbag, seeking some semblance of action I could take, but Leigh was quicker, his movements smooth and assured as he retrieved my bag from its crumpled state beside the bed.

"But I spoke with my contact in the Department and had Jarod released and all charges dropped," he explained, offering the bag to me, his actions bridging the gap between his words and my rising panic.

Our eyes met in a fleeting connection, a silent exchange laden with a mix of gratitude and lingering concern. "Thank you," I murmured, the words barely escaping, a whisper of relief amidst the whirlwind of emotions, acknowledging his intervention and the complexity of the situation that continued to unfold.

"The two of you make a good pair. A somewhat disastrous pairing, perhaps, but well-suited nonetheless." The words hung in the air, and I couldn't help but respond with a mix of irritation and disbelief. My hand found its way to Leigh's bicep, delivering a thump that was more than a mere gesture—it was a physical manifestation of my frustration.

Leigh, seemingly undeterred by my reaction, continued, "But with the proper training, I think you could both make for a very formidable team." As he spoke, he extended his arm, his hand unfolding to reveal another Portal Key nestled in his palm. "I think we should give him this."

The suggestion hit me like a physical blow, intensifying the throbbing in my head, my eyes straining against the pressure of the moment, feeling as though they might escape their confines. "You're crazy!" The words erupted from me, a volatile outburst mirroring the inner turmoil Leigh's proposal had ignited.

His laughter in response to my exasperation only fuelled my ire, my glare intensifying as I sought to convey the depth of my disbelief and frustration.

Leigh's amusement didn't last, his demeanour shifting as he countered, "I'm not the one who, in only twenty-four hours, tried to steal from a casino and survived the attack of a deadly shadow creature."

"Panther. It was a shadow panther," I interjected, a hint of insistence in my tone, unwilling to let the details of my ordeal be generalised.

Leigh's expression softened, his gaze finding mine, a serious undertone cutting through his earlier levity. "You can't deny it, Beatrix," he said, his voice taking on a note of sincerity. "You've got some fine skills there." His acknowledgment, while possibly meant as a compliment, only served to add another layer of complexity to the concoction of thoughts and emotions swirling within me, leaving me to ponder the implications of his words and the potential path they suggested.

As Leigh's proposal hung in the air, I found myself inhaling deeply, an involuntary response as I mulled over the ramifications of his suggestion. My mind raced, entertaining the prospect of aligning myself with Jarod in a capacity so intimate, so fraught with potential complications. *Could reintegrating our paths, this time under the mantle of Guardianship, be a boon, or would it simply weave a more intricate web of challenges?* The idea tugged at me, a mix of allure and apprehension. Yet, amid these swirling thoughts, a stark realisation struck me—I was still grappling with the essence of my own role as a Guardian. *How could I possibly contemplate extending this labyrinthine journey to Jarod?*

"At least think about it," Leigh urged, breaking into my internal debate with a voice that bore the weight of expectation.

My reply was almost reflexive, a loud exhale marking the release of pent-up tension as I yielded, if only slightly. "Fine," I admitted, a word that carried more resignation than agreement.

To my surprise, Leigh's reaction was immediate and vivid, his eyes expanding with a blend of anticipation and excitement, his demeanour brightening as if my tentative acquiescence was a beacon of hope. "You'll give the Portal Key to Jarod?" he queried, his voice tinged with an enthusiasm that seemed to stretch beyond the confines of the room.

But I was quick to temper his expectations, the reality of my indecision still anchoring me firmly to the ground. "I'll think about it," I clarified, stressing the point to Leigh once more. This wasn't a commitment, merely a concession to consider the possibility, to turn it over in my mind amidst the tumult of doubts, fears, and the nascent flicker of curiosity about what such a future might entail.

"Either way," Jarod articulated, his voice carrying a note of casual suggestion as he engaged in a stretch, his back cracking in response to the movement. His arms extended, pulling his shoulders back in a deliberate motion, emphasising the seriousness of his advice despite the nonchalance of his actions. "You should at least visit him. Tell Jarod that he should probably keep a low public profile for a while."

I couldn't help but scoff at the idea. "Jarod, keep a low public profile. Unlikely." The words slipped out laced with skepticism, reflecting my doubt about Jarod's capacity for discretion.

Leigh's tone sharpened, a hint of urgency creeping in. "I'm serious, Beatrix," he insisted, pausing to let his words sink in before gesturing towards the tangible proof of our predicament—the contents of my wastebasket. "It's a serious situation."

My response was an involuntary eye roll, a gesture betraying my exasperation with the insistence Leigh imposed on us. "Fine, but you're coming with me," I declared, unwilling to navigate the upcoming challenges solo.

"I am?"

"Yes, well, you are the one that got me onto this horrendous rollercoaster in the first place," I retorted, my words firm, leaving no room for argument as I rummaged through my handbag in search of my phone. "So yes, you are coming too," I reaffirmed, my stance unwavering.

"Okay," Leigh acquiesced, his energy undiminished as he wielded his device, casting an array of lights across my wall, transforming the mundane surface into a kaleidoscope of colours, reminiscent of a vibrant Christmas display.

Phone in hand, suspended in the half-light of decision, I felt Leigh's gaze on me, his perceptiveness cutting through the momentary stillness. "I guess there's no need to hide it anymore, now that you have your own Portal Key," he remarked, an undercurrent of resignation in his voice, acknowledging a shift in our shared duties.

Yet, even amidst his revelations, the persistent ringtone sliced through, a reminder of the world persisting beyond our immediate turmoil.

"What are you doing?" Leigh's voice, edged with urgency, broke the tension.

"Calling Jarod," I retorted, my impatience surfacing as I struggled to comprehend his apparent obliviousness to my actions. My brow furrowed with my growing irritation.

"Turn it off, quick," Leigh urged, his hand reaching out, swiping the phone from my grasp in a swift, almost desperate gesture.

In the brief interaction, Jarod's voice momentarily pierced the room, "Beatrix?" A fleeting connection, cut abruptly as Leigh terminated the call.

My suspicion deepened as I regarded Leigh, his actions puzzling, sparking a flurry of questions. "Probably best that we don't pre-warn him," he reasoned, yet his words did little to quell my burgeoning doubt.

"I think it's a bit late for that," I countered, my tone laced with a mix of sarcasm and frustration, reclaiming my phone just as Jarod's name flashed again across the screen.

"Don't answer it," Leigh interjected swiftly, a note of desperation in his voice.

"Why the hell not?" My scowl deepened, my patience fraying at the edges as I grappled with his erratic instructions, yet I complied, rejecting the call in a swirl of confusion and agitation.

"Even better, turn your phone off," he pressed on, his tone brooking no argument.

"What?" My confusion escalated, teetering on the edge of exasperation. The drama unfolding was more than I had the bandwidth to handle, my mind screaming for a reprieve, yearning to telegraph my frustration to Leigh, who seemed oblivious to the mounting stress his directives were causing.

"It'll make him panic when he can't reach you," Leigh's voice was steady, his reasoning clear, yet it did little to quell the turmoil brewing within me.

My response was a narrowed gaze, my eyes transforming into sharp points of skepticism as my brows drew together, a result of the inner tension clashing with exhaustion. The idea flickered through my mind, a tempting whisper: *There's still time to call Jarod back and fabricate a small white lie. I could easily claim it was a mistaken dial*—a plausible excuse in our ever-connected world.

I exhaled a soft sigh, my mind teetering between two daunting prospects. On one hand, dragging Jarod deeper into the maelstrom of Clivilius could send our already precarious journey spiralling into darker chasms. Yet, the thought of navigating the murky waters of Guardianship without his presence seemed even more daunting—a solitary venture into the unknown that I was loath to undertake.

"Beatrix," Leigh's voice cut through my reverie, sharp and demanding attention. "What are you doing?"

My fingers continued their dance across the phone's screen, crafting a message with deliberate calmness. "I'm messaging Jarod," I stated plainly, my voice a steady contrast to the flurry of activity under my fingertips.

Leigh's expression shifted to one of surprise, his dark eyes widening. "I thought we agreed that you were going to turn your phone off?"

His words hung between us, but my resolve was firm. "You agreed to that," I countered, a hint of defiance colouring my tone as I completed the message. The thought of Jarod embarking on a frantic search if I vanished from the digital world was unappealing. "He'll only come looking for me if I turn my phone off, and I don't fancy a wild goose chase around town," I explained, sealing my decision with practical logic. "I've told him I'm on my way to meet him."

**10:17AM Beatrix:** *On my way to meet you at our usual rendezvous*

Leigh's reaction was a mix of surprise and resignation, his body language shifting as he leaned back against the desk, a silent observer to the unfolding plan.

Almost instantly, my phone buzzed with Jarod's reply.

**10:18AM Jarod:** *Wrest Point?*

I couldn't suppress an eye roll, a small chuckle escaping me. The thought of returning to Wrest Point, a place now tangled with memories and risks, seemed ludicrous. *There's no way in hell we're going back to that place anytime soon*, I silently vowed.

The room was suddenly awash with the vibrant, pulsating lights from Leigh's Portal, casting dancing shadows across the walls.

"And where are you going?" My curiosity piqued as I watched the colours flicker.

"To Jarod's," he stated matter-of-factly, as if it were the most natural decision. "I've registered the location of his house with my Portal Key."

My astonishment was evident, my eyes widening as I processed his words. "Of course you have," I replied, the incredulity dripping from every syllable.

Leigh's expression shifted to one of mild apology. "Oh, sorry," he offered. "I forgot you're a new Guardian. You wouldn't have access to his location yet."

"No," I conceded, acknowledging the limitation but dismissing its significance. "But that doesn't matter."

A smile of relief spread across Leigh's face. "I'll meet you there then?"

"Unlikely," I shot back, a playful edge to my voice.

"What?" Leigh's confusion was almost comical.

I couldn't contain my amusement at his baffled expression. "We're not going to his house."

"We're not?"

"Come on, I'll drive us," I declared, a plan forming in my mind as I headed for the door. The muffled sounds of my parents' voices floated up from downstairs, prompting me to shut the door swiftly behind me. "On second thought, let's meet at Luke's." It was a safe bet, a location I knew my Portal

Key could access and far removed from the complications of any engagement with my parents.

Leigh nodded, understanding dawning. "See you in a minute," he said, before disappearing through the Portal.

My fingers flew over the phone's screen as I sent a clarifying message to Jarod.

**10:22AM Beatrix:** *No! The other rendezvous*

As the message sent, I steeled myself for what lay ahead, the weight of my decisions pressing heavily as I navigated through the maze of our intertwined fates, stepping into the unknown with a mixture of determination and trepidation.

# CAMPING

## 1338.209.7

Stepping into Clivilius, the abrupt transition from the dimly lit room to the brilliant outdoors was jarring. My hand shot up reflexively, a shield against the harsh, unyielding sun that seemed to scrutinise my every move. The sand beneath my feet offered an uncomfortable welcome, each step producing a distinct squelch as my shoes protested against the dry, coarse grains.

I moved with purpose, distancing myself from the Portal, my eyes scanning the translucent screen that flickered with location images, finally securing a mental image of my destination: Luke's house. It was a new routine that was still a little jarring, yet the ease of the practice did little to ease the sense of urgency that thrummed through my veins.

"Hey, Beatrix!" The voice, unexpected and intruding, shattered my focus. I cast an irritated glance over my shoulder, only to find Kain Jeffries anchoring himself to the scene, an unwelcome distraction. Recognition dawned; not only had our paths crossed at the morning's campfire, but our acquaintanceship, courtesy of Jamie's familial ties, had laid a foundation for this interaction.

Kain's posture, casual as he lounged against the dune, contrasted starkly with my internal tumult. His legs stretched out before him, he seemed almost part of the landscape, a figure painted against the backdrop of ochre dust.

Internally, I groaned. Time was a luxury I couldn't afford, yet there was Kain, beckoning me over with a wave that suggested a conversation I was keen to avoid. Opting for a diplomatic approach, I feigned misunderstanding, offering a wave in return that I hoped conveyed cordiality rather than invitation.

Turning back to the task at hand, my focus narrowed on the Portal's screen, now a gateway not just to a location but to the next chapter of this unfolding saga. Luke's house materialised on the display, demanding my concentration. With a final, resolute look, I committed the image to memory, the screen before me transforming into a whirl of colours and energy, a visual echo of the turmoil brewing both within and around me.

❖

The study, enveloped in a quasi-darkness, felt almost alien; the blinds were still a firm barrier against the outside world, casting long shadows that danced across the room. As I stepped in, the crunch of the shattered light globe underfoot echoed ominously. That unsettling sound sent a shiver racing down my spine, a visceral response to the memories it evoked.

My gaze drifted, landing on a dark, ominous smudge on the door—a bloodied handprint. For a heartbeat, the sight jolted me, until the realisation dawned: the blood was my own, a macabre token of my earlier ordeal. The hallway extended before me, no less foreboding, marked by the grim path of dried blood smears that adorned the walls, a visceral breadcrumb trail of the night's horrors.

With a hesitant pause, I stilled, straining my ears for any hint of the shadow panther's presence. The silence that greeted me was profound, almost tangible, heightening the sense of isolation.

"Leigh?" My voice broke the silence, a mix of hope and apprehension lacing my words as I edged forward. "Leigh, are you there?" I needed the reassurance of his presence, a lifeline amidst the palpable remnants of fear.

Then, without warning, a figure materialised in the doorway at the hall's end. The shock of it—a dark silhouette framed against the dim backdrop—wrenched a loud gasp from my throat as my body recoiled instinctively. Every nerve was alight, the sudden appearance igniting a fresh surge of adrenaline.

"Leigh," the word emerged as a half-whisper, half-sigh, relief flooding through me as I clung to the familiarity of his presence. My breath, stolen by the shock, gradually returned as I steadied myself, grounding my presence in the here and now.

"What the hell happened in here?" Leigh's inquiry came from the living room, his figure momentarily vanishing from the doorway.

"I told you. I was attacked by a shadow panther last night," I called back, my voice steady despite the rapid drumming of my heart, as I hastened down the hall to join him.

Upon entering the room, a groan escaped me involuntarily. "Shit," I muttered under my breath, my eyes sweeping across the disarray. The living room, now a graveyard of camping supplies, seemed to echo the turmoil of the previous night.

Leigh crouched to examine a shattered camping light, his voice tinged with a mix of curiosity and concern. "It really is quite the scene in here."

His words lingered in the air, a heavy understatement of the night's horrors. My brow creased slightly, a silent acknowledgment of the ordeal he had yet to comprehend. *You really have no idea*, I thought, my gaze drifting to the tiles that now bore the gruesome imprint of the night's events, their pattern reminiscent of a grotesque boysenberry swirl.

Pulling myself from the grim tableau, I addressed the immediate, pressing matter, "I should really take all this gear to Clivilius first. I did promise Paul."

Leigh's query followed, "What about Jarod?"

"Jarod will wait," I asserted. His expression, a blend of concern and skepticism, seemed to question my priorities.

Leigh's eyes stared at me with disbelief, and his furrowed brow urged me to reconsider.

"I know Jarod. Trust me, he'll wait for me," I reinforced, my voice carrying a strong assurance.

Leigh's gesture, offering me a sleeping bag, was a silent show of support. "I wish I could help you," he said, his tone laden with genuine regret.

"It won't take me long," I reassured, more for my sake than his, as I prepared to transport the gear. "I'll just leave it all beside the Portal."

With a final glance at the disarray, I summoned the Portal, the living room wall igniting with its vibrant hues. Stepping through, I embraced the warmth of Clivilius once more, the realities of both worlds weighing heavily as I navigated the fine line between duty and personal allegiance.

❖

"Beatrix!" Kain's voice cut through the air, laden with urgency, as he made his way toward me with a determination that matched the harshness of the Clivilius landscape. "I need crutches." His sudden approach felt like an ambush just as I set foot on the dusty terrain.

Waving him off with a hint of impatience, "You'll have to talk to Luke," I said, my focus divided as I placed the sleeping bag beside the Portal.

"But look at my leg," Kain pressed, drawing near with a limp that underscored his plea.

Glancing at his leg, the pragmatist in me responded without sugarcoating, "Looks like it's bleeding." My tone was detached, a defence mechanism against the day's accumulating stresses.

Kain's gaze followed mine, a mix of resignation and frustration in his voice as he acknowledged the wound, "Not again."

The mention of Glenda was instinctive, a logical suggestion in a world that seemed increasingly devoid of logic. "You should probably go and visit Glenda."

But Kain's response was unexpected, his words hitting me with an unforeseen weight. "Glenda's gone."

The words sent a shiver through me, the implications unsettling. "Gone? Is she—" I paused, the question heavy on my tongue, "Dead?"

Kain was quick to clarify, though his news did little to assuage the growing sense of unease. "Oh, no, she went with Charity and Jamie to hunt the Portal pirate."

The revelation puzzled me, my mind grappling with the bizarre turn of events. *What an odd thing for Glenda to do*, I thought, skepticism and worry intertwining. A doctor's presence on such a perilous venture seemed incongruous, and her absence left a tangible void within the settlement's fabric.

With a brief shake of my head, I attempted to clear the cloud of confusion. There were more immediate issues demanding my focus, yet the undercurrent of concern for Glenda and the settlement's well-being lingered, a silent echo amidst the commotion of my own obligations.

"You'll still have to ask Luke for crutches," I reiterated to Kain, positioning myself in front of the Portal, the words laced with a hint of apology. "Sorry."

"Bea–" Kain started, but I cut him off with a deep inhale, bracing myself for the relentless tide of tasks that lay ahead.

Kain's persistent interruptions were a distraction I could ill afford, yet I knew avoiding him entirely would be impossible.

"Shit," Leigh's expletive drew my attention as he clumsily sloshed water across the kitchen tiles, a feeble attempt to cleanse the blood and fear that had consumed the space.

"Everything alright?" My voice carried a mix of concern and curiosity as I hefted several small boxes, my gaze shifting to Leigh's hunched form.

Engrossed in his task, Leigh didn't raise his head, his focus fixed on dragging a bath towel through the murky mixture of water and blood. "Yeah," he panted, the word barely escaping as he toiled on the floor. "All good here."

I paused, my mind wrestling with the futility of our actions. The house, tainted by recent misadventures, felt like a sinking ship, and any effort to restore order seemed increasingly like rearranging deck chairs on the Titanic. With every new development, the likelihood of police intervention grew, threatening to upend our precarious existence here. Yet, despite the inevitable sense of doom, there was a strange comfort in witnessing Leigh's dedication, a silent solidarity as we navigated the storm together, each of us clinging to our roles amidst the uncertainty.

Kain had remained remarkably silent throughout the remainder of my trekking back and forth with camping supplies, despite his intermittent glances in my direction, each filled with an almost tangible yearning. Those bright, blue eyes of his, usually so full of jest and laughter, now conveyed a depth of plea that tugged at the very fabric of my resolve. Yet, despite their luminous allure, I had managed to shield my willpower from their silent entreaty. There was an urgency that gnawed at the edges of my focus, compelling me to expedite my task for a forthcoming rendezvous with Jarod.

As I manoeuvred through the labyrinth of responsibilities that shackled me to the settlement, the weight of Kain's silent appeals grew increasingly burdensome. With each passing moment, with every step laden with duty, the echoes of Leigh's words reverberated more resolutely within the confines of my mind. The notion of bestowing a Portal Key upon Jarod began to morph from a mere suggestion into a tangible solution, a necessary concession to alleviate the relentless tide of obligations that threatened to engulf me.

Guardianship, a mantle I had donned merely a day prior, was already proving to be an odyssey of unforeseen trials and tribulations. The notion that my tenure had scarcely eclipsed a day seemed almost farcical, given the plethora of tasks and decisions that had cascaded upon me. In this maelstrom of duty and expectation, the idea of augmenting our ranks with another Guardian appeared not just appealing, but essential for my own sanity.

With the relocation of the camping supplies nearing completion, the sight of Paul's silhouette cresting the dune unleashed a wave of weariness that etched a grimace across my features. The impending interaction loomed over me, an unwelcome spectre at the feast of my already depleted reserves of patience. Paul's approach, marked by an air of expectation, seemed to herald yet another requisition of my time or resources, a pattern all too familiar in the recent hours.

As he drew near, the lines of his intent already taking shape, I pre-empted his request with a suggestion to seek assistance from Luke. The words, "You'll have to ask Luke for crutches," spilled from my lips, a mix of fatigue-laced resignation and a faint glimmer of hope that this redirection might spare me from further demands on my already overstretched capacity to care.

Paul's gaze shifted towards Kain, who offered nothing more than a resigned shrug, his earlier plea seemingly evaporating into a silent acquiescence. As Paul's eyes found mine again, the weight of his question hung in the air between us. "Have you seen Luke?" he inquired, his voice carrying a mix of urgency and subtle concern.

I halted my actions, allowing myself a moment to sift through my recent memories. "No, I haven't seen him since that initial encounter when I first arrived," I replied, my voice tinged with a hint of introspection. The image of Luke, passing us with that characteristic briskness, flickered briefly in my mind's eye.

Observing Paul's reaction, I noted the furrows deepening on his brow as he rubbed his chin thoughtfully. Despite the encroaching shadows of my own exhaustion and the nagging tendrils of irritability, a spontaneous smile broke through my weary façade. There was something inherently engaging about Paul, perhaps a reflection of the light-hearted interludes that Gladys and I had shared with him. His idiosyncratic gestures and the animated expressions that danced across his face provided a peculiar sort of comfort, a fleeting respite from the relentless demands thrown at me.

After what seemed like an eternity in contemplation, Paul's demeanour shifted, signalling the end of his silent deliberations. His voice, now imbued with a newfound decisiveness, broke the lingering silence. "Beatrix," he began, anchoring his gaze onto mine, "I need you to source us a couple of caravans or motorhomes. They will make our living and sleeping arrangements a little more comfortable and also, hopefully, provide us with more safety than the tents currently do."

I hesitated, the weight of Paul's suggestion anchoring my feet to the ground while my mind raced through the myriad of implications. His ability to assume command in times of uncertainty had left an indelible mark on me. "But I don't have enough money for that kind of expense. How am I supposed to get them?" I blurted out, the words slipping from my lips before I could corral them into silence. The financial aspect of his request loomed large, casting a shadow over the initial flicker of possibility his words had ignited.

"You've got a Portal, a place to escape to where nobody can catch you," Paul retorted, his tone laced with a mix of encouragement and challenge. He paused, allowing the gravity of his statement to sink in, before adding, "I'm sure you have the creative abilities to pull the mission off," his words punctuated by a cheeky smile and a quirky hand gesture that resembled someone enthusiastically stabbing at their food with a fork.

I squinted at him, suspicion threading through my curiosity. *Did Luke spill the beans about the cutlery?* The thought that my purposeful collection of restaurant silverware was no longer a secret caused a ripple of unease. Yet, despite my rising skepticism, Paul's infectious energy began to seep into my veins, igniting a spark of reluctant excitement. His words, "a mission," echoed in my head, teasing out a reluctant smile from the corners of my lips.

The notion of embarking on a covert operation, armed with the enigmatic power of the Portal Key, sparked a thrill I hadn't known I craved. *Could this be the adventure that would wrench me from the mundane chains of my current life?* The idea of weaving through the fabric of reality, untouchable and elusive, sent a surge of adrenaline through my system. My heart, a once complacent companion, now hammered against my chest with a fervour, urging me to leap into the unknown.

Caught in the tug-of-war between reason and impulse, I found myself teetering on the brink of a decision that could either be a brilliant escapade or a reckless folly. "A mission, you say?" I echoed, the words tinged with a burgeoning sense of daring. The monotony of life with my parents, once a stifling cocoon, now felt like a shell begging to be shattered. *Was I ready to step through the Portal, not just as an escape, but as a challenger to my own limits?* The thought was both terrifying and exhilarating.

The façade of calm I erected on my face felt as fragile as a house of cards in the breeze, but it held as I uttered, "Sure. I'll do it." The words felt like stones in my mouth, heavy with the weight of the commitment they carried.

Paul's expression transformed instantaneously, his satisfaction blooming like a flower in fast-forward before it was swiftly overshadowed by a new concern. The quick shift only added to the knot of apprehension tightening in my stomach.

I bit my tongue, the taste of my own restraint bitter, as I braced for his next words. "By the way, where's Duke?" he inquired, his casual tone belied by the intensity in his eyes.

The question hit me like a splash of cold water. Duke. The poor dog's whereabouts suddenly became a glaring vacancy in my memory, an oversight that sent a pang of guilt through me. In a scramble to cover my tracks, I retorted, "What do you want first, Duke or the caravans?" My attempt at diversion, to sound nonchalant, belied a desperate hope that my oversight wasn't as transparent as it felt.

Paul's response, a medley of sighs and indecision, did little to ease the churning of my thoughts. "Get them in whatever order works the best for you," he said, his voice a mix of resignation and laissez-faire that I wasn't used to hearing from him. "I don't want to be too prescriptive... or restrictive."

I nodded, a bit too eagerly, perhaps, using the motion to mask the scoff itching to break free. Over the years, I had honed my ability to read others at the poker table, a skill that now allowed me to see the cracks in Paul's composed exterior. I clung to the hope that my own façade was more impenetrable, that my internal turmoil and the frantic search for Duke in the recesses of my memory were not as apparent as they felt.

❖

The list of tasks before me—Duke, Jarod, caravans—felt like a jigsaw puzzle with pieces from different boxes. I stepped into the cleanliness of the living room. Discussing Duke's whereabouts with Leigh was a conversation I wasn't ready to have, especially with the nagging guilt that I couldn't place Duke's last location. The caravans posed another problem; without the necessary funds, I knew I'd have to resort to less conventional means to acquire them. "Jarod it is," I murmured to myself, deciding to tackle the most straightforward task first.

Leigh's voice cut through my internal deliberations. "I'm ready to get going, if you are?" His hands left damp imprints on his clothes.

"Yeah," I responded, the word a buoy in the sea of my swirling thoughts. "I'm ready too."

"I assume Jarod isn't far from here?" he inquired, his brow furrowed slightly in anticipation of the journey ahead.

The geographic placement of Jarod's location flickered through my mind. Not too far, but not conveniently close either. "I'll call us a taxi," I declared, trying to sound more confident than I felt about our mode of transportation.

Leigh's counter was swift and logical. "I'm not sure that's a good idea. Our movements can be tracked. We'd be safer walking."

I was momentarily at a loss, my mouth opening and closing without producing sound, my mind scrambling for a solution. It was then that my gaze inadvertently swept across the kitchen, landing on the glint of metal in the corner of the bench. Jamie's car keys.

"What are you doing?" Leigh's curiosity piqued as he watched me move closer to the window, leaning over the sink to get a better view of the driveway.

"Bingo," I whispered, a surge of relief washing over me. The keys chimed in my grasp as I snatched them up, their jingle like music to my anxious heart. "Come on," I urged Leigh, my head gesturing toward the front door with newfound determination. "I'll drive us."

# PROPOSITION

## 1338.209.8

The main street of New Norfolk unfurled before us like a tapestry of everyday life, its vibrant hum punctuated by the quaint charm of its stores. As I steered the car to a stop, I could sense Leigh's curiosity peaking, his gaze ensnared by the antique store's inviting façade. "Is that where we're going?" he inquired, his voice a blend of bemusement and intrigue.

"No, not quite," I responded, my lips curving into a playful smile, savouring the little surprise I had in store. "We're headed to a little shop just over here," I indicated, nodding towards a modest establishment across the street, its unassuming appearance belying the vital role it was about to play.

Stepping into the pet shop was like entering a different realm, one ruled by a symphony of animal sounds and a kaleidoscope of movement. The air was thick with the scents of sawdust and animal dander. The shop was a riot of life; cages and tanks were arranged in meticulous rows, each housing its own little universe. Cats lounged with feline nonchalance, their eyes tracking our movements with detached interest. Puppies tumbled over each other in their eagerness to play, their yaps and barks a vibrant soundtrack to the shop's lively atmosphere. Rabbits and guinea pigs huddled in corners or nibbled on food, while the aquarium section was a mesmerising display of colour and movement, exotic fish gliding through their watery domains.

The familiar timbre of Johnny's voice sliced through the ambient noise of the pet shop, pulling me back from my brief immersion in the animal kingdom around us. "Beatrix, I haven't seen you here for a while," he called out, his approach marked by the swish of his green apron.

"I know, I've been busy," I responded, offering him a smile tinged with regret. My words, simple on the surface, carried a deeper significance—a coded message between old allies. "But I needed to pick up a few things for my reptiles, so I figured I'd stop by." The casual mention of reptiles was our agreed-upon signal, a subtle indicator of the true nature of my visit.

Johnny's acknowledgment was swift and understanding. "Ah, of course," he replied, his nod laden with unspoken knowledge. "You're wanting to see the other stuff?" His casual question, paired with a discreet gesture towards a nondescript door at the back of the shop, signalled the transition from public storefront to the clandestine purpose of our visit.

"Please," I confirmed, feeling a spark of anticipation ignite within me. My eyes, I hoped, conveyed the gratitude and urgency I felt, unable to express in words.

We navigated past the final row of tanks, their inhabitants oblivious to the layers of human intrigue unfolding around them. Johnny opened the door, revealing a small, dimly lit room that felt worlds away from the lively storefront we had just left. The hatch in the floor was already open, an invitation to the secrets that lay beneath.

With a brief nod of thanks to Johnny, I led Leigh to the staircase. The narrow steps descended into the basement's gloom, a stark contrast to the shop's vibrancy. Each step downward felt like a further detachment from the ordinary world above, our descent marking our transition into the realm of covert operations and hidden agendas.

The staircase creaked beneath our feet, its echoes bouncing off the close walls, amplifying the mix of anticipation and unease that emanated from Leigh. His presence behind me was a steady reminder of the shared journey we were on, his emotions palpable in the close confines of our descent.

At the staircase's end, the subterranean room unfolded before us, dimly lit yet unmistakably alive with an undercurrent of clandestine energy. Jarod stood at the room's core, a python draped around him like a statement of his connection to the wild and unpredictable.

"Maggie!" I couldn't contain my excitement, my voice a blend of joy and surprise as I approached the familiar creature. My fingers reached out, brushing against her scales, the sensation familiar and comforting. Maggie's response, a gentle flick of her tongue, felt like a silent acknowledgment of our bond.

"Hey, Beatrix," Jarod's voice, laced with a playful undertone, pulled my attention from Maggie. His smile was infectious, his eyes a spark of mischief in the dim light. "Glad you could finally show up."

A tinge of embarrassment coloured my response. "Sorry I'm late," I admitted, my voice carrying a note of regret. The myriad tasks that had delayed my arrival seemed trivial now, in the face of Jarod's casual acceptance. "I had to finish up a job before I could come," I added, skirting around the core of our visit, not yet ready to dive into the depths of our purpose here.

Jarod's shrug was a testament to the timelessness of our underground surroundings. "No problem, we've got all the time in the world down here," he said, his voice a blend of ease and detachment. "So, you've changed your mind about us working together again?"

His question hung in the air, a challenge and an invitation, stirring a whirlpool of thoughts and emotions within me. The weight of our past collaborations, the successes and the frictions, all came rushing back, mingling with the present tension and the uncertain future. In this secluded world, away from the sun's reach, the possibility of reigniting our partnership sparked a complex tapestry of hope, doubt, and determination.

Introducing Leigh to Jarod felt like bridging two worlds—my past with Jarod, tangled and complex, and my present, with Leigh, still so fresh and undefined. "I wanted to introduce Leigh to you properly," I said, using the introduction as a buffer to momentarily divert from Leigh's tempting offer. "You remember him from the casino the other night, don't you?" My hand swept toward Leigh, presenting him as more than just another face from the crowd at the casino.

"Yeah, I remember," Jarod responded, his hand extending toward Leigh with a hint of reluctance. The handshake was a formal acknowledgment, yet the air buzzed with an unspoken tension, a dance of unfamiliarity and caution. Leigh's grip was firm, despite the obvious unease that shimmered in his gaze.

Leigh's voice, laced with a mix of wonder and apprehension, broke the momentary silence. "So, what do you have down here?" he inquired, his eyes scanning the shadowy corners of the basement, where the outlines of various cages and tanks hinted at the hidden life within.

Jarod's reply, delivered with a playful wink, was quintessentially him—vague yet intriguing. "Oh, all sorts of things," he said, his tone light yet laden with the promise of secrets nestled in the depths of this underground sanctuary. "You never know what you might find in the secret basement of a pet shop."

I couldn't help but roll my eyes at Jarod's flair for the dramatic. Some things never change, and Jarod's love for mystique was one of them. Yet, beneath the surface of our banter and the curious glances exchanged between Leigh and Jarod, a current of seriousness pulsed through me.

Surrounded by the dim light and the peculiar chorus of sounds from the concealed creatures, my heart raced with a cocktail of emotions. The familiarity of Jarod's presence, the novelty of having Leigh by my side, and the gravity of our clandestine meeting—all these elements wove together, heightening my sense of urgency. It was time to peel away the veneer of casual introductions and cryptic exchanges. It was time to delve into the heart of why we were here, in the shadowy underbelly of New Norfolk, standing amidst the whispers of hidden beasts and buried agendas.

"Jarod, we need to talk to you about something of the utmost importance," I announced, my tone shedding any remnants of casual banter.

I watched as the levity drained from Jarod's face, replaced by a focused attentiveness. "What is it?" he inquired, his usual lighthearted demeanour giving way to earnest concern.

Leigh, caught up in the moment's urgency, looked to me, his eyes flickering with a mix of resolve and uncertainty. Without waiting for my cue, he spilled our secret. "Beatrix and I are Guardians," he declared, his voice a mix of pride and nervous energy.

Jarod's reaction was unexpected—a chuckle, as if the gravity of Leigh's words hadn't fully landed. "Come again?" he asked, an eyebrow raised in bemusement.

Leigh started to repeat himself, but I intervened, steering the conversation in a direction that might allow better context. "Do you know why you were released from police custody so easily?" I questioned, my tone firm, aiming to draw his attention to the larger picture while masking my annoyance at Leigh's premature revelation.

Jarod's hand instinctively moved to the cut above his eye, a reminder of the brutality he had faced. "I wouldn't say it was that easy," he retorted, the humour fading from his expression as he recalled the unjustified violence from Officer Cribthorpe at the casino.

The remembrance of Cribthorpe stirred a potent mix of anger and revulsion within me. The officer's unprovoked aggression towards Jarod and his sleazy advances towards me at the casino were vivid in my memory, fuelling a burning desire for justice. Standing there, in the dimly lit basement, surrounded by the sounds of unseen animals, I felt a surge of resolve. It was time to reveal the depth of the corruption we were up against and to enlist Jarod's help in our fight—not just as a former ally, but as a fellow victim of the system we were determined to challenge.

"I was told they had made an error of judgment and that all charges had been dropped." His voice, tinged with skepticism, echoed Leigh's words to me earlier about the so-called 'error of judgment.'

I felt a surge of urgency, needing to make Jarod understand the gravity of our position. "They were going to bring you down, Jarod, but Leigh put a stop to it. He has–" My words were cut short by Leigh's cautionary glance, a silent plea to tread carefully with our revelations.

"Beatrix," Leigh's warning was clear, yet I knew we needed Jarod's trust and cooperation. I nodded subtly, acknowledging his concern, then turned back to Jarod. "It's okay," I said, striving for a balance between transparency and discretion. "Leigh has connections in the police department. Connections that can only protect us for so long." My words were deliberate, designed to underscore our shared vulnerability and the transient nature of our safety net.

"Hang on a minute. Let's go back to this Guardian thing," Jarod demanded, his gaze shifting between us, seeking the truth in our faces.

The tension in the room was palpable, a tangible cloud of doubt and suspicion. It was then that Maggie, ever perceptive to the emotions around her, began to move restlessly on Jarod's shoulders. I watched her stretch out toward me, a silent witness to our human complexities. Stepping closer, I allowed her to transition to my shoulder, her presence a welcome, grounding contact. Her tongue flickered against my skin, a reminder of the natural world's simple realities amidst our web of human intrigues and uncertainties.

The basement's dim light seemed to focus on the Portal Key in Leigh's hand, a beacon of our otherworldly connection. "We have devices, called Portal Keys," Leigh elaborated, his voice steady, but I could sense the undercurrent of awe he felt for the technology he held. The device, simple in design yet profound in function, gleamed subtly in his palm, a testament to the extraordinary portal it accessed.

"An alternate reality," I chimed in, keen to provide clarity but also to underscore the weight of our revelation.

Leigh's next words were tinged with a hint of uncertainty, his eyes flicking to mine as if seeking reassurance. "We're not really sure what it is," he admitted, his honesty painting a picture of our still-unfolding understanding of the Portal keys' powers.

Impatience nipped at my calm, prompting a sharper response than I intended. "It doesn't really matter what it is," I retorted, my gaze locking with Jarod's. I needed him to grasp the seriousness, not get lost in the details. "This is where Jamie is."

Jarod's question, "Can he get back?" was laced with genuine concern.

Leigh's response, "No," resonated with finality in the cramped space. "Anybody that passes through the Portal that isn't a Guardian becomes trapped in that new world forever."

Seizing the moment to solidify our case, I added, "Clivilius." The name of the alternate world rolled off my tongue, imbued with a sense of otherness yet tinged with a strange familiarity. "The world is called Clivilius." Naming it felt like giving shape to our fears and challenges, an attempt to make the intangible tangible, to bring Jarod fully into our circle of trust and shared destiny.

Leigh extended the Portal Key to Jarod, a serious expression on his face. "Beatrix and Jamie could really use your help. We want you to take this device and become a Guardian like us."

Jarod's incredulity was a palpable force in the cramped, shadow-laden space, his head shaking a visible sign of his struggle to reconcile our words with reality. "You've both lost your minds," he declared, his voice tinged with a mix of skepticism and concern.

His disbelief stung, but I understood it. The realms we spoke of were beyond the ordinary, challenging the very fabric of what we accepted as reality. "It's true," I insisted, my voice firm, bolstering Leigh's claims. "We need all the help we can get."

Jarod's frown deepened, his mind visibly wrestling with our assertions. "I see," he uttered, the gears of his thoughts turning audibly in the silence that followed. "Look, Beatrix, you know that I'll do anything I can to help you, but this all sounds so unbelievable. How can I trust that this is true?" His question, honest and raw, echoed in the dimly lit room, hanging in the air like a challenge.

"I know it's hard to believe," I confessed, acknowledging the vast chasm between our extraordinary reality and the mundane world most lived in. "I was just as skeptical the first time I heard about Clivilius, Guardians, and Portal Keys. But it really is all true." My words were a bridge, an attempt to span the gap between disbelief and the astonishing truth.

Jarod's response was immediate, a reflex born of a life spent discerning truth from fiction. "Okay, prove it," he demanded, his arms folding defensively across his chest. His challenge, a clear demand for tangible evidence, hung between us, a new hurdle to overcome.

The Portal Key felt cool and significant in my grasp as I presented it to Jarod, its presence a tangible link to the extraordinary truths I was trying to convey. "This is my Portal Key," I stated, imbuing my voice with a sense of gravity to match the item's importance. "There are five in total for every Guardian group, and they are the only way to open the Portal."

Jarod's gaze lingered on the device, his expression a mixture of curiosity and skepticism. "How do I know I can trust you?" he pressed, his eyes searching mine for deceit. "How do I know this isn't some kind of trap?"

His doubt stung, more than I anticipated. After all we'd been through, the notion that he would question my sincerity now felt like a bitter pill to swallow. "You have to trust your instincts, Jarod," I urged, striving to inject a blend of confidence and sincerity into my tone. "I know it's hard to believe, but I promise you it's all real. And anyway, since when have you ever doubted trusting me before?" The irritation in my voice was palpable, my frustration at his mistrust breaking through my composed exterior.

Jarod paused, his hand absentmindedly stroking his chin, a gesture I recognised as his thinking pose. "I suppose that's true," he conceded after a moment, his skepticism beginning to wane. "And we've done some pretty crazy shit before."

I latched onto his acknowledgment, eager to reinforce the bond of our shared past and the extraordinary nature of our current situation. "Exactly!" I exclaimed, feeling a glimmer of hope. "Just think of this as another one of those times." My words were an invitation, a call to embrace the unknown with the same trust and camaraderie that had seen us through past challenges.

I nodded toward Leigh. The moment Leigh activated his Portal Key, reality as we knew it seemed to pause, bending to the will of the device. The burst of light from the key was not just illumination—it was a spectacle of colour, a visual symphony that captivated the senses. As the cabinet beside me became the canvas for this display, its surface dancing with colours more vivid than nature itself, I couldn't help but relive the awe of my first encounter with a Portal.

"Shit," Jarod's reaction was a mix of disbelief and wonder, his voice barely above a whisper as his gaze fixed on the transformed cabinet. "I've never seen anything like this before."

I couldn't suppress my smile, buoyed by his astonishment and the shared experience of witnessing something truly beyond the ordinary. "It's incredible, isn't it?" I echoed his sentiment, my eyes still on the mesmerising colours. "The Portal is a gateway to other worlds, and the Portal Keys are the only way to access it. Each Portal Key has an owner and can only be used by that owner. I can't enter through Leigh's Portal, and he can't enter through mine."

The reality of our situation crystallised as Leigh stepped through the Portal, his form swallowed by the cabinet only to emerge elsewhere, in a world unseen and unimaginable to those who've never crossed the threshold. The Portal snapped shut behind him, leaving behind a lingering echo of its presence.

"Holy shit," Jarod's whisper was a testament to the impact of what he'd just witnessed. "He just walked through the side of a fucking cabinet."

"Well, technically he's now in Clivilius," I clarified, grounding the magical in reality, or at least the version of reality we were now a part of.

Jarod's struggle for words was palpable, his mind grappling with the implications of what he'd seen. The line between the possible and the impossible had not just been blurred; it had been erased and redrawn in fantastical hues. Standing there, in the aftermath of the Portal's closure, I knew we had crossed a pivotal threshold in our mission. Jarod's understanding of our world—and his place within it—was forever altered, just as mine had been when I first encountered the enigmatic beauty of a Portal.

The return of Leigh through the Portal was as surreal as his departure, the cabinet erupting into a kaleidoscope of colours before settling back into its mundane state. Jarod's reaction, a mix of awe and disbelief, resonated deeply with me.

"That's fucking insane," Jarod exclaimed, his voice a cocktail of excitement and bewilderment as he edged closer to the colours.

Leigh's subtle gesture, a mere flick of his hand, extinguished the vibrant display, returning the cabinet to its ordinary state. The transition from the extraordinary back to the ordinary seemed almost anticlimactic, yet it underscored the immense power at our minds fingertips.

"So, are you in?" Leigh's question cut through the thick air of wonder, grounding us back to the reason for our gathering.

A mischievous smile played at the corners of Jarod's mouth.

"Come on, Jarod. You know we make a formidable team. Imagine what you could do with power like this," I said to him.

Jarod's smile, tinged with mischief, hinted at the adventurer within him, yet his hesitation spoke volumes. "I need some time to let it sink in and consider my options. And I have a few loose ends I need to tie up before I can fully commit to anything," he confessed, his internal struggle evident in his furrowed brow and contemplative gaze.

Leigh's nod was one of empathy, a recognition of the permanency of the choice Jarod faced. "That's a reasonable request. Take all the time you need to think things through. We'll be here when you're ready."

I echoed Leigh's sentiment with a nod of my own, understanding the importance of Jarod making this decision independently. The urgency of our situation pressed against my mind like a ticking clock, reminding me of the stakes we faced. Yet, I recognised that true commitment couldn't be rushed or imposed. Jarod's journey to acceptance and understanding was his own.

The shift in conversation from the ethereal to the practical was jarring, yet necessary. The pressing needs of the caravan mission given to me by Paul, grounded me back to the reality of my situation, a world where resources were as crucial as courage. "In the meantime, I need to borrow some of your cash," I stated plainly to Jarod, acutely aware of the stash he kept.

"I'll pay you back as soon as I can." My promise hung in the air, a half-truth at best. The complexities of our situation, intertwined with the potential of never needing to settle debts in a traditional sense, clouded the sincerity of my assurance. Yet, it was a necessary façade, a part of the dance of trust and cooperation we were engaged in.

Jarod's compliance was a relief, his actions as he led us to the safe a blend of familiarity and routine. Watching him unlock the safe, the ease of his movements spoke of a man well-acquainted with the dualities of security and risk. As he counted out the bills, the crisp sound of the currency being separated was oddly reassuring in the dim, cluttered space of the basement.

"Take what you need," Jarod's words were generous, yet I detected the underlying tension, a subtle acknowledgment of the stakes at play. I accepted the money, feeling its weight not just in my hands but in my conscience. This cash, a tangible representation of trust and alliance, would fuel my next steps.

The thought of the caravans, another piece in the puzzle of my Guardian responsibilities, loomed in my mind. The funds in my hand were more than just currency; they were a lifeline, a means to secure a crucial element of my mission. As I pocketed the money, I couldn't shake the blend of gratitude and the heavy sense of responsibility that came with it.

"Do you need some too, Leigh?" Jarod asked, the simplicity of the question belying the depth of its implications.

Leigh's reaction was immediate, his surprise evident in his wide eyes, but quickly replaced by a casual acceptance. "If you're going to be handing it out like that, sure," he responded, a grin playing on his lips.

My shock at Leigh's nonchalance was palpable. To accept money so freely from someone who was, in essence, still a stranger to him, struck a discordant note in my mind.

Leigh, perceptive to my discomfort, addressed me directly. "Funding our Guardian activities is a never-ending battle. I've learned never to turn down an opportunity when it's presented," he explained, his voice carrying a hint of pragmatism born from experience.

My glare lingered on Leigh, unsoftened by his justification. In this murky world we navigated, where lines blurred between right and wrong, his readiness to embrace such pragmatism shouldn't have felt unexpected to me, yet somehow it caught me off guard.

Maggie's hiss cut through the tension, a serpentine reminder of the natural instincts that governed even our extraordinary world. Leigh's hand retracted from his reach for my shoulder, a small concession to the discomfort he had unwittingly provoked.

"I'll leave the two of you to discuss things," Leigh announced, his tone a mix of respect and resignation. As he activated his Portal Key, the basement was once again awash in the ethereal glow of the Portal's colours. "It was good to see you again, Jarod," he offered, a farewell that bridged the gap between acquaintances and newfound allies.

With Leigh's departure, the weight of the moment settled on my shoulders. The dance of colours faded, leaving behind the outcome of our choices, and the alliances we forged. Jarod's presence, the tangible cash in my possession, and Leigh's pragmatic acceptance of our circumstances—all converged in a moment of clarity. My path was fraught with moral ambiguities, but my commitment to our Guardian cause remained the beacon guiding me through the darkness.

❖

As Jarod and I delved deeper into the intricacies of Clivilius and the life of a Guardian, a flame of purpose ignited within me, a feeling I hadn't truly experienced since the sorrowful days following Brody's passing. The conversation wasn't just about plans and strategies; it was a rekindling of the bond Jarod and I shared, a revival of a camaraderie that had once been a cornerstone of my life.

My mind, ever wandering, drifted to Maggie, my cherished python. She wasn't just a pet; she was a companion, a silent confidante who had been by my side through thick and thin. The memories of our time together at the antique store were vivid, filled with moments of silent understanding and mutual companionship. When circumstances forced me to leave her behind, it was with a heavy heart and a promise to myself that our separation would be temporary.

Now, as possibilities unfolded before me, the dilemma of Maggie's future weighed on my mind. The stark reality was that she couldn't traverse the worlds with me. The rules that governed our travels between Clivilius and Earth were unyielding, especially for those not bound by the Guardians' call.

Yet, as I glanced around the dimly lit basement, an idea began to form. With Jarod's support and the resources at our disposal, perhaps there was a way to create a haven for Maggie and other creatures like her. The notion of building a sanctuary in Clivilius, a safe haven where Johnny could care for them, offered a glimmer of hope.

The plan was fledgling, filled with 'maybes' and 'what ifs,' but it was a start. The thought of providing a sanctuary not just for Maggie but for other beings caught between worlds sparked a new sense of determination in me.

The sudden vibration of my phone, persistent and insistent, pulled me sharply away from the world of Guardians and Portals, dragging me back to a reality I had momentarily escaped. My mother's calls had been a background noise, easily dismissed until now. The text on the screen, abrupt and alarming, cut through the basement's dim light like a cold blade:

**Wendy Cramer 18:17PM:** *Why the hell is there a dead dog wrapped in a blanket in your bathroom!?*

The words seemed to echo in my mind, each one a hammer blow to my composure. "Shit," slipped from my lips, a whisper of confusion and growing horror. Jarod's voice, the conversation we were having, it all receded into a blur as the urgency of the message took hold.

"I need to go," I said, my voice a mix of urgency and fear. The room, with its secrets and plans, suddenly felt suffocating, the weight of my mother's message urging me to action.

Jarod's concern was palpable, his brow creased as he stood up. "Is everything okay?" he asked, his voice a blend of confusion and worry.

"I don't know," I confessed, my heart racing as scenarios and possibilities whirled chaotically in my mind. "I need to go home and find out what's going on. I'll see you soon." My words felt hollow, an inadequate response to the turmoil that churned within me.

"Wait, Beatrix," Jarod interjected, his determination cutting through my panic. "I'll come with you. If you really want me to become a... Guardian... then you need to be able to trust me too. You shouldn't have to face whatever this is alone."

My hesitation was a tangible thing, a moment suspended between Jarod's offer of companionship and the daunting prospect of confronting the unpredictable drama that awaited me at home. The image of my mother, bewildered and distressed by the inexplicable presence of Duke, gripped my mind. Duke, who I had unintentionally brought back to Earth and left in a place he shouldn't have been. The severity of the situation, the potential repercussions, it all weighed heavily on me.

"No, Jarod," I finally uttered, my voice steady despite the turmoil inside. "I appreciate the offer, but I have to do this alone. You know how my mother can be when she is stressed." My words were an admission of the delicate balance I needed to maintain, a balance that might not withstand additional variables, even well-intentioned ones.

Jarod's laughter, a brief respite from the tension, echoed in the basement. "Yeah, I've experienced the wrath of her stress firsthand, remember," he said, a hint of levity in his voice that quickly faded into a solemn expression.

"How could I forget?" I responded, the memory of his previous encounters with my mother adding a layer of shared history to our current predicament. But there was no time for reminiscences. Duke's situation, the urgent need to address the confusion and distress at home, pressed on me with increasing weight.

Stepping through the Portal, I braced myself for the confrontation ahead. The myriad possibilities of what might unfold raced through my mind as I crossed the threshold, leaving Jarod and the basement behind.

# FAREWELL DUKE

## 1338.209.9

"Luke?" My voice barely cut through the silence, a sharp whisper that betrayed my shock at the sight of his familiar silhouette. It loomed against the backdrop of the glaring hallway light, an intrusive luminescence that invaded the serene sanctuary of my bedroom. This brightness contrasted starkly with the whimsical dance of colours emanating from my Portal, painting abstract stories on the walls—stories abruptly interrupted by Luke's unexpected presence.

As he pivoted on his heels, a swift, fluid motion that carried a hint of urgency, the Portal's vibrant light receded, as if startled into submission. The room was suddenly engulfed in darkness, a consuming void that seemed to amplify the tension hanging in the air.

"What the hell is Duke doing here?" Luke's whisper, though hushed, cut through the darkness with an edge of accusation, a sharpness that hinted at barely contained agitation.

I felt my hands rise, almost of their own accord, a subconscious shield against the onslaught of his words. "Luke, I can explain," I stammered, the words emerging as a fragile defence, a feeble attempt to bridge the chasm of misunderstanding widening between us. My mind was a tumultuous whirlpool, swirling with questions about how Luke could have unearthed Duke's presence.

"Whose idea was it? Jamie's?" His questions flew like arrows, each one laden with suspicion and the weight of unspoken accusations.

"No," I countered sharply, my head shaking in a reflexive dismissal, even as my heart raced with the anxiety of confrontation.

"Paul's?"

"It was mine," I confessed, the words hissing between clenched teeth, a turbulent mixture of defensiveness and regret churning within me. The confusion within me swelled, a tumultuous sea threatening to engulf my resolve. *How could anyone besides Paul or Jamie have known?* It was a question that loomed large, its shadow cast over the room, adding to the oppressive weight of the darkness.

"What... Where... What the hell were you thinking?" Luke's voice fractured, a reflection of his internal turmoil, escalating in pitch as his composure began to unravel. Each word punctuated the growing rift, his confusion and disbelief mirroring the chaos that threatened to overwhelm my own thoughts.

In this charged moment, the room felt like a battleground of emotions and unspoken truths, the darkness around us a fitting backdrop for the turmoil within, each of us isolated on our islands of misunderstanding, trying to bridge the gap with words that seemed woefully inadequate.

A humanly figure emerged from the shadows behind Luke, materialising like a ghost. With a discernible click, a stark, unforgiving light flooded the room, banishing the shadows and laying bare the tension that hung in the air like a thick fog.

"Beatrix!" Mother's voice sliced through the tension. Her tone was one of surprise, tinged with an undercurrent of curiosity. "I didn't hear you get home." Her words, innocuous on the surface, sent a ripple of panic through me.

*Oh, please no*, I pleaded inwardly, my mind racing with dreadful scenarios. The hope that my mother hadn't been the one to spill the beans to Luke clung to me, fragile as a spider's web. Yet, recalling the cryptic message I had received earlier, that dreaded possibility now seemed highly plausible.

"And Luke, when did you–?" Her voice trailed off, the unfinished question hanging in the air like an ominous cloud.

"We haven't been home for long," I interjected hastily, my voice a blend of urgency and feigned nonchalance. I was desperate to steer the conversation away from dangerous waters, to prevent my mother from delving into a line of inquiry that would surely lead to an uncomfortable revelation. "Luke and I were just discussing where we should bury Duke," I fabricated smoothly, the lie slipping from my lips with practiced ease.

"Your father is taking care of it," my mother retorted, her voice laced with a hint of disapproval. She stood with her hands planted firmly on her hips, her posture radiating a mix of authority and disappointment.

I could feel Luke's gaze on me, intense and questioning. His eyes, wide with disbelief and a hint of accusation, sought answers I didn't have. I was as adrift in the sea of uncertainty as he was, unaware of my parents' clandestine plans.

Suddenly, a sound from outside shattered the uneasy stillness—a car door slamming shut, followed by the growl of an engine springing to life. It was a clarion call, propelling Luke and me toward the bedroom window with a shared impulse.

We peered out, our faces close, our breath fogging the glass. Outside, the backyard was shrouded in darkness, the silhouettes of trees swaying gently in the night breeze. There was no sign of the car or its occupants, only the enigmatic dance of shadows and the whisper of leaves, as if nature itself was complicit in the night's secrets.

"Where is he going?" The words tumbled out of my mouth as I spun around, my hip colliding awkwardly with the edge of the dresser, sending a sharp jolt of pain up my side. But the physical discomfort was a mere backdrop to the turmoil swirling in my mind.

Mum's expression shifted, a gentle softening around her eyes that contrasted with the tension that had etched itself onto her features moments earlier. "To yours, Luke," she revealed, her voice carrying a hint of reluctance, as if she was a reluctant bearer of inconvenient truths.

"Tell him we'll meet him there," Luke interjected quickly, his tone laced with an urgency that seemed to stem from a well of unresolved emotions. His fingers fidgeted with the small Portal Key, its metallic surface glinting in the light as it rolled between his digits, betraying his growing restlessness.

"Luke!" My voice was a sharp hiss, cutting through the air as I reached out, grabbing his arm with a firm grip to halt his retreat. It was a desperate bid for connection, for understanding, in a moment brimming with confusion.

"What?" His retort was swift, a snap born of frustration as his piercing eyes met mine. In that instant, they seemed to darken, a storm brewing behind his glare, reflecting the tumultuous sea of emotions churning within him.

My gaze dropped to the device in his hand, a silent plea for discretion. "Not here," I whispered, my voice a mere breath, yet heavy with implication. It was a reminder of the secrets that the Portal Key represented.

Luke's response was immediate and visceral. His hand clenched around the device, his knuckles whitening with the intensity of his grip.

Seeking to divert attention from the Portal Key and its associated risks, I turned my eyes back to my mother. "I'll call Dad and ask him to come back here," I declared, attempting to inject a note of assertiveness into my voice as I reached for my phone.

"I doubt he'll answer you while he's driving," mother countered, her voice steady, imbued with the practical wisdom that often underscored her words. "You know he's sensible like that." Her words, meant to be reassuring, instead felt like another layer of complexity added to the already intricate tapestry of our predicament, reminding me of the intricate dance of decisions and consequences we were all entangled in.

I knew mother was right, yet the stubborn ember of hope inside me refused to be snuffed out. My finger hesitated over the call button before pressing down, a small act of defiance against the tide of rationality. The dial tone hummed in my ear, a prelude to silence, but then a faint, mocking echo of a ring floated up from downstairs.

"Oh, I think that might be your father's phone," mother's voice cut through the tension, her words laced with a tinge of realisation as she pivoted on her heels, her movements swift with a newfound purpose as she exited the room to investigate.

"Shit," the curse slipped from my lips, a whisper of frustration as I trailed after her.

"Beatrix," Luke's voice, sharp and commanding, halted me in my tracks. His hand found my arm, a firm grip that drew my attention back to him. "Let's get out of here," he implored, his voice a blend of determination and desperation, tugging me back toward the sanctuary of my room.

"What about Mum?" The question emerged from me, a flicker of concern, even as I was drawn back into the room by Luke's insistent pull.

Luke's brow furrowed, a shadow of worry crossing his features. "I'm sure she'll just assume that we left through the front door," he reasoned, his eyes locking with mine, silently beseeching me to acquiesce.

"Fine," I conceded with a shrug, a gesture of reluctant agreement, though a part of me clung to a sliver of rebellion. "I'll meet you there in a minute."

His eyes narrowed, a flicker of suspicion igniting within them as he gauged my sincerity.

Exhaling a loud, exasperated huff, I sought to dispel his doubts. "I'm just going to run downstairs and slam the front door. It'll make it more believable," I explained, a plan forming amidst the maelstrom of thoughts. "I've already got enough explaining to do with Duke. I don't need to add our silent vanishing to the list."

"Okay," Luke relented, his expression easing, a hint of trust breaking through the clouds of his skepticism.

"But in case she catches me, don't wait for me," I added, laying out a contingency plan, preparing for the worst while hoping for the best.

"We've got nowhere else to be," he responded, his shoulders drooping in a gesture of resigned acceptance.

"I know," I acknowledged, a note of agreement in my voice, even as I braced myself for the potential storm of interrogation that awaited. "But you know mother's not going to let me get away so easily without a full assault of questions."

Luke's grunt was loud, a gruff sound that carried a mix of frustration and resignation. "Don't get caught then," he advised, a simple directive that hung between us, heavy with unspoken implications, as we stood on the precipice of our next uncertain steps.

Giving Luke a final nod, an unspoken pact sealed between us, I pivoted and darted out of the room, my footsteps a hasty patter against the floor. The urgency thrummed through me, a clear directive: *I need to hurry if I'm going to get to the front door before Mum returns with Dad's phone.* The thought was a mantra, propelling me forward, my heart racing in tandem with my steps.

As I reached the front door, my hands, slick with a sheen of nervous sweat, fumbled with the smooth, cold metal of the knob. My attempts to turn it were futile; it was locked, an unforeseen obstacle in my hasty plan. A soft groan threatened to escape my lips, but I stifled it, aware of the need for stealth.

Then, like a thunderclap shattering the silence, my mother's voice rang out, "Beatrix!" The sharpness, tinged with worry, struck me, freezing me in place. The temptation to bolt, to dash away from the looming confrontation, surged within me. Yet, caution held me fast—*it's too risky*, I admonished myself, and with a deep, steadying breath, I turned to face her.

"Where's Luke?" The question was direct, her gaze piercing, as her eyes narrowed and her brow creased with an amalgam of concern and suspicion.

"He's just left to go meet father at his place," I responded, my voice steadier than I felt. The truth, or a version of it, slipped from my lips with an ease that belied the tumult churning within me.

There was a pause, a heavy, laden silence as my mother's stare bore into me. It was as if she were trying to peel back the layers, to discern the veracity of my words. I stood there, under her scrutinising gaze, acutely aware of the impending deluge of questions that would surely follow. In that moment, suspended between truths and half-truths, I braced myself for the interrogation I knew was inevitable, a storm on the horizon that was swiftly drawing near.

"Beatrix," my mother's voice was a soft murmur, a stark contrast to the sharpness that had pierced the air moments earlier. She advanced towards me with hesitant steps, each one measured and laden with an unspoken tension. As she halted, a weary sigh escaped her lips, her shoulders drooping as if burdened by an invisible weight.

The subtle shift in her demeanour drew me in, igniting a flicker of concern within me. The issue at hand, veiled in mystery, beckoned my focus, urging me to probe deeper. I decided that Luke's wait could be extended by a few crucial minutes.

Stepping away from the obstinate front door, I bridged the gap between my mother and me. "You said earlier that you and Dad had something that you wanted to discuss with me. What's the matter?" The question emerged from me, tinged with a mix of curiosity and apprehension, my pulse quickening with each passing second.

"We really should wait for your father to return," she deflected, her hand fluttering in a dismissive gesture, her eyes darting away from mine, as if the truth was too burdensome to be borne in her gaze alone.

Yet, I couldn't let it lie. A knot of anxiety tightened in my stomach, the possibilities swirling in my mind like dark storm clouds. "Are you sick?" The question was out before I could temper it, my voice threaded with a raw concern.

She responded with a shake of her head, her grey locks swaying softly, a silent reassurance that at least one of my fears was unfounded.

"Is it my father?" The words were heavier, sinking with the weight of another dreaded possibility.

"No, Beatrix," she responded, her eyes finally lifting to meet mine, a clear, if troubled, connection. "It's about your sister."

"Gladys?" The name slipped out, laced with surprise. The thought that my sister would be the subject of such a sombre family discussion was unexpected, disorienting.

"Do you have another sister that your father and I don't know about?" Her attempt at humour, a light jest in the heavy air, barely grazed the surface of the tension that enshrouded us.

My impatience bubbled to the surface, manifesting in a sharp gesture for my mother to expedite her revelations. The urgency of the situation with Luke and Duke gnawed at my conscience, yet the unfolding mystery demanded my immediate attention.

"I didn't think anything of it at the time, but the name kept bothering me," she confessed, her voice a murmur laced with unease, reflecting the worry etching deeper into her features.

"What name?" My inquiry was laced with genuine confusion, my brow furrowing as I tried to sift through my memory for any significant mention.

"Cody," she announced, her tone imbued with a matter-of-factness that belied the gravity of the revelation.

"Cody?" The name echoed in my ears, a sudden jolt that forced me to mask my reaction, to hide the surge of anxiety that name provoked.

"Yes," she affirmed, her eyes locking onto mine, as if trying to unearth the secrets buried in my reaction. "You asked us a few days ago whether your father or I had heard of anyone named Cody."

"I vaguely remember," I lied, the memory crystal clear in my mind now, taunting me with the consequences of my past inquiries.

My mother's posture shifted, a physical manifestation of her discomfort, as the air around us thickened with unspoken tensions.

"Perhaps we should sit?" she proposed, a gentle nod toward the living room suggesting a more formal setting for the discussion.

I hesitated, torn. The reminder of my responsibilities toward Luke and Duke tugged at me, yet the gnawing curiosity and the potential implications of my mother's information held me rooted to the spot. "Can you give me the abridged version now and then when I get home with my father you can tell me the full version?" I proposed, seeking a compromise that would quell my rising anxiety while not abandoning my commitments.

"That sounds reasonable. I'll do my best," she acquiesced, her steps toward the living room slow and measured, as if each one carried the weight of the impending disclosure.

Trailing behind her, my thoughts churned tumultuously, a whirlpool of anticipation and dread. As my mother launched into the narrative of her recent visit to Gladys, I leaned against the wall, my body seeking support as my mind wrestled with the flood of incoming information. I was on the brink of reminding her to condense her tale when her words struck a chord, snapping my focus back with the precision of an arrow hitting its target.

She detailed the mundane beginnings of their visit—my father's chore of lawn mowing and her accompanying him, a veneer for her true intent of indulging in neighbourly gossip. With Gladys absent, my mother had utilised the spare key to enter the house. Once inside, she nonchalantly brewed herself a cup of coffee, an act so ordinary yet now tinged with the prelude to something more sinister.

Seated at the kitchen table, her gaze had wandered to the window, a casual glance that morphed into a scrutinising stare as she noticed a man—an anomaly in the otherwise serene domestic landscape. This stranger, lurking with an unsettling presence, had drawn my mother out, her protective instincts flaring as she confronted him. His refusal to reveal his identity and his abrupt departure only deepened the mystery, painting his intentions in shades of dubious grey.

The narrative took a sharper turn as my mother connected this encounter with my casual mention of Gladys's possible romantic involvement. The subsequent discussion with my father had unveiled a chilling coincidence: he too had encountered the man, who claimed he was waiting for Gladys. This detail, a seemingly innocuous thread in the fabric of daily life, now seemed like a glaring signal, a piece of a puzzle that I couldn't yet complete but which undeniably bore the mark of significance.

The uncertainty swirling around the stranger's identity gnawed at me, yet I clung to the belief that Cody, despite the mystery shrouding him, was not a figure to fear. "Cody and Gladys have been seeing each other for a few months now," I ventured, my voice a blend of reassurance and a subtle plea for understanding, aiming to soothe my mother's evident anxiety. "Cody might look tough, but he is completely harmless."

Her eyebrow arched, a silent but potent expression of skepticism. "Oh, really? From the way you were asking about him the other morning, I would have guessed that you hadn't met the man before?" The words were sharp, a mirror reflecting my own deception back at me.

A wave of unease washed over me, my nerves tightening like strings on a violin. I swallowed, my throat suddenly parched as I realised the depth of the corner into which I had painted myself. *My mouth has really gotten me into trouble this time*, the thought echoed in my head, a grim chorus accompanied by the sensation of my tongue tracing the arid landscape of my lips.

"Best you talk to Gladys about it," I deflected, the words tumbling out as I rose from the chair, eager for an escape from the escalating scrutiny. "I had better go and see Luke." The excuse was flimsy, a transparent veil over my growing desperation to retreat from the conversation.

As I moved toward the door, a heavy sigh from the living room trailed after me, laden with unspoken words and lingering tensions. "Yes, well, that is another matter we will talk about when you and your father get back," my mother's voice reached me, a reminder of the unresolved issues that awaited.

With a quick glance ensuring my mother's absence, confirmed by the mundane sounds of kitchen activity, I executed my plan. I unlocked the front door, and opened and closed with a deliberate clamour, a theatrical performance meant to deceive. Yet, instead of embarking on a covert trek back to my sanctuary, I opted for a more direct escape. Pressing my hand against the Portal Key, I activated the device against the door, the familiar hum and swirl of colours enveloping me as I stepped through, leaving behind the kitchen's clatter, my mother's suspicions, and the looming spectre of family secrets yet to be unravelled.

❖

Navigating the shadowy expanse of the study, I felt a shroud of darkness envelop me, an almost tangible presence that seemed intent on consuming every speck of light. The hallway stretched before me, its obscurity only challenged by a weak luminescence emanating from the living room, a distant beacon in the oppressive gloom. Approaching the doorway, I paused, drawing in a deep breath to steel myself for the unknown, every sense alert and straining to detect any hint of movement or life.

A sudden, soft sound arrested my progress. Faint, yet unmistakably human, sniffles sliced through the silence, pulling me toward their source with a mix of apprehension and urgency. Treading lightly, the plush carpet beneath my feet muffling my approach, I moved closer, drawn by the increasing clarity of the emotional display unfolding just beyond the doorway.

"Luke?" My voice, a hushed murmur in the quiet, broke the stillness, laden with concern and confusion.

The only response was a loud snort, a stark, raw sound that punctuated the continued sniffling.

"Luke?" I repeated, my concern deepening as my hand, almost of its own accord, reached for the light switch, flooding the room with illumination and revealing the poignant tableau before me.

There he was—Luke, an image of vulnerability, seated cross-legged on the bed. The sight tugged at my heartstrings, his eyes brimming with unshed tears, red and swollen from crying, his cheeks glistening with the trails of his sorrow. In his embrace, cradled with a tenderness that belied his usual strength, was Duke.

Luke sniffled again, a sound that resonated with the rawness of his emotions, painting a picture of a moment caught between personal grief and the shared understanding of loss.

"Oh, Luke," I murmured, the words barely escaping as a sigh, my heart sinking under the weight of his sorrow. The dilemma of whether to draw closer or maintain a respectful distance tugged at me, yet the silent plea in Luke's demeanour guided my steps closer, until I found myself sitting delicately on the edge of the bed, the space between us charged with shared grief.

"I could have done more," Luke's words emerged through a haze of tears, his voice a fragile thread frayed with regret.

With a gentle, tentative motion, I reached out, placing my hand on his shoulder, an anchor in the tumult of his despair. "I know you did everything you could, Luke. You're a great dog dad, and Duke was lucky to have you." The words felt inadequate, too feeble to shoulder the weight of his mourning, but they were all I had, offered with a sincerity that I hoped would provide a sliver of comfort.

Luke's gaze, heavy with loss, lifted to meet mine, a silent testament to his inner turmoil. "I just wish I could have done more. I feel like I let him down." His voice cracked, laying bare the depth of his self-reproach.

In response, my arms instinctively wrapped around his shoulders, an embrace meant to shield him from the barrage of his self-criticism. "You did everything you could. Duke knew how much you loved him, and he was grateful to have you and Jamie as his family." My voice wavered, betraying the struggle within me to remain composed, to be the pillar he needed in this moment of vulnerability.

Silence enveloped us, a heavy, suffocating cloak. I wracked my brain for words of consolation, for some magic phrase that could mend the fracture in Luke's heart, but the harsh reality loomed large – no words could rewind time, no assurances could resurrect Duke. In this moment, all we had was each other, a shared understanding of the pain that comes with love and loss, a silent acknowledgment that sometimes, being present is the most profound solace we can offer.

The silence that enveloped us was thick, a tangible entity that seemed to press down on us with the weight of unsaid words and unshed tears. It was in this heavy quietude that I gathered the shards of my courage to pierce the stillness. "What are you going to do with him?" My voice was a whisper, feather-light, aiming not to disrupt the fragile peace that had settled between us but to offer a diversion, however slight, from the torrent of Luke's sorrow.

"I don't know," came his reply, each word steeped in desolation, echoing the turmoil that clouded his eyes.

Pushing forward, I broached the practicalities that our extraordinary circumstances demanded. "That Charity woman said it's too dangerous to bury Duke in Clivilius. His body will attract creatures worse than shadow panthers." The words felt cold, clinical, but necessary, a grim reminder of the perilous world that had claimed Duke as its victim.

Understanding flickered in Luke's gaze, a silent acknowledgment of the harsh reality that Clivilius, with all its untamed beauty, harboured dangers that now cast a long, dark shadow over our grief.

The moment Luke stood, the shift was palpable, a transition from mourning to action, Duke cradled tenderly in his embrace—a poignant symbol of the vulnerability and love that bound them. I trailed behind him, my own heart heavy, witnessing the transformation of the man I knew—a pillar of strength now grappling with a loss that threatened to undermine his fortitude.

Outside, under the expanse of Hobart's wintry sky, Luke's request was a whisper against the backdrop of our grim task. "Beatrix, I don't want to go back yet. Can you get me a shovel or something from the Drop Zone?"

"Sure," my response was tinged with hesitation, an echo of my internal struggle to find my role in this tapestry of grief and duty. Despite the uncertainty that knotted my stomach, my resolve was clear—I would stand by Luke, offering my support in whatever form it needed to take, navigating the precarious balance between the reality of his loss and the necessity of moving forward, one painful step at a time.

Back in Clivilius, I moved with a singular purpose, my strides quick and determined as I navigated the terrain to the Drop Zone. The weight of the task ahead lent urgency to my steps, a resolve to not let anything—or anyone—hinder my mission. With the shovel secured, I made my way back to Luke, the tool feeling awkward and heavy in my hands, a foreboding reminder of its intended use.

The backyard lights cast a soft glow over the garden, a serene backdrop to the sorrowful task awaiting us. Luke was at the garden's edge, under the apricot tree, its branches a silent witness to his grief. The space around the tree was now cleared of weeds, a small act of preparation for the final resting place of his beloved Duke.

"Duke loved this garden," Luke's voice was a low murmur, laden with a mix of nostalgia and sorrow, as he began to dig into the earth. The sound of the shovel slicing through the soil was a harsh intrusion into the night's quiet.

Together, we worked in a heavy silence, the rhythmic shovelling punctuated only by the occasional clink of metal against stone. The hole grew steadily, a dark void in the soft earth, until it was time to lower Duke, his body gently wrapped in a sheet, into his final resting place. Standing there, looking at the small mound of dirt that now marked Duke's presence and absence, a wave of finality crashed over me. *Duke is gone, and there's nothing we can do to bring him back*, the thought echoed in my mind, a sombre refrain to the day's tragic chorus.

Luke's words of farewell were a soft-spoken tribute, a final acknowledgment of Duke's impact on his life. But it was the subsequent collapse of his composure that struck me the hardest. His emotional dam, held back by sheer will, finally gave way, and his sobs broke the night's stillness. Collapsing at the base of the apricot tree, his figure seemed to fold in on itself, a physical manifestation of his overwhelming grief. Watching him, his head buried in his hands, shoulders quaking with each sob, I felt an acute sense of helplessness, my own heart aching not just for Duke, but for Luke, witnessing his unbridled anguish in the shadow of the tree that had once brought us all joy.

The despair that had etched itself onto Luke's face was palpable, mirroring the tumultuous churn of the soil where Duke now rested. His gaze, fixed on the disturbed earth, seemed to seek answers in its dark expanse.

"We have no resources, almost no money, no security," Luke's words spilled out, each one laden with a burden of anxiety and uncertainty. His voice, usually so sure and steady, now carried the weight of our precarious situation. "What are we going to do? Do we really have any hope of helping the Bixbus settlers survive?"

In response, I closed the space between us, my movement more instinct than decision, and sat beside him. My arm found its way around his shoulder, an attempt to meld my strength with his, to share the load of his heavy doubts. "We'll figure something out," I murmured, the words more a declaration of intent than a statement of fact, my own mind clouded with the same concerns.

When Luke leaned against me, his sigh was a tangible release of pent-up fears and frustrations, resonating deeply within me. "I don't know, Beatrix. It feels like everything is falling apart."

The urge to reassure him was strong, to counter his despair with unwavering optimism, yet reality held my tongue. The acknowledgment that we might indeed be in over our heads was a bitter pill, its truth undeniable yet hard to voice.

But then, amidst the swirling doubts, a spark of inspiration ignited within me. "Hey, why don't you grab your laptop?" The suggestion sprang forth, a lifeline thrown into the turbulent sea of our sorrow. "I have an idea." My voice carried a new note of determination, a harbinger of a plan yet to be unveiled.

Luke's skepticism was evident in the slow, measured way he rose, his gaze still lingering on his recent loss beneath the apricot tree. Yet, there was a flicker of curiosity, a subtle shift towards the possibility of action, a step away from the mire of despair.

As I cast a final, silent farewell to Duke, a promise that his memory would be honoured not just with grief but with our continued fight for survival, I followed Luke inside. The weight of leadership and the responsibility to those dependent on us hung heavily in the air, but with a new resolve kindling within, I stepped forward, ready to face the challenges ahead, together with Luke.

❖

Seated at the kitchen table, the laptop's glow cast a soft light in the dim room, creating an island of illumination in the surrounding darkness. I pulled up a chair beside Luke, our heads bending together over the screen as we dove into the depths of the internet, searching for something, anything, that might offer a semblance of hope, a thread to grasp in our current predicament.

After navigating through a maze of options, a spark of possibility caught my eye. "Look," I said with a surge of excitement, pointing to the display. "They have next day delivery. I think this might work until we can figure out a more permanent solution." The words tumbled out, infused with a tentative optimism, as I highlighted the advertisement for temporary fencing solutions.

Luke's demeanour shifted, a glimmer of hope breaking through the veneer of worry. "Do you think we could order enough to protect the entire settlement?" His voice, tinged with a newfound energy, mirrored the flicker of possibility that the idea had ignited.

"I'm not sure," I confessed, my enthusiasm tempered by realism. "But it's worth a try. And in the meantime, we can look into other options." My fingers danced across the keyboard, assembling a modest order, each click a small step toward regaining a semblance of control, a gesture of defiance against the uncertainties that besieged us.

As I keyed in the Owens' property in Collinsvale as the delivery address, the reality of our situation settled over me. The order, set to arrive the next day, was a stopgap, a temporary bulwark against the looming threats that cast a long shadow over our endeavours.

"I know this is just a temporary solution, but it's a start. It should be enough to give Jamie, Paul, and the other settlers the security and protection that they need," I voiced my thoughts to Luke, finding solace in the shared sense of purpose that bridged the gap between desperation and action.

Luke's smile, rare and precious in these trying times, was a beacon of shared resolve. "Yeah, it will. And it will give them some peace of mind too. They've got every right to be worried about the shadow panthers and other unknown dangers that might be lurking around."

As we sat there, united in our determination, staring at the confirmation screen, a seed of hope was sown in the fertile ground of our collective resolve. A burgeoning confidence grew within me—a belief that in the gathering of more Guardians, lay our strength and our hope to surmount the obstacles that lay ahead.

*4338.210*

*(29 July 2018)*

# CONNECTIONS

## *4338.210.1*

Rubbing my tired eyes, I stretched my arms heavenward, a silent goodbye to the early morning blue skies of Clivilius, cradling the day's nascent light like a tender secret. The skies here always held a different kind of serenity, a calmness that Earth's horizon seldom matched. I stepped forward, my body moving instinctively toward the Portal's ever-welcoming glow, a kaleidoscope of rainbow energy that shimmered and danced like an aurora borealis on steroids. The air around it hummed, charged with an unseen power, and I could feel the hair on my arms stand on end as I approached.

Entering the Portal felt like diving into a cool, vibrant ocean of light. For a moment, everything was an explosion of colours, a sensory overload that never failed to leave me awestruck. It was like being at the heart of a star, witnessing the birth of light itself. Despite the countless times I'd made this journey, the wonder of it never dulled. It was a reminder of the vastness of our universe, the endless possibilities that lay stretched out before us, a tapestry woven from the very fabric of space and time.

But today, my mind was preoccupied, tinged with a hint of frustration. I was in Clivilius for a visit that lasted less than a minute, a brief interlude in a journey that should have been more straightforward. I transitioned from my bedroom, a cozy, familiar space filled with the remnants of my dreams, into Luke's living room, a stark contrast with its own unique ambiance—warm, inviting, a testament to his personality.

The Portal and our Portal Keys, these marvels of technology and magic, continued to fascinate me. They allowed Luke and me to share and use locations on Earth, wherever either of us used our Portal Keys. The concept was groundbreaking, revolutionary even. It had changed the way we interacted with space, turning what was once a vast expanse into a mere step away.

Yet, despite its convenience, a part of me found the whole process odd, even annoying. *Why did I have to pass through Clivilius every time I wanted to transfer to a different location on Earth?* The detour felt unnecessary, a redundant step in what should have been a seamless journey. It would have been much easier, much more logical, to step out of my bedroom and arrive directly at Luke's house. *Why the extra step? Was it a flaw in the technology, or perhaps a safety measure we weren't aware of yet?*

"Hello?" Luke's voice echoed down the hallway, slicing through the fog of my discomfort.

"Hey, Luke," I managed, my voice carrying a mix of relief and curiosity. I had barely taken a few stealthy steps into his domain, yet here he was, aware of my arrival as if alerted by some invisible signal.

"You're up early," he remarked, his voice carrying a hint of surprise as he emerged into the shared kitchen and living area.

"I didn't sleep very well," I confessed, suppressing a yawn that fought its way out, revealing my unrested state. My arms reached for the ceiling in a futile attempt to stretch away the lingering shadows of a restless night. "I've already taken more pain killers than I probably should, and my head is still pounding." The words tumbled out, a testament to my frayed edges and the persistent ache that throbbed behind my eyes.

"Tell me about it," Luke sympathised, his voice carrying a note of understanding that wrapped around me like a warm blanket. It was comforting, knowing I wasn't alone in my discomfort, that shared pain could be a bridge rather than a barrier.

Compelled by a sudden, gnawing hunger, I turned toward the fridge. My hand wrapped around the cold metal handle, pulling it with a hope of finding something to quell the hunger pangs. The door swung open, revealing an interior as barren as my hopes. A few lonely items stared back at me, a silent testament to neglect or perhaps a Guardian lifestyle too busy for grocery shopping.

"Alcohol already?" Luke's voice laced with humour, his smirk a playful challenge in the soft morning light. The comment, meant to tease, struck a chord, igniting a spark of irritation within me.

"Fuck off. I'm not Gladys," I retorted sharply, the words slicing through the air, a knee-jerk defence against a comparison I found less than flattering.

"Sorry," he offered, his apology tinged with a residual chuckle, unable to fully mask the amusement that twinkled in his eyes. His mirth felt like salt in an open wound, though I knew his intentions were far from malicious.

"We have muesli bars," he said, shifting the topic with an ease that spoke of familiarity, opening the pantry to reveal a box of what he must have considered a suitable breakfast substitute. The sight of the unopened box, its contents so starkly at odds with my growling stomach, did little to improve my mood.

My frown deepened, a silent scream of frustration. *Seriously!? A muesli bar for breakfast? I'm starving!* The thought echoed in my head, a chorus of discontent at the meagre offering.

"They're choc-chip," he added, a chuckle lacing his voice, as if the mere mention of chocolate could somehow sweeten the deal.

Despite my irritation, the persistent growling of my stomach betrayed my hunger, forcing a slight relaxation of the tension etched into my face. "Fine," I conceded, a reluctant surrender, gesturing for him to toss me the box.

Catching the bars with a practiced ease, my hands moved with the precision and grace of a seasoned thief, a nod to skills honed in a past that seemed both distant and vividly close. Tearing open the package with a haste born of hunger, I shoved half the bar into my mouth, the rough texture of the muesli contrasting with the smooth, melting chocolate chips.

Walking across the living room, the familiar surroundings a backdrop to the morning's minor drama, I chewed thoughtfully, the initial rush of frustration giving way to a begrudging acceptance. "Any plans for today?" I inquired, my voice muffled by a mouthful of muesli, seeking to bridge the gap that the morning's exchanges had widened, even if just a little. The stray chocolate chip on my tongue, a sweet interloper, offered a small, tactile reminder that not all was amiss.

"You're going to visit Grant Ironbach and bring him to Clivilius," Luke stated, his tone casual as he tore into a muesli bar, seemingly oblivious to the weight his words carried.

I halted mid-stride, the remnants of the muesli bar in my mouth turning to sawdust. Swivelling to face him, my expression darkened into a scowl. The simplicity of his statement belied the complexity of the task, a complexity he knew all too well.

"It'll be good practice for you," he added, as if sensing my hesitation, trying to package the mission as a beneficial exercise.

My eyebrow arched, skepticism painting my features. *Did Luke really think that response would mollify me?* "People aren't my thing," I declared, my voice flat. It was a well-known fact, an unspoken agreement among those who knew me—I preferred the silent companionship of animals to the unpredictable nature of people.

Luke's demeanour shifted, the levity draining away. "I already have to get Adrian," he explained, his voice laced with a seriousness that commanded attention.

"Who's Adrian?" My curiosity piqued, I probed for more information, eager to divert the conversation from my apparent impending task.

"He's a construction engineer. Runs his own company," Luke elaborated, a hint of respect creeping into his tone as he spoke of Adrian's credentials. "He did the building inspection for this place when Jamie and I bought it. Nial is great with fences, but I think the group needs more... professional help."

Chewing thoughtfully on the muesli bar, the chocolate chips offering a faint consolation, I conceded, "I suspect you're right there." Acknowledging the necessity didn't ease the discomfort of the assignment, but it lent perspective to Luke's request.

Luke, seemingly emboldened by my acknowledgment, continued to outline his plan. "I'm going to arrange to meet with him at the Collinsvale property tomorrow morning."

A long and loud honk shattered the morning tranquility, its discordant note slicing through the calm of Luke's house. Instinctively, I moved towards the large window, my steps quick and silent, a remnant of a past where stealth was often a necessity. The venetian blinds, their slats like the bars of a cage, offered a narrow view of the world outside. My fingers, deft and precise, parted them just enough to allow my eyes to scout the source of the intrusion.

A surge of panic shot through me as my gaze landed on the familiar vehicle parked across the road. The driver, a ghost from a chapter of my life I hoped was closed, sat unaware of my scrutiny. I recoiled from the window as if burned, the blinds snapping back into place with a soft clatter.

"I wouldn't worry about it," Luke's voice, calm and reassuring, reached me. "There are always hoons on that road." His casual dismissal of the situation was meant to comfort, but my heart raced with a different truth.

"No," I countered, my voice firm, my head shaking with more vigour than I intended. "I think the house is being watched." The words hung in the air between us, heavy with implications I wasn't sure I wanted to fully explore.

Luke's brow furrowed, a visible sign of his concern. He rubbed his forehead, a gesture I'd come to recognise as his way of processing unwelcome news. I stood there, caught in an internal tug-of-war, debating how much of my suspicion to share, how much of my past I could allow to bleed into our present.

"Did you recognise the person?" His question was direct, his gaze intent on mine.

"No," the lie slipped out smoothly, a practiced deceit. "It was too quick." I maintained the charade, my head shaking in feigned uncertainty.

"Have another look then," he suggested, his hand gesturing towards the window, an invitation to confirm or dispel my fears.

With a reluctance that I hoped appeared genuine, I approached the window again. My fingers, now trembling slightly, parted the blinds for a second glimpse. "He's gone!" The words heightened my anxiety, the blinds fluttering back into place as I stepped away.

"Gone?" Luke echoed, his voice steady, a stark contrast to the storm of adrenaline coursing through me.

*Why the hell is Karl parked across the road?* The thought screamed in my mind, a torrent of worry and suspicion. *It can't be good, whatever the reason.* "We'd better get out of here for a while," I announced, more to myself than to Luke, the decision made in the grip of my escalating fears.

Without waiting for a response, I acted on instinct, my Portal Key in hand. Its familiar weight was a small comfort as I aimed it at the living room wall. A press of a button, a flicker of light, and I stepped through the portal, leaving Luke's house—and the threat lurking outside—behind. My heart still raced, the echo of the car horn mingling with the myriad of possibilities and dangers that Karl's presence implied.

❖

The moment I stepped through the Portal, the Clivilius sun greeted me with its unrelenting brilliance, forcing my eyes to squint as they adapted from the gloomy Tasmanian morning to the vibrant intensity of this alien world.

"Hey, Beatrix," Paul's voice, unexpectedly close, jolted me from my transitional reverie. I spun towards the sound, my heart skipping a beat, not yet accustomed to the immediate shift in surroundings that portal travel entailed.

Paul wasn't alone. Beside him stood the new guy, the one with the expertise in fences. Despite our introduction the previous night, his name danced just beyond my grasp, an elusive detail amidst the whirlwind of names and faces I'd encountered since my arrival in Clivilius.

"We're glad you're here. We've been waiting for either you or Luke. Nial has come up with this amazing theory about how we might be able to establish a connection with Earth and communicate–" Paul's enthusiasm was palpable, his words tumbling out in a rush of excitement and anticipation. Yet, despite the potential significance of his news, my focus wavered, pulled away by a nagging concern.

As Paul's voice became a distant buzz, my gaze drifted back to the Portal. A knot of worry tightened in my stomach. *Where the hell is Luke?* The question echoed in my mind, a persistent drumbeat of anxiety. He should have been right behind me, stepping through the portal in his usual, unflappable manner.

But the Portal remained silent, its translucence undisturbed by any further arrivals. The absence of Luke, unexpected and unnerving, cast a shadow over the Clivilius sun, the bright day suddenly tinged with an undercurrent of unease.

"Beatrix?" Paul's voice cut through my worrisome thoughts, louder this time, tinged with a hint of urgency as he tried to reel me back to the present.

Whipping around to face him, my frustration bubbled to the surface. "What!?" The word came out sharper than I intended, a reflection of the tension gnawing at me.

Paul recoiled slightly, his arms lifting in a gesture of peace. "You're not even listening, are you?" His accusation stung, the earlier vibrancy in his expression dissolving into a look of disappointment.

"I was with Luke. He should have been–" My voice trailed off as my gaze drifted back to the Portal, its surface a silent testament to my unease. The smooth, shimmering expanse offered no answers, only reflecting back my own worried expression.

Paul interrupted, his voice a mix of reassurance and mild frustration. "I'm sure Luke's fine. He's always getting himself into and out of trouble." His attempt to lighten the mood felt hollow, missing the mark.

"Yeah, but–" I countered, the words heavy with a mix of concern and fatigue. Arguing seemed futile, yet I couldn't shake the feeling of discontent.

"We need your help with our experiment," Nial chimed in, his voice a new element in the conversation, pulling my attention towards him.

Though I acknowledged Paul's point about Luke's knack for navigating danger, my instincts screamed otherwise. "Maybe I should go check on him," I suggested, the need to ensure Luke's safety outweighing my curiosity about their experiment.

"As long as Luke has his Portal Key, he'll be fine," Paul tried to reassure me again, seeking validation from Nial with a quick glance.

Nial's response was a noncommittal shrug, not quite the solid reassurance he sought.

"Come on, Beatrix," Paul pressed, his demeanour shifting to one of earnest persuasion. "Help us. It's for the safety of our community."

I sighed heavily, the weight of the situation pressing down on me. *Is Paul right?* The question echoed in my mind, mingling with a cocktail of concern and skepticism. *As long as Luke hasn't lost his Portal Key, he would never get caught, right?* The thought was meant to be reassuring, yet it fluttered in my chest like a trapped bird, its wings beating against the confines of uncertainty.

"Fine," I relented, the word tasting of resignation on my tongue.

Paul's demeanour transformed instantly, his face alight with the kind of delight that one might exhibit upon solving a perplexing puzzle. His enthusiasm, although infectious, couldn't fully penetrate the shroud of my worries.

"What do you need me to do?" I inquired, my voice laced with a reluctant curiosity.

His grin widened, as if he had been eagerly awaiting this very question. "We're going to try to establish an internet connection." The simplicity with which he stated this goal belied the complexity of the task at hand, especially here, in Clivilius.

My eyebrows furrowed, skepticism creeping into my gaze as I echoed his words internally. *Internet connection? What do they want that for?* The idea seemed out of place in our current setting, an odd blend of our past life on Earth with the vastly different reality of Clivilius.

Paul, perhaps sensing my confusion, hastened to elaborate, his words tumbling out in a rush to fill the silence. "Luke gave us Nial's laptop," he paused, allowing Nial to lift the laptop, its familiar yet out-of-place presence a silent confirmation of their intent. "But we can't really do much with it without an internet connection."

I shrugged, a gesture of bemusement mixed with a tinge of helplessness. "What do you want me to do about it?" My expertise did not lie in the realms of digital connectivity, especially not here, far from the infrastructure and resources we took for granted on Earth.

Paul opened his mouth, presumably to lay out their plan, but Nial interjected, his voice carrying a mix of determination and frustration. "The idea was for me to use the business accounts to order some fencing supplies so we can secure the property. The business doesn't have much money, but I have enough credit to get the basic supplies we need." His explanation painted a picture of their struggles, a pragmatic approach to fortifying our new haven.

He sighed, a mirror to my own earlier exhalation, his gaze falling to the laptop in his hands. "I've tried to put the order together, but everything is web-based. There's not much I can do without an internet connection." His words highlighted the irony of our situation—stranded on an alien world, yet hindered by the absence of a tool as earthly and mundane as the internet.

The absurdity of it all tugged at the corners of my mind, a bizarre blend of past and present, of Earthly concerns in an unearthly locale.

"Which is why we need you, Beatrix," Paul's words broke through my thoughts, his tone laced with a mix of urgency and hope.

My confusion only deepened. "How can I help?" I questioned, my voice a blend of curiosity and skepticism. *I'm not a walking Wi-Fi router, after all.* The peculiarities of our situation seemed to be pushing us toward increasingly bizarre solutions.

"It's simple," Paul said, a spark of optimism in his eyes as he moved towards the Portal's screen. "Do you have Wi-Fi at home?" he inquired, as if the answer might unlock the next step in their ambitious plan.

"Of course," I responded, a touch of incredulity in my voice. "Who doesn't these days?"

"Go to your house and leave the Portal open. We'll get the laptop as close as we can and see if we can pick up the Wi-Fi signal," Paul laid out the strategy, his words painting a picture of a makeshift bridge between worlds.

The plan, while unconventional, sparked a glimmer of possibility within me. "I can do it from my room. That should give me enough privacy," I conceded, finding myself drawn into their experiment, the chance to contribute to our collective well-being outweighing my initial reservations.

"Let's do it," Paul's enthusiasm was infectious, his words a clarion call to action.

Minutes later, the familiar surroundings of my bedroom were bathed in the prismatic hues of the Portal. Impatience nibbling at my composure, I leaned through the bedroom wall, the boundary between worlds blurring around me. "Any luck?" I called out, my voice tinged with a mix of hope and anxiety.

I found Paul and Nial crouched in the Clivilius dust, the stark, orange terrain a vivid backdrop to our technological endeavour. Paul looked up, his expression mirroring my own concern, while Nial's voice, tinged with disappointment, delivered the unwelcome news.

"It's not detecting any signal at all," he admitted, the lines on his forehead deepening with the weight of his words.

The ripple of disappointment that coursed through me was unexpected, a testament to how Paul's fervour had subtly woven its way into my own sentiments. *Paul's enthusiasm really is infectious*, I mused internally, a grudging respect for his relentless optimism dawning within me. I hadn't realised until that moment just how much I had been pulled into the tide of their excitement, how much I wanted their experiment to succeed.

"Can you get the Portal closer to the router?" Paul's question sliced through my reverie, his eyes alight with the kind of determination that refused to acknowledge defeat.

My brow furrowed in concentration as I visualised my home, trying to pinpoint the router's exact location. *Living room?* The image of the small black device, unassumingly perched on a coffee table near the couch, came to mind, its mundane appearance belying its significance to our current endeavour.

"I can try. I don't think I'm alone," I confessed to the men, the potential complication of my family's presence casting a shadow over the plan.

With a swift movement, I retreated into the room and shut the Portal, severing the connection to Clivilius momentarily. I checked the time, my mind racing through the likely whereabouts of my family members. My father should be at work by now, assuming his punctuality held. The sudden crash and a frustrated expletive from the ensuite confirmed my mother's presence—and her usual battle with the overburdened towel rail.

Her misstep, albeit minor, was a stroke of luck for me, granting a narrow window of opportunity. I hastened to the living room, my steps quick but silent, mindful of not drawing attention. Standing beside the router, I extracted my Portal Key, its familiar weight a comfort in my hand. I aimed it at the wall adjacent to the router, the potential gateway to bridging our worlds with a sliver of Earthly normality.

With a deep breath, I slid my finger across the activation button, a flicker of hope kindling within me. The Portal sprung to life, its colours swirling, a silent yet vibrant beacon of our efforts to tether these two worlds together.

"Shit," escaped from my lips in a hushed exhale, my eyes widening in horror as the large picture, which had adorned the wall moments before, vanished into the Clivilius landscape.

Tentatively, I pushed my head through the Portal, my heart sinking at the sight that greeted me. Paul and Nial were engulfed in a cloud of displeasure, their forms dusted with fragments of what used to be the picture's glass frame.

"What the hell, Beatrix!" Paul's voice pierced the tense air, his frustration palpable as he stripped off his shirt in a frantic motion, rushing towards Nial. The latter sat in the ochre dust, his posture one of resigned pain, his left hand awkwardly trying to stem the flow of blood from the small lacerations on his right.

"Sorry, I didn't think—" My words faltered, guilt knotting my stomach. The sentence hung unfinished, a feeble attempt at an apology for a mishap I hadn't foreseen.

"There's still no Wi-Fi signal," Nial interjected, his tone a mix of pain and irritation. He brushed off Paul's offered shirt, his bloodied hand leaving a stark imprint on Paul's chest as he pushed the help away.

Paul's expression darkened, a frown etching deeper into his features. "Bring the router through," he instructed, his focus shifting back to Nial's wounds in a renewed effort to provide some semblance of first aid.

Doubts clouded my mind, skepticism about the effectiveness of their plan mingling with the guilt of the accident. Yet, feeling responsible for the disturbance, I complied with Paul's request. Unplugging the router, I clutched it in my hands, as I returned to Clivilius.

Handing the router to Paul, I watched as his expression morphed into one of perplexity. "What the heck am I supposed to do with this?" he blurted out, frustration lining his words as he pushed the device back toward me.

"But you just asked me for it," I retorted, my confusion mirroring his. The abrupt change in his attitude caught me off guard, throwing a wrench into the already tense atmosphere.

"You need to keep it plugged in," he stated, his teeth clenched, conveying a mix of urgency and impatience.

With a heavy sigh, I retreated to the living room, the weight of the situation pressing down on me. Plugging in the router, I watched the lights blink in their mechanical dance, a silent countdown to another attempt at bridging worlds.

Just then, a sharp cry of frustration from the ensuite sliced through the silence. "She's still distracted," I murmured to myself, a sliver of relief cutting through the tension as I acknowledged my mother's continued preoccupation.

Finally, the router's light steadied, signalling readiness. Clutching the device, now a lifeline of sorts, I made my way back to Paul, ensuring it remained connected to the power source.

Back in Clivilius, Nial and I huddled around Paul, our eyes glued to the laptop's screen as he navigated the unfamiliar territory of inter-dimensional Wi-Fi. The air was thick with anticipation, each click and scroll magnified by our collective breath-holding.

"We've got something!" Paul's exclamation shattered the silence, a beacon of hope as he pointed to the sole Wi-Fi network listed on the screen.

My heart skipped a beat. *Are we really about to connect Earth and Clivilius?* The enormity of the moment wasn't lost on me. A cocktail of excitement, anxiety, and disbelief churned within me as we stood on the brink of achieving something that felt akin to a miracle, a testament to human ingenuity and the relentless pursuit of connection, no matter the realm.

"We're connected!" Paul's voice was a mix of triumph and urgency as he passed the laptop to Nial.

"Shit," came Nial's strained exclamation, the device nearly slipping from his grasp, his bloodied fingers struggling against the laptop's smooth surface.

"You really need to get that cut looked at," I insisted, concern etching my voice as I eyed the makeshift bandage, now soaked through and ineffectual.

Paul glanced at me, a mix of gratitude and determination in his eyes. "He will once we get this order through." His tone brokered no argument, the weight of our situation anchoring his words.

I rolled my eyes, a gesture more out of habit than true annoyance. Deep down, I knew the stakes. Despite the absence of shadow panthers lately, the unknown threats lurking beyond our makeshift sanctuary sent a shiver through me. The potential of unseen dangers, perhaps even more menacing than those we had encountered, loomed large in my mind.

"How much longer do you need?" I asked, my voice tinged with a growing edge of impatience, the silence stretching too thin over the undercurrent of our collective anxiety.

"Nearly done," Nial muttered, his focus unwavering as his fingers danced over the keyboard, the screen reflecting in his intense gaze. "I'm using a previous order as a base."

"Think you can get us enough to at least make a small perimeter fence?" Paul's question hung in the air, his eyes locking with Nial's in a silent exchange of hope and determination.

"Yeah. If we can get it all, should be enough to give us room to expand," Nial's response carried a weight of intent and determination that filled the space between us.

"Expand?" The word echoed in my head as I repeated it aloud, surprise lacing my voice. The concept of growing our little enclave in such a hostile environment hadn't fully occurred to me until now.

Nial paused, his fingers halting their frenzied dance over the keyboard. Lifting his gaze to meet mine, the intensity in his eyes was startling. "I don't want to be here alone forever," he stated, a stark flatness in his tone that belied the depth of his sentiment.

A wave of unease washed over me, the idea of dragging more souls into this uncertain and dangerous world causing my stomach to churn. "He's not serious, is he?" I whispered to Paul, seeking some semblance of reassurance.

"We've all left family we love behind," Paul's voice was soft, a thread of shared sorrow woven through his words. The hint of moisture in his eyes spoke volumes of the sacrifices each of them were making to be here, even if it hadn't been entirely their own choice.

Interrupted by Nial's practical inquiry, "Where am I getting all of this delivered to?" the moment of shared vulnerability passed.

Paul's reaction, a mix of alarm and realisation, was almost comical, pulling an involuntary chuckle from me amidst the tension. "We can use the Owens' Collinsvale property," I offered, a semblance of a plan beginning to form.

"What timeframe are we looking at?" I pivoted the conversation toward logistics, kneeling beside Nial to input the delivery details into the system he had accessed.

"I've selected all local materials and put a priority flag on it. There will likely be multiple deliveries, the first one arriving tomorrow," Nial announced, a hint of pride in his voice as he leaned back slightly, the glow of success on his face.

As Nial reclaimed the laptop, a semblance of normality returned, though it was short-lived. "I'll let Luke know and we'll keep an eye out for the delivery," I asserted, pushing myself up and shaking off the dust that clung to my clothing. The mention of the urgent order Luke and I had placed felt like a necessary interjection, a contribution to our collective efforts. "Oh, and I don't know how I forgot, but last night Luke and I also placed an urgent order for temporary fencing. It should arrive tomorrow."

"That's awesome! Thanks Bea—" But his words were swallowed by the sudden chaos that erupted.

"Shit! We've lost it!" Nial's alarmed shout sent a jolt of panic through me as I watched the laptop skid into the dust, an ominous prelude to his next words.

"Lost what? The order?" Paul's question pierced the mounting tension as he lunged for the laptop, his movements a blend of desperation and hope.

"The internet con—" Nial's explanation was brutally interrupted by the abrupt entrance of the router's power cable, whipping through the Portal like a malicious serpent, narrowly missing us before thudding into the ground.

"Beatrix, close the—" Paul's command was half-formed, his voice tinged with urgency, but my reactions had already kicked in.

With a swift, decisive movement, I manipulated the Portal, its vibrant display shifting to a translucent veil. My heart pounded, a frantic drum in my chest, echoing the tumult of the moment.

"What the hell just happened?" Nial's voice trembled slightly, his eyes locking onto mine, searching for an explanation in the tumult.

"I'm not sure," I admitted, my own voice tinged with a blend of fear and disbelief. The thought that my mother could inadvertently be involved flitted through my mind, sending a shiver down my spine.

"Your parents?" Paul's question, echoing my internal fears, made me pause. The idea of my mother, curious and unwitting, meddling with the Portal and inadvertently hurling the power cable through, was plausible yet terrifying.

*She'd more likely be stupid enough to touch the Portal and then be forced to come here. Whomever did this, assuming it was a person, knows...*

"No," I asserted, my voice stronger as conviction took hold. "It must be someone familiar with Portals." The realisation that we might not be alone, that someone else knew of and could manipulate the Portal, sent a chill through me.

The gasps from the men punctuated the implications of the situation. Paul, ever practical, shifted focus. "But you got the order through?" His eyes were on Nial, seeking some sliver of positive news amidst the mayhem.

Nial, still grappling with his minor wounds, managed a nod. "Yeah... I... think so," he stammered, his uncertainty mirroring our collective unease.

A surge of resolve washed over me. Clarity cut through the confusion. I needed answers. *If my mother wasn't responsible, then who was in my house? Was it safe?* The questions spiralled, each one fuelling a growing determination to uncover the truth.

The soft whisper of Clivilius, delicate and haunting, echoed in my mind: *You have no choice.*

"When Luke returns," I instructed Paul, my hand gripping his shoulder in a gesture meant to convey both comfort and resolve. "Send him straight to my bedroom." The urgency in my voice was unmistakable.

"Of course," Paul replied, his nod conveying understanding and agreement.

With no time to spare, I turned away from them, stepping forward, determined to confront whatever—or whoever—awaited me.

# CARAVANS

## 4338.210.2

Stepping into my bedroom, the door let out a loud, creaky whine as I closed it behind me.

"What the hell were you thinking, Beatrix?" Leigh's voice pierced the heavy air, his figure rigid with disapproval. He was standing closer than I anticipated, his finger waving accusingly in front of my face, making me acutely aware of the seriousness of his rebuke. "Leaving the Portal open like that," he continued, his disappointment palpable, his head shaking in a rhythm that seemed to accentuate each word. "If I hadn't arrived first and thrown that power cable through the Portal to get your attention, your mother could have caught you with the Portal wide open. Do you have any idea how dangerous that is?"

I retreated a few steps, the back of my legs brushing against the edge of my bed, seeking physical distance from his reproach. Defensive yet cornered, I felt my face flush with a mix of shame and frustration. "It was Paul's idea," I muttered, my attempt to deflect sounding feeble even to my own ears.

"I don't care whose idea it was," Leigh retorted sharply, his voice rising in intensity. The room seemed to shrink under the weight of his words. "You should have known better than to leave the Portal open. You know how risky it is to leave it unguarded." His statement, firm and unequivocal, left little room for excuses, emphasising the danger and irresponsibility of our actions.

Feeling my resolve waver, I huffed, a mixture of defiance and desperation fuelling my response. I crossed my arms over my chest, a barrier against the onslaught of criticism, yet also a shield masking my own creeping doubts. "You might care when you hear what we just discovered," I countered, clinging to the hope that our findings might shift the focus from my lapse in judgment to the potential implications of our discovery, eager to redirect the conversation from blame to revelation.

Leigh's hands dropped to his sides, a subtle yet poignant shift in his demeanour as he took a step back, his eyes narrowing into slits of suspicious curiosity. His gaze felt like a spotlight, dissecting my every move, every flicker of emotion that might cross my face.

"Hmph," I snorted, my attempt to mask my nervousness with a veneer of indifference. I walked over to my desk, the familiar softness of the carpet under my feet offering a strange comfort. Opening the lid of my laptop, the screen came to life, casting a soft glow that seemed to momentarily push away the intensity of the situation.

"Well?" Leigh's voice, now laced with a blend of curiosity and impatience, broke the transient calm. He was approaching me again, his presence looming like an inquisitive shadow. "What is this amazing discovery you're so proud of then?"

I pursed my lips, a frown etching itself onto my face as I wrestled with the conflicting emotions swirling within me. "I wouldn't say I'm feeling proud," I confessed, my voice a mixture of defensiveness and reluctant humility.

A few moments of silence enveloped the room, the only sound being the faint hum of the laptop as I navigated through it, opening a new web browser.

"Well?" Leigh prodded once more, his impatience now tinged with a note of urgency. "Come out with it. What have you discovered?"

"Oh, right," I muttered, a sudden realisation dawning on me that Leigh was actually awaiting a substantive explanation, not just the promise of one. I rubbed my temple, feeling a slight throb of a headache beginning as I looked away from the screen. "Paul and Nial discovered that as long as we keep the router connected through the Portal, they can access the internet in Clivilius," I explained, the words tumbling out with a mix of astonishment and apprehension.

"That's actually quite ingenious," Leigh conceded, his tone shifting from accusatory to contemplative. He began rubbing his forehead, lost in thought. "How have we not thought to try that before?" he muttered to himself, seemingly oblivious to my presence for a moment, his mind wandering through the implications of our discovery.

"I don't know," I replied, a hint of sarcasm lacing my words as I rolled my eyes, feeling a mix of annoyance and relief. Leigh's musings, while reflective of the potential of our discovery, also highlighted the isolation I felt, even in his company, as we navigated the uncharted territories of our actions and their consequences.

"May I borrow your devices?" Leigh's request floated through the air, almost innocuous, yet laden with a reminder of the tangled web we'd woven with our experiments.

"You'll have to wait until I bring them back from Clivilius," I retorted, my voice laced with a hint of irritation. The reminder served as a subtle jab, pointing out his own role in the chaotic dance of actions and consequences surrounding the Portal's usage.

Leigh began to pace, his movements erratic, like a caged animal seeking an escape. "Can you get them now?" he pressed, his voice tinged with a blend of urgency and impatience, echoing off the walls of my cramped bedroom.

"Not right now," I responded, my tone flat, dismissive. I watched him pace, feeling a mixture of annoyance and detachment. "I have other things to do besides fetching equipment for you." My words hung in the air, a clear demarcation of my growing frustration with the situation and with Leigh's persistent demands.

"But, Beatrix—" he started, his voice trailing off as if he was grappling with the urge to argue or persuade.

I cut him off with a wave of my hand, a clear signal of my dwindling patience. "Go away, Leigh. I'm busy," I snapped, my focus returning to the laptop screen in front of me, though the pixels now seemed to blur, reflecting my inner turmoil.

There was a brief pause, a momentary silence that felt heavy with unspoken words and tensions. "Beatrix... ah, never mind," Leigh finally conceded, his voice a mixture of resignation and frustration. With those words, he activated a Portal on the wall of my bedroom, the familiar swirl of colours and energy framing his silhouette as he stepped through and vanished, leaving me alone with my thoughts and the eerie quiet that followed.

I let out a sigh of relief as the quietude enveloped me, the absence of Leigh's presence allowing a momentary respite from the day's tumultuous events. Alone in my room, I was left with my thoughts and a pressing task that demanded my attention: sourcing caravans for the settlers in Bixbus. The task felt daunting, a venture into uncharted territory, but necessity is the mother of invention—or in this case, the catalyst for a deep dive into the digital realms of the internet.

Positioning myself in front of my laptop, I took a moment to gather my thoughts, the soft hum of the machine in sync with my racing mind. "That's what we have the internet for," I muttered to myself, an attempt to bolster my confidence as my fingers danced across the keyboard, entering the search query into the bar.

My initial search led me to Hobart's online marketplaces. It was a city I knew like the back of my hand, its streets etched in my memory, its quirks and corners familiar territory. Starting here felt like anchoring myself to a known point on a vast, uncharted map.

The glow of the screen illuminated my face as I delved into the listings, the digital pages filled with possibilities. Each caravan I came across felt like a small beacon of hope, a potential home for someone in Bixbus. I scrutinised photos, compared prices, and read descriptions with a meticulous eye, aware of the weight of my decisions.

When a few promising options caught my eye, I felt a surge of cautious optimism. Under the guise of Sophie, my new online persona, I messaged the sellers, crafting each inquiry with care, mindful of the balance between obtaining necessary information and maintaining my anonymity. The internet was a tool, but it was also a place where identities could be unravelled with ease. *Protecting my privacy is critical*, I reminded myself, reinforcing the mental walls I needed to ensure were built around my online persona.

As I arranged meetings and corresponded with sellers, the room around me felt both confining and expansive—confining in its physical boundaries, but expansive in the possibilities that the laptop before me unlocked. It was a portal to a world as vast and complex as the one Leigh had just exited through, a reminder that gateways come in various forms, each with its own set of rules and risks.

❖

I arrived early at the designated meeting location, a decision driven by a mix of nervous anticipation and the strategic desire to observe unnoticed. The park in Hobart was a familiar one, yet it took on a new guise through the lens of my current mission. Its tall trees stood like silent sentinels, and the clusters of bushes offered covert nooks and crannies, creating a picturesque setting that belied the serious nature of my visit.

The crisp air of the park carried the faint whispers of winter, a chill that nipped at the edges of my resolve. I wrapped my jacket tighter around myself, a physical shield against the cold and a metaphorical one against the uncertainty of the task ahead.

Reviewing the seller's description once more, I scanned the area. My eyes settled on a retired couple seated on a bench near a formidable oak tree, basking in the weak winter sun. The scene was almost idyllic, the couple embodying a picture of serene retirement. The husband, tall and lean, had an air of quiet dignity, his thick white hair contrasting with the deep hues of the park. His smile, gentle and welcoming, seemed to invite conversation. Beside him, his wife, with her shorter stature and rounder frame, radiated warmth. Her blue eyes sparkled with the kind of liveliness that suggested a deep fondness for life.

Taking a deep breath, I felt the persona of Sophie cloak me, a necessary guise to navigate the delicate dance of the transaction ahead. This alter ego was not just a name but a fully crafted character, complete with her own backstory and demeanour, designed to interact with the world in a way that Beatrix currently could not afford to.

With each step toward the couple, I could feel Sophie taking over, her confidence seeping into my posture, her smile curving my lips. It was a performance, yes, but one that required immersion into the character to ensure its success. As I drew closer, I mentally rehearsed the lines, the questions, and the casual demeanour I would need to adopt to make the interaction smooth, yet unremarkable.

The couple looked up as I approached, their expressions open and welcoming, unaware of the layers of fiction that cocooned our impending interaction. In this moment, under the watchful boughs of the oak tree, I was Sophie, here to discuss a caravan, the intricacies of my true mission tucked away beneath layers of pretence and smiles.

"Hello, you must be Sophie," the husband greeted, his voice carrying a warm timbre that seemed to echo the gentle smile on his face. As he stood and extended his hand toward me, the sunlight glinted off his silver hair, lending him an almost ethereal quality.

"I'm Jack, and this is my wife, Mary. Thanks for coming along." His introduction was as inviting as his demeanour, a stark contrast to the knot of tension that had formed in my stomach.

"It's no problem at all," I responded, infusing my voice with as much ease as I could muster, despite the undercurrent of nervous energy that pulsed through me. Shaking Jack's hand, I felt the firmness of his grip, a subtle reminder of the reality of the situation amidst the swirling charade.

"I'm very interested in the caravan you have for sale. Can you tell me more about it?" I inquired, aiming to project the image of an earnest buyer, even as my mind juggled multiple layers of personas and motives.

"Of course," Jack replied, his enthusiasm evident as he began guiding us toward the caravan parked in the nearby carpark. The walk felt longer than it probably was, each step a delicate dance of maintaining my façade while absorbing the details around me.

He continued speaking as we walked toward the caravan. "We've owned this caravan for several years now, and it's served us very well."

As the caravan came into view, its sleek, modern design stood out, its shiny white exterior adorned with a bold blue stripe that added a touch of elegance. Jack's pride in the vehicle was palpable, his voice imbued with a fondness that likely stemmed from a myriad of memories created within its confines.

Mary, with a grace that complemented her husband's, added her own insights, her voice weaving through the details of the caravan's interior with practiced precision. "The interior is just as impressive," she chimed in, painting a picture of plush furnishings and comprehensive amenities that promised comfort and convenience. Her description of the cosy kitchen, the comfortable sleeping area, and the spacious seating area crafted an inviting image, while the mention of an outdoor awning conjured visions of leisurely days spent under the sun.

Each word they spoke was designed to sell, yet there was an authenticity to their pitch that resonated with me, even through the layers of my pretence. As Sophie, I listened intently, nodding and smiling at appropriate intervals, all the while the real Beatrix inside cataloged every detail, acutely aware of the stakes involved in this transaction beyond the mere purchase of a caravan.

"It sounds like a wonderful caravan," I offered, layering my voice with as much enthusiasm as I could muster, despite the internal skepticism that nagged at me. The caravan, while perfectly suitable for the settlers' needs, was a far cry from what I would have chosen for myself in a different life. Yet, the necessity of the moment dictated my actions, not personal preference. "Can you tell me more about its history and maintenance?" I inquired, my fingers discreetly crossed behind my back, a silent plea to the universe that my questions would steer the conversation in the right direction.

Jack's response came with a sense of pride, his posture straightening slightly as he spoke. "We've always taken excellent care of the caravan," he assured me. His words painted a picture of meticulous attention and care, a testament to the vehicle's reliability and the joy it had brought them. "We've kept up with all of the necessary repairs and maintenance, and we've never had any major issues with it. It's been a reliable and enjoyable vehicle for us, and we hope it will be the same for you."

Mary chimed in, her voice carrying a tender note as she spoke of their attachment to the caravan. "We've put a lot of love and care into the caravan over the years, and it shows in every inch of it." Her statement resonated with sincerity, reinforcing the narrative of a cherished possession rather than a mere piece of equipment.

"I can see that," I responded, my smile a well-crafted façade as I absorbed their words, recognising the emotional value they placed on the caravan. It was more than just a vehicle to them; it was a vessel of memories and experiences. "I'm interested in making an offer. Can we discuss the price you listed?" I ventured, steering the conversation towards the practicalities of the transaction, the final hurdle in this elaborate dance of negotiation.

"Of course," Jack replied, his tone open and amenable, signalling a readiness to engage in the discussion of numbers.

"We're quite flexible on price," Mary interjected, her glance toward Jack revealing a shared understanding, a united front in the face of this pivotal moment. Their flexibility offered a glimmer of advantage, a small but significant leverage in the negotiation process.

My nervous fingers thumbed the wad of notes stuffed in my purse, the paper currency a tangible reminder of the importance of this transaction. "What discount can you give me if I pay in cash?" I inquired, my voice steady despite the internal churn of anxiety and anticipation.

"Cash?" Mary echoed, her reaction a blend of surprise and curiosity. Her eyes, a testament to years of life's experiences, widened slightly, betraying a flicker of unexpectedness at the proposal.

Jack shared a brief, loaded glance with his wife. It was one of those silent exchanges that spoke volumes, a testament to years of partnership where words become secondary to understanding. With a subtle nod from Mary, the decision was made. "We'll knock twenty percent off the listed price," Jack declared, his voice firm yet fair.

"That sounds reasonable to me," I responded, a sense of satisfaction bubbling within me. The comparison to antique negotiations flitted through my mind, a comforting analogy that momentarily eased the tension. I stifled the urge to let a triumphant grin break through my composed exterior.

"Great," Mary responded, her hand extending with an expectation that mirrored her earlier surprise. Her gesture was as eager as it was decisive, a bridge to the conclusion of our dealings.

With a shared eagerness to seal the deal, I counted the notes with meticulous care, ensuring the accuracy of the exchange. The crisp rustle of the banknotes as they transferred from my hand to Mary's felt like the final note in the symphony of our negotiation.

"Do you need a receipt with that?" Jack's question, cautious and considerate, momentarily pierced the bubble of triumph. I paused, a brief interlude where the implications of that choice hung in the balance. *No receipt, no name, and no evidence!*

Shaking my head, I opted for the path of less documentation. "Um, no, I don't need a receipt," I assured, my tone laced with an amiable sincerity. The absence of a paper trail was a strategic choice, aligning with the need for discretion. "Just the keys," I added, my smile warm and appreciative, a mask that veiled the intricate dance of motives and decisions playing out beneath the surface.

"Congratulations," Jack intoned, his voice imbued with a mix of satisfaction and a hint of sentimentality as he handed over a small set of keys. The metal felt cool and heavy in my hand, a tangible symbol of the transaction we'd just completed. "She's all yours."

"Thank you," I responded, my voice measured, my grasp on the keys tight. They were not just keys to a vehicle but to a new chapter for the settlers, a responsibility that weighed on me as much as the metal in my palm.

Mary's sudden attention to the time broke the momentary reflection. "Oh, look at the time," she exclaimed, her eyes darting to her watch, a well-practiced gesture that signalled a shift in the interaction. "We promised we'd visit the grandchildren," she explained, her face alight with the soft glow of familial affection.

"You remember, don't you dear?" she prodded her husband, a gentle tug on his arm reinforcing her words.

"The grandchildren... oh, the grandchildren. Of course," Jack echoed, a touch of feigned forgetfulness in his tone, perhaps a playful acknowledgment of the routines and rhythms that defined their aged lives.

"It's fine," I assured them, a dismissive wave serving as my blessing for their departure. The undercurrent of my gesture was one of relief, eager to end the charade and turn my full attention to the task at hand. "I can handle it all from here," I asserted, more to myself than to them. The couple's departure marked the end of one act and the beginning of another, this time with me as the sole player on stage.

The truth was, I didn't care what details the couple may have been concealing with their abrupt departure. I had purchased the caravan for a great price.

*And it's not like anybody will be taking the caravan anywhere once I get it to Clivilius anyway,* I reminded myself, waving to the couple as they departed.

As they walked away, I allowed myself a moment to watch them go, their figures gradually blending into the park's tapestry. Turning back to the caravan, I felt a steady transition from the role of Sophie back to Beatrix, the weight of my true intentions settling back onto my shoulders.

"It's just a temporary shelter," I muttered to the empty air, my gaze lingering on the caravan.

❖

With the newly purchased caravan securely in tow, I stepped out of Jamie's car. The gentle breeze toyed with my hair, unruly strands escaping my ponytail's grasp in a playful defiance of my attempts at order.

Frustration bubbled up as I wrestled with the hair tie, yanking at the rebellious locks in a vain effort to impose some semblance of control. The strands fluttered in front of my eyes, a veil of annoyance that momentarily distracted me.

"Beatrix!" Luke's voice, tinged with an unmistakable note of excitement, cut through my momentary preoccupation with my hair. His tone, brimming with energy, was a sharp contrast to the practical concerns dominating my mind.

I couldn't help but roll my eyes inwardly, wondering what could possibly have him so enthusiastic. I shook my head and refocused on the task at hand. "Can you two unhitch the caravan?" I asked, voice tinged with a hint of impatience, my hands still preoccupied with the futile task of taming my hair.

But Luke, ever caught up in his own world of discoveries and experiments, seemed to barely register my request. "I need to test something with you," he said, his words carrying a weight of urgency that suggested his latest fascination wasn't just a mere distraction but something he deemed critically important.

Paul's interruption, marked by his perplexed expression, instantly brought me back to the logistical challenges at hand. "How am I supposed to move the caravan back to the camp if it's not connected to a vehicle?" he asked, his tone a mix of confusion and mild exasperation.

I released a heavy sigh, a sign of my growing annoyance, yet I was conscious to temper my visible frustration. "You've got other vehicles here," I retorted with a hint of impatience, the words slipping out sharper than I intended. "Surely, one of those has a tow bar you can use." It seemed so obvious to me.

Paul grunted in frustration, and I couldn't help but feel a little annoyed at his behaviour.

"You're doing a lot of grunting today," Luke teased his brother with a chuckle and a playful slap across the shoulder.

"I can always bring you another vehicle with a tow bar?" I offered Paul, who reluctantly began unhitching the caravan again.

As Luke redirected his attention to me, his question cut through the momentary respite. "I can't go through your Portal, and you can't go through mine, right?" he inquired, his eyes alight with the curiosity that so often drove his actions.

"Right," I replied, my eyes narrowing in caution as I tried to anticipate where he was going with this line of questioning.

"So, what if that also means that I can't open my Portal if you have yours open and vice versa?" Luke's question hung in the air, his smile one of satisfaction at the potential revelation. It was a hypothesis that, if correct, could redefine our understanding of the Portals' operations and limitations.

The realisation hit me like a sudden gust of wind, sending a ripple through my thoughts. "The router!" I gasped out, the pieces of the puzzle clicking together with startling clarity. The memory of the Portal remaining stubbornly open while we fiddled with the laptop and Luke's absence during that time coalesced into a singular, alarming picture.

"Exactly!" Luke's voice, laced with a mix of excitement and validation, confirmed my conclusion. "I'm pretty sure my Portal Key wasn't working at the same time that you had your Portal active with that blasted router." His words, though spoken with a hint of frustration, resonated with a sense of breakthrough, as if we'd just uncovered a critical rule in the elusive handbook of Portal mechanics.

"Shit," I whispered under my breath, a wave of dread washing over me. This wasn't just a minor hiccup; it was a potential flaw in our lifeline, a glitch in our gateway between worlds that could have dire consequences. *Just another complication to add to Guardian life!* The thought was both sardonic and sobering, a reminder of the ever-present danger and complexity woven into the fabric of our entanglement with Clivilius.

Luke's next instructions snapped me back to the present, a plan already forming in his mind. "I have a small truck with fence supplies to bring through. Beatrix, go somewhere safe on earth and wait for two minutes. Give me enough time to get this truck here. I'll leave my Portal active for another few minutes and in that time, you keep trying your Portal Key," he said, the rapid pace of his words matching his decisiveness.

"Yeah, good idea," I responded, my voice steady despite the swirling mix of anxiety and determination inside me. Testing Luke's theory wasn't just a matter of scientific curiosity; it was a vital step in understanding the limitations and risks of our Portals, a way to gauge the thin line we tread between control and calamity.

As I nodded in agreement, a chilling image flashed through my mind—the menacing shadow of a panther, its eyes glinting with predatory intent. The thought of being trapped, unable to activate my Portal and escape such a threat, sent a shiver down my spine. My life, our lives, depended on the functionality of these Portals, on understanding their quirks and constraints.

"What about the internet?" Paul's question pierced the tense atmosphere, his curiosity seemingly untamed by the implications of our discovery.

"Not now, Paul," Luke snapped. Without another word, he stepped through the Portal, his figure dissolving into the swirling vortex, leaving behind a palpable void charged with unanswered questions.

Confused at Luke's abrupt departure, I cast Paul a curious glance. He shrugged in reply.

"I have another caravan appointment to get to," I said, the words a reminder of the never-ending list of tasks that awaited me. My role, it seemed, demanded constant movement, a relentless push forward, regardless of the personal toll.

Slipping back into the driver's seat of Jamie's car, I ignited the engine, its roar a brief respite from the cacophony of concerns that echoed in my mind. As the vehicle lurched forward, carrying me back through the Portal, a sense of unease clung to me like a shadow. The life of a Guardian was fraught with challenges, each day a navigation through uncertainty and danger. This latest complication with the Portals added another layer of complexity, another potential peril in our delicate dance between worlds.

As the familiar yet always unsettling sensation of passing through the Portal enveloped me, my thoughts lingered on Luke's theory. The possibility of being stranded, of facing insurmountable obstacles with no escape, was a daunting prospect. The very essence of my missions hinged on the ability to traverse this gateway between worlds, and any threat to that capability was a threat to my own safety.

❖

The thrill of the second successful caravan purchase pulsed through me as I navigated the vehicle through the swirling energies of the Portal. A sense of accomplishment washed over me, a silent acknowledgment of my growing adeptness in this unorthodox role. *I bet that must be the fastest caravan sale ever*, I mused internally, a wry smile playing at the corners of my lips. I was indeed getting the hang of this, mastering the art of quick, efficient transactions in a world where every second mattered.

Sophie, my crafted alter-ego, had once again proven her worth. Meeting Lisa and Malcolm at a local cafe in Blackmans Bay, I slipped effortlessly into the persona, the mask fitting more comfortably with each use. The casual setting of the cafe, with its hum of background chatter and clinking of coffee cups, had provided a perfect cover for the transaction. Waving a handful of cash had simplified matters significantly, reducing the need for prolonged discussion and haggling. It was transactional, impersonal, but incredibly effective.

The absence of a receipt and the use of a fake name left a clear boundary between my Guardian identity and these brief, commercial interactions. Apart from a vague physical description, there was nothing to link me, Beatrix, to the caravan or the transaction. The reliance on cash, a deliberate choice, added another layer of anonymity, erasing any digital footprint that could trace back to me. In my mind, I doubted Lisa and Malcolm would bother with the formalities of recording such a cash-heavy transaction for tax purposes, especially under the informal circumstances of our exchange.

Back in Clivilius, the satisfaction from the recent acquisition dissipated quickly, replaced by a growing sense of disturbance. "He's still here," I murmured under my breath, my eyes fixating on Paul as he moved around the first caravan, which, to my frustration, had not budged an inch from its original spot.

Reluctantly, I conceded to let Paul use Jamie's car to transport the caravan back to the camp, a decision that now felt like a compromise against better judgment. I observed, almost in disbelief, as the car's wheels churned through the thick, Clivilian dust, sending clouds of the arid soil swirling into the air.

The duration of Paul's absence stretched, each passing moment amplifying the tension that knotted in my stomach. Yet, eventually, he returned, his presence a silent affirmation of the task's completion. But any relief I felt was short-lived.

Against my expressed wishes, Paul took it upon himself to attach Jamie's car to the first caravan, his determination evident in his brisk movements and focused expression. The sight sparked a surge of irritation within me, a mix of anger at his unilateral decision and anxiety over the potential consequences of his actions.

As Luke joined Paul, the two brothers engaged in a conversation just out of my earshot, their huddled figures a visual representation of my exclusion from the dialogue. "I need the car back, Paul!" My voice, laced with a blend of exasperation and urgency, sliced through the distance, but it seemed to make no impact on the duo.

Feeling a blend of desperation and indignation, I approached, intent on unhitching the caravan myself. My actions, however, were uncoordinated, fuelled by a cocktail of frustration and haste. "C'mon, Paul, just help me unhitch it," I found myself pleading, my hands coming together in a gesture of near supplication. My voice softened, "Luke?" I called out, locking eyes with him, my gaze sharp, imploring.

Luke's retreat was as swift as it was frustrating, his arms raised in a gesture that spoke more of avoidance than surrender. "I have stuff to do," he declared, his voice carrying a note of finality that left no room for negotiation.

Paul's mention of needing more wood felt almost trivial in the moment, a mundane concern juxtaposed against the pressing issue of the caravan. My focus was singular—on the caravan still hitched to Jamie's car, essential for my next task. Paul's wood dilemma seemed a distant, almost inconsequential matter.

"I'll take care of the wood," Luke's voice, offering a semblance of solidarity to Paul, barely registered as he gave his brother a comforting squeeze on the shoulder—a gesture of support that I yearned for in that moment of escalating stress.

"Luke?" My voice, tinged with a mix of desperation and frustration, trailed off after his retreating figure as he vanished through the Portal, leaving me to grapple with the situation at hand.

"I'll only be five minutes," Paul's plea echoed, his words attempting to bridge the gap between request and assurance. Yet, they landed with a hollow thud against the backdrop of my growing exasperation.

"Fine," I murmured, my acquiescence more a surrender to the circumstances than a genuine concession. The weight of defeat settled heavily upon me as Paul, his face lit up with a victorious smile, climbed into the driver's seat, oblivious or indifferent to the turmoil churning inside me.

With a sense of resigned determination, I slumped into the Clivilian dust, a cloud of fine particles rising around me, settling on my skin and clothes, a gritty reminder of the planet's unyielding nature. There, seated in the dust, I resolved to wait stubbornly for Paul's return, a silent protest against the day's trials. My mind, however, couldn't help but wander, tracing the potential paths of the day's decisions, each one a thread in the intricate tapestry of our survival in Clivilius. The wait wasn't just a physical one; it was a mental journey through the complexities and challenges of my new life as a Guardian, each moment laden with the weight of decisions yet to come.

# MISSION CHARLIE

## *1338.210.3*

As the sun began to set, casting a warm, golden hue over the horizon, our small group of Bixbus settlers gathered around the bonfire, their faces illuminated by the flickering flames. The air was filled with the comforting crackle of the firewood and the subtle scent of smoke mingling with the tantalising aroma of food. Life in the settlement had taken a turn towards the slightly more comfortable, a change I embraced wholeheartedly.

I stood a little apart, observing the scene, the corners of my mouth turning up in a subtle smile. The arrival of camping supplies and power generators had transformed their daily existence, and I couldn't help but bask in the quiet pride of facilitating that change. It was a clever manoeuvre, securing these essentials along with the third caravan purchase of the day. I knew the value of being prepared, of seizing opportunity when it presented itself, even if luck played its part in the acquisition of the power generators.

The fatigue from the day's endeavours weighed on my shoulders, a physical manifestation of the mental gymnastics I, or rather Sophie, my shrewd alter-ego, had performed. Sophie was the mask I donned when negotiations demanded a tougher, more assertive presence, a façade that allowed me to navigate the complexities of trade and diplomacy with greater ruthlessness and anonymity. Now, as the evening wore on, I allowed myself to shed that persona, sinking into the more reflective, introspective side of Beatrix.

A large pot of chilli was making its rounds among the settlers, a communal offering that seemed to warm not just the body but the soul. I watched as hands, rough from the day's work, ladled the rich, aromatic stew into bowls, steam rising and blending with the cool evening air. The chilli was a simple yet hearty fare, with chunks of tender beef and beans bathed in a spicy tomato gravy that promised warmth and satisfaction. Accompanied by a small basket of warm, crusty bread, it was more than just sustenance; it was a small luxury in our rugged existence.

The chatter and occasional bursts of laughter among the settlers provided a satisfying contrast to the underlying tension that permeated the camp. Despite the joviality, there was a palpable sense of vigilance, a collective awareness of the unknown dangers that lay just beyond the camp's perimeter, in the darkening wilderness. It was a reminder that, despite our small victories and moments of comfort, we were never truly at ease.

I listened to the conversations, the stories, and the shared experiences, feeling both a part of this community and a spectator. My mind wandered to the days ahead, the challenges we would face, and the resilience we would need to muster. And yet, in this moment, there was a semblance of peace, a fleeting sense of belonging that I cherished. Here, amid the flickering shadows and the comforting presence of fellow settlers, I allowed myself a moment of respite, a moment to simply be Beatrix, unburdened by expectations and roles, basking in the humble yet profound joy of our shared human experience.

❖

As the meal concluded, the remnants of the chilli vanished into the satisfied bellies of the settlers, the atmosphere around the bonfire shifted subtly. The group began to disperse, a slow, almost reluctant scattering of bodies and spirits. Some sought the sanctuary of their new caravans and tents, while others, like moths drawn to a flame, lingered by the fire, immersed in hushed conversations.

I remained a silent observer for a moment, watching as the night deepened. Among the dwindling group, my attention was particularly captured by Grant Ironbach, the esteemed Director of the Bonorong Wildlife Sanctuary in Hobart, and his sister, Sarah. Their presence here, in Clivilius, sparked a blend of curiosity and intrigue within me. My previous encounters with them had been brief yet memorable, and their unexpected appearance in our settlement piqued my interest.

I had heard through the grapevine—Luke's offhand comments—that a visit to Grant was on the agenda. Yet, the reality of his presence here, far from the sanctuary he so passionately dedicated his life to, was a puzzle that tugged at my mind. In the whirlwind of my duties and Paul's missions, I hadn't had the opportunity to delve into the hows and whys of their arrival. The notion that Grant would abandon his sanctuary without a compelling reason seemed unfathomable.

Spying the young wildlife enthusiasts on the outskirts of the group, engaged in a lively conversation with Paul, I approached cautiously.

"Grant," I interjected, my voice a mix of familiarity and intrigue as I approached the circle, my hand outstretched toward the tall figure whose presence commanded attention. Grant's stature, robust and assured, was complemented by his short, brown hair, which seemed to shimmer slightly under the firelight.

As I drew closer, the group naturally parted, allowing me to directly address him. Paul, understanding the moment's significance, stepped aside with a subtle nod, acknowledging the personal connection that needed its space to rekindle.

"Beatrix," Grant responded, his voice carrying a weight of sincerity. His green eyes, bright and discerning, met mine with a spark of recognition. Our handshake was firm, a testament to the strength and candour that defined him. "It's been a while."

"Perhaps a little too long," I admitted, feeling a twinge of nostalgia mixed with the current of unfolding events. The words floated between us, laden with unspoken acknowledgments of the time that had slipped away since our last encounter.

"You've met my sister, Sarah, haven't you?" Grant asked, motioning toward the woman standing beside him.

"I have," I answered. I turned to her, noting the elegance of her white sundress, which contrasted with the rustic backdrop of our gathering. It fluttered gently in the night breeze, mirroring the grace of her demeanour. Her sandals, a simple yet chic choice, revealed toes adorned with playful colours, hinting at a personality that embraced both sophistication and a touch of whimsy.

Sarah's nod and smile were infused with warmth, acknowledging our previous acquaintance and the thread of connection through the wildlife sanctuary. "Thank you for having the wildlife sanctuary added to the list of supported charities," she expressed, her gratitude genuine and her smile reaching her eyes.

My response was a blank stare, a momentary pause as I processed her words, a silent bridge between past actions and their lingering echoes in the present.

"Charlie Claiborne's charity event at MONA," Grant added, his elbow gently nudging mine, a friendly gesture that brought a hint of informality to our exchange. "I'm curious how you managed that one."

My cheeks flushed with heat as the memory of the charity event at MONA surged to the forefront of my mind, vivid and unbidden. "It was nothing," I murmured, attempting to infuse a tone of nonchalance into my voice while internally cringing at the recollection. I was eager to steer the conversation away from past endeavours and towards the present, peculiar circumstances that had brought us together. "So, what brings the two of you to this barren place?" I inquired, a hint of curiosity piercing my feigned indifference.

Paul's glance was sharp, a silent reprimand that I felt more keenly than any spoken word. I met his eyes briefly, offering a shrug that I hoped conveyed my regret without undermining my position. My question lingered in the air, unabated and pointed.

"Work," Sarah's reply was succinct, her voice steady, yet there was an undercurrent of something deeper, a resonance that hinted at layers yet to be uncovered. Her single word response, laden with meaning, piqued my interest further.

"Oh?" The word escaped me, a reflexive expression of my surprise at the brevity of her answer. Grant, sensing my curiosity—or perhaps driven by his own agenda—elaborated on their mission, his words sketching the outline of a project that was as ambitious as it was unexpected.

"In short, we've agreed to do an initial assessment of the place and provide recommendations on how a wildlife sanctuary can be established here." His explanation, while informative, opened a floodgate of questions in my mind, each one vying for precedence.

"You have?" My response was automatic, a mix of intrigue and a burgeoning sense of unease. There was a piece of the puzzle missing, a gap in the narrative that left me feeling unmoored. The notion of a wildlife sanctuary here, in this untamed land, was both exhilarating and daunting, a dichotomy that resonated with the very essence of Clivilius.

"We're only here for a week or two," Sarah said, giving Karen a brief greeting wave as she approached.

Sarah's acknowledgment of Karen's arrival did little to distract me from the weight of the revelation. "And after that?" The question sprang from my lips, unfiltered and raw, a direct conduit to the churn of thoughts and emotions swirling within me.

Grant's response came amidst the distraction of Karen's approach, his words slicing through the burgeoning chaos of my thoughts. "Bonorong won't manage itself forever," he stated, a simple declaration that carried the weight of inevitability.

The impact of Grant's words was visceral, a metaphorical blow that left me momentarily unsteady, my thoughts reeling as I processed the implications. With my brow knitted in confusion and eyes wide with a mix of shock and dawning comprehension, I instinctively turned toward Paul, seeking an anchor in the tumult of my emotions.

Paul, for his part, appeared distinctly uncomfortable, his chuckle tinged with nervousness as he shifted his weight from one foot to the other, reminiscent of a dancer caught in an awkward rhythm. His usually composed demeanour was frayed at the edges, betraying the tension of the moment.

"Shit," the word slipped out, a whispered exhalation that carried with it the weight of my sudden realisation. The pieces of the puzzle that had just clicked into place only served to highlight the gaps in my understanding, amplifying my sense of unease.

As Grant seamlessly merged into the conversation with Sarah and Karen, I found myself being gently but firmly guided away by Paul. Our steps carried us to a quieter spot, a temporary refuge from the buzz of the gathering, where our isolation mirrored the seriousness of Paul's demeanour.

"Beatrix," he began, his voice a low, sombre cadence that seemed to resonate with our secluded discussion. "I have another mission for you," he revealed, each word deliberate, infused with an urgency that commanded my full attention.

My response was a sharp hiss, a mix of frustration and incredulity. "What, besides keeping from Grant and Sarah the fact that they won't be going back to Bonorong!?" The words tumbled out, edged with a blend of anger and despair.

A fleeting thought crossed my mind, a glimmer of hope amidst the turmoil. "Or can they?" I asked.

The silent shake of Paul's head, accompanied by a muted "No," extinguished that flicker of hope, sealing the reality of their permanence in Clivilius. His nonverbal response was a clear, unequivocal confirmation of the path laid out before us —a path marked by subterfuge and the looming shadow of undisclosed truths.

*Shit*, I cursed inwardly, the word echoing the earlier expletive but laden with a deeper sense of foreboding.

"My dog, Charlie, is currently in Broken Hill with my wife and kids. I miss her dearly and I know she'd love it here," Paul said.

My heart tugged in sympathy, yet my mind recoiled at the suggestion, especially in the shadow of Duke's recent passing. "Hang on a second," I found myself saying, the words sharp with a mix of incredulity and concern.

The air around us seemed to thicken as I addressed the absurdity of the idea. "We've only just dealt with Duke's death yesterday and you already want to bring another dog to this godforsaken place?" My voice, laced with a cocktail of emotions, echoed slightly in the open space.

Paul's response, a mixture of hesitation and resolve, did little to alleviate my growing unease. "She'll make a great early warning system," he argued, his words seemingly practical yet tinged with a hint of desperation. The notion of replacing Duke so swiftly, using Charlie as a mere tool for the camp's security, unsettled me deeply.

"You're unbelievable," I retorted, the frustration evident in my tone. The idea of bringing another innocent life into our tangled web of challenges felt increasingly reckless. "Not only do you want to bring another animal here, but you want me to dognap her!"

"I know it sounds crazy, but–"

"Yeah, you're right!" I interrupted Paul, my voice rising as I spoke. "It is crazy!"

"Please, Beatrix," Paul begged. "Claire isn't very good with pets."

As my gaze unintentionally caught Grant and Sarah's figures entering my peripheral vision, a fleeting thought crossed my mind. With their expertise and compassion, perhaps Charlie would indeed find a semblance of safety and care here. This realisation, however, did little to ease the moral dilemma I faced.

The conflict raging within me—between my loyalty to Paul, my concern for Charlie, and my reservations about the plan—left me teetering on the edge of a decision I wasn't ready to embrace. Yet, despite my reservations, the weight of Paul's plea and the unspoken promise of support from our new arrivals nudged me toward reluctant acquiescence.

With a heavy sigh, signalling the internal battle I had just endured, I yielded. "Fine," I huffed, the word heavy with resignation. In that moment, I felt the weight of not just Duke's loss or Charlie's impending arrival, but the broader realisation of our precarious existence in Bixbus, where each decision seemed to lead me further into uncharted territories, laden with unforeseen consequences.

*4338.211*

*(30 July 2018)*

# CHARLIE INTERRUPTED

## 4338.211.1

Inhaling deeply, I drew in the rich, intoxicating scents of the motorhome's fresh new leather interior, a luxury that tingled my senses with its novel allure. "Idiot," I murmured with a smirk, my voice laced with a mix of amusement and disdain, watching the waving dealership owner shrink in the motorhome's side mirror. His oblivious cheerfulness contrasted sharply with my covert intentions. Perched smugly in the driver's seat, I felt the faux-leather beneath me, its plushness a reminder of the façade I had to maintain. The indicator clicked rhythmically, a metronome to my escalating excitement, as I turned the large vehicle onto the main road, the vehicle that I was apparently only taking for a test drive. "You're never going to see us again," I chuckled softly, the sound a blend of thrill and guilt, my face glowing with the triumph of my deceit.

The plan had taken shape rapidly, spurred by necessity and a touch of desperation. I'd given myself an early start, fully aware that the day ahead was a labyrinthine quest – finding Paul's dog and delivering her to Clivilius was no minor errand. The impromptu flight from Hobart to Adelaide last night was a testament to my resolve, a whirlwind decision that set the stage for today's caper. This morning, fresh off the plane, I had zeroed in on my target: a motorhome dealership in the bustling heart of Adelaide. Initially, I had considered sourcing a caravan or two, a logical and less conspicuous choice. But impatience gnawed at me, urging me toward a bolder, more audacious move.

Seated in the back of a taxi, the city's early light casting shadows and highlights across my path, I revisited my plans. A motorhome, luxurious and unmistakably conspicuous, was far more extravagant than the humble caravans I had first considered. Yet, as the taxi weaved through the awakening streets, my resolve hardened. I had no intention of parting with a single cent for the vehicle. The motorhome wasn't just a means of transport; it was a statement, a bold stroke in the grand scheme I was weaving. *Besides*, I rationalised, *the new inhabitant of this motorhome would surely relish the upgrade from a simple tent.* This thought, a blend of justification and self-assurance, cemented my resolve as I stepped out of the taxi, ready to play my part.

The dealership was a canvas of possibilities, the vehicles lined up like chess pieces, awaiting their role in my plan. As I manipulated the old dealership owner, a sweet concoction of charm and guile, I couldn't help but marvel at the ease of it all. The keys in my hand were not just metal and plastic; they were the keys to the next phase of my mission, a mission that was as much about liberation as it was about deception.

With every kilometre that stretched behind me, the excitement mingled with a twinge of guilt, a reminder of the thin line I was treading. But in the grand tapestry of my endeavours, these moments of doubt were mere threads, overshadowed by the vivid hues of determination and purpose. As the motorhome hummed along, a steel beast under my control, I couldn't shake off the exhilaration of the chase, the rush of bending rules to craft my own narrative. In this mobile fortress, I wasn't just Beatrix; I was a maestro orchestrating a symphony of moves, each one leading closer to my elusive goal.

And then, as if the universe itself conspired to temper my daring escapade, the adrenaline rush that had fuelled my audacity dissipated abruptly. I found myself ensnared in a tedious crawl through roadworks, the kind that stretches like an endless ribbon of inconvenience across the asphalt. The orange cones and warning signs seemed to mock my urgency, creating a glaring contrast to the freedom I had just tasted. Glancing at the digital display on the dashboard, the time stared back at me, a silent reminder of the ticking clock in this high-stakes game of deception I was playing.

The reality of my situation began to gnaw at the edges of my confidence. How long would it be before the dealer, with his unsuspecting smile and trusting eyes, reached for the phone to dial the fake number I had left in his hands? A shiver of anxiety rippled through me at the thought, an unsettling reminder of the fragility of my plan.

For a fleeting moment, doubt crept in, whispering questions of morality and consequence. "The guy did take a copy of your license," I mumbled to the empty air around me, my voice a mix of worry and frustration. My fingers began a restless dance on the edge of the steering wheel, tapping out a rhythm of growing impatience and uncertainty.

But then, as if flicking a switch, I shifted my mindset, invoking a personal pep talk to quell the rising tide of apprehension. "But I'm not in Tasmania now," I reasoned, trying to inject a dose of reassurance into my wavering resolve. The geographical distance felt like a thin veil of safety, a fragile barrier between me and the potential fallout of my actions.

With each kilometre that rolled under the motorhome's tires, I fortified my resolve, reminding myself of the ultimate goal. "Once I've taken the motorhome to Clivilius, there will be absolutely no evidence." The words were a mantra, a beacon of hope in the murky waters of my ethical dilemma. I clung to the idea that the ends would justify the means, that my actions, however questionable, were in service of a greater good.

*And besides, the police are already investigating Luke.* This thought offered a twisted comfort, a reminder that my misdeeds were but a drop in an ocean of larger schemes and darker deeds. "If we are going to keep the settlement alive and supported—".

My foot slammed the brake in a sudden, instinctive jolt, my hand sounding the horn in a burst of warning. The sharp, blaring sound cut through the air, a clear signal to the audacious driver attempting to usurp my space. "My vehicle's bigger than yours!" I bellowed, the words muffled by the closed windows, my voice a mix of anger and indignation. *The audacity of some people,* I thought, feeling a surge of irritation at the cheeky attempt to undermine my command of the road.

But the moment of disruption passed, and I refocused, returning to the pressing concerns that gnawed at my mind. "It's only a matter of time before the police come after both of us," I muttered, voicing the looming threat that shadowed our every move. My gaze drifted to the Portal Key, its innocuous appearance belying the immense power it harboured. Positioned between my legs, it was a constant reminder of the fine line I walked between audacity and recklessness.

*It's our ultimate escape,* I reassured myself, the thought offering a flicker of confidence in the swirling uncertainty. *With this amount of power, it would be near impossible for us to get caught.* The logic was sound, the strategy clear, but the assurance was fleeting, dissolving as quickly as it had formed.

Memories of Luke's recent ordeal intruded, a jarring reminder of the precariousness of our situation. The drama unfolded vividly in my mind's eye – the tense moments with the Portal activated too long, the near-miss with Detective Jenkins. Luke had been lucky, far too lucky, and the reality of our vulnerability settled heavily upon me.

That final thought, the image of Luke's narrow escape, sent a nervous shudder skittering across my shoulders. Despite the power at our fingertips, despite the careful calculations and bold manoeuvres, the risks we faced were starkly real, tangibly close.

I needed a hideaway, a secluded nook far from prying eyes, to hand over this motorhome to Paul. Time seemed to sprint, each glance at the clock amplifying the urgency of my mission. The tranquility of my solitude was shattered by the shrill ring of my mobile phone, an unwelcome intrusion that jerked my focus away from the winding road ahead.

My eyes flickered to the passenger seat, where the phone vibrated with persistence. The screen flashed an ominous "Unknown Number," a harbinger of potential complications I was not in the mood to confront. With a sigh bordering on resentment, I picked up the phone.

Reluctantly, I answered, the speakerphone filling the cabin with the clarity of the incoming voice. I perched the phone precariously on my thigh, a balancing act that mirrored the tightrope I was walking in my current endeavour.

"Beatrix?" The voice was familiar, yet it took a moment for the fog of recognition to clear. I responded with a guarded "Yeah," my mind racing to place the voice, to anticipate the angle of the conversation.

"It's Sergeant Charlie Claiborne," the voice identified itself, sending a jolt of alarm through me. My response was visceral, a whispered curse slipping through my lips as the phone nearly slipped from its precarious perch.

"Shit!" The word was a hiss of frustration, a release of the tension that tightened around my chest. Claiborne's voice, now tinny and distant, filtered through the speaker, urging me not to disconnect. "Beatrix, don't hang up!" he called, a note of urgency in his tone.

Slowly, with a deliberate lack of urgency, I retrieved the mobile, bringing it closer, my ear bracing for what I perceived as inevitable bad news. The world outside became a blur, the bustling road ahead a mere backdrop to the unfolding drama in my hand. "What do you want?" I asked, my tone dripping with reluctance.

"Your sister is in trouble," Charlie's voice came through, weighted with a seriousness that instantly tightened my stomach.

"Gladys?"

"Yes."

A long sigh was my only immediate response, a brief respite as I attempted to corral my spiralling thoughts. My focus shifted momentarily to the road, a futile attempt to anchor myself in the present.

Charlie's voice cut through the tense silence, "There's been an incident at the Owens' property in Collinsvale." His words felt like a cold splash of reality, jolting me.

"What do you know about that?" I snapped, irritation and fear intermingling, creating a cocktail of emotions that threatened to overwhelm my composure.

"Not a lot. Forensics are there now." The mention of forensics sent a shiver down my spine, a chilling indication of the complexity of the situation.

"Forensics?" My voice rose in pitch, a clear sign of the panic that was starting to claw at my insides. "Where's Gladys?" The urgency in my question was palpable, a mix of sisterly concern and a deep-seated fear of losing one of the few constants in my tumultuous life.

"Apparently she's involved in an ongoing pursuit." The words were like a punch to the gut, each one amplifying the dread building within me.

My eyes bulged. "What the hell does that mean?" The demand for clarity was desperate, a plea for something solid to grasp onto in the maelstrom of uncertainty.

"I don't have any further details." Charlie's admission, meant to be informational, felt like an abandonment, leaving me to navigate the turbulent waters of speculation and worry alone.

"What the fuck are you doing, Gladys," I whispered under my breath, the motorhome decelerating as I veered off the main road, steering toward an avenue that promised the seclusion I desperately needed. The trees seemed to lean in closer, their shadows enveloping the vehicle, mirroring the growing unease in my heart.

"I know I shouldn't be so direct on this type of line, but I need to know, Beatrix. Is Gladys a Guardian?" Charlie's question pierced through the growing tension, his words laden with a significance that sent a jolt of surprise coursing through me.

His unexpected insight into our world caught me off guard, and for a moment, I grappled with the extent of trust I could afford to place in him. "Not that I know of," I replied, my voice a careful blend of caution and candour. There was a dance of truths and half-truths we were performing, and I wasn't ready to reveal all my cards just yet.

"If Gladys isn't going to go to Clivilius, she needs to be careful. She needs to get the cops off her tail. And don't ever return to that Collinsvale property." His words, a blend of warning and advice, weighed heavily on me.

"You're the sergeant," I countered, my confusion and frustration bubbling to the surface. "Can't you call off the chase?"

"There's only so much more I can do to protect you all. They're onto me, Beatrix." The gravity in Charlie's voice was unmistakable.

"What do you mean they?" I pressed, seeking clarity, but his next words sidestepped my inquiry, adding layers to the mystery.

"Don't try and make any contact with me, Beatrix," he instructed, a note of finality in his tone that signalled the closing of a door, the narrowing of our options.

My mouth opened, but no words emerged, just a silent echo of my racing thoughts. "Be careful, Beatrix," he added, a parting gesture of concern that hung in the air as the line went dead, leaving me enveloped in silence, save for the soft hum of the motorhome and the whisper of leaves brushing against its sides.

Pulling the motorhome over to the side of the road, I allowed the engine's gentle purr to fall into silence, mirroring the stillness of the phone in my hand. My fingers hovered over the device, torn between the urge to reconnect with Charlie or to seek out Gladys. After a moment teetering on the edge of indecision, I dialled Gladys.

"Beatrix," her voice crackled through the speaker, a lifeline in the swirling uncertainty.

"Gladys, listen to me," I started, urgency threading through my words as my hands began to betray a tremble, the onset of panic creeping in. "The police know it's you in one of those cars, and they're at the Owens' property now."

"How do you know that?" Her question, simple yet loaded, punctured the bubble of my constructed calm.

*How much do I tell her?* The internal debate was swift, a rapid assessment of risks and necessities. Opting for caution, I chose a veiled truth over full disclosure. "I have a contact that has an informant in the Hobart Police, and they've just called to warn me." The words flowed with a practiced ease, a testament to the necessity of such half-truths in our precarious existence.

A heavy pause followed, laden with unsaid fears and unasked questions.

"I'm at the property now. Don't come here," I instructed, weaving a lie with the ease of a seasoned fabricator. The words were a strategic manoeuvre, a play to keep her safe, or at least safer than she would be heading into a known danger zone.

As I ended the call, a part of me recoiled at the ease of the deception. Yet, I rationalised, the lie was a necessary shield, a protective measure in a game where the stakes were perilously high. I knew my next steps would lead me to the Collinsvale property, not as a harbinger of doom but as a seeker of truths and a protector of kin.

With a determined turn of the key, the motorhome's engine hummed back to life, its steady thrum a backdrop to my erratic thoughts. My mission now was twofold: find a secluded spot to activate the Portal and transport the motorhome to Clivilius, all while mulling over the newfound ally in Sergeant Charlie Claiborne. The idea that our inside help might extend beyond him flickered through my mind, a glimmer of hope in a sea of uncertainty. *It's definitely a possibility*, I mused, acknowledging the silent network of Guardians whose reach and influence were perhaps more extensive than even Leigh knew.

As I drove the large vehicle, a newfound sense of purpose straightened my posture, my eyes scanning the environment with a mix of caution and newfound confidence. The ease with which I'd taken the motorhome now seemed like a minor feat compared to the broader canvas of our endeavours. *Maybe Charlie can help erase any trace of my involvement from the police records*, I pondered, allowing the notion to fuel a sense of optimism, manifesting in a broad grin that spread across my face.

In a moment of whimsy and longing for connection, I rolled down the window, letting the world in. The breeze greeted me like an old friend, playful and invigorating, carrying with it the scent of the outside world. It danced through my silver hair, the strands brushing against my skin in a ticklish caress that I chose to endure, a small price for the momentary freedom it offered.

My eyes caught sight of an ideal location – the back wall of a supermarket, inconspicuous enough for my purposes. With a careful turn of the steering wheel, I guided the motorhome toward it, the vehicle's bulk handling the curb with a noticeable jolt. The unexpected bounce triggered a sneeze, an abrupt, humanising interruption to my stream of strategic thoughts.

As I realigned my focus, the mundane grey of Adelaide's sky transitioned into the vibrant, almost surreal azure of Clivilius. The abrupt shift was disorienting, the familiar yet always startling transition jolting me back to the immediacy of my actions.

"Shit!" The expletive tore from my lips as instinct took over, my foot crashing down on the brake with all the force of my burgeoning panic. The motorhome lurched, a beast of metal and momentum protesting as it ground to a halt. Dust clouds mushroomed around us, a gritty, choking veil that obscured the figure lying ominously still before the vehicle. The harsh screech of the brakes was a physical assault, a discordant symphony with the frantic hammering of my heart.

Frozen in a moment of dread, I inched forward in my seat, my knuckles white from their death grip on the steering wheel, a tangible expression of my shock and fear. Leaning over, I peered out through the windscreen, the barrier between me and the potential catastrophe outside. "Is he dead?" The question slipped out in a whisper, a fragile thread of sound barely piercing the heavy silence that enveloped me. My eyes stung, not just from the biting dust but from the acute, pressing fear of what this could mean, of what I might have done.

Then, like apparitions in this chaos, Luke and Paul materialised, their sudden presence snapping me out of my paralysing horror. They moved with a purpose I couldn't muster, reaching for the man with a practiced urgency. As they dragged him from beneath the motorhome's imposing frame, I remained transfixed, the scene unfolding with a surreal clarity.

The door of the motorhome creaked ominously as I nudged it open, the sound slicing through the tense silence. My foot, trembling slightly, found the small instep, serving as a temporary anchor before I jumped down from the cab, my movements jerky with a blend of adrenaline and remorse.

"I'm so sorry," the words tumbled out as I rounded the vehicle, my voice laced with genuine concern. "Are you okay?" I inquired, though the question felt woefully inadequate given the circumstances.

Luke was already there, his gaze analytical as he surveyed the man's condition. "I don't see any blood," he remarked, a statement that offered a sliver of relief amidst the swirling worry.

Paul's attempt at a rudimentary medical check was almost comical under different circumstances. "How many fingers am I holding up?" he asked, his fingers wobbling slightly, an unintentional testament to our collective unease.

The man's response was a mute one, his eyes cloudy and unfocused, offering no recognition or understanding of Paul's inquiry.

"He's high," Luke deduced, his voice carrying a note of certainty. "And most likely dehydrated. You'd better take him back to camp." His diagnosis was clinical, a brief respite from the emotional turmoil that gripped me.

The arrival of Nial and Kain added new layers to the unfolding drama. "Everything okay?" Nial's question, though well-intentioned, felt almost rhetorical amidst the obvious disarray.

Paul's voice broke through the tense air, practical yet tinged with concern. "Can you two take him back to camp?"

Nial's exclamation cut sharply into the moment, his recognition of Adrian injecting a personal, jarring note into the proceedings. "Shit! Adrian. What the hell are you doing here?" His words, laced with incredulity and frustration, echoed my own startled confusion. Watching him step forward, the repeated slaps to Adrian's face seemed both an attempt to elicit clarity and a release of pent-up exasperation.

Paul's query, "You know him?" seemed almost rhetorical in the context of our tightly-knit community, where personal connections were as intertwined as the paths that crisscrossed our landscape.

Luke's comment, "Not surprising. Hobart's a small place," offered a dry slice of reality, a reminder of our interconnected existences, where personal histories often collided with the present with unpredictable force.

I observed, my heart heavy, as Nial's firm grip on Adrian's shoulders conveyed a mixture of determination and concern. "Let's get you to camp," he said, his voice steady.

Kain's agreement, "We'll come back," was a quiet vow, his assistance in helping Adrian to stand a testament to their collective responsibility for one another.

Paul's silent nod was a sombre seal on the exchange, a mutual understanding that resonated among them. As they departed, a reflective mood settled, a collective contemplation of the unpredictable dance of fate and choice, and the unspoken acknowledgment of the fragile thread that connected each moment, each decision, in the intricate weave of our lives in Clivilius.

As the trio receded into the distance, ensuring they were far enough away not to overhear, I couldn't contain the whirlwind of questions and emotions churning inside me. The need for answers, for some semblance of understanding, was overwhelming.

"What's going on, Luke? Why the hell is Gladys in a bloody car chase with the police?" The words spilled out, my voice laced with a rising tension that mirrored the turmoil within. The situation felt surreal, a narrative unfolding with us at its core, yet spiralling unpredictably.

Luke's response was infuriatingly calm, almost detached. "Things didn't go quite according to plan with Adrian," he said, initiating an explanation that seemed painfully obvious.

*No shit!* The thought blared in my mind, a silent scream of frustration. My irritation wasn't just with the situation but with Luke's nonchalant demeanour. The realisation that Adrian's life had hung in the balance, that my actions could have ended tragically, was a heavy weight, a confrontation with the potential consequences of our intertwined lives.

"Clearly," Paul interjected, his casual tone striking a dissonant chord within me. The undercurrent of tension was palpable, the gravity of our predicament hanging over us like a dark cloud.

Luke's account continued, outlining a series of decisions and actions that seemed increasingly reckless. "We chased after him when he took off," he explained, as if the choice was a mere footnote in their day.

"You couldn't just let him go?" My question was tinged with incredulity, a reflection of my struggle to reconcile their actions with what they expected to achieve.

Our attention was abruptly drawn to a commotion near Adrian's ute, the scene unfolding like a tableau of discord.

Adrian's voice, firm and laced with a hint of defiance, cut through the air. "I'm just getting the rest of my gear," he declared, pushing Nial away with a force that spoke volumes of his agitation and desperation.

"He'd already seen the Portal," Luke interjected, redirecting our focus to the pressing concern—my sister's precarious situation. "I know he's high, but I didn't think it was wise to let him go. Who knows—"

My response was instinctive, a sharp glare aimed at Luke. "Wise?" The word escaped my lips soaked in incredulity and tinged with anger. I couldn't wrap my head around his logic, or lack thereof. "You didn't think it was wise to let him go, yet you had no qualms with racing through the streets and attracting the attention of the police?" My voice climbed, a crescendo of frustration and disbelief. Each word I uttered was a pointed barb, aiming to puncture the bubble of his flawed reasoning.

Luke's reaction was telling—eyes narrowing, lips parting, but no sound emerging. It was as if my words had struck a chord, or perhaps, he was grappling with the weight of his own decisions.

Paul cut through the mounting tension with a question aimed at unravelling the sequence of events. "And how did you finally get him here?"

Luke's answer, while straightforward, unveiled the extent of their desperate measures. "We came through a wall of the toilet block at Myrtle Forest," he confessed.

"And my sister?" The urgency in my question couldn't be masked, my patience fraying at the edges as the seconds ticked away, each one a potential harbinger of worsening scenarios for Gladys. The tension knotted within me, a silent acknowledgment of the looming crisis. *This is going to get worse, isn't it,* I chastised myself internally, a bitter taste of apprehension settling in as I awaited Luke's response.

His expression, a mix of concern and discomfort, did little to quell the rising storm within me. His brows knitted together, his face flushing a deep shade of red, a visual testament to the severity of his next words.

"I told her to run," Luke admitted, his voice laced with a mix of defensiveness and regret.

"Fuck's sake, Luke!" The expletive burst from me, a spontaneous release of pent-up frustration and disbelief. *How could he think running was a viable solution?* The anger and worry twisted inside me, coalescing into a throbbing pulse that echoed the frantic beat of my heart.

Driven by a cocktail of emotions, my actions became automatic. Huffing in exasperation, I powered up the Portal's screen, the glow casting a surreal light on the scene. My steps were quick, propelled by a mix of determination and fear as I moved towards the swirling colours of the Portal.

"Where are you going?" Luke's voice trailed after me, tinged with a blend of concern and caution. "It's too dangerous, Beatrix. The police were right behind us."

His warning barely registered. My focus was laser-sharp, my resolve unshakeable. Without breaking my stride or turning to face him, I offered a silent, defiant gesture—the middle finger. It was a succinct, powerful message of my intent and feelings towards his advice.

Then, with a final step, I embraced the vibrant whirlwind of the Portal, allowing it to envelop me, to whisk me away from the escalating tension. It was a leap, not just through space but through the fragile boundaries of our realities, driven by the unyielding force of sisterly bonds and the turbulent undercurrents of our shared plight.

# DOUBLE TROUBLE

## *1338.211.2*

"Shit!" The expletive slipped from my lips, almost reflexively, as my feet lost their grip on the slick, muddy ground of Myrtle Forest. Just moments after stepping through the Portal's shimmering veil and into the chaos of a storm, I was grappling with the earth, my hands slapping down into the cold, wet muck to prevent a full-on tumble.

The sirens were a harrowing backdrop, their wails intensifying as they drew nearer, slicing through the sound of the relentless rain. I squinted through the downpour, my gaze sweeping over the mud-drenched vicinity. The entrance to the small toilet block, now just a gateway to further turmoil, offered no shelter, no respite from the mounting dread.

"Where are you, Gladys?" The question was a whisper torn away by the howling wind, a fragile thread of hope in the storm's fury. I pressed on, hugging the building's wall, seeking some clue, some sign of my sister amidst the deluge.

My pace was urgent, a rapid dance with desperation as I skirted the edge of the structure. The world seemed reduced to the rhythm of my heartbeat, the lash of the rain, and the urgency of finding Gladys.

As I rounded the corner, time seemed to slow, my breath catching in a tight chest. There it was—Gladys's car, an oddly angular shadow against the toilet block, its door flapping open like a broken wing in the violent wind. "Shit," I breathed out again, the word a soft echo of my racing thoughts.

The sight of the car, deserted and askew, ignited a flurry of scenarios in my mind, each more unsettling than the last. The deepening frown on my face and the creases marking my forehead were telltale signs of the worry gnawing at me. The storm outside mirrored the turmoil within, each flash of lightning illuminating a landscape fraught with uncertainty and danger. In that moment, standing in the tempest's embrace, I was a sister consumed by concern, poised on the edge of actions born of desperation and love, ready to brave the storm's wrath to find Gladys.

Approaching the car, a sense of urgency pricked at my skin, sharper than the raindrops lashing around me. "Gladys," I called out, my voice sharp yet hushed, a desperate whisper against the storm's roar, hoping against hope she might hear and respond.

Leaning into the open door, a quick scan confirmed my fears—she wasn't there. The car's interior, damp and abandoned, offered no clue, no hint of her whereabouts.

With a heavy heart, I withdrew from the empty vehicle, my eyes darting around, piercing through the curtain of rain, searching for any sign of her. *Could the dense trees nearby offer her shelter, or had she ventured further into the forest's deceptive embrace?*

Then, a sound—a car door slamming shut—jolted me back to the pressing reality. Adrenaline surged, mingling with the cold rain soaking my skin. *What do I do?* The question echoed in my mind, a tumultuous blend of fear and determination. With a reflexive gesture, my fist met the car's side in a thud of frustration.

The knowledge that the police were now on the scene tightened the vice of anxiety around me. Time was slipping through my fingers, each second critical, each decision pivotal. *I can't go after her,* I reasoned, the forest trail beside the vehicle looming as a daunting, uncertain path. Yet, returning the way I came was equally untenable, a direct path to the officers now scouring the area.

With my heart pounding, a beacon of raw, frantic rhythm in my chest, I felt my body react, almost of its own accord. My legs propelled me, not towards the forest, but back towards the toilet block—a structure that suddenly seemed like the only available sanctuary in this maelstrom of uncertainty and fear.

Tucked inside the musty confines of the toilet block, the voices outside sliced through the tension like a blade. "Karl, check this out," called a female officer, her voice piercing the heavy air and sending a shiver down my spine.

A hard lump formed in my throat, the name 'Karl' reverberating through my mind like a dire omen. *Detective Karl Jenkins?* The thought was a stone in my stomach, the implications of his presence tightening around me like a vice.

"Well, this doesn't make sense," came Karl's unmistakable reply, a statement that spurred my curiosity despite the gnawing fear. His voice, familiar yet foreboding, spoke of confusion, of puzzles unfolding just beyond the thin barrier that concealed me.

I edged closer to the door, my every sense strained to catch the fragments of their exchange, desperate for any scrap of information that might reveal their thoughts, their progress, their suspicions.

The female officer's voice floated in, muffled and distant, "Just end here... just disappeared." Her bafflement was a small comfort, a sign that our tracks, our traces, still defied easy explanation.

Karl's analytical mind pieced together the scene with a logic that was both impressive and terrifying. "There wouldn't be much left of that wall if they'd driven into it," he reasoned, unwittingly brushing against the truth of Luke's otherworldly escape.

My heart hammered against my ribs, a frantic drumbeat echoing my spiralling thoughts. They were discussing the very anomaly I had exploited, the wall I had traversed from another realm. *That makes sense*, I consoled myself, clinging to the sliver of advantage our secret knowledge provided.

"There's still this second set of tracks," the female officer's voice rose in volume.

"Shit!" The curse slipped from me, a whisper of dread. The mention of a second set of tracks—a clear sign they were on Gladys's trail—tightened the knot of anxiety in my chest. I was cloaked in shadows, yet felt starkly exposed, the walls of my temporary refuge seeming to press in closer with the weight of impending discovery.

In that cramped space, every sound amplified, each moment stretched taut with tension, I was a sister ensnared in a web of fear and determination, bracing for what might come next in the relentless pursuit of finding and protecting Gladys.

"It's here!" the woman's voice pierced the tense air, a declaration that sent a surge of adrenaline coursing through me. Their discovery was inevitable, yet the confirmation hit with the force of a physical blow.

"They must have taken off on foot. There's nobody here," Karl's voice boomed, analytical yet laced with an undercurrent of frustration. His deduction was a double-edged sword, offering a sliver of respite that Gladys was not there to be caught but also indicating their readiness to pursue.

In that moment, a loud crack of thunder rolled across the sky, its rumble magnifying within the confines of the toilet block. The sound was a startling intruder, merging with my escalating heartbeat, each thunderous beat echoing the turmoil inside me.

Startled, I jostled against the hand dryer, an inadvertent nudge that sent a broom crashing against the sink. The clatter was jarringly loud in the cramped space, a reckless giveaway of my presence.

"Shit!" The curse was a whisper of dismay, a reaction to my clumsy betrayal of silence. I was teetering on the edge of discovery, every sound amplified, every breath a potential alarm.

Karl's instinct was swift and authoritative. "Police!" His voice was a clarion call, demanding and assertive. "Come out slowly with your hands up." The command was clear, a directive that left no room for ambiguity, his law enforcement training kicking in with full force.

With a surge of panic-fuelled clarity, I made a split-second decision. Dashing into the furthest cubicle, I moved with a quiet desperation, gently closing the door to create a barrier, however flimsy, between myself and the imminent threat. Locking it silently, I sought to become invisible, to blend into the very fabric of the space that concealed me.

Huddled in that small, confined space, I was a blend of racing thoughts and stifled breaths, a mixture of fear, frustration, and an unwavering determination to evade capture. The looming possibility of what lay beyond that thin cubicle door was a palpable presence, as I stood silent and immobile, waiting for the next move in this high-stakes game of hide and seek.

The squelch of slow, heavy footsteps invading the block sent a wave of panic through me. Each step was a countdown, drawing closer, threatening the fragile veil of my hiding place.

Grimacing in disgust at the surroundings, I made a swift, silent decision. The toilet seat clacked softly as I closed it, then I carefully perched atop, trying to minimise my contact with the less-than-sanitary surface. My body tensed, ready for flight or concealment, whichever became necessary.

Outside, the wind's mournful howl through the rooftop vents mingled with the fierce clamour of thunder, a tumultuous symphony that mirrored the chaos unfolding within and around me. *Do it, Beatrix,* I urged myself, the command a silent mantra. The stakes were too high, and the pressing need to evade capture and find Gladys propelled me towards the only route of escape I had left, fervently hoping Luke's use of his Portal Key wouldn't interfere with mine.

As I slid my finger across the activate button of my Portal Key, a wash of colours burst forth, transforming the drab cubicle into a kaleidoscope of escape. A fleeting moment of relief sparked within me, a tiny star in the overwhelming night of my predicament.

Then, a loud thud shattered the tense silence, a sound so forceful it seemed to vibrate through my very bones. Wood splintered, tiny projectiles flying through the confined space as the door was kicked open with daunting force. My eyes, wide with shock and fear, locked with Karl's for a split second, an eternity encapsulated in a brief exchange of glances before the door swung shut again.

Time stood still, then rushed forward. I didn't pause to consider, to weigh my next actions. With the door rebounding closed, I seized the moment, the colours in front of me not just an escape but a lifeline. I leapt, diving into the swirling vortex on the cubicle wall, landing amidst the soft dust of Clivilius. *Close!* I mentally commanded, the word a gasp of relief as much as an instruction, urging the Portal to seal shut behind me, cutting off pursuit, leaving the danger behind, if only for a moment. In that instant of transition, the collision of worlds, I was a fugitive, a sister, a desperate soul seeking refuge, propelled by an unyielding drive to protect, to survive, to persevere.

❖

As I brushed the ochre dust from my knees, my eyes surveyed the empty surroundings. Everyone had moved along since my last visit and Paul's distinct voice carried in the wind from the direction of the Drop Zone.

One step was all I managed in Paul's direction before the weight of my situation anchored me in place. With Gladys entangled in a perilous chase and the police scouring the Collinsvale property, the luxury of time was not on my side. Conversing with Paul, as comforting as it might have been, could not take precedence.

*You could ask Sergeant Charlie for help*, the fleeting suggestion darted through my mind, a tempting prospect yet fraught with risk. But the echo of Charlie's stern admonition not to make contact reverberated in my memory, dousing the spark of that idea.

*Leigh?* The question hung in the air, my body stretching, a series of cracks along my spine breaking the silence as I mulled over my limited options.

A deep, resigning breath escaped my lips as I acknowledged the stark truth: *We need to work this out ourselves.* It was a silent concession to our autonomy, a recognition of the thin line we tread between seeking assistance and maintaining the fragile web of secrecy that enveloped our actions.

With a determined step, I crossed the threshold of the Portal, entering the Collinsvale property. My entrance was so abrupt that I nearly collided with the wall directly in front of me. Stopping just in time, I felt the cold, unyielding surface of the barren wall mere inches from my face, its starkness a harsh welcome.

I spun around in a swift one-eighty, my movements tinged with a hint of desperation. My left foot inadvertently struck the door, propelling it to swing shut with a click that echoed ominously through the room. The sound, small yet significant, marked my silent re-entry into a world fraught with tension and peril.

My heart hammered against my ribs, a frantic drumbeat echoing the surge of adrenaline coursing through me. Two officers, their figures outlined against the archway that bridged the cluttered living room and the dining area, were engrossed in examining the contents of the clear plastic bags they held. I froze, my breath caught in the tight clasp of anxiety, wondering if the sound of my entrance had betrayed my presence.

They were absorbed in their discussion, their attention fixed on the items they had collected, seemingly oblivious to my presence. A wave of relief washed over me as they exited the room, their departure allowing me to exhale the breath I didn't realise I'd been holding.

The immediate danger may have receded, but the intrusion of loud voices from outside yanked my focus to the window. Treading lightly, I navigated toward the large pane that offered a view of the front veranda and the expansive yard beyond. The raised voices, a distinct tone of contention between a man and a police officer, piqued my curiosity and heightened my alertness.

From my position in the room, the scene outside remained obscured, the angle and distance denying me a clear understanding of the unfolding dispute. With a surge of caution, I glanced back, ensuring the door to the living room was securely closed, a barrier between me and potential observers who might traverse the adjacent hallway.

The closed door wasn't just a shield; it was a possible escape route. The smooth wooden surface stood as a silent sentinel, ready to serve as my portal back to Clivilius should the need arise. In this moment, nestled within the walls of a unfamiliar space now fraught with danger, I was acutely aware of the delicate balance I navigated—a blend of observation and readiness, each sense attuned to the slightest hint of discovery, every thought shadowed by the prospect of a swift retreat.

With meticulous care, I lifted each foot, placing it down with the utmost caution as I inched closer to the window. My body was low, almost merging with the shape of the couch to avoid any detection. The lace curtains brushed against my face as I peered out, seeking a clearer understanding of the tense dialogue unfolding just beyond the glass.

The voices were more distinct now, yet their clarity battled against the drumming rain assaulting the corrugated iron roof of the front deck. Craving a better grasp of the words exchanged, my fingers gingerly edged the window up an additional inch, the minimal movement a calculated risk to enhance my eavesdropping without revealing my presence.

"I need to search the truck," asserted an officer, his tone firm yet courteous as he offered the sanctuary of his broad umbrella to the man I deduced was the truck driver.

"It's just a standard delivery," the man countered, his voice tinged with a blend of annoyance and urgency as he thrust a paper into the officer's grip.

A silent curse slipped from my lips, "Shit," as anxiety surged within me. My mind raced, grappling with the sudden realisation of our connection to the scene outside. *Had Luke and I inadvertently tied ourselves to this delivery by using our real names?* The memory of our fence order nudged its way to the forefront of my thoughts, mingling with the fear of our potential exposure.

"I'm sorry. I can't let you leave yet," the officer's words to the driver were firm, a declaration that the situation was far from resolved.

As I crouched there, a witness to the interaction that could very well ripple back to me and Luke, a mix of dread and resolve settled over me. I was caught in a limbo of observation, the stakes mounting with every word exchanged outside. In that moment, the room felt both like a sanctuary and a trap, each passing second a thread in the tightening web of our entangled circumstances.

The driver's heavy sigh was a tangible wave of surrender to the situation. As he lit a cigarette, the glow briefly illuminated his resigned expression, indifferent to the rain's onslaught.

Having absorbed the key details of the conversation, I carefully nudged the window shut. The need to consult with Luke pressed urgently against my thoughts with a sense of immediacy as I retreated to the room's shadowed corner, seeking a semblance of privacy among the haphazard stacks of science and nature magazines.

Crouching there, a blend of urgency and caution governed my movements. I retrieved my phone, its screen a beacon in the dimness, and dialled Luke's number. A wash of tentative relief swept over me as the dial tone hummed in my ear—a hopeful indicator that Luke was within reach, somewhere on this tumultuous planet of ours.

When the dialling ceased, replaced by the subtle sound of breathing, a surge of mixed emotions coursed through me. The repetitive plea in my mind, 'Luke, please pick up,' halted abruptly, giving way to a torrent of words as I began to speak.

"I'm at the Collinsvale property," the words tumbled out of me, a rush of confession to Luke, my heart pounding with every word. "The police are taking it very seriously, Luke. They've bagged evidence and everything."

My focus fractured as a loud metallic rattling from the truck outside pierced the tense silence, a jarring reminder of the ongoing activity just beyond these walls.

"Get the fuck out of there, Beatrix!" Luke's voice cut through, sharp and urgent, a clear command that snapped my attention back to the imminent danger. His tone was laced with an intensity that mirrored my own rising panic.

The murmur of soft voices began to swell from the adjacent room, their approach like the ominous crescendo of a suspenseful score. Time was running out.

"I will as soon as I hang up. Where are you?" I pressed, urgency knotting my voice, seeking his location, a plan, anything to anchor the growing dilemma.

A brief silence filled with the sound of rain hinted at Luke's hesitation or perhaps his caution. "I'm at the property," he finally revealed, his words striking me with a blend of shock and an odd sense of solidarity.

"Where?" The question leaped out, my eyes widening in disbelief and a flicker of respect for his audacity. Luke's presence here, in the lion's den, was as reckless as it was brave.

A small, involuntary smirk crept across my face, a momentary lapse in the tension. *But then, I came here too*, I acknowledged silently, a thread of kinship weaving through the worry. Here we were, both ensnared in a dangerous dance of our own making, each step fraught with risk, yet bound by a shared determination to navigate the storm we'd summoned.

"I'm going to save that fencing order," Luke's voice came through, laced with a resolve that didn't quite mask the absence of specifics about his location. His determination was palpable, even through the phone, yet it left me grappling with a mix of admiration and frustration at his vague response.

"Let me help you," I blurted out impulsively, the words escaping before I could tether them to any concrete plan of action. The urge to be part of the solution, to not just stand by, was overwhelming, even if I hadn't fully conceptualised what that involvement might entail.

A sudden thud echoed nearby, a sound of something heavy making contact with the floor, followed by an unmistakable expletive. The proximity of the noise jolted me, an urgent reminder of the ever-present danger lurking just beyond my hideout.

"No! Go to Clivilius. You need to continue with the missions Paul is giving you," Luke's voice came through, firm and directive, attempting to steer me towards a path he deemed safer.

An officer's voice cut through the background, "Better bag that too," sending a cascade of chills down my spine.

"And you need to find your sister!" Luke added, the weight of his words amplified by a significant pause, underscoring the dual urgency of our mission and the personal stakes at hand.

"Luke, stop being such a stubborn prick. You can't do all of this yourself," I retorted, my voice a mixture of concern and reprimand. Despite my scolding, doubt clouded my mind, echoed by the view of the closed living room door. *What awaited me on the other side? More officers, more obstacles?*

Luke's response carried a surge of tension, his voice rising, "You think I don't know how much trouble we're in? But if we lose that fencing delivery, those caravans you are sourcing are the camp's only line of protection." His words, a blend of fear and determination, painted a stark picture of our predicament.

Then, silence. The line went dead, leaving me enveloped in a sudden, oppressive quiet.

"Luke?" The word slipped out in a hiss, a futile call to a now unresponsive device. The phone's black screen mocked me, a silent witness to the abrupt end of our connection.

I tried to redial, but the lack of a dial tone hinted at Luke's deliberate choice to go dark, a strategic move to avoid detection.

With a mix of urgency and caution, I crouched low, navigating through the room. My movements were deliberate, each step calculated to avoid the clutter of magazines and the mundane obstacle of the coffee table situated near the room's heart. My destination was the window that offered a view of the truck and the unfolding drama outside.

Leaning forward, my gaze fixed on the stationary vehicle, I strained to see through the curtain of relentless rain. And then, there he was – Luke, his movements reminiscent of a shadow, blending with the environment in an almost ninja-like manner. My eyes tracked his progress until he disappeared from my line of sight, obscured by the truck's bulk.

A sudden movement caught my peripheral vision – an officer, turning sharply, heading toward Luke's last known location. "Shit!" The word was a whisper, a soft exhalation of rising panic. My mind raced, weighing the scant options, the potential outcomes of this dangerous game of cat and mouse we were both entangled in.

Despite Luke's clear directive for me to stay out of it, the gnawing sense of urgency within me couldn't be quelled. Luke needed help, whether he admitted it or not. My hands, almost of their own accord, pushed the window open once again, grasping for the nearest substantial object—a weighty book that felt solid and promising in my grip. With a swift motion, more instinctual than calculated, I hurled the book through the window, watching it descend with a satisfying thud onto the rain-soaked wooden slats of the front veranda.

The sudden noise had its intended effect. The officer paused, his attention diverted from Luke to the unexpected disturbance. From behind the blinds, I became a shadow, a wisp of movement just beyond perception. My heart raced, the adrenaline coursing through me was both a catalyst for action and a reminder of the peril I was flirting with.

I was acutely aware of my appearance, starkly out of place in this high-stakes tableau. The last thing I needed was for the officer to spot me, to realise that the figure lurking behind the window was not one of his own.

Time seemed to stretch, the officer's silhouette framed against the grey, rain-drenched backdrop as he weighed his next move. His decision process was interrupted by another book I sent flying through the window, a desperate bid to keep his focus away from Luke.

"Who's there?" His voice cut through the sound of the rain, sharp and demanding, as he took a step toward the house. The tension in his tone mirrored the tightening in my chest.

With the blind meticulously returned to its original position, I retreated deeper into the living room's relative safety. The officer's view through the window was obstructed, forcing him to take a longer route if he intended to investigate further. In the back of my mind, a thread of hope spun out, wishing that my diversion provided Luke with the precious seconds he needed, though I harboured doubts about the existence of any coherent plan on his part.

The resurgence of loud voices outside snapped me back to the immediate reality, reminding me of the other officers' presence, whom I had momentarily dismissed from my mind. My focus shattered, and in a clumsy bid to move swiftly, my foot caught on a stack of nature magazines. The resulting cascade of paper and the jarring thump of my body hitting the floor broke the room's tense silence.

Scrambling across the carpet, I sought refuge in the room's corner, a strategic position that allowed me a clear view of the door while keeping me concealed. The walls seemed to press in, the space shrinking as the gravity of my situation settled heavily upon me.

With the Portal Key in my trembling hand, I aimed it at the door, a lifeline within my grasp. My finger slid across the activation button, a familiar motion now laden with a desperate urgency.

"Shit, Luke!" The words slipped out in a hiss, frustration and fear intermingling as my finger frantically swiped across the activation button, each attempt as futile as the last. The pounding in my chest escalated to a deafening crescendo, overshadowing the rising clamour of voices outside just as the ominous silhouette of a foot appeared in the doorway.

In that moment, my mind was a maelstrom of panic and desperate hope. *Close your damn Portal, Luke!* The thought was a silent scream, an internal plea for him to sever whatever connection might be interfering with my escape.

With what felt like the weight of the world pressing down on me, I made one final, desperate swipe across the Portal Key. My breath hitched, time seemed to suspend, and then, miraculously, a small ball of light burst forth, colliding with the door that exploded into a vivid spectrum of colours, a vibrant gateway amidst the encroaching peril.

Instinct took over. I launched myself towards the luminescent door, the Clivilius dust rising to meet me as I tumbled through. The familiar yet alien terrain greeted me, a welcome contrast to the room I had fled. Without hesitation, I mentally issued the command to close the Portal.

Landing on the other side, the dust clinging to my skin, I lay there for a moment, allowing the reality of my narrow escape to sink in. The portal's closure severed my connection to the immediate danger but also to Luke and the unresolved situation I'd left behind. Lying in the Clivilius dust, I was safe, yet the turmoil of my emotions — relief, guilt, worry — swirled within me as tumultuously as the storm I'd just evaded.

# DISHEVELLED SISTER

## *1338.211.3*

The knowledge that I needed to find my sister swirled relentlessly in my mind, rendering my stay in Clivilius a fleeting affair. With a mission from Paul to retrieve his dog, Charlie, in Broken Hill, I found a distraction to keep my restless thoughts and idle hands engaged while I awaited word from Gladys.

In Adelaide, I had become adept at charting Portal locations, allowing me to resume my journey with ease. Having fulfilled my daily commitment to the new upgraded settlement housing, a wave of satisfaction washed over me. It was time to seek out transportation, and I opted for a modest, independent car hire company. Their lack of communication and coordination played to my advantage. Having previously deceived the motorhome dealer with a fabricated number, I decided to test my luck once more. Success was mine again as the clerk barely glanced at my license before ticking a box, neglecting even to make a copy. A smirk danced on my lips as I hit the accelerator, the open road unfolding before me.

The car, though not the latest model, possessed an essential feature—an inbuilt navigation system pointing me towards Broken Hill. My travels had rarely taken me beyond the urban sprawl of the mainland's major cities, with Melbourne holding a special place in my heart as a favoured retreat. Yet, here I was, embarking on an adventure into the vast expanse of the Australian outback, an area uncharted by my own experiences. The irony of the situation wasn't lost on me—I was en route to commit a dognapping, of all things!

My mind, ever the relentless wanderer, drifted back to the car I was driving through the vast and quiet landscapes. This vehicle, just like the others before it, was destined to join the expanding collection of the Clivilian fleet—unreturned, unnoticed. A part of me revelled in this new norm, this life of subtle defiance. "I really could get used to this life," I whispered to myself, a hint of amusement in my tone as I caught sight of the green road sign heralding my approach to Gawler.

The thought lingered, a smirk playing on my lips, even as a part of me wrestled with the moral implications of my actions. It was a thrilling yet unsettling dance between right and wrong, freedom and responsibility.

The cabin of the car, filled with the sounds of an upbeat track, momentarily insulated me from the world outside. Yet, my thoughts were elsewhere. "She's had plenty of time," I mumbled under my breath, the music's energy now clashing with my growing impatience and concern. My fingers, slightly trembling, reached out to lower the volume, cutting through the song's climax as I sought a moment of quiet to connect with Gladys.

Balancing my phone on my thighs, a sense of urgency took hold. I dialled Gladys's number, the beep of each digit echoing in the suddenly quiet car. Activating the loudspeaker, I placed the phone beside me, my eyes flickering between the road and the device, waiting for that familiar voice to break through the silence.

The phone rang, cutting sharply through the car's stillness. Once, twice, thrice—it was a countdown, each ring heightening my anticipation and anxiety. After countless attempts that had only met with the indifferent tone of voicemail, this call felt weighted with significance.

Then, a click, a breath, and Gladys's voice filled the car. Relief washed over me, mingled with a surge of questions and concerns. I pulled over to the roadside, the gravel crunching under the tires, signalling a pause in my journey. The engine idled, a soft purr against the backdrop of silence, as I braced myself to dive into a conversation laden with pent-up worries and looming decisions.

"Where the hell are you, Gladys?" I screeched into the phone, the urgency in my voice mirroring the pounding of my heart. "Are you safe? Did they catch you?"

Her response, "I'm fine, Beatrix," was less than convincing, her voice a thin veil over underlying distress. "Please can you come and get me?" she implored, her plea cutting through the static of distance and fear.

I glanced out the car windows, the vast open fields stretching endlessly, the nearest semblance of civilisation—a cluster of distant houses—seemed to mock my desperation. A flicker of hesitation washed over me, the isolation of my surroundings pressing in, amplifying the gravity of the situation.

"Of course," I replied, my voice steadier than I felt, propelled by a surge of determination to aid my sister. "Where are you?" I inquired, ready to traverse any distance, to navigate any obstacle.

"I'll send you my location."

"Great!" I responded, clinging to the lifeline she offered, yet the brief respite was shattered by a sudden loud revving of an engine in the background of Gladys's call. My pulse quickened, dread coiling in my stomach.

"Dickhead!" Gladys's shout pierced the tense air. My mind raced, envisioning every conceivable danger, the worst scenarios playing out in vivid detail.

"Gladys?" I called out, my voice tinged with fear, the spectre of her being caught by authorities looming large. Her heavy sigh was a gut punch, the weight of her exhale carrying more than just air—it bore the burden of her predicament.

"Beatrix, please hurry," she urged, her words a blend of desperation and resolve.

"I'll find you as fast as I can. I promise," I vowed, the finality of the call echoing in the silent car. The line went dead, leaving me with a churning mix of determination and trepidation. The stillness of the car contrasted sharply with the turmoil within me. With a deep breath, I steeled myself, igniting the car back to life, ready to confront whatever lay ahead in my relentless pursuit to safeguard my sister.

Pulling back onto the main road, my mind raced as fast as the car's engine. I was acutely aware of my surroundings, eyes darting for the perfect secluded spot to activate the Portal. The realisation hit me with clarity—Gladys would need a ride, and here I was, in possession of a vehicle that could very well serve that purpose. Luke's past feats of transporting inanimate objects between worlds sparked a plan in my mind. *Why not take the car with me to Clivilius and then back to Earth?* It was audacious, yet the circumstances called for boldness.

As I navigated the outskirts of Gawler, my eyes caught a narrow side road, veering away from the main thoroughfare. It promised the seclusion I required. With a decisive turn of the steering wheel, I ventured down the path, the car's tires crunching the gravel beneath. I drove down Marlowe Lane for a few kilometres until I reached an abandoned farmstead, identified by a decrepit sign "Old Fenwick Place." This farm, once bustling with activity, had long been deserted, its fields now overrun with wild grass and its structures succumbing to time and the elements. Its dilapidated barn providing the perfect secluded backdrop with its large, flat wall ideal for the Portal's activation.

I pulled up close to the barn's broad side, the structure standing solitary amidst the sprawling fields, a silent witness to my extraordinary endeavour. With the car positioned, I stepped out, my heart pounding with a mix of excitement and apprehension. The Portal device felt heavy in my hand, not in weight but in potential.

Activating the Portal against the barn's flat, weathered surface, I watched in awe as the familiar shimmering gateway materialised, its edges blurring into the surroundings. "This is freaking brilliant!" I couldn't help but exclaim aloud, a smile breaking across my face as I gazed at the portal, which now stood as a testament to my quick adaptation and problem-solving.

With no time to lose, I climbed back into the car, drove through the shimmering surface of the Portal, and emerged into the dusty landscape of Clivilius. The transition was seamless, the car's tires kicking up clouds of extraterrestrial dust as I braked. My arrival seemed to go unnoticed, a small mercy in the urgency of my mission.

The ingenuity of my plan filled me with a rush of exhilaration. I had managed to bend the rules of physics and reality to my will, an empowering realisation. However, the criticality of my mission to rescue Gladys allowed no time for self-adulation.

I manoeuvred the car, reversing it through the Portal, mirroring the path previously trodden by small trucks, and emerged in Luke's driveway. The seamless transition between worlds was nothing short of miraculous, a testament to the power at my fingertips.

With my vehicle now Earthbound once more, my thoughts refocused on Gladys. The urgency to find her injected a new wave of determination into my veins. Her location pinged continuously on my phone, a digital beacon guiding me towards her.

As I drove, I noted the rain beginning to ease, the clouds parting as if in acknowledgment of my resolve. Yet, the potential sight of Gladys, possibly in distress or danger, cast a shadow over the relief brought by the clearing skies. My sister's safety was paramount, and as the distance decreased between us, so did the barrier to our reunion.

❖

Within a mere twenty minutes, the insistent voice of the GPS indicated I was nearing Gladys's last known location. The stability of her location pin, barely shifting since she'd sent it, knotted my insides with growing anxiety. Such stillness hinted at distressing possibilities: *was she injured, or had she sought refuge in the numbing embrace of alcohol?* I leaned forward, eyes narrowing as I scanned the horizon through the windshield.

As I crept closer, a vehicle materialised at the roadside ahead, its presence oddly conspicuous in the sparse surroundings. My pace slowed to a crawl as I neared, the details becoming clearer. The car, emblazoned with the bold lettering "Tassie Independent," seemed out of place in the quiet landscape. Beside it, a scene unfolded that tugged at my heartstrings and spiked my pulse with a cocktail of relief and dismay.

A young couple, their expressions a mix of concern and frustration, stood beside a middle-aged woman whose posture was all too familiar. The woman's erratic movements and the glint of a wine bottle in her hand painted a clear picture even before my mind accepted it. My breath caught as I watched her take a clumsy swing at the man, the bottle arcing through the air with dangerous unpredictability.

A wave of realisation washed over me, and I exhaled a heavy sigh, my initial shock giving way to a pang of sibling responsibility. "And taking swipes at a reporter, no less," I murmured, the scene before me confirming my worst suspicions. Gladys, in her state of inebriation, was the centre of this roadside spectacle.

As I edged past the car, I rolled down the passenger window, the cool air carrying the sounds and scents of the altercation inside. "Gladys! Get in the car!" My voice, firm yet laced with a sisterly blend of exasperation and concern, cut through the chilled air. I beckoned to my dishevelled sister, hoping to extricate her from the mess and shield her from the consequences of her actions. In that moment, my role shifted from rescuer to protector, determined to pull Gladys away from the brink of a potentially ruinous escapade.

Gladys's approach was anything but subtle; she staggered towards me, her movements erratic, bumping into the young man who had been part of the roadside tableau. With a mixture of determination and disarray, she yanked the passenger door open and slumped into the seat, the empty wine bottle clutched between her thighs like a trophy of her defiance.

"Shit, Gladys," I exhaled, a cocktail of frustration and concern bubbling within me as I took in her dishevelled state. My gaze flicked to the bottle, its contents long gone, symbolising the extent of her escapade. "You really had to drink now?" My tone was a blend of incredulity and resignation. It wasn't the first time alcohol had been her refuge in moments of turmoil, yet the timing couldn't have been worse.

Gladys's response was swift, laced with the sharpness of someone cornered. "You would have done the same," she snapped, her words sharp like a knife, cutting through the tension in the car. She then turned away, her gaze fixed on the passing landscape, a clear signal she was shutting down the conversation.

With a deep breath, I refocused on steering the car away from the scene. The reporters, momentarily forgotten, lingered in my rearview mirror, their presence a nagging reminder of the potential fallout from this incident. They would no doubt relish recounting the spectacle of a dishevelled woman, seemingly emerging from the wilderness, engaging in a public display of intoxication.

As I navigated the car onto the road leading home, my mind raced with scenarios of the morning headlines, each more sensational than the last. The thought of Gladys, and by extension, our family, being the subject of local gossip and scandal was a bitter pill to swallow. All I could hope for was that the reporters' attention had been more focused on aiding Gladys than documenting her downfall. Yet, the seed of worry planted itself firmly in my thoughts, the possibility of our private drama becoming public spectacle hanging over us like a dark cloud.

As we made our escape, the tranquility inside the car was abruptly shattered when Gladys wound down the passenger window, allowing a rush of frigid, damp air to invade the warm cocoon I had cultivated within the vehicle. My eyes widened in disbelief as I watched her casually discard the empty wine bottle into the wilderness, an act of carelessness that seemed to epitomise her current state of mind.

Reacting instinctively, I slammed on the brakes, the car coming to a jarring halt as the tires squealed against the road, the smell of burnt rubber briefly permeating the air. "Go and get it," I ordered, my voice stern, my gaze fixed on her with a mix of frustration and disbelief. It was as though every time Gladys was involved, the threshold for chaos was invariably lowered.

"We're better off without it," she retorted with a dismissive huff, her indifference stoking my irritation. "Gladys," I exhaled, a mixture of exhaustion and exasperation in my voice. *Why did every interaction have to be a battle of wits and wills?* "It's evidence now," I explained, trying to pierce through her haze of inebriation with logic, emphasising the risk her impulsivity had posed. "It has your DNA all over it."

Reluctantly, with an even more pronounced huff, she exited the vehicle to retrieve her discarded mistake. Meanwhile, I leaned over to the back seat, retrieving the small overnight case I'd packed. It was a habit borne of necessity—being prepared for any eventuality, knowing all too well how quickly circumstances could spiral when Gladys was involved.

Unzipping the case, I extracted a towel, unfurling it with a snap before meticulously lining Gladys's seat with it. It was a small act, but one that spoke volumes of the forethought I'd been forced to adopt. As I settled back into my seat, waiting for Gladys to return, I couldn't help but mutter to myself, "Lucky I'm going on a road trip." It was a reminder of the perpetual readiness required in the whirlwind that was life with my sister, a life where normality was often a fleeting guest.

As Gladys trudged back to the car, bottle in hand, her expression was a mixture of defiance and irritation. She cast a disdainful look at the towel before her gaze shifted to me, as if questioning my motives without uttering a word.

"I don't want you getting your wet shit all over the clean seats," I stated plainly, cutting through any pretence. It was practical, straightforward, and necessary, given the state she was in.

With a roll of her eyes that spoke volumes of her current mood, Gladys dropped herself onto the towel-covered seat, the impact echoing her frustration as she slammed the car door shut. I exhaled a silent breath of relief, grateful that the towel remained, an unspoken boundary between chaos and order within the confines of the car.

As we merged back onto the road, the familiar landscape passing by, Gladys broke the silence, her voice laced with a mix of confusion and a hint of concern. "Where are we going?" she inquired, noting our deviation from the usual path home.

"I'm taking you to Luke's house," I replied, my voice steady but carrying an undercurrent of tension.

"Why not home?"

I clenched my jaw, the frustration of having to justify the plan to her adding another layer of strain. "The police know it was your car involved in the car chase, Gladys. They've already found where you left it at Myrtle Forest." I let the words hang in the air momentarily. "You can't go home now. Not ever."

Her response was a soft plea. "I want to go home, Beatrix. Snowflake still needs me." Her words tugged at my heartstrings, a reminder of the personal stakes involved, yet they also underscored the impossibility of returning to a semblance of our old lives.

The car's windows briefly clouded over as I exhaled a heavy sigh. The pain of losing Duke was still a tender wound for us all, and the thought of neglecting Snowflake's wellbeing was unbearable. "I'll park the car at Mum and Dad's, and we can walk to your place from there," I conceded, making a sharp turn to head towards my home.

Navigating the familiar streets, I approached our parents' house—or rather, the house that once felt unequivocally like mine too. A sense of displacement washed over me as I pondered over what 'home' meant now. My hand unconsciously brushed against the lump of the Portal Key in my pocket, a tangible reminder of my current, transient existence. The packed overnight bag in the backseat stood as a testament to my unsettled life; the car, the road, and the in-between spaces felt more like home than any fixed address could.

Pulling into the driveway cut my spiralling thoughts short. The sight of the house evoked a mosaic of memories, each window reflecting fragments of a past that seemed both intimately familiar and strangely distant.

I turned to Gladys, who was now gathering her scattered senses, and spoke with a tinge of caution in my voice. "Probably best you don't go inside," I advised, acknowledging the complex web of explanations that awaited her should our parents witness her current state. My own exit from the car was a blend of reluctance and resolve, stepping out into the reality of our situation, while part of me longed for the simple comfort of stepping back into a past that no longer existed in the same way.

As I circled the car to join Gladys, I couldn't help but pause, observing her as she stared at her own reflection in the window. The sight tugged at my heartstrings. Her shoes were a mess, drenched and caked with mud, while her trousers bore the vivid green marks of recent encounters with grass. Up close, her dishevelled state was even more apparent. *And the forest still clings to her*, I mused sombrely, reaching out to gently remove a twig and a few stray pine needles that had entangled themselves in her hair.

Gladys, seemingly oblivious to the bits of nature she'd inadvertently collected, tightened the towel around her like a makeshift shield against the world. "Let's go," she said, her voice a mixture of resignation and urgency, the stress of the day carving deeper lines of worry into her face.

I responded with a silent nod, abandoning my initial plan to enter the house. Instead, I retrieved my bag from the back seat, a symbol of my current nomadic existence, and followed Gladys. We tread quietly, mindful of our surroundings as we headed towards her street, each of us lost in our thoughts yet acutely aware of the potential for prying eyes.

The spectre of legal repercussions loomed over us, a shadow that darkened with every step towards what was supposed to be a sanctuary. *There's only so much that Sergeant Charlie can do to protect us*, I pondered internally. The hope that he might interfere just enough to buy Gladys time was a thin thread of comfort, but in our current state, even the smallest reprieve felt like a lifeline. As we moved stealthily, the weight of our predicament pressed heavily upon me, a confronting reminder of the fine line we were walking between evasion and facing the consequences head-on.

❖

As soon as we opened the front door, Snowflake, the embodiment of home and normality, was there, her presence a bittersweet reminder of simpler times. Gladys, her emotions raw and visible, dropped to her knees with an audible thud, embracing the cat in a scene that juxtaposed her tumultuous day with a moment of pure, unconditional love.

But peace was fleeting. My peripheral vision caught the ominous crawl of a patrol car down the street, its slow progression toward us setting off alarms in my mind. "Shit," I hissed under my breath, urgency lacing my voice. With a quick, decisive elbow nudge, I ushered Gladys and Snowflake inside, shutting the door with a quiet but firm click that seemed to seal us off from the encroaching threat outside.

"What is it?" Gladys's voice was tinged with confusion and fear, her gaze lifting to meet mine as she clutched Snowflake closer, seeking comfort in the cat's familiar purr.

"The police are here," I stated, the weight of those words heavy between us. My hand found her shoulder, guiding her with a gentle but insistent pressure, propelling us toward the relative safety of the spare bedroom at the back of the house.

The air in the hallway felt unnervingly cold, making the hairs on my arms stand on end as we hastened our retreat. Once inside the room, while Gladys secured the door, I moved with practiced speed to close the blinds, shrouding us in semi-darkness. Each pull of the cord was a silent acknowledgment of our precarious situation, the dimming light a metaphor for the uncertainty and danger that now lurked just beyond our walls. In those moments, the house no longer felt like a sanctuary but a fragile barrier between us and a reality we weren't ready to face.

The tension in the room was palpable as we sat huddled against the bed, our bodies rigid with anxiety. The sudden, jarring knock at the front door sent a shockwave through me.

"Police!" The announcement came loud and clear, penetrating the walls of our supposed sanctuary. Snowflake, sensing the tension, sought refuge under Gladys's arm, her instinctual search for safety mirroring our own.

For a moment, there was silence—a brief, tantalising hope that they might leave. My breath held in anticipation, released in a premature sigh of relief, only to be caught again by the sound of the side gate being forcefully opened. My heart raced as the silhouette of an officer passed the window, the brief pause of their shadow sending a surge of adrenaline through me.

"Intrusive pricks," I muttered under my breath, my whisper laced with bitterness. My gaze fixed on the window where the shadow had passed, resentment boiling at the invasion of our privacy, at the disruption of our lives by those who claimed to serve and protect.

Gladys, seemingly numb to the escalation, offered only a shrug in response. The dim light accentuated the dark circles under her eyes, visual markers of the toll this ordeal was taking on her. Her expression, a mix of fatigue and resignation, painted a picture of a woman pushed to her limits, enveloped in a weariness that seemed to seep into her very bones.

The flicker of a nascent plan sparked in my mind, casting a momentary glow of hope amidst our dim surroundings. "Gladys!" My voice, though hushed, was urgent, slicing through the tension to seize her attention.

"What?" Her reply was a whisper, her eyes locking with mine, searching for a fragment of hope or a new direction.

"I think you should come to Clivilius with me," I proposed, the idea bold, yet offering a sliver of escape.

"I can't," she replied instantly, her hands automatically finding comfort in Snowflake's fur, her actions grounding her even as her world spun out of control. "The police will leave in a minute. They can't enter," Gladys tried to reassure herself more than me, her voice a fragile thread of optimism in the heavy air, despite the reality we'd witnessed so far.

Observing her, I could almost feel the turmoil churning within her, the weight of our dire circumstances pressing down on her spirit. When her tears began to fall, they were silent testaments to her inner struggle, streaking down her face in a quiet surrender to the fear and stress that had been her constant companions.

Despite the surge of sympathy that swelled within me at her display of vulnerability, I knew that comfort alone would not shield us from the dangers we faced. "Gladys," I pressed on, my voice firm yet not devoid of warmth, compelling her to meet my gaze. "Luke and I can't protect you if you stay here, you know that."

Her acknowledgment came through sobs, a raw, heartbreaking sound in the quiet room. "I know," she conceded amidst tears, clinging to a thread of hope. "I just need a few more days. Give me time to settle Snowflake with

Mum and Dad," she implored, her plea not just for time but for a semblance of normality, for a chance to secure at least one aspect of her life before plunging into the unknown.

*I don't think you have a few more days, dear sister,* the unfortunate truth echoed in my mind. The silent sigh that escaped me was heavy with resignation and unvoiced fears. "And what are you going to tell them? You know you can't tell them the truth—" My words hung in the air, pregnant with the weight of our predicament. The idea of bringing our parents to Clivilius briefly flickered through my mind, a fleeting fantasy born of desperation. The scratches on my arm seemed to pulse in response, a physical reminder of the harsh realities of Clivilius. I chastised myself internally for even entertaining such a thought. Our parents, with their serene and settled lives, would be fish out of water in that alien world.

"Just a few more days. I'll sort it, I promise," Gladys implored, her voice threaded with a mix of determination and despair. I could see the plea in her eyes, the silent vow to protect what little normality she could salvage.

My response was a roll of my eyes, a mix of frustration and reluctant acceptance. Gladys's attachment to Snowflake was unshakeable, a bond that, even now, she fought to preserve. My thoughts momentarily shifted—*Speaking of fur babies, where is Chloe?*—but the tension of our current situation clouded any potential concern Gladys might have shown for her other pet. Assuming Chloe was somewhere safe within the house, I suppressed the urge to ask, not wanting to add another layer of worry to Gladys's already burdened shoulders.

The lengthening stillness outside was unnerving. My fingers, acting on their own accord, delicately parted the blinds just enough to allow a sliver of vision. My gaze scoured the exterior, vigilant for any lingering presence of the officer who had so boldly invaded our peace.

"Looks like they're gone," I confirmed, my voice a mix of relief and caution as I turned back to Gladys, signalling it was safe to leave our temporary refuge. As we made our way to the kitchen, "No doubt they'll keep checking here for you," I added, a grim reminder of the scrutiny we were now under.

"I know," she acknowledged, her resignation clear as she sought solace in the familiar ritual of uncorking a new bottle of shiraz. Her actions unfolded with a resigned inevitability, the pop of the cork echoing like a subdued cry for normality.

"Gladys, don't," I found myself saying, a plea tinged with concern as I watched her pour a generous amount of wine into a glass. It wasn't just the wine; it was what it represented —a descent into a cycle I feared she wouldn't escape from.

My warning fell on deaf ears, dismissed with the casual ease of someone too weary to heed caution. She savoured a deep sip, the sound of the glass returning to the countertop resounding like a gavel in the quiet kitchen.

"I'm going to have a shower. Tell Luke that I'm alright, would you?" Gladys's words were almost casual.

"Sure," I replied, my voice tinged with a hint of resignation as my lips formed a tight line. Paul's directive echoed in my mind, a reminder of the obligations waiting for me beyond these walls. "I've left a car near Gawler. I need to finish driving to Broken Hill before nightfall," I declared, the sense of purpose lending a slight edge to my voice.

Gladys halted, her curiosity piqued as she lingered in the doorway. "Broken Hill?" she echoed, her head tilting slightly, her gaze searching mine for clues. "What's in Broken Hill?"

"Paul has sent me on a mission," I stated, feeling a spark of determination ignite within me, pushing aside the fatigue that clung to my bones.

"A mission?" Gladys repeated, a playful smirk breaking through her previously sombre demeanour, injecting a moment of lightness into the heavy atmosphere.

Irritation flickered within me at her echo. "Are you really going to just stand there and repeat everything I say?" I challenged, my frown deepening.

Her chuckle, light and fleeting, filled the space between us. "I'm going for a shower," she reaffirmed, finally moving away, allowing the conversation to close.

Alone now, I reached for Gladys's abandoned wine glass, the remnant scent of shiraz wafting up to tease my senses. I allowed myself a moment, inhaling the rich, complex aroma, a brief respite from the unending drama. Yet, as I set the glass down, a stern inner voice reminded me to maintain focus. *That's enough.*

Compelled by the need to fulfil my own tasks, I initiated the Portal activation in Gladys's home, a new anchor point in our ever-expanding network. The familiar whirl of colours and energies enveloped me, offering a temporary escape from the weight of Gladys's reality.

Stepping through the Portal, I left behind the house's muted tensions, the lingering scent of wine, and the sound of shower water—a poignant reminder of the normality we were both desperately clinging to. Onward to Broken Hill, to the mission, to the next chapter in this unfolding saga, with the hope that, somehow, I'd navigate through the storms awaiting me on the other side.

# THE OTHER SIDE

## *1338.211.1*

"You've got to be kidding me," I muttered under my breath, my eyes narrowing as I observed Paul's hurried approach. His enthusiasm was palpable, even from a distance, and while normally infectious, today it felt like just another layer of complexity I wasn't in the mood to unravel.

"Beatrix!" he shouted, his arms flailing in an attempt to capture my attention. "Beatrix, wait up!"

A heavy sigh escaped me, a silent question to the universe: *Is there ever any escape from Paul?* It wasn't that I didn't appreciate his energy; it was just that sometimes, like now, I craved a moment of solitude, a brief respite from the whirlwind that was my life.

"What is it?" I inquired, mustering a semblance of patience as Paul caught up, his breaths quick and his eyes alight with urgency.

"Have you got Charlie yet?" he asked, the anticipation in his voice almost tangible.

"Not yet, sorry. I've been distracted dealing with Gladys," I admitted, the frustration of juggling too many crises at once evident in my tone.

"Oh, is she alright?" His concern was genuine, a reminder of the camaraderie we shared despite the chaos.

"Yeah. She's fine now," I reassured him, though the simplicity of the statement belied the complexity of the situation.

"That's good to hear," Paul said, mopping a bead of sweat from his forehead.

An idea sparked as we conversed, a realisation that Paul's presence could be advantageous. "When you do see Luke," I started, a plan forming, "can you please tell him that Gladys is safe and at home? She's going to pack a few things and stay with our parents for a while until—" I halted, mid-sentence. There was no need for Paul to be burdened with all the details.

His expression shifted to one of curiosity, but he nodded. "Of course," he agreed, a note of solidarity in his voice.

"Thank you," I responded, offering him a smile that carried a mix of gratitude and relief. In this tumultuous sea of events, it was a comfort to know that there were still points of connection, moments of support, even if they came wrapped in Paul's relentless enthusiasm.

"So, how far did you get?" Paul's inquiry snapped me back to the present, his curiosity never waning.

"Get?" I echoed, momentarily lost in the whirlpool of my thoughts.

"To Broken Hill?" he clarified, his energy undiminished, hands still animatedly moving in sync with his words.

"Oh," a light scoff escaped me as I felt a tinge of embarrassment for momentarily forgetting the crux of our conversation amidst my own tumultuous reflections. "I managed to get somewhere on the outskirts of Adelaide. I've left the hire car at my parents but registered the location near Adelaide first. I'm about to go to my parents to collect the car and then I'll continue from where I left off," I explained, laying out my plan with a newfound clarity.

"That's amazing that you can travel so easily like that," Paul remarked, his admiration evident in his tone, a glimmer of fascination in his eyes reflecting the marvel of the technological capabilities at our disposal.

A smile, broad and genuine, spread across my face. "I know," my acknowledgment came with a mix of satisfaction and a hint of awe at my own experiences.

As I considered the whirlwind of events, a sense of surrealism washed over me. The ability to traverse such distances and tackle a cascade of crises in mere hours was something out of science fiction, yet here I was, living it. The thought that, in just one day, I'd journeyed from Hobart to Adelaide, returned to assist Luke save a critical fence delivery, ventured into the wilds of Tasmania to extricate Gladys from an alarming police evasion, and was now on the cusp of reaching Broken Hill—all of it underscored the extraordinary nature of my new Guardianship.

This reflection brought a momentary pause, a breath in the relentless pace of my day. It wasn't just about the distances covered or the tasks undertaken; it was about the sheer capability and resilience demanded by this new world I was navigating. The pride I felt was tinged with a sobering recognition of the weight of responsibility that this power entailed.

"I'll let you get going then," Paul said, stepping back, his understanding of the urgency and importance of my mission clear in his parting words.

As I faced the Portal, ready to transition between worlds once more, a sudden thought halted my departure. "Make sure you keep the Portal clear. I need to drive the car in and out. Wouldn't want to hit anybody."

"Oh, absolutely," Paul's quick assurance was a balm to my rising anxiety about the logistical complexities awaiting me.

"Thanks."

"And Beatrix?" His voice caught me as I was about to step through the Portal.

"Yeah?" I paused, looking back at him.

"You should probably record several Portal locations on your journey. They may come in handy later," Paul suggested, offering a piece of solid advice.

I nodded, acknowledging the wisdom in his words. "Good idea. I'll do that."

"I recommend Burra and Yunta. If I ever need to stop on my way, they're the usual places," he added, providing specifics that grounded his advice in practical experience.

"Got it," I affirmed, storing the information mentally as I finally stepped into my bedroom, the transitional space before my next leap.

True to my word, I executed the manoeuvre with the hire car, guiding it through the Portal's shimmering threshold. The transition was seamless, a testament to the blend of technology and magic that had become my new normal. I emerged precisely where I had left off, on the quiet outskirts of Gawler.

Settling back into the driver's seat, I felt the car's engine hum to life under my command, a steady companion in the solitude of my mission. As I merged onto the Barrier Highway, the vast expanse of the road stretched before me, a tangible symbol of the journey ahead.

Pressing down on the accelerator, a surge of excitement coursed through me. This wasn't just another drive; it was an adventure into the unchartered outback. "Broken Hill, here I come!" I declared, the words echoing in the confines of the car, a mix of determination and excitement fuelling my voice.

# OUTBACK

## *1338.211.5*

    The transition from the gentle undulations of rolling hills to the vast, monochromatic expanse of the outback marked a noticeable shift in my journey. The landscape unfurled in endless shades of brown, a canvas that mirrored the dryness I associated with Hobart's harshest summer days. It was a sobering reminder of nature's indifference, its capacity to drain life and colour from the world in the face of relentless heat.

    Despite being winter, the trees, sparse and sapped of vitality, stood as ochre sentinels against the arid backdrop, their presence more a testament to survival than to life. It struck me, the parallel between this place and my home during those scorching weeks when the sun seemed intent on leaching every drop of moisture from the earth, leaving behind a landscape gasping for relief.

    As the outskirts of the next town appeared on the horizon, I eased off the accelerator, the change in speed a reluctant concession to civilisation's boundaries. The sign greeting me was a beacon of progress on my path: "Welcome to Yunta," I announced to the empty car, a hint of triumph lacing my voice despite the solitude of my audience. The town's name, a mere marker on a map, now signified my entry into the true heart of the outback, a milestone in my trek across this vast country.

    However, the satisfaction of this achievement was short-lived. A sudden realisation struck me, pulling a frustrated "damn it!" from my lips. In my focused pursuit of Broken Hill,

I had neglected Paul's sage advice to register a Portal location in Burra. The oversight was more than a mere lapse; it was a missed opportunity, a breach in my preparedness that gnawed at me with the insistence of an unresolved chord.

The endless expanse of the road stretched before me, my journey already stretching several hours and covering vast distances that seemed to meld into a blur of monotonous scenery. Paul's advice to register multiple Portal locations along this extensive route echoed in my mind, a nudge of wisdom I begrudgingly acknowledged. While the solitary freedom of the drive had its charms, with Taylor Swift's anthems for company and the road's rhythm under my wheels, the reality was: this was not a voyage I wished to repeat with any regularity. "And I still have two-hundred kilometres to go before I get to Broken Hill," I muttered to myself, the music's energy dimming as practical concerns took the forefront.

As I manoeuvred around a dormant semi on the roadside, the sight of Yunta's petrol station loomed as a beacon of civilisation in the sparse outback. The town, with its meagre population and scattering of humble dwellings, seemed an unlikely hub for two sizeable petrol stations. Yet here they stood, sentinels of the vast wilderness, catering to those who ventured along this outback path. My pre-trip research had painted Yunta as a crucial pit stop before Broken Hill, a fact that now presented a reluctant necessity rather than a mere point of interest.

I had harboured hopes of bypassing this stop, driven by a desire to conserve resources and maintain a low profile, especially given Gladys's precarious situation. The last thing I needed was to leave a breadcrumb trail for anyone trying to piece together my movements. Yet, as I pulled into the station, the reality of my need for fuel overshadowed these concerns. The car's thirst for petrol was palpable, the sound of fuel coursing into the tank a reminder of my dependency on these finite resources in the vast, unforgiving landscape.

The bell above the door of the petrol station jingled, a familiar yet always slightly jarring sound, as I stepped into the confined space, leaving the cold outside world behind. Instantly, the pungent fumes of fuel, so thick and invasive, quickly dissipated, a fleeting discomfort replaced by the engulfing, almost comforting, aroma of freshly cooked hot chips. The scent was potent, invoking an immediate, visceral reaction. My stomach, neglected and empty, growled angrily, a fierce reminder of its discontent, having been ignored for several hours longer than it was accustomed to—a silent protest against my neglect.

The interior of the petrol station was dimly lit, the fluorescent lights flickering sporadically, casting an uneven glow over the aisles crammed with an assortment of snacks. I weaved my way between them, my steps slightly hurried, driven by the gnawing hunger. My eyes scanned the shelves, an array of colours and shapes blurring into one as I reached for a bag of sugary lollies, their bright packaging catching my attention.

Clutching the bag, I beelined for the service counter, the tiles underfoot showing years of wear, a mosaic of countless, hurried visits like my own. The counter, cluttered with an assortment of items aimed at tempting last-minute purchases, stood as a barrier between me and sustenance.

A moment of realisation washed over me, a wave of frustration mingled with resignation. I've been too heavy-handed on the petrol, I sighed internally, the words echoing in the confines of my mind, a silent rebuke. My purse, a small, worn thing burdened with the task of carrying my essentials, felt unusually light as I rummaged through it. The realisation that I didn't have enough cash to cover the transaction was an unfortunate reminder of my miscalculation.

Reluctantly, I searched for my bank card, the plastic cold and impersonal, my reluctant saviour in this moment of need. *I can hardly get petrol back out of the car now*, I mused, the thought tinged with a mix of humour and bitterness.

"I don't really have much choice," came the deep, gruff voice of the man who had joined the queue behind me, his tone carrying a weight of resigned inevitability. His words seemed to hang in the air, dense with an unsettling finality. "Nobody wants the damn thing. I think I'm just gonna 'ave to shoot him."

The casual mention of such a drastic action sent a shiver down my spine, my eyes widening in shock. My empty stomach, already a knot of hunger, twisted further, morphing into a gnarly, uncomfortable mass, as if reacting to the harshness of the man's intentions.

Turning slightly, I caught a glimpse of the man. He was burly, his face etched with lines of a hard life, eyes reflecting a stark, uncompromising reality. His presence felt overwhelming, his aura heavy with a mix of resignation and a peculiar, grim pragmatism.

The woman behind the counter, a fixture in this small, transient world of the petrol station, didn't seem at all perturbed by the man's startling declaration. Her face remained impassive, a mask of professional detachment, as if the talk of shooting was no more remarkable than a comment about the weather. She extended the card reader toward me with a steady hand, her demeanour unflinching, a true embodiment of routine desensitisation.

"That's a bloody shame, mate. That Vincent was alright, he was," chimed in a second voice, rough yet tinged with a hint of sympathy, a contrast to the first man's stoic resignation.

This new voice belonged to another patron, his expression a mix of concern and morose acceptance.

"Yeah, he was. But me new bitch don't like him much. Carries on like a right pork chop, she does. Barkin' and nippin' at the old fella's legs. Broke through the skin the other day, she did. Even drew a bit of blood."

The conversation unfolded behind me, painting a vivid, albeit grim, picture of domestic discord, a clash between old and new, the inevitable yielding to the ruthless, unspoken laws of survival and coexistence.

My fingers clumsily grasped at my purse, nearly letting it slip through in a rush to tuck it away into the confines of my handbag. The conversation unfolding behind me was unsettling, its content darkly mundane in this all-too-normal setting, creating a morbid atmosphere that left me disconcerted.

"Would ya be able to eat him if ya shot him?" the second man's inquiry pierced the air, its timing impeccably poor as I turned to leave the counter, provoking an involuntary gasp from my lips. The question, so blunt and raw, anchored my feet to the spot for a moment, curiosity and horror mingling within me as I couldn't help but turn my gaze toward the two men.

The owner of Vincent, a scruffy figure in a checked flannel shirt that seemed to mirror the ruggedness of his lifestyle, responded with a nonchalant shrug. "Nah, I don't reckon he'd taste much good. Too old a goat now, he is. He'd be all tough and stringy I reckon."

A wave of grim relief washed over me at his words. *At least that's something*, I mused silently, a sliver of solace found in the knowledge that the man's pragmatism didn't extend to consuming his aged goat, despite the bleakness of its fate.

As the man replaced me at the counter, laying out his items to be scanned, the mundanity of the transaction juxtaposed starkly with the grim nature of their earlier discussion. "Good to see you, Bill," the woman's voice, a beacon of normality, cut through the heavy atmosphere, her greeting to the man creating a semblance of everyday civility amidst the otherwise disquieting exchange.

With the bell's chime ringing above me as I exited, the sounds and sights of the petrol station receded. I stepped back into the outside world, the weight of the conversation lingering in my mind, a reminder of the complex tapestry of life's narratives, where the ordinary and the extraordinary, the mundane and the morbid, intertwine in the most unexpected places.

Small puffs of breath formed in the cold air, each one a visible testament to the chill, as I looked up at the darkening late afternoon sky. The transition from day to night seemed to mirror my own internal shift, a mixture of resignation and determination setting in. I wasn't particularly fond of these shorter winter days, their briskness and the swift descent into darkness always seemed to bring a tinge of melancholy. Yet, the vast swathes of flat ground that stretched out before me promised a lingering twilight, offering a sliver of hope that daylight would hold long enough for me to reach the proximity of Broken Hill.

As I pulled away from the petrol pump, my gaze inadvertently landed on a silver Toyota Land Cruiser parked along the fence ahead. It was unremarkable at first glance, but what caught my eye were the several large dog cages mounted on the back. Inside one, through the crisscrossing wires of the cage, I could clearly make out a dark-haired goat. "Vincent!" The name escaped my lips in a gasp, a sudden surge of recognition flooding through me. My eyes locked onto the goat, Vincent, as I slowly drove past. He seemed oblivious to his fate. My stomach churned, mimicking the tumultuous sea, as images of Vincent's potential fate—

lying in a pool of his own blood—invaded my thoughts, unbidden and unsettling.

"I can't let this happen," the words were a whisper, a soft but firm declaration to myself, as I suddenly braked and shifted the car into reverse. This was not a moment for passivity; it was a call to action, however impulsive it might have seemed.

Exiting the car, I cast several quick, stealthy glances toward the station's front door, hoping for the mundane chatter within to continue, a cover for my impending intervention. "Please keep on talking," I mumble-pleaded to the universe or perhaps to the oblivious patrons inside, as I made my way to the cages.

With each step, my resolve hardened. The chill in the air seemed to sharpen my senses, focusing my thoughts on my new rescue mission. I was about to step into a situation fraught with uncertainty, propelled by a sudden, deep-seated conviction that I couldn't stand idly by. Vincent's life, however small or inconsequential it might seem in the grand scheme of things, mattered in this moment, and I was inexplicably, irrevocably drawn into his story.

The back door of the car creaked open, its hinges protesting with a sound that seemed to underscore the gravity of what I was about to do. Around me, the world seemed to pause, the late afternoon air holding its breath as I prepared to enact my hastily forged plan. After a couple of heaped armfuls of hay, torn from one of the several bales I had noticed behind the cages, the stage was set. It was time to rescue Vincent.

Approaching the cage, I could hear Vincent's bleats—each one a thunderous echo in my ears, amplifying the urgency of the moment. When I pulled him from his exposed confinement, the reality of his weight hit me with unexpected force. My knees buckled under the strain, and I found myself slamming painfully against the side of the Land Cruiser. The impact sent a jarring pain through my back, a physical echo of the turmoil inside me.

As I struggled to regain my footing, Vincent, perhaps sensing his chance for freedom, broke free from my faltering grasp. His hooves landed with a heavy, definitive clop on the concrete, a sound that seemed to reverberate with my racing heartbeat. "Shit!" The expletive slipped from my lips in a hiss, a rare loss of composure as I quickly moved to Vincent's side.

My hands, though shaking, were guided by a practiced familiarity, swiftly steering Vincent's head toward the open car door. There was a moment, fraught with tension, where I feared he would resist. But then, as if understanding the seriousness of his situation—or perhaps sensing my desperation—Vincent obliged. With a final, resonant bleat, he jumped into the back seat, his body finding refuge among the hay I had scattered in haste.

With Vincent secured, I gently closed the door, turning my attention to the unexpected audience that had gathered during the commotion. Half a dozen brown hens had swarmed around the car, their clucking reaching a frenetic pitch as they witnessed Vincent's escape. My eyes met the gaze of the apparent leader, her beady eyes holding a challenge, a silent plea that I couldn't ignore. They seemed to understand the stakes, their own fate mirroring Vincent's in the cruel arithmetic of farm life.

"Oh, come on then," I conceded, my voice a mixture of resignation and newfound resolve. The decision to extend my impromptu rescue to these feathered bystanders was impulsive, yet it felt like the only acceptable choice in a world where the lines between right and wrong were suddenly drawn in stark relief. My actions today, born of a spontaneous empathy, were shaping the trajectory of not just my own story, but those of Vincent and now these hens, all of us intertwined in a shared narrative of escape and survival.

❖

The air was heavy with the scent of rust and dust as I guided my newly acquired menagerie toward a large dilapidated shed, its wooden frame groaning under the weight of years. The decision to find this secluded spot was driven by a need for discretion, a lesson learned the hard way from a previous oversight of not registering an outback Portal location. Such a mistake was not one I could afford to repeat, especially now with the stakes so unexpectedly elevated.

I manoeuvred the car carefully, its headlights cutting through the shed's pervasive gloom, illuminating the expanse of wall that would soon become our passage. With a sense of solemnity, I activated the Portal device, its mechanics whirring to life with a promise of passage. The once inert wall was now a canvas, painted with the swirling, vibrant colours of the Portal, a spectacle that seemed almost surreal against the shed's rustic backdrop.

The swirling colours intensified, casting a mesmerising glow that enveloped the car, the goat, the hens, and me in a cocoon of light and energy. The air around us seemed to hum, charged with the potential of imminent transition. I gripped the steering wheel, the car's engine a steady purr amidst the crescendo of the Portal's activation.

With a deep, steadying breath, I edged the car forward, the boundary between our current reality and Clivilius beckoning just ahead. The sensation of crossing was unlike anything I could have anticipated— a confluence of exhilaration and trepidation, as the fabric of our existence stretched and melded into new possibilities.

As we passed through the Portal, the concept of time and space momentarily lost its meaning. We were in flux, between what was and what could be, the future unfurling with each passing second. It was a leap not just through space but into a future where the fates of a woman, a goat, and a flock of hens were irrevocably intertwined, propelled by a shared journey into Clivilius.

❖

The air was charged with tension as Paul stood there, hands resting on his hips, his expression a mix of bewilderment and exasperation. The unimpressed pout that formed on his lips spoke volumes before he even uttered a word.

"Beatrix?" he asked, his voice laced with a burgeoning frustration that I knew all too well.

"What?" My response was terse, a reflection of the sudden tightness in my chest as I braced for the impending confrontation.

"Why is there a goat in the back of the car?" His question, though simple, was laden with a deeper incredulity, his palm outstretched toward the unexpected passenger as if to emphasise the absurdity of the situation.

"Oh," was all I managed initially, my mind racing as I moved swiftly to the car's back door. The latch clicked softly as I opened it, revealing Vincent, who seemed blissfully unaware of the commotion his presence had caused. "This is Vincent," I said, introducing the old goat as if the formality could somehow smooth over the irregularity of the scenario. I took a handful of hay from the backseat, using it to coax Vincent out of his temporary refuge.

Vincent emerged with a happy bleat, his hooves kicking up small clouds of dust as he playfully adjusted to his new surroundings before settling down with the straw, a simple pleasure amidst the unfolding drama.

"What the hell am I going to do with a goat?" Paul's question hung in the air, his incredulity palpable. I could only offer a helpless shrug in response, my own uncertainty mirroring his.

"Are you trying to get us all killed?" The intensity of Paul's rebuke hit me harder than I expected.

"I didn't have a choice. Bill was going to kill him," I defended, the justification sounding thin even to my own ears.

"Who's Bill?" The confusion on Paul's face deepened, the situation spiralling further into the realm of the absurd.

"Vincent's owner," I explained.

Paul's eyes widened, his initial frustration giving way to a dawning realisation of my actions. "So, you decided to kidnap his goat instead!?"

My eyes rolled, a silent counter to Paul's critique, which felt more like an affront to my intentions than a rational argument. "Look at him," I urged, my hand gently stroking Vincent's head, feeling the coarse texture of his hair under my fingertips. "He's so happy now." It was a plea for empathy, a call to acknowledge the simple joy evident in Vincent's demeanour.

"I don't think he's going to be very happy when he gets eaten by a shadow panther," Paul retorted, his voice laced with a mix of sarcasm and concern. His statement, meant to inject a dose of reality into the situation, only served to heighten my irritation.

Annoyed at his inability to grasp the immediacy of the compassionate choice I had made, I looked up at him, my gaze sharpened with frustration. "He can live in one of the motorhomes," I declared, presenting what I saw as a perfectly viable solution, my voice imbued with a sense of triumph.

"Beatrix!" Paul's response was a sharp rebuke, slicing through the air between us. "We're not keeping Vincent in a motorhome. Those are for people." His tone was adamant, brooking no room for debate, a clear line drawn in the sand of our moral battleground.

Undeterred, I leaned in, my action deliberate, as I placed a quick kiss on Vincent's head, a gesture of solidarity with the creature I had saved. "Then Vincent's death is on you," I countered, my words heavy with implication, my glare laden with a challenge, pushing the weight of the ethical dilemma squarely onto his shoulders.

Paul's reaction was a physical manifestation of capitulation, his hands thrown up in a gesture of defeat, his sigh a resonant symbol of his begrudging acceptance. "Fine. I'll find Vincent a safe home." His words, though reluctant, were a concession, a sign that despite his protests, the undercurrent of humanity that I knew resided in him had been stirred.

With a sense of relief washing over me now that Vincent's immediate future seemed less grim, I turned my attention to the next order of business. "Time for accident number two," I muttered under my breath, a mischievous smirk playing at the corners of my lips as I approached the boot of the car. The sense of illicit excitement was palpable, a guilty pleasure in unveiling the next chapter of my impromptu rescue mission.

"Beatrix, what are you...?" Paul's voice trailed off as he came to stand beside me, his sentence dissolving into the cool air as his gaze fell on the unexpected cargo. I could feel his exasperation without looking at him, the weight of his sigh speaking volumes.

"Well, I couldn't just leave them behind," I said, my voice a blend of defensiveness and justification as I gestured toward the hens. They continued their gentle rummaging through the hay, oblivious to the larger ethical debate they were unwittingly a part of.

"You're in Yunta, aren't you?" Paul's question cut through the air, his tone laced with a resigned familiarity, as if the pieces of an unseen puzzle were falling into place in his mind.

His question, more an assertion than an inquiry, warranted only one response. "Yes," I admitted.

"I thought so," Paul mused, his gaze lingering on the hens with a mixture of curiosity and resignation. "Were they on the side of the road?" he asked, tilting his head slightly, his eyes not leaving the feathered ensemble in the boot.

"Um... basically," I replied, the ambiguity of my answer a thin veil over the truth of their acquisition. It was probably best, I reasoned, that Paul remained unaware of the specifics surrounding the hens' sudden change in circumstances. The less he knew about the minutiae of their 'abduction,' the better. After all, the road to saving these creatures was paved with good intentions, even if it meant bending the rules just a tad in their favour.

Paul's actions were gentle and deliberate, as he reached into the boot and carefully extracted one of the hens. His calm demeanour was almost soothing. "I'm not surprised," he remarked, a hint of amusement in his voice as he placed the chook on the ground, watching it acclimate to its new surroundings. "There are always chickens running around that town when I pass through," he said, his casual acceptance of the situation brought a small, nervous laugh from me. *Well, I guess they were running around the town,* I echoed in my thoughts.

"You still need the car to get to Broken Hill, don't you?" Paul's question snapped me back to the present, his hands now busy with a second hen. The bird's wings flapped in a brief, frantic ballet, sending feathers drifting into the air like dandelion seeds before it settled down, grounding itself in this new chapter of its existence.

"Yeah," I replied, my voice steady as I assisted Paul with the remaining chickens. Each bird seemed to carry its own story, a narrative abruptly intersected by my intervention. As we transferred them from their temporary haven in the boot to the open air, I felt a twinge of responsibility for their well-being.

The sound of the boot slamming shut resonated, a definitive end to this part of our journey. The hay, once a bed for the hens, now lay in darkness once again, its purpose momentarily fulfilled.

"Can you bring the car back once you've found Charlie?" Paul's question was practical, a reminder of the ongoing mission.

As I observed Paul's meticulous handling of the single brown feather, a simple byproduct of my current operation, my fascination with his actions bordered on amusement. The feather, innocuous yet symbolically laden with the day's events, became the centre of an unexpected spectacle as Paul, perhaps driven by curiosity or some unspoken ritual, brought it to his nose. The feather's unexpected journey toward being a makeshift nostril accessory turned comical as it nearly got inhaled, transforming Paul into a sneezing spectacle. His series of rapid sneezes disrupted the fragile peace, scattering the chickens and ruffling even Vincent's calm, each sneeze sending them into a flurry of motion and sound.

Amid the ensuing chaos, with chickens darting and Vincent vocalising his disapproval, a chuckle escaped me. The scene unfolding was like a slapstick comedy, an interlude of light-heartedness. "I'll bring the car back," I declared to Paul, a statement of responsibility amid the disarray, and with a smile, I slid into the driver's seat, the familiar space a welcome enclosure.

The act of closing the door felt like sealing myself off from the immediate dilemma, a momentary respite as I prepared to rejoin the broader, unpredictable journey ahead.

The engine's hum was a comforting constant as I navigated back onto the Barrier Highway, the road stretching out before me like a promise of continuity amidst change.

"Broken Hill, one hundred and ninety-nine," the road sign's bold letters declared, a beacon of direction in the vast, open landscape. My foot pressed against the accelerator, a physical affirmation of my commitment to the journey, while my fingers found the stereo's volume control, an instinctual reach for the comfort of music. As the sounds of Taylor Swift filled the car, a sense of companionship enveloped me, the music a reminder of normality and personal space in a day that had been anything but typical.

# RAGS

## 4338.211.6

The cloak of night had fully descended, shrouding the vast, open landscapes in an impenetrable darkness, punctuated only by the occasional glimmer of distant stars. The "Welcome to Broken Hill" sign emerged from the abyss, its faded letters momentarily illuminated by the car's headlights, offering a silent, almost mocking greeting. The excitement of arriving at this remote outpost was tempered by the night's obsidian embrace, denying me the vibrant, rugged welcome I had envisioned.

The fatigue from the drive was a creeping, insidious force, gradually weighing down my eyelids and dulling my senses. The thrill of the journey had waned, replaced by a growing sense of isolation and an unsettling quiet that seemed to envelop everything.

Navigating the town's quaint streets to find Paul's house was an exercise in patience. The charm of the town's naming conventions lost its appeal quickly, morphing into a frustrating puzzle. Roads and lanes, so whimsically similar in name, became a labyrinth in the dim glow of the streetlights.

Upon arrival, Paul's house presented itself as a tableau of abandonment. The structure, modest and unassuming, was swallowed by the shadows, its windows dark and lifeless. The absence of a car in the driveway, coupled with the sight of neglected mail peeking out from the letterbox, painted a picture of a home forgotten by time, or perhaps deliberately left behind.

A pang of disappointment washed over me as the realisation set in – there was no sign of Charlie. The purpose of my arduous journey, the reunion I had longed for, seemed to slip further away with each passing moment. The house's unyielding doors, locked and indifferent, were a physical manifestation of the barriers that now stood between me and my goal.

Defeated and with the gnawing emptiness in my stomach becoming ever more insistent, I had no choice but to retreat to Clivilius, empty handed.

Manoeuvring the car to the side of the Portal after entry to avoid any collisions, exhausted, I promptly exited the vehicle. Closing my door, the slam of another door closing echoed through the cool evening air, causing the hairs on the back of my neck to bristle with warning.

"Beatrix!" Paul called out, jogging toward me, firestick in hand.

My eyes narrowed, trying to make out the silhouette of the person that followed not far behind him. *Karen!*

"Beatrix!" Paul huffed, panting as though he had just sprinted a marathon. His face was flushed, beads of sweat glistening on his forehead under the dim light of the firestick. "Did you find her?"

"Sorry, Paul," I replied, biting the inside of my cheek, a mixture of frustration and disappointment churning in my stomach. "I couldn't find her."

"Really?" asked Paul in surprise, dribbling saliva down his chin as he continued to pant. His eyes, wide with disbelief, searched mine for answers, for hope.

"Is everything okay here?" I asked, suddenly concerned for Paul's wellbeing. His laboured breathing was unsettling.

"We've been chasing those blinkin' chickens of yours," answered Karen, hands on hips as she heaved deeply. Her voice was laced with irritation, yet there was a hint of amusement in her tone.

Confused, my brow furrowed.

"Well," began Paul, a satisfied grin spreading across his face, his eyes twinkling with a mixture of mischief and pride, "You gave me an idea earlier. I was going to wait for you to return, but then I figured that they'd probably be better in separate cars anyway."

I continued to stare blankly at Paul, my brain struggling to process his words amidst the mental and physical exhaustion that clung to me like a second skin.

"The chickens," he emphasised, as if the word itself should explain everything.

"Yeah, I got that part," I replied, my voice laced with confusion and a growing sense of incredulity. "What about the chickens?"

Karen groaned loudly.

"I've taken Glenda's car–" Paul started again, oblivious to Karen's growing irritation.

"You mean we," Karen interrupted, her voice sharp, a clear assertion of her involvement.

"Of course," Paul corrected himself quickly, a flash of embarrassment crossing his face. "We've taken Glenda's car to the Drop Zone and decided to turn it into a hen house."

I gasped audibly, my mind reeling at the absurdity of the idea. "You've put the chickens in a BMW?" The words felt ridiculous even as they left my lips, the luxurious car an absurd sanctuary for poultry in a world where luxury had lost all its meaning.

"I take that back," said Karen, her voice firm, her face set in a mask of determination and slight annoyance. "The idea was all yours, Paul."

I rubbed my temple, a headache brewing at the forefront of my mind. *What the hell was wrong with Paul? Chickens in a BMW?*

"It's not as though we really had many options," cried Paul, in an attempt to defend his decision. "We can't very well leave them running freely around camp. They're a threat to all of us."

"He's not wrong," agreed Karen, nodding her head slightly.

"We can't risk them attracting any more wild creatures," Paul added, his eyes scanning the horizon as if expecting a threat to emerge at any moment.

A deep frown smothered my face, my brows knitting together in a mixture of concern and disbelief. "So, you'd rather sentence them to a torturous death out here... alone?"

"Beatrix, don't be so foolish," scolded Karen, her beady eyes penetrating mine, sharp and unyielding. Her stance was firm, her resolve clear, as she continued, "You know as well as I do that we can't let our love for the preservation of nature surpass the logical faculties that the universe has bestowed upon us."

*Oh my God, what a freak*, I told myself silently as my eyes rolled. Karen's words felt like a slap, a jarring blend of condescension and pseudo-philosophical rambling. It's true, I have a deep passion for nature and wildlife, but logical facilities bestowed upon the universe... what the hell does that even mean!? In this moment, the absurdity of our situation – arguing over chickens and philosophical principles while the world crumbled around us – struck me with full force, a poignant reminder of the strange new reality we were all navigating.

Simultaneously, almost as though the new Clivilius universe were sending us instant messages, all three of our bellies grumbled. The sound, embarrassingly symphonic, seemed to echo around us.

"I'm so hungry," Karen confessed, her hand gently rubbing at her belly, a look of genuine discomfort crossing her face. "I'm not sure I've eaten today."

Paul's eyes suddenly lit up, and my heart skipped a beat in preparation for what request might follow next. His sudden change in demeanour was startling, almost as if a switch had been flipped, transforming his concern into an eager anticipation.

"You're in Broken Hill now, aren't you, Beatrix?" Paul asked, his tongue running salaciously along his lower lip, a gesture that seemed overly dramatic for the context. The sight was unsettling, out of place amidst the desolation that surrounded us.

Cringing, I replied in the affirmative, albeit reluctantly. My voice was a reluctant whisper, betraying my unease at the direction this conversation was taking.

The pleasurable, almost sexual groan that escaped Paul's moistened lips sent a reprehensible shudder down my spine. It was a sound that seemed to belong to another world, one far removed from our current struggles and concerns.

"I think there is some food being prepared back at camp, but–" Paul paused, his eyes seemingly rolling back into his head as he got lost in his own fantasy. The moment stretched uncomfortably long, filled with an awkward silence punctuated only by the uneasy shuffling of our feet.

After what felt like an eternity, during which Karen and I exchanged concerned glances, silently questioning the sanity of our companion, Paul continued. "You must get us some Rags chips. They are simply divine."

"Rags?" I queried, latching onto the least bizarre aspect of the conversation, a welcome distraction from the unsettling display I'd just witnessed.

"They're on Oxide Street," Paul said quickly, a hint of fervour in his voice. "You can't miss the shop. Simply the best chips you've ever tasted!"

I remained somewhat hesitant, my mind still reeling from the oddity of Paul's behaviour. Yet, given that he looked as though he was deeply fantasised by the idea, I decided to agree to the suggestion rather than engage in further conversation. It seemed a small concession, a way to bring some semblance of normality back to our interaction, even if the thought of Paul's earlier groan still lingered uncomfortably in my mind.

❖

Thankfully, Paul's chicken and chip shop of choice wasn't a long walk, and the seemingly vague directions he had given me began to make some sense as the trip unfolded. The location I had chosen for the Portal, while discreet, was central to most of the important sites in Broken Hill, and, as I have now discovered, also close to the home of the best chicken and chips in Broken Hill. *Paul will owe me for this one*, I thought as I made my way past the car wash next door, its silence contrasting sharply with the bustling activity of the evening, and towards the shop entrance.

The glow of the neon sign flickered in the dusk, casting an amber hue on the cracked pavement. I paused momentarily to take in my surroundings, feeling a slight chill in the air that made me pull my jacket tighter around me. The instantly recognisable smell of BBQ chickens filled the air like a thick invisible fog, permeating every corner of the street and weaving its way into the fabric of my clothes. It was a comforting, almost nostalgic scent that momentarily eased the weight of the day's worries.

I observed the shop's façade, noting the peeling paint and the warmth emanating from within, visible through the fogged-up windows. A sense of anticipation built up inside me, mingling with an odd sense of displacement—a feeling that was becoming all too familiar in my travels.

And from the way Paul had reacted, I could now easily imagine that if the smell could be bottled up into an aftershave lotion, Paul would be a repeat customer. The thought of someone walking around, exuding the essence of BBQ chicken, was so absurd that it brought a slight, involuntary smile to my face. I found myself wondering whether, in some corner of the universe I had yet to explore, such a scent was considered the height of sophistication.

*Imagine smelling like a BBQ chicken.* The strange thought tickled my mind, offering a brief respite from the complex web of emotions and responsibilities that came with my journey.

Despite the chill in the air, several young children ran about barefoot outside the shop door, their laughter piercing the evening's calm. Their young mother, a figure of frazzled determination, scrambled after them, trying to herd them away from the busy road. "Stay away from the bloody road," she scolded, her voice a mix of worry and weariness. Her arm lifted in a swinging motion, warning of the consequences should they stray too close to danger again. Witnessing this, my smile quickly inverted into a frown, a pang of empathy striking me for the harried mother.

At the same moment, a plump, middle-aged lady bustled out of the shop, her arms cradling a white plastic bag almost overflowing with fried goodies. The aroma of the food wafted out, mingling with the evening air. Her flip-flops slapped against the soles of her feet with each hurried step she took on the pavement, creating a rhythm that seemed out of sync with the chaotic dance of the children.

"Did you grab some gravy?" a bearded man called out from the open window of his dark-coloured ute, parked haphazardly at the curb. His tone was casual, yet there was an undertone of expectation, as if this tiny detail could make or break his evening.

"Shit," the plump woman muttered under her breath, her moment of triumph deflated by the forgotten gravy. She turned on her heels with a sigh, her body language a mix of frustration and resignation, and retreated back into the shop.

*I guess she forgot*, I figured, observing the scene unfold with a mix of amusement and sympathy. The busyness of the place, the cacophony of voices, and the flurry of activity were beginning to overwhelm me, making me second guess whether the chips really were going to be worth the effort.

Seizing the moment, I followed the plump woman into the shop. As I stepped inside, a harsh buzzer cut through the hum of conversation, announcing my entrance. Instantly, I was engulfed in a loud hive of activity. The space was cramped, filled with the chaotic ballet of patrons and staff moving in a tight choreography. I navigated the small space, positioning myself slightly off to the right in front of the large shop window, beside the end of the counter, where I could observe without being swept away by the current of customers.

My eyes were drawn to the back wall, where a row of vats filled with hot oil bubbled menacingly, frying what I assumed were the shop's famed crinkle-cut chips. The air was thick with the scent of frying food, a smell that was at once appetising and overwhelming. Along the side wall, directly behind the counter, the chicken rotisseries turned slowly. The sight that unfolded before me was jarringly brutal in its culinary efficiency: blackened, headless chicken carcasses rotated in an unending cycle, their skin glistening as oil and juices popped and dribbled down the sides, collecting in trays below.

A sudden, visceral reaction clenched my stomach, and a wave of empathy washed over me. *Oh no!* I silently gasped, my heart sinking as I watched the grim spectacle. The reality of the meal, the stark, unvarnished truth of what it meant to eat meat, was laid bare before me in a way I couldn't ignore. *I can't look*, I cried to myself, turning my head away, a hand instinctively coming up to cover my mouth. *Those poor chickens!*

"Hey, you!" a voice to my left boomed, snapping me out of my unsettling reverie. Dazed, I turned, finding myself face to face with the plump woman who'd just re-entered the shop.

"You're standing in the way of the buzzer. You need to move," she said, her tone a mix of annoyance and urgency, gesturing towards the door where I had inadvertently stationed myself.

"Oh," was all I could muster, my voice a faint echo of my internal turmoil. I awkwardly took a step forward, clearing the path. With the commotion inside the shop, the constant buzz had blended into the background noise until now.

"What can I get for you?" came a man's voice, pulling my attention to the counter. The server, a middle-aged man with a stained apron, looked at me expectantly, ready to take my order.

"Hmm?" I uttered, still somewhat disconnected from the moment as I turned my attention to him.

"What would you like?" he rephrased, his voice carrying a hint of impatience amidst the bustling environment.

"Ah," I finally managed, gathering my thoughts and deliberately avoiding the unsettling view of the rotating chickens behind him. *What was it Paul wanted?* My mind scrambled to recall the order. *Ah, yes.* "I'll have a large chips with chicken salt, please," I stated, more confidently this time.

"Would you like gravy with that?" he inquired, a routine question that momentarily brought me back to the plump woman's forgotten gravy.

"No, thank you," I replied quickly, eager to conclude the transaction and step away from the unsettling display. He nodded and shuffled off to fulfil my request, leaving me with a moment to collect my thoughts and adjust to the shop's frenetic energy.

Between the rotating chickens and the congested waiting area, I quickly decided that I needed some fresh air. *It's all a bit too much in here*, I thought, as I pushed the door open. The buzzer sounded its harsh alert, marking my exit, and the familiar smell of BBQ chickens wafted over me once again. Despite its persistence, it was a welcome respite from the overwhelming atmosphere inside. *It's still better than inside*, I concluded, taking a deep breath of the cooler outside air.

Oxide Street was buzzing with activity around me. Cars whizzed past, their engines a constant hum in the background. The drive-through line for KFC diagonally across the street snaked around the corner, while traffic was backed up at the roundabout to the left, congesting the road outside. *Wow, chickens must be really popular in Broken Hill*, I mused to myself, a hint of amusement in my thought. *Or is this an outback obsession?*

Lifting my gaze up the street to my left, my attention was caught by a strange, hooded figure. He was leaning against the wall of the building across the road, an island of stillness in the bustling environment. His hands were buried deep in his trouser pockets, and his head was dipped forward, obscured by the hood of his sweater. Despite the lack of visible eyes, I couldn't shake the feeling that he was staring directly at me. A cold shiver ran down my spine, unsettling me further.

Curiosity piqued and a bit unnerved, I subtly shifted my stance to face the hooded figure more directly. "What the hell?" I whispered to myself, a reflexive response as the man suddenly stirred. As if sensing my scrutiny, he abruptly turned and started down the side street, his movements quick and purposeful.

*Who is he and why the peculiar interest in me?* The questions echoed in my mind, fuelling a mix of curiosity and apprehension. My instinct was to follow, to uncover the reason for his mysterious presence and interest. Yet, I hesitated, torn between the urge to investigate and the instinct to maintain my distance from potential danger.

"Oi, you." The voice, tinged with impatience, snapped me back to the present. I turned to face the source, the plump woman who'd just exited the shop. She was clutching her plastic bag more securely now, the forgotten gravy now in her possession. Her interruption steered my focus away from the mysterious man and back to the reason I was here.

"Yes?" I responded, a bit taken aback by her abruptness.

"Your order is ready. They're looking for you inside," she informed me, her voice a mix of helpfulness and haste, as if keen to get back to her own business.

"That was quick," I replied, a note of surprise in my voice. With a polite nod, I manoeuvred past her, re-entering the shop's chaotic interior.

"Ah, here she is," announced the man with the red apron from behind the counter, a beacon of familiarity in the bustling space. "Your order is ready. Come down here to the register, and I'll ring it up for you."

Weaving through the cluster of customers, I reached the far end of the counter, positioning myself in front of the register. The man with the red apron, his age evident in the deep lines etched across his face, began to process my order. His hands, skinny and slightly trembling, moved over the register's buttons with painstaking slowness. His fingers fumbled, tracing frustrated circles in the air as he struggled to locate the correct keys.

*Oh my God*, I thought, a surge of impatience washing over me, at this rate, *I'll be here all evening!* Watching his struggle, a mix of sympathy and exasperation bubbled inside me.

Finally, the man behind the counter looked up, a quirky smile playing on his lips as he peered over the top of his square glasses. "That will be $8.50, unless I can tempt you with some cheeseslaw to go with your crunchy chips?" he offered, his tone light and inviting.

I couldn't help but let a little giggle escape. "What in the world is cheeseslaw?" I asked, genuinely curious and slightly amused by the novelty of the concoction.

"Why, it's only the best salad in Broken Hill," he replied with a hint of pride in his voice. "It's made of cheese, shredded carrot, and a bit of mayonnaise." His description was straightforward, yet it carried a sense of local charm.

*Is that all? How is that a salad?* I pondered internally, bemused by the simplicity of what was considered a delicacy here. *It really doesn't take much to please these people*, I mused, a wry smile tugging at the corners of my mouth.

"In that case, I had better get some cheeseslaw as well, thanks," I replied, my tone light, a soft smile spreading across my face. *Paul is going to love me!* I thought, already anticipating his reaction to this local specialty.

The man's fingers resumed their dance across the register keypad, a few more seconds of awkward fumbling before he triumphantly announced, "That will be $12.50 now, thank you."

I handed over the cash, watching as he tackled the next challenge: bagging the items. His hands clumsily navigated the task, a few stray chips escaping their container and tumbling to their demise as he placed the bag of chips into a larger plastic bag. Despite the minor losses, he maintained his cheerful demeanour, finally handing me the bag with another smile.

"Here you go. Have a lovely evening, miss," he said, his eyes twinkling behind his glasses, a blend of kindness and weariness etched into his features.

Hastily retreating from the shop, my smile broadened, tinged with a mix of relief and amusement as I reflected on what could only be considered my first real outback experience. "Well, excluding Yunta," I muttered under my breath, a quiet acknowledgment of my growing collection of uniquely outback encounters. *And what an experience it was!*

Stepping back onto the street, I scanned my surroundings for any sign of the strange hooded man, but he was nowhere to be seen. *Maybe I really am imagining things,* I pondered, a slight frown creasing my brow. *Too much of this Broken Hill dust must be affecting my brain,* I concluded with a half-hearted chuckle, trying to brush off the eerie feeling. *It's definitely time to get out of here.*

With new determination, I began my trek back to the Portal, the bag of chips and cheeseslaw swinging by my side. The rustle of the plastic bag and the occasional clink of the container inside served as a steady rhythm to my steps. Despite the reassurance of the busy street around me, a part of me remained on edge, prompting me to glance over my shoulder every now and then... *just to be safe.*

❖

Finally, I returned from the shop, the distinct aroma of Rags chips heralding my arrival as I stepped into Clivilius. The scent, rich and inviting, immediately captured Paul and

Karen's attention, and I couldn't suppress a small, satisfied smile at their reaction. But the chips were just the beginning. With a flourish that might have seemed over-the-top in any other context, I presented a container of cheeseslaw, a recent discovery that promised to be more than just a side dish.

"This," I announced, elevating the container to almost ceremonial importance, "is cheeseslaw. Apparently, it's a game-changer." I observed their faces closely, detecting the spark of intrigue and the ripple of anticipation that crossed their features.

"Indeed it is," Paul echoed, his voice tinged with a zeal that matched the fervour in his eyes. His hand darted towards the container with a speed driven by his burgeoning satisfaction. As they combined the cheeseslaw with the chips, diving into the taste test, I watched their expressions transform. The fusion of the rich, cheesy flavour with the chips' salty crunch created a symphony of taste, eliciting a reaction that bordered on the reverential.

"Wow, this is amazing," Karen's voice rang out, her face alight with a kind of joy that was infectious. Seeing her so happy over something I had brought felt surprisingly fulfilling. The simplicity of a local delicacy had sparked such a pure, unadulterated pleasure.

I found myself nodding in agreement, my own taste buds revelling in the unique blend of flavours. "Should we share this with the rest of the camp?" Paul's voice broke through my thoughts, carrying a hint of hope that perhaps we could keep this culinary discovery to ourselves just a little longer. Internally, I echoed his sentiment, feeling a selfish tug to keep this small joy just between us three.

Karen, her attention still half on the delightful mix she was enjoying, simply shrugged and offered a contented grin. That nonverbal exchange was all the confirmation we needed;

tonight, the cheeseslaw and chips were our little secret indulgence.

As we continued to savour the flavours of Broken Hill, the weight of my responsibilities as a Guardian of Bixbus momentarily lifted. The act of sharing this meal, finding a moment of camaraderie and simple happiness, provided a brief respite from the complexities and uncertainties that had filled my day. Surrounded by friends, enjoying a piece of local culture, I felt a lightness, a reminder that there were still moments of normality, moments of sheer, uncomplicated joy to be found. It was these instances, however fleeting, that added a silver lining to the challenging journey I was on.

# SAFE

## 4338.211.7

Standing around the campfire, the soft murmur of voices mingled with the crackle of flames, casting a warm, flickering light across Luke's weary features. Despite his recent induction as a Guardian, only a week ago, the optimism that once shone in his eyes seemed to have dimmed. Deep lines etched into his forehead betrayed the weight of his new responsibilities. Observing him, a pang of apprehension stirred within me. *Is this the imminent future awaiting me?* The question lingered in my mind, heavy with foreboding.

The scars I bore, painful reminders of my own tumultuous introduction to Clivilius, seemed to echo with a shiver across my shoulders. Even in my relatively short tenure as a Guardian here in Bixbus, the changes were noticeable. The population was growing, the transition from temporary tents to more permanent caravans and motorhomes marking a significant shift. Recently, everyone had thrown themselves into constructing a basic but functional chainlink fence around the camp's perimeter.

Yet, beyond the reassuring boundaries of our makeshift fortification, the vast, uncharted wilderness stretched out, a constant reminder of the unknowns that lay waiting. The landscape, so reminiscent of the open expanses I had traversed on my way to Broken Hill, held an eerie silence. Apart from the goat and the scattered chickens that I had collected along my way, there was a palpable absence of life, a void that seemed too vast to be merely empty. The sudden recollection of the shadow panthers that lurked in the periphery of our new home sent a chill down my spine.

I forced a deep breath, trying to anchor myself in the moment, away from the spiralling thoughts of what other mysteries and threats might lie beyond our small enclave.

"That's everyone," Nial announced, his voice echoing slightly as he secured the metallic gate with a resounding clang. He and Paul stepped into the small, enclosed settlement, their silhouettes briefly framed against the dimming sky.

Luke, observing the finality of the gate's closure, remarked with a hint of dry humour, "It feels a bit like a zoo here now." His words floated across the cool air as his brother joined our small assembly with a heavy sigh that seemed to carry the weight of the day.

"Except this time, I think we are the animals locked in the cage," Paul said, his voice tinged with a mix of resignation and irony.

The comparison struck a chord, and I couldn't help but think of the more literal captives we had. "I'm not so sure that the goat and chickens that you've locked in the car and left out there would agree with you," I told Paul, my tone laced with a gentle reproof as I gestured vaguely towards the Drop Zone, where the unsuspecting animals awaited their fate.

Luke interjected, "It won't always be this way." He rubbed at his brow, a gesture of weariness yet determination, and turned to me. His eyes met mine, seeking to instil a sense of hope. "Beatrix and I will bring you more supplies tomorrow."

I nodded, feeling the weight of responsibility settle on my shoulders yet again. "Yeah, I'll get you as many motorhomes as I can over the next few days," I affirmed, my voice steady, bolstered by the resolve in Luke's gaze.

"And you've got some skilled people here now. You'll have a little village built and buzzing with enthusiasm in no time,"

Luke asserted, his voice laced with a hope I found both comforting and daunting.

"I wouldn't go that—" I started to inject a dose of realism into his sunny outlook, only to be cut off by Paul's interjection.

"Speaking of motorhomes and supplies, Luke can give you my house keys." Paul's statement, seemingly straightforward, carried an undercurrent of resignation. He paused, turning to Luke with a look that seemed to seek confirmation.

"Yeah," Luke responded, his voice steady. "I've got them all in a safe space." His assurance was matter-of-fact, yet it couldn't entirely mask the underlying tension that the subject stirred.

"If Claire and the kids really have gone to Queensland, I doubt they'll return anytime soon," Paul continued.

I noticed Luke's right eye twitch as he gave his brother a look filled with unspoken questions and perhaps a hint of worry. The complexity of their shared history and unspoken fears seemed to momentarily bubble to the surface.

Meanwhile, Paul, either oblivious to or choosing to ignore Luke's silent interrogation, turned his gaze back to me. "You may as well bring anything from the house that looks useful," he instructed, his voice carrying a note of finality, as if in handing over his keys, he was also relinquishing a part of his past, a chapter he was perhaps ready or resigned to close.

"Include furniture with that," Kain's voice cut through our conversation, drawing our attention as he approached with the awkward yet determined gait that his new crutches dictated. "I could really do with a good couch to rest my leg."

Luke's expression tightened with concern, the lines on his forehead deepening as he addressed Kain's discomfort. "Has it still not healed fully?" he inquired.

"No," Kain responded tersely, a flicker of frustration crossing his features. "I don't seem to be as privileged as Joel."

"Any news on that front?" Luke's question seemed to probe for more than just an update, perhaps seeking a glimmer of hope.

"No," Kain's reply was succinct, the concern etched on his face growing more pronounced as the daylight waned around us, the shadows deepening and blending with the lines of worry on his brow.

"We've not seen anything of Joel, Jamie, or Glenda," Paul interjected, his voice adding another layer to our collective anxiety.

"Give them a couple more days," Luke suggested, though his words seemed to float more on hope than conviction.

"And then what?" My question cut through the strained optimism, seeking something more concrete, a plan or a promise we could hold onto.

Luke's shrug was a silent admission of uncertainty, a gesture that felt unsettlingly inadequate in the face of our growing concerns.

Paul sighed, a sound heavy with the weight of unspoken fears, just as Kain's scoff broke the tense silence. "You've really got no idea what you are doing, do you, Luke?" His words, sharp and laden with his own mix of fear and frustration, were a jarring reminder of our precarious situation.

"It's not that easy," I found myself snapping back, rushing to Luke's defence.

"You don't have to tell me that," Kain shot back, his voice hard, his words not just a retort but a reminder of his own struggles and pain.

My mouth opened to respond, to defend, to argue—caught in the crossfire of emotions and the harsh truths of our existence here.

"And while I think of it," Paul's voice broke through the mounting tension, his words cutting through the air with a decisiveness that momentarily redirected our focus. "My car is still parked at the Adelaide airport carpark. Can you collect it for me and bring it here?"

I shifted my gaze from Kain, whose stubbornness lingered in the air like a thick fog, to Paul, feeling the shift in the conversation's direction. "Sure," I muttered, my agreement quick but laced with the remnants of the previous disagreement.

Luke's reaction was almost instantaneous, his face brightening with a kind of eager helpfulness. "Oh," he exclaimed, the idea clearly sparking a sense of purpose in him. "I am flying from Hobart to Adelaide first thing in the morning. I won't have time to collect Paul's car, but I can register a Portal location to make it easier for you, Beatrix."

"Thanks, but there's no need to fly, I've already registered several locations in Adelaide," I informed him, my tone gentle yet firm, aiming to ease any unnecessary burdens from his shoulders.

Luke's expression shifted, his initial enthusiasm melting into a look of thoughtful concentration. "Oh," he uttered, a simple acknowledgment that seemed to carry a weight of realisation or perhaps disappointment.

I watched him, my eyes narrowing slightly, trying to decipher the underlying currents of his thoughts. Despite the clear logic of my explanation, Luke's pensive demeanour hinted at deeper layers, unspoken considerations or perhaps personal reflections triggered by the mention of Adelaide. *It seems like a no-brainer to me*, I thought, puzzled by his reaction but aware that each of us, in our own way, was navigating the complexities of our new realities, sometimes caught in the tangle of our thoughts and the unspoken narratives that played out within us.

Finally, Luke's demeanour shifted as he raised his head, a new resolve in his voice. "I've already got my flight booked. I may as well use it. Besides, I might find something useful at the airport. In any event, it'll give you a much closer point of entry for collecting Paul's car."

"Alright," I conceded, masking my initial reservations with a nonchalant shrug. Internally, I acknowledged the logic in his plan, though a part of me craved the simplicity of a direct task. *My list of tasks from Paul is growing quicker than I can keep up with*, I reflected, feeling the weight of responsibilities piling onto my shoulders.

The conversation took another turn as Paul, his eyes sharpening with curiosity, probed his brother. "What are you actually going to Adelaide for, Luke?" His suspicion was palpable, echoing my own silent questions about the necessity of this trip.

Luke's brief hesitation was telling, a subtle crack in his usually composed exterior. "I'm thinking I might bring our parents and siblings to Clivilius," he declared, his voice gaining strength with the admission. The idea was bold, perhaps reckless, and it resonated with a mix of potential promise and undeniable risk.

I couldn't contain my reaction, a gasp escaping my lips unbidden. "Is that a good idea?" The question burst forth, driven by a surge of concern for the myriad implications of such a move.

To my surprise, it was Paul who responded, not Luke. "It'll be a lot more mouths to feed, but I think you are right. I think they could really help us here." His endorsement was unexpected, a rare alignment with his brother's plan.

The conversation left me with a swirling mix of thoughts. Bringing Luke's family to Clivilius wasn't just a logistical challenge; it was a gamble, one that could either fortify our community or strain it further.

"How many?" I queried, the mention of additional mouths to feed igniting a flicker of concern within me. The logistics, the resources needed—it all started to tally up in my mind.

"Only Adelaide?" Paul's question was pointed, an attempt to gauge the scope of Luke's plan.

"I think so, for now," Luke's response was measured, hinting at a larger plan yet to unfold.

Paul's gaze shifted back to me, providing specifics, "Parents and three brothers."

"Two brothers," Luke interjected, his correction slicing through the growing tally in my mind.

The sudden change threw me off, and I wasn't alone; Paul's puzzled look mirrored my own confusion.

"Eli is still visiting Lisa in the United States," Luke added, filling in the blanks and drawing a map of his family's global footprint.

"Girlfriend?" I ventured, trying to piece together the familial connections.

"Sister," they responded in unison, a brief moment of brotherly synchrony in an otherwise fragmented conversation.

"Oh, you've got a big family," I remarked, my mind unconsciously moving to count the members, an attempt to grasp the full picture of what—and who—Luke's plan entailed.

"Yep," they agreed together again, a simple affirmation that carried the weight of expanded responsibilities and altered dynamics for our community.

Paul, always focused on the immediate tasks at hand, pressed on, "Are you going to bring them to Bixbus tomorrow?"

Luke's shrug was nonchalant, but the undercurrent of his words suggested a depth of uncertainty. "I'm not sure yet. I still haven't worked out the best way to approach them." His gaze lingered on the flickering shadows cast by the firelight, lost in contemplation, before he sought external input. "Any ideas?" he directed at Paul, a subtle admission of his need for guidance.

Paul's response was a shrug, his silence hanging in the air momentarily before his expression shifted, eyes widening as if a lightbulb had flicked on in his mind. "I suspect that all you need to do is find a way to convince dad, and the rest will easily follow." His voice carried a confidence that seemed to pierce through Luke's uncertainties.

Luke's reaction was contemplative, his hand absently stroking his stubbled chin. "Hmm," he intoned, considering the new angle Paul offered. "I think you're onto something there." It was clear that the dynamics within their family were complex, hinging significantly on the patriarch's stance.

As their conversation unfolded, I found myself adrift in a sea of confusion. *How did their father wield such influence? Was it respect, fear, or something more profound that bound them to his will?* The notion of one person having such sway over a family's collective decisions was both intriguing and mildly alarming. *Is he some sort of controlling sociopath?* The question skated dangerously close to judgment, but the curiosity was unavoidable, a natural response to the unfolding narrative of their family dynamics.

Luke's voice snapped me back to the present, "Come on, Beatrix," he said, a gentle nudge out of my internal musings. "Let's get you these keys." His words, simple and practical, pulled me from the whirlpool of thoughts about family influences and control.

❖

The wardrobe door, its white paint chipped and worn, groaned on its track, revealing a sparse collection of empty hangers that swayed slightly with the motion. "Where are your clothes?" I inquired, my voice tinged with confusion. The practicality of transporting clothes to Clivilius puzzled me, especially when Luke had the luxury of returning here whenever he wished. *And to wash them*, my thoughts added, as I tried to piece together the rationale behind his actions.

Luke, stretching on his toes, reached toward the top shelf, his back momentarily to me. "They're in the other side of the wardrobe," he stated, his voice carrying an edge of obviousness that I hadn't detected.

I winced slightly as his fingers grazed the shelf, the sound of wood against skin echoing subtly in the room. "Got it," he declared, a hint of triumph in his voice as something metallic clinked against the wood. Watching him withdraw his arm from the closet's upper reaches, I noted the shift in his balance as he settled back on his heels.

My hand instinctively moved toward the jingling keys in Luke's grasp, but he, seemingly lost in his next task, knelt down without handing them over. My eyes tracked his every move, curiosity piqued, as he extracted several pairs of shoes from the bottom of the wardrobe. The realisation that the keys might not be Paul's sparked a twinge of nervous excitement in me. *What was Luke hiding, or rather, what was he about to reveal?*

Luke's meticulous fingers delved into the carpet, his actions precise and knowing. I watched, fascinated, as he peeled back a section of the floor covering, unveiling a gleaming metal underneath. "You have a safe buried in your wardrobe floor?" My voice carried a mix of awe and disbelief as I lowered myself beside him, my curiosity piqued.

"You have a safe buried in your wardrobe floor?" I asked incredulously, carefully bringing myself to my knees beside Luke.

The key, now in Luke's steady hand, found its home in the lock effortlessly. He paused, a moment of anticipation hanging between us, before answering with a confident and somewhat mischievous, "Of course." His grin, broad and unrestrained, hinted at secrets about to be unveiled.

With a decisive turn, the lock yielded with a satisfying click, and Luke lifted the lid. I leaned in closer, my breath catching at the reveal. The interior was a trove, lined with zip-lock bags bulging with contents that spoke of hurried packing or meticulous hiding.

"Here's Paul's," Luke announced, his hand selecting a specific bag from the collection. He handed it over with a casualness that belied the anticipation of the moment.

The bag's plastic crinkled under my touch, an oddly mundane sound in the midst of the unfolding mystery. My fingers traced the outlines of a phone, a wallet, and various scraps of paper within. Each item, seemingly ordinary, was imbued with a sense of importance, fragments of a life temporarily tucked away, now handed over to me. The weight of the task, the trust implied, and the secrets just beneath the surface sent a shiver of responsibility through me. I was not just retrieving belongings; I was delving into the private world of another, a world hidden away in zip-lock bags in a buried safe.

Questions bubbled up inside me, each one vying for escape, but the most pressing emerged first. "Is there a bag for everyone?" My voice carried a mix of curiosity and a tinge of concern as I considered the implications of such meticulous compartmentalisation.

"Yeah. I figured keeping things grouped by owner would be the best way to manage," Luke's response was practical, his tone matter-of-fact, reflecting a level of organisation that was both impressive and slightly unnerving.

I was about to nod in agreement, acknowledging the sensibility of his method, when Luke's next action interrupted my train of thought. "Oh, apart from this one," he said, presenting another bag to me.

My eyes instinctively narrowed, scrutinising the new item. Inside, a collection of driver's licenses peered back at me, their laminated surfaces gleaming under the artificial light. "Why keep all the driver's licenses separate?" I queried, the question laced with a mix of confusion and a burgeoning sense of intrigue.

Luke's reaction was swift and a tad evasive. Without addressing my inquiry, he reclaimed the bag, promptly returning it to its hidden haven. The swift dismissal of my question hung in the air, thick with unspoken explanations and Luke's apparent desire to keep certain things under wraps.

Choosing not to delve deeper into the enigma of Luke's organisational logic, I shifted my focus to the zip-lock bag containing Paul's items. "What's all this?" My inquiry broke the brief silence as I sifted through the contents, fingers brushing over scraps of paper filled with a jumble of numbers and letters.

"It's the notes I've been making for Paul. It includes all the important stuff like the codes to unlock his phone and access his bank accounts," Luke elucidated, his tone carrying a hint of pride in his thoroughness.

His explanation offered a glimpse into a side of him I hadn't fully appreciated before—meticulous, methodical, and undeniably prepared. A part of me admired his foresight and organisation, traits that were becoming increasingly vital in our unpredictable world. Yet, as I knelt there, the scraps of paper in hand, a silent acknowledgment of Luke's complexity settled over me. His actions, so calculated and precise, revealed a depth of responsibility and perhaps a burden that he carried quietly.

Paul's keys, each meticulously labelled, clinked in front of my face, momentarily pulling my attention away from the scribbled notes and codes. Even in the dim light, I could clearly see Paul's name etched on the small tag attached to the keychain. The level of organisation was almost comforting.

"Feel free to access the safe whenever you need to. Leave the key at the back of the top shelf," Luke instructed, his voice steady, imbuing the simple directions with a sense of ritual, of trust bestowed.

"Of course," I replied, acknowledging the responsibility he was entrusting me with. The safe wasn't just a physical container; it was a repository of trust, of shared secrets and mutual dependence.

"And only turn the mobile phones on when you need to use them," he added, his tone shifting slightly.

"Why's that?" I asked, as my nose scrunched in thought.

"I don't know whether police really can track our exact locations from a phone when it is turned on, but I'd rather not take any chances to find out." Luke's admission was candid, a rare concession to the limits of his knowledge.

I shrugged in response, the gesture laden with my own uncertainty. The mysteries of technology and surveillance were beyond my expertise, and like Luke, I preferred caution over potential peril.

Luke's guidance didn't end there. "And don't reply to any messages or answer any calls unless they are from me." His words were firm, leaving no room for misinterpretation.

I nodded, a quick, jerky motion that conveyed my understanding and acceptance. The instructions were clear, each one a thread in the web of our collective security.

Luke's voice carried a new note of caution, a shift that drew my focus back to him. "Oh," he interjected, adding another layer to his instructions. "Use the cash sparingly and be sure to make a note of any bank transactions on the relevant paper." His eyes met mine, ensuring I understood the importance of financial discretion.

I nodded once more, my mind already ticking through the implications of meticulous financial tracking. The importance of every cent spent was not lost on me, especially in our precarious position where resources were as valuable as the air we breathed.

As Luke's thoughts spilled out, the weight of our financial reality began to sink in. "Finances don't go too far. I'm really not sure how we're going to keep up paying for supplies and materials to help them build the new settlement," he admitted, his voice laced with a rare hint of vulnerability.

My lips tightened, drawing into a thin line as I absorbed the implications of his words. The financial strain wasn't just a personal burden—it was a collective one, threatening the very foundation of the new world we were striving to build.

Luke's contemplative voice broke through my reverie. "I think we're going to need to get creative," he mused, his gaze drifting off, perhaps envisioning unconventional solutions to our looming economic challenge.

His words resonated with me, sparking a mixture of apprehension and resolve. Creativity wasn't just a luxury; it was a necessity, a crucial element in navigating the uncertain terrain of our new existence.

An unexpected spark of inspiration struck me. My demeanour shifted, a softening of my features, an illumination in my eyes signalling a sudden shift in thought.

"What is it?" Luke inquired, pausing in his financial fretting, clearly noticing the change in my expression.

A sly smile crept across my face as I leaned into the newfound idea. "I know how we can get more cash," I declared, the corners of my mouth lifting in a knowing smirk. "Lots of cash."

His curiosity piqued, Luke pressed, "How?" His surprise was evident, a mix of skepticism and hope colouring his tone.

I shook my head, a playful secrecy taking hold. Stuffing Paul's keys into my pocket, I stood up, feeling the weight of the impending adventure. "Never mind about the details. I think the less you know the better. Leave it to me and Jarod."

"Jarod?" Luke's voice cracked slightly, panic igniting in his eyes as he mirrored my actions and stood. The mention of involving Jarod seemed to stoke his anxieties, adding fuel to the fire of his apprehensions.

My grin persisted, undimmed by his worry. "Just trust me on this one, Luke," I assured him, my confidence perhaps more for my benefit than his. Without lingering for rebuttals or further questions, I exited the bedroom, my steps carrying me toward the living room, toward action.

As I activated my Portal Key, the wall before me erupted in a kaleidoscope of buzzing colours, signalling the gateway to my next move.

"Beatrix," Luke's voice trailed after me, a blend of concern and urgency in his call.

I paused, turning to face him as I stood before the swirling portal. His expression was a tangle of fear and plea for caution.

"Please be careful," he implored, his brow knitted in deep worry.

The words sparked a light chuckle from me, a mix of bravado and nonchalance as I replied, "Well, I can't promise that one." My laughter, though light, didn't fully mask the underlying tension of the risks ahead.

Eager to communicate with Jarod, I knew my plan, however audacious, demanded immediate action. The message I sent was succinct yet laden with urgency.

**19:03PM Beatrix:** *I'm coming for Maggie.*

*TO BE CONTINUED...*

Printed and bound by CPI Group (UK) Ltd, Croydon, CR0 4YY
01/04/2024
03757241-0007